An Inspection so Sweet

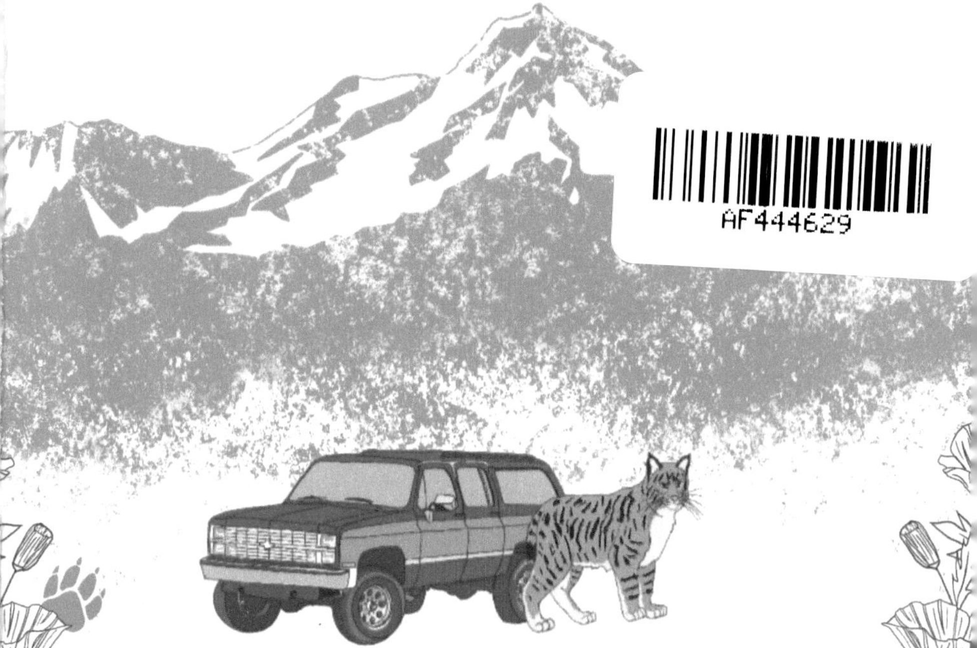

Kelly Virens

To request permissions, contact the publisher at Portfireflirt@gmail.com

Do not use any part of this book for AI purposes. It is seriously damaging to the environment and the creative industry.

Hardcover: 979-8-9986774-0-3
Paperback: 979-8-9986774-1-0
Ebook: 979-8-9986774-2-7

First paperback and hardback edition June 2025.

Edited by Brittany Gossin, Kai Yee Goh, & Kristen Hamilton
Cover art by SubtleServal

Map, interior art and layout by Kelly Virens

Port FIreflirt Bindery
P. O. Box 278083
Sacramento, Ca 95827

Author's Note:

This is my step into the paranormal romance genre. I am not sure if I actually managed the right formula but it was a ton of fun to fall into this world. While set in the same universe as Old Giants, this one is different. Each one stands on its own but is very interconnected with the others.

This is set in the town of Mt. Shasta, California. I took some liberties here but tried to remain as true to Siskiyou County as possible. I realize that Reyes, if employed by the county would not work in Mt. Shasta as it's not the county seat, nor would Camille be able to open a bakery under the circumstances she does, but we can suspend a bit in disbelief for the sake of a fun sometimes tense paranormal romance.

Content Warnings:

Open door scenes: *Chapters 24 & 25*

Unwanted brief assault (Not by either MC): *Chapter 41*

Animal injury (Sitka lives! I promise!): *Chapter 35*

Profanity

Minor periods of isolation

Oppressive parents/coven

Minor injury, not graphic or very descriptive

Cami + Reyes Campsite
Reyes's Cabin
The Meadow
CITY HALL
BAKEWELLS
The Apothecary
The Bakery
Willow's Shop
The Story of:
An Inspection so Sweet
Willow's House
To Seattle
Mt. Shasta
Interstate 5
Sacramento River
Hedge Creek Falls
Mossbrae Falls
McCloud
McCloud Dance Hall
CA 89
To Lassen
Camille's Cabin
Dunsmuir
To Sacramento

To anyone who has been towards a mold that did not fit and away from one that did.

Art by Chelzd_art

Prologue

Headlights illuminated the royal blue sign on the side of the road. Words written in a goldenrod brush script lit up along with the image of golden poppy flowers.

Camille Thornwell had only stopped once on the eight-hour drive from Seattle—in some small town in Oregon she didn't learn the name of. The only things she needed to do were to change her rental car out and pawn a few items that she was more than happy to part with. These items meant her doom and with any luck, getting rid of them meant escaping her fate that had been arranged for her. The last task involved buying a burner phone. After sending herself some vital information, she factory reset her old phone and slipped it into a slot on the nearest big rig trailer she saw.

With an hour left until she arrived at her accommodation, she repeated the check-in instructions that she had memorized silently to herself. Tonight, she would slip into the small cabin nestled on the cliff above the Sacramento River in the dark of night and when she awoke, she would remain in the shadow of Mt. Shasta.

She wasn't sure what awaited her here, or if she would even be staying long. All she knew was tomorrow she would take her first steps alone, free of the Thornwell name.

Chapter 1

Two months later

Camille was so close to opening the bakery she dreamed of in the small town of Mt. Shasta, California. It was named after the massive mountain that could not be missed just to the east of town. Since moving to Siskiyou County, the space had been signed for, she had keys in hand, the paperwork was all filed, and the last bit of renovations were being wrapped up.

Today was a perfect day for a hike to reward herself for all the hard work she had done.

She had always loved hiking. The crunch of dirt under her boots and the cool breeze brought a sharp focus to Camille's senses. It was important to be aware of one's surroundings after all, even if she had grown more comfortable since arriving here. One thing she had finally let herself do was stop looking over her shoulder so much. The animals were no threat to her, nor were the elements. Camille knew to prepare for those things.

The real threat were others like her and the ones who shared her name.

Other witches.

Her family would have never let her have this, so she had fled the Thornwell Coven.

All of it.

She knew she would have to weave lies with people she met. Non-magic users or humans couldn't know what she was. Witch hunts were certainly proof of that. So she would have to be careful here regardless of how safe it was starting to feel.

That mountain could be seen from so far away, and she could feel it watching her. Not that she could really explain the feeling she got when she looked at Mt. Shasta, and she did often look, but it felt as though it was curiously waiting.

Maybe it was waiting in a way. Be it for her to find a new kind of magic here or something more, she wasn't sure. Part of her secretly wished it was the mountain saying she was home.

As she continued to walk, a prickling sensation of unease crept into her gut. It brought her to an abrupt halt. The sensation was not the fear that she had been found. She didn't sense any witches nearby, just a few ordinary humans, nothing to be concerned with.

Then she heard it.

A cry from an animal. It was painful. That was the unease that had crept into her gut, leaving it feeling almost scratchy. Her deeper connection with the earth as a green witch always tapped into her veins and she could not ignore these. Something needed help.

Bad things happened to the environment often, and there was little she could do on a grand scale, but this? This wrongness was close and she might be able to help the animal.

She promptly picked up her pace to a swift sprint. When she came to a ledge, she discovered a bobcat had its leg stuck in a trap.

"Oh no! Poor thing," she lamented and without a second thought, Camille scrambled down the embankment. The soil was dry and loose as it was early summer. The dirt slid, causing her to stumble and fall to her hands and knees. The cold rush of air followed by the sharp sting of scrapes hit her. Still, she pressed on, ignoring the large gash on her leg since she had opted for knee length leggings today.

"Shhh, I got you," she said softly. The cry from the bobcat held a pain she could feel.

It did not hiss or growl at her, nor try to swipe or bite her, it just simply watched her work pensively. She could usually keep animals calm with the intent she would cast outward. Another part of being a green witch was that she could feel the very roots pulse through the earth. Oftentimes animals would send their intent out into the soil as well. It was a mutual method of nonverbal basic communication.

As she dug in her pack for a salve to staunch the bleeding and gauze from the first aid kit, a low growl slipped out of the bobcat, causing her to still. Her eyes fixed on the sage green of the bobcat's eyes as it shifted its gaze past her. Frantic heavy footsteps came to an abrupt halt behind her.

"Are you alright?" a man's voice asked. "A bobcat? Please move away slowly," he instructed.

Camille narrowed her eyes in annoyance, not turning around yet. This was just a clumsy, loud human. Not a witch, fae, or any other magical being. Any other magic being would know this poor cat was not a danger to anyone.

"I'm fine. I'm trying to help the injured animal; it's hurt." She realized the redundancy of her statement and sighed. Then she set her supplies down and finally turned around to look at this human.

Slowly, her mouth fell open ever so slightly. His russet skin and short, messy black hair against the backdrop of the tall sugar pines and clear blue sky was a sight she committed to memory. He was stocky, and dressed in a blue T-shirt with cargo pants. He wore a black baseball cap with a patch of the highway sign for Interstate 5 and a stretchy looking blue fabric was draped around his neck, likely acting as bandana.

He looked rugged, as though he belonged on these trails, and there was a warmth in his amber eyes that was alluring to her.

"Okay, and they get hurt out here all the time. It's a wild animal in its natural environment. Move away from it before it scratches you," he said, concerned. He hadn't taken his eyes off her, she noted.

She realized she had been staring at him and quickly averted her gaze. "I'm not going to just leave it out here. It's paw is injured. It will become prey for a mountain lion or something and attract predators to the trail where people are. Then it's a manhunt for another innocent animal." Her eyes went back to him.

He stood there dumbfounded, letting his jaw fall agape. "It's not a dog or a child though. It might have something."

Camille rolled her eyes. "Does it look like it has rabies? I know how to tend to its injuries."

"I have a buddy who works at a wildlife rescue in Trinity County. He can come get it."

"And leave it out here to suffer? Just go about your day, sir. I am alright. I can help it."

"But you can't just handle an injured bobcat."

"Listen, I can help it and your buddy doesn't need to come out here from wherever Trinity County is. I just need to get back on the trail and I can put it in my car."

"Trinity is like two hours southwest of here," he replied. "You can't just pick it up and put it in your car!"

"Again, I'm not leaving it here. Then what, your buddy gets here and releases it in Trinity, away from its home?"

He just stared at her, once more dumbfounded. They remained locked in each other's gaze for a moment longer until Camille sighed and set to work.

"Sorry, little kit, this might hurt," she said and wedged her trekking pole into the trap, attempting to pry it open but struggling.

"Wait! What if there is rust on the trap? Or the animal bites you? What are you doing? This is so dangerous," he pleaded.

Then before she realized, he was kneeling beside her and pressing down on a latch, releasing the trap and the animal. She smiled at him, slightly stunned.

"It's an older model trap, but they always have releases on them. Are you hurt?" he asked her.

"Did you set the trap?" She leveled him with her gaze.

"What? No. I just know how they work. I would never. These traps shouldn't be anywhere near this trail."

"Thank you." Camille nodded and began to tend to cleaning its paw and wrapping it. She kept her intent focused on the cat, urging it to stay calm.

"You're welcome?" He paused for a moment. "I will give you the number, he can come pick it up I guess, but I really don't think it's a good idea to keep it. I will get you animal control's number too."

"Listen, I really appreciate your help, but I'd feel better seeing to it that the animal is healed and able to return to its home. Not locked up in a cage or relocated hours away, or worse," Camille explained and took off her jacket. The cool air hit her skin, but she had certainly experienced much colder. She would experience much colder in the shadow of Mt. Shasta, too, when winter came.

She could feel his gaze on her skin as she only had a fitted tank top on. Not wanting a look of disgust from him, Camille ignored it. She was sweaty and dirty, not very proper looking as her mother would say. Besides, her priority was the cat.

"Okay, easy," she said in a soft voice and wrapped the cat up, swaddling it in her arms. It purred softly.

"I guess I have seen it all," he said, standing up when she did. "Let me help you back up the embankment. I will carry your pack."

"Thanks," she relented and began walking.

"You are limping and your leg is bleeding," he exclaimed.

"It's just a scrape from getting down here. I will be fine."

"I have a first aid kit," he said in a rush.

"I do too. I will tend to it in the car. I don't live far from here, just in Dunsmuir," she said as though it wasn't a big deal. It really wasn't for her. Sure, the scrapes stung but it wasn't the first time she had gotten an injury on a trail.

"That's still a twenty-minute drive."

"I appreciate your concern, but I will be fine. I promise you." She really was not sure where his concern was stemming from. If she had come back from a hike injured, her parents would have chastised her for being so careless. They wouldn't even have mentioned a first aid kit or going to see a healer.

He sighed in defeat. "Fine. Let's go, there is an easier way up," he said, walking a little further away where it wasn't as steep.

Once they were back on the trail, he helped her slip her backpack on. He was as soft and gentle as ever, holding out one strap then the other so she wouldn't have to set the bobcat down. It was still very calm, though she could see its eyes tracking his movements.

"Thank you again." She looked at him with a smile. "Sorry if I sounded accusatory about the trap. I just think they are horrible things."

"They are. I will alert Fish and Wildlife about it. Hopefully there are no others." His gaze was still fixed on her and they briefly traveled to her lips and back up. He seemed nervous when he met her eyes, as if he had been caught. "My name is Reyes."

"Camille," she offered, then took in the warm rich amber of his eyes again. She found them lovely if she were being honest with herself.

"Camille," he said softly and the slightest smile graced his lips. "That is beautiful."

She was not the most well-versed with flirting. Usually when there was flirting involving her, she would come to find out it was seldom ever genuine. Her name and family held a lot of power, given that they owned and ran Thornwell Academy—a prestigious academy for witches.

Yet Reyes didn't know anything about her and he was not only showing concern but curiosity lingered in his eyes. She knew she felt a curiosity about him. *No, he isn't flirting. He is being nice.*

The thought did cross her mind though. How odd it would be if she gained a familiar and found a love interest on the same day. It sure would make Mt. Shasta special. Her eyes shifted to the mountain behind him. It was always watching.

She had read that it was a magical place and the stories told over the years were endless about its power.

Something told her that Reyes respected the mountain too. She usually trusted her instinct and didn't get a bad feeling about him. It was more excitement than anything else.

Not that she knew anything about this guy. Though she wouldn't mind seeing him again, but chastised herself for the brazen thought.

"So are you from here?" she asked, trying to distract herself.

"No, I'm from San Jose, Silicon Valley. Tech boom, all that stuff. I moved up here about six years ago. It's home now. How about you?" he asked.

She frowned as they started walking. "I'm from Washington. Tacoma. Moved here recently."

"Any particular reason you moved to Mt. Shasta?"

"It looked nice."

Reyes laughed and it sent some sort of current through her. It was the same sort of curiosity as when she looked at him, of wanting and belonging. That urge to get to know him.

"So are you like a veterinarian?" Reyes asked.

"No. I'm just good with animals."

"No schooling or training?"

"I have worked with them, had some classes," Camille replied.

Reyes nodded and they stopped in front of the car she had bought a few days after arriving. He promptly opened the door to the backseat for her once she clicked the key fob that she'd kept in her pocket.

"Let me get you the card for my buddy, Seth, and animal control. I'm in that blue truck over there. Let someone look over the animal at least. They won't put the cat down if that's what you are worried about."

"Okay." Camille removed her pack once the animal was set on the seat. It watched them.

Reyes nodded and ran over to the behemoth of a truck with the camper shell and faded blue paint. The doors alone looked heavy to open. He slammed one shut, causing her to jump. The bobcat rotated its ears around as he walked back up.

"Give them a call and please be careful on your drive home. Tend to your injuries before you try to tend to the cat."

She nodded quickly and they stood looking at each other for an awkward amount of time before he let out a quick exhale.

"See ya, Camille," he said, then promptly turned and hurried to his truck. She watched him for a moment longer but didn't want to hear the door slam so she got in her car and closed the door.

"Well that was interesting," she said to the cat. Then she drove off.

Chapter 2

Reyes backed his truck into the usual spot off to the side and parallel to his double garage. Glancing over, he thought he really should clean the garage out this weekend. It had been a while. Then again, it wasn't as though he wanted to park his truck in the garage. The other bay stored his small boat on the trailer.

With a shake of his head, he focused on grabbing his backpack and keys before heading to his front door. He still hadn't replaced the batteries in the garage door opener and he made a mental note to do that too.

Once inside, Reyes tossed his stuff down and sighed, realizing he had left the lid off the jar of peanut butter and the knife on the counter. He cleaned up the remains of breakfast and set to tracking down batteries. Repeating the word 'batteries' over in his mind helped keep his focus as he rummaged through cabinets.

"I know I have some," he groaned, trying to organize the cabinets in the process.

This was normal behavior for him though. So easily distracted. He had to pat himself down, checking that he had his wallet, keys, cellphone, and ID badge every morning before work. Fortunately, he had gotten in the habit of patting himself down on the weekend for everything but the badge which he left in his truck.

Work policy would have him put the badge in his glove box, but half the time he forgot and left it in the cupholder. He wasn't worried about it getting stolen though. His A-frame cabin was at the end of a dirt road with only two other neighbors a good distance away. Motion lights and cameras would go off if anyone pulled into the driveway. The only times he cringed at not following that work policy was when he met up with friends after work. Still, Reyes was forever grateful for the checklist on his work forms. They likely kept him employed for he knew he would surely miss something if not for all the boxes on the county health inspection forms.

As he continued to search, he thought about her.

Camille. You would think I'm a mess, he laughed to himself. *Right, as if she would ever be over here.*

The thought did stick with him though. Her eyes were a beautiful sage green, and her strawberry blonde hair had been tied back with a silky looking green bandana. Some sort of embodiment of spring in a bright and bold woman. Then the way she handled the bobcat as though she was an expert with wildlife, yet she said she wasn't a veterinarian.

Dad would love talking to her. He chuckled again at the thought of her and his wildlife biologist dad talking about animals. Though his dad's specialty was wolves.

Reyes hoped she was alright and had tended to her leg. He already felt like he had made a bad impression on her so he didn't want to linger. Confidence had only seemed to wane in him as of late.

Still, he could not forget the way she looked up at him. As though she were awestruck. No one had ever looked at him like that. Then he had to go and make an ass of himself about the cat. As he thought about it, he found it odd how calm the cat was as she wrapped its paw.

While he was comfortable here, he was also lonely at times. He had friends. In fact, his best friend and co-worker, Evan, wasn't far.

Yet he wasn't sure why he was worried about ruining his chance with her. He didn't even know her. She honestly sounded amazing and was very pretty. He figured he didn't have any chance with her even if he hadn't insisted the bobcat be taken somewhere else.

He was never good at relationships and now with Mt. Shasta being such a small town, he had pretty much resigned himself to being single.

As nice as it had been to have someone to go places with and come home to, he didn't want to end up in a situation like his last relationship. That hadn't been good for either party. He had made plenty of mistakes. His ex, Jodie, had made plenty too. They were done and had been for nearly a year now. All he could do was learn from it and try to break his bad habits if someone else did come along.

Reyes groaned, realizing he likely hadn't actually remembered anything he was supposed to have learned with Camille. Someone might have come along and he had blown it. But it was a bobcat, a wild and unpredictable animal. *That she had picked up and swaddled like a baby...how in the hell—*

The sound of his phone ringing pulled him out of his wandering thoughts and he shot up, hitting his shoulder on the upper cabinet door he hadn't closed.

"Ow!" he groaned, then rushed over to his phone. It was his mom. He answered the video call and slumped down at the table, noting he should clean that off too. It was cluttered and mail needed to be sorted.

"Hey, Mom," he answered.

"Hi, honey, you look out of breath. Is this a bad time?"

"He was probably working on something." Reyes heard his dad interject before he joined his mom on the couch at his childhood home in San Jose.

"No, it's fine. I was just looking for something. I was on a hike earlier and hadn't freshened up."

"It's not too hot there, right?"

Reyes knew her concern was valid; it could get warm in Siskiyou County. Luckily, the town usually stayed pretty cool.

"No, it's still cool. It's only mid-March. I was planning on cleaning the garage out."

"Well don't overexert yourself with it," his dad noted.

His parents called often enough, and the reminders and concerns for his scatterbrained habits were normal. He knew they just wanted to make sure he was alright given how far away from them he lived. Their concern only grew after the relationship with Jodie had ended, as if he would suddenly deteriorate from being alone.

"Your father and I were planning to come visit; it's been a while and we just saw your sister recently."

"Yeah, Andi told me about that. She said it was fun and that Weylyn was ecstatic to see you." Reyes laughed.

"It was a good trip. Though your nephew asked about when he would see you again. You should consider coming up with us. You could fly out of Sacramento or come down to San Jose and fly up with us."

Reyes thought about it for a moment. "When are you going back up there?"

"Not sure. It will be after we come to visit you," his mom answered.

"Alright, I will think about it."

"We will send you some dates to come visit. Does that sound good?"

"Yeah. Send them over and I will request time off work." Reyes sat back in the chair.

"Maybe we consider Christmas at your place. Andi and Nick can come down with Weylyn?" his dad chimed in.

It took everything in him not to groan at the thought of that many people in the cabin. It was plenty big for one or two people, but it was still an A-frame cabin with the second level being a large open loft bedroom. Jodie hated it, but it provided such a good view of the mountain. It also offered little in the way of privacy when guests were here. His parents usually stayed with him and took the bedroom downstairs, but with them, his sister, brother-in-law, and nephew, it would be cramped. Not to mention how heavy the snow could get here—their cars might get stuck.

Still, he knew he had picturesque accommodations for a holiday with his family. He was sure his sister had places to take his nephew near Seattle and that they got snow, too, but this was a place they could just walk out into the snow with sugar pines and fir trees right in the yard.

Then Camille crept into his mind again, and he imagined her with them all. The thought of seeing her again made him smile. Not that he knew when that might be. He wasn't even sure why he was thinking about her. Soon, he found himself lost in thoughts of going on a hike with her and a trail of animals trotting behind them as if she were a forest princess that befriended all the animals or something. Of course, the bobcat would be right beside her.

"Reyes." His mom's curious tone caught his attention.

"What?" he stammered, feeling heat burn his cheeks. *That's ridiculous,* he said in his head.

"What has you so deep in thought?"

"Nothing." He tried to divert. "Hey, Dad, I know wolves are your specialty, but what do you know about bobcats?"

"Have you noticed one hanging out in the yard? Maybe going for some of your fishing stuff? You should clean that up and scare the cat away. Maybe report to Fish and Wildlife? Generally they are not aggressive towards humans but they're still wild animals."

Reyes glanced up at the high-peaked ceiling where the rafters met. "Yes, I know it's a wild animal," he groaned. "And no, there isn't one on the property that I have seen. I just saw one on the trail."

"Don't try to pet them."

"Dad. I know. I'm thirty-five, not five," Reyes relented and hoped Camille hadn't been injured by the bobcat. "Send me some dates and I will get back to you."

"Alright, Son, we love you and are looking forward to spending time up there soon."

"Love you both too. Take care," Reyes replied and they ended the call with a pleasant farewell.

He set the phone down and set to cleaning the table, feeling accomplished.

Chapter 3

Camille parked next to the small rustic cabin she was renting. It was painted white but it certainly could use a touch-up coat. The property had a variety of accommodations including Airstreams, a row of hotel rooms, and more modern cabins. They had one very fancy cabin she had seen online but those options were, of course, much more expensive than the rustic cabins.

The rustic cabins were single rooms connected to a small kitchen with small bathrooms that boasted a rustic experience from 1923, but with Wi-Fi. It was plenty comfortable and sat overlooking the Sacramento River. The freight train down below was loud and slightly jarring in the middle of the night but she had gotten used to it.

Sitting in her car, she watched for anyone that may be walking by then glanced at the cat, willing it to be calm. Camille grabbed her daypack and unlocked the door, leaving it open as she drew the curtains closed and looked around once more before rushing to her car and gently picking up the bobcat. After pushing the car door shut with her hip, Camille made it inside and closed the door.

Once the bobcat was set on the bed, it laid its head down and purred. She set some lunch meat down for it since it was all she had on hand. Stopping at the store and leaving the animal unattended in her car was not a risk she was willing to take, so she had headed straight home and cleaned the animal's wound. After applying a light antiseptic infused with some healing herbs, the cat's rapid breathing and panting slowed.

"There you are, little one," Camille said softly to the cat as she wrapped a soft cloth around its paw. "Come back and I will remove it if you don't get it off before then."

After she was done, she glanced at the old notebook that lay beside them. It had her notes on animal care and familiars from her lessons as a student at Thornwell Academy. While her coven had founded the prestigious academy in the Seattle region, she was still expected to prove her worth. She was guaranteed an opportunity to attend, but nothing else—no special accommodations, and no handouts aside from the acceptance. Her parents would have likely disowned her had she declined and she always wanted to prove her worth.

Then again, that was before she realized they already had a plan for her. No amount of hard work would have changed that. Her older brothers had been part of that plan unknowingly to her at the time. All of them were essentially sold off into marriages that benefited Thornwell, gaining wealth from other covens seeking to join with Thornwell. To cement their place with heirs and bloodlines. Yet her brothers just acted as though this was business as normal. They didn't even put up a fight.

To their credit, her older brothers had seemed happy in their unions if not a bit distant with their spouses. They appeared to be good parents to her nieces and nephews.

But Camille wouldn't retain the name with her betrothal. Her betrothed was a wretched excuse for a man. She despised Leland Talbot for his arrogance and insults. Producing heirs with him sounded like a nightmare. It was a rude awakening when she realized just how little autonomy she had in the Thornwell coven despite being an heiress.

Thornwell was a well-known name. Holding enough wealth, power, and numbers to be deemed a legacy by the witch council of Washington.

Leaving was such a hard choice and yet it was such an obvious one. Ever since that betrothal had been announced, every day just grew darker for her. She had packed the clothes that would fit in a suitcase, all of her academy notebooks, and as many of her tomes she had acquired as she could. They were her only resource now. Her cauldron was the first thing she had packed.

Camille found herself petting the cat, feeling the small rumble of its purr under her hand. "You were a very good cat to endure the pain in such a controlled manner. The window is open so when you want to leave, you may go." Her soft words hovered in the air and she knew it wasn't the words that the animal would understand so much as the intention. Speaking the words made it mutually known to her and the earth.

This was something she had learned in her familiar classes—one of many electives she took. Her parents had said it was good that she was eager to learn, but some of the electives she took were silly and pointless. Familiars included. She never did understand why her parents were so against them.

Upon proving herself as was expected, she became a professor. She had taken as many electives as she could, always being worried she might miss out on what she was truly good at since her parents had deemed baking a waste of time. So she had studied a lot, opting to be a student teacher for a long time. She graduated later than most due to her large transcript of classes and areas of studies.

Others would often compliment her enchantments, unlike her parents. The most they would ever say to her was there was always room for improvement.

Camille was determined to make it on her own now. She had to. At thirty-seven and truly on her own for the first time, it was both terrifying and liberating.

Ever since arriving here, she would find herself getting lost in what she had done. She missed parts of the academy—her favorite window seat in the library, seeing her students understand something they were stumped on, and her favorite meals being prepared. The small apartment on academy grounds that she had made her own was her safe haven. She often baked for her neighbors and colleagues who all raved about the treats. Though she kept a respectable distance from them and they did her. She was the daughter of a legacy family, after all.

The daughter they sold off to Talbot.

Leland.

Refusing to give him any more space in her life, she looked at the bobcat.

How cute and comfortable it looks. How gentle a soul she has. What if she did become my familiar? No, that might not be wise. Thornwells don't concern themselves with familiars, she thought. *But you could have one now. If the cat wanted to choose that. Would you deny it?*

If it wanted to choose that path for itself, of course Camille would let it decide. She would let her intentions be known and simply allow the cat to decide to become her familiar, but never demand it be so. A familiar bond was a mutual trade. It was in no debt to Camille, even if that was how the old rules went.

She would let the cat decide.

Because what stood before her now was a new start, one she could choose. She had felt it the very moment she saw the peak of the mountain about thirty minutes after crossing into California from Oregon.

From what she had read about the mountain, some believed this to be where physical and metaphysical worlds met. Some even believed it to be the center of the universe. She wasn't sure what she believed, but she could not deny the presence it had. Or the magic resting in this massive formation on the horizon. It was the second highest peak in the Cascade

Range. Second only to her home mountain of Rainier, which was the entity of her former home.

She had felt Mt. Shasta looking at her. It held such a presence in this area and it had almost felt as though it welcomed her.

Then again, maybe that was her delusion. It was a shiny new place she was reaching for with everything in her. The feeling of that mountain's shadow felt safe though. It felt like a weighted blanket—she could still move, but she was secure. It was that shadow the mountain left on her in this cabin every day. The trees broke the sunset's path, shielding her from the lies she was living and the truths she was running from.

This little bobcat had curled up on her bed and was sleeping soundly by the time she came back to herself, affirming her belief that this place would be safe. It might be foolish to hope but she wanted to.

She thought back to meeting Reyes earlier today. He was not like anyone she had been with in the past. Her parents wouldn't approve of him, wouldn't approve of a human. Then again, why did she care? She was not under the Thornwell coven anymore. They had bartered her off anyway. Reyes obviously was concerned for her, maybe even for the animal too. She hadn't sensed any malice from him but she would still be on her guard. One eye over her shoulder as always, of course.

"What if this is home? What if I could stay?" she asked herself. After putting the books away in the small closet of the cabin, she grabbed her current notebook off the end table and set to making some of her enchantments.

Her preferred medium for enchanting was simple syrups of sugar and ground-up herbs for her pastries. She would bake some things in the small cabin over the next few days to test recipes out.

"If you are still here in the morning, I will offer the bond," she said to the animal.

Once Camille was done with that, she decided to run to the store and get some raw meat for the cat and a few other things she needed.

When she returned, the cat had woken up and was watching her with curiosity. Camille put the animal's dinner down and set to prepare hers, all the while the window was open for the cat to leave through, but it hadn't. And so, she went about her night—researching the area, recipes, and reading. Occasionally, she wondered what Reyes was doing, who he was, and what his life entailed. The image of his smile gave her a sense of warmth.

As slumber began to claim her, she imagined that mountain watching over the land. Steady and steadfast. It would watch over Reyes, wherever he was. He had established a life here. It would watch over her, trying to find her footing free from chains.

And when she awoke the next morning, she felt safe. She had dreamed of him. Of her and Reyes sitting on the tailgate of his big, blue truck with the bobcat curled up next to her, looking at that mountain.

When she fully emerged from the dreamy state, she realized the bobcat was still curled up next to her.

"Do you want to be my familiar? I've never had one before," she said softly, pushing her intent out towards the cat and for Mt. Shasta to hear. The cat purred and headbutted her hand. "Let's eat and relax before I make the bonding circle. If you want to go, you really are free to go. I would never keep you here against your will."

The cat let out a small chuff and nudged her hand once again.

So Camille got up and made them both food and when it was mid-afternoon, the cat was still there, watching her.

"Are you sure, little one?" she asked once more, knowing the mountain was watching. She was a stranger on this land regardless of how safe the mountain's shadow felt.

When the cat purred again, she set to create a circle in chalk on the floor with a star pointed towards Mt. Shasta and placed herbs in the appropriate sections of the star. The cat leapt into the center and Camille smiled, fixing on its sage green eyes. She spoke the words, setting the intention. Pressing the point of her dagger to her finger, she let one bead of blood fall on the cat's head.

"Sitka." Her voice along with the cat's purr filled the space and magic wove an invisible thread between them.

She could almost feel Mt. Shasta watch the thread form and offer a blessing to the new bond. An extra glimmer of warmth filled the space with her and Sitka.

Chapter 4

A few times that following week, Camillie took Sitka on some trails she found nearby. She figured midmorning on a weekday was the best time to try to strengthen her bond with the bobcat. So far, Sitka had been very responsive around the cabin and on drives. The cat didn't seem to mind the car and always came back to the cabin. Camille had gotten in the habit of letting her out at night and leaving a window open and usually at some hour in the night, she would feel Sitka cozy up against her, helping with the cold nights.

Next week, Camille would be frequenting the bakery to get ready for opening. She knew she didn't want to leave her familiar stuck in the cabin all day, but she also didn't want to be away from her when the bakery was open either. So she tried to work on a system that would allow Sitka to be out in the wild some days and in the bakery on others. Of course, Camille also knew Sitka couldn't just walk through town during the day to go to the wild either. So off they went on a trail. Sitka kept pace with her, which wasn't surprising.

"You probably have a favorite area here in Siskiyou, don't you?" she asked the cat, though she knew it wouldn't answer. It just looked at her then stared ahead. "I never thought I'd have a familiar."

Camille knew how crazy she would appear to anyone else on this trail. A chuckle slipped out of her at the thought of Reyes seeing her talking to the bobcat he seemed so scared of.

"Reyes." A smile formed on her lips after she said his name. "I wonder what you are doing right now. What would it be like to actually hike with you?"

Her mind began to wander through thoughts of him. She wondered if she would bump into him again, if he lived near the mountain. The area certainly wasn't densely populated. She had heard of his hometown but she had never been there. She hadn't been off Thornwell grounds much to really explore other than Seattle or Tacoma.

Of course everyone would occasionally sneak out. Some did it more often than others. She had only started doing it more often before she left.

The fact that she was even here now on her own caught up to her once again. She had really just left everything behind; she actually *managed* to. Then again, she knew she had only managed to do so because everyone overlooked her. She was perfectly obedient; she did everything she had been told to do, abided by her parents' commands. Just like her namesake, to serve.

Until she hadn't. It was odd to be free from the dictatorship of the Thornwell coven, and from witches with power and skill to use said power. Somewhere along the way, she had learned that even witch covens could fall from grace and lose their way. Thornwell cared only for wealth and status. They cared only for molding wealthy witches in their image. To snub their nose up at those less than them. Camille had never grown out of her love of foraging, hiking, and baking. 'Things that children did who didn't grow up' as her parents and eventually her peers had said.

At some point witches couldn't waste precious time doing those things. They needed to be working on gaining more power, forming alliances and unions, and eventually producing and raising heirs too. At least that was how they explained it to her, countless times.

When her own union had been announced, Camille had the bitter harsh realization she was a bargaining chip and little more. Her two older brothers had been bargaining chips, too, and they didn't even tell her. Her oldest brother, Rainier, hadn't said anything to her middle brother, Galen. She was furious when she found out that was how it worked. She felt betrayed and foolish. They put in so much hard work into instilling discipline in her only to barter her off. To make her more "marketable."

Leland Talbot. The very name of her betrothed made her sick to her stomach. He was so arrogant, and he absolutely made it known how much he loathed her. He would scoff loudly whenever she walked by, speak loudly to his friends about how dirty Camille was with her hands touching dirt and sweating like a pig out in the sun. Then, as if that wasn't bad enough, her parents would reprimand her for being upset about it.

You should stop doing those things. You are a Thornwell, not a peasant. How do you expect to find a suitor when you act so far below them? Act like a Thornwell.

Tears made her vision blur and despite the cry scraping at her throat, she forced it down and took a deep breath. It hurt worse, as if she were pushing so much anger and years of hurt back into her. All the things she had been told felt like shards of glass forced into her soul. As if the more she did it, the more immune to it she would become.

A soft nudge and gentle vibration on her leg pulled her attention downward.

Sitka.

In an instant, Camille knelt down and scratched the bobcat's fluffy cheeks and a laugh slipped out of her.

"Thank you." Camille was so grateful for her familiar. How could her parents have scoffed at the idea of one?

Her mind wandered back to Reyes now too. How she had met both within moments of each other. She had been dirty and sweaty from her hike. Still, Reyes stayed to help her. He was sweaty too. His eyes had widened and his mouth had gaped open, but she didn't think it was out of disgust. It certainly wasn't a look she had gotten from Leland or any of the other partners she had been with. She seldom hiked with anyone that could be deemed a suitor.

Yet Reyes smiled after he said her name and said it was beautiful.

The whimsy daydreams of this place could run wild in her head. A small mountain town free from Thornwell's expectations. But Camille was not that much of a fool, despite how often her mother had told her she was. Regardless of who may come into her life now here, she would make something of herself. She wanted to. She had a bakery to run and a future to build.

After her hike, she freshened up and took to trying one of her enchantments in the form of a simple syrup in a berry banana bread. Luckily, she had plans to let others try it out.

Camille was grateful she had met Willow Calarook, the only other witch in Mt. Shasta. It had been another chance meeting shortly before she had met Sitka and Reyes. One afternoon when she was locking up after one of the few renovations she had to do at the bakery, she heard the door to the shop next to hers open. The bright purple aura of the person staring back at her was that of a witch. The two women simply stared at each other for a moment before the other witch smiled and introduced herself as Willow. They talked for hours in Willow's apothecary shop and exchanged phone numbers. Camille was grateful for a friend who seemed so kind and down to earth. She was also a green witch, dealing with scent-based enchantments.

They had met up a few times, always at the house Willow was renting. It was a small, brightly colored two-bedroom, one-bathroom house in the town of Mt. Shasta. She would be heading over there tonight and introducing her to Sitka for the first time. She had never pried much into Willow's story for fear of having to cover her own up.

Once they reached Willow's house, Camille hesitated with her knuckles hovering over the front door. She looked down at Sitka and knew this was a lot to spring on someone, witch or not, but Sitka was Camille's familiar now.

"Alright, let's see how you do with Willow, Sitka." Camille knocked on the door and waited.

The light sound of the lock releasing took up the air and the door opened, revealing a smiling Willow. "Hey, how are you?" Willow said, not even looking down until Sitka began to purr. "Oh, hello." She smiled then looked back at Camille. "You got a familiar?"

"Yeah. It kinda happened on a hike the other day. I hope it's alright, I know she's not exactly a house cat."

"She seems rather docile. Besides, I can't leave your familiar out in the cold; that would be rude and a good way to ensure I was on her bad side. What's her name?"

"Sitka."

Willow knelt and let the bobcat sniff her hand. "Hello, Sitka." Sitka rubbed her head and acceptance was made. "Come in; tell me about it."

"Well, I felt something off in the air and slowed my pace. New area and all," she noted.

"Of course. Intuition is important."

"Then I heard her cry and headed towards the sound." Camille went on to tell the rest of the story. She purposely left out the Reyes encounter, not wanting to talk about him. He had crept into her mind more often than she cared to admit.

"Aww, a warm welcome to Mt. Shasta. How is the bakery going?"

"I have a few last-minute county and city things to take care of that should be wrapping up this week, but I think I might actually open the following week. I am excited. It's been a while since I got to bake."

"That's great to hear. You were a teacher before you moved here, right?"

"Yeah. I got a little busy with that." Camille maintained the facade as usual. She had been run into the ground with such rigorous programs at

Thornwell Academy, but of course she wasn't going to tell Willow about her past.

No one would leave a legacy. No one except you. You betrayed your coven. That stigma of the betrayer label rang loud and clear in Camille's mind. It was hard to wrap her head around that the council might deem her as one. An outcast witch. If her parents requested it, the council would certainly oblige. Every witch she saw would know she had betrayed with a mark branded into her flesh.

Willow's cheerful tone pulled her out of her anxious, fearful thoughts. "Are you going to do a few test runs? I will be your first customer too. And don't worry about the lack of advertising, it certainly has gained some attention that the old deli is becoming a bakery. Everyone is excited. The street stays pretty busy with foot traffic."

Camille picked up her bag, revealing the loaf she had baked, grateful for the topic change. "I had some overripe bananas and berries a little past their prime so I made a loaf. It's more like a pound cake though. We can try it out, maybe with some butter or whipped cream. I'm happy to leave some here if you like."

Willow's eyes lit up. "Oh this looks amazing. Is it enchanted?"

"Yes, it should last a few days and boost the joy receptors ever so slightly. But let me know if it's overpowering. I need to test these things of course. I can't have a whole town doped up on my enchantments." She chuckled.

"I'm excited." Willow beamed and got up to get a knife and small plates. "I have some chai on the stove if you want some."

"Yes. It's my favorite," Camille replied happily, and they both got settled.

Willow loved the pound cake and Camille thought the chai was amazing. Willow noted how perfect the enchantment felt, and how the serotonin boost hit in a subtle way. She also mentioned that the flavor of the syrup didn't overpower the other flavors. It certainly was a bit of an ego boost to Camille, but she felt bad for feeling good about it. As though she had wasted her skill on something so trivial. At least that was what her parents would have said.

Some bout of worry brought Camille to bite her lip for a moment before she spoke. "You were really the only witch here before me?"

"Yep. Just me. I looked when I first moved here. I always keep an eye open. A few have passed through, of course, but you are the first to move here."

"Didn't it get lonely?" Camille asked. The sadness echoed in her tone. Thoughts of whether she had to leave and start over plagued her. Maybe it wasn't a matter of if but when. Only now there was a paper trail of her existence here, even if it was under the fake name of Bakewell. She had been lucky she hadn't gotten caught sneaking off grounds when she had gotten the false identification documents.

"It did. I wished I had someone I could just be myself with, that I wouldn't have to hide myself from. But you are here now and we are business neighbors."

"What was your coven like?"

"It's a little complicated. The Calarook Coven lives in Astoria, Oregon. We are smaller but very tight knit. However, they encourage us to spread our wings. We are always welcomed back though. I visit my parents and family once a year. How about you, were you part of a coven?"

"Not a big one." The first of a half-truth. "They were not fond of me leaving given our smaller numbers, and said I should do more, be stronger." That last part wasn't a lie.

"What? You are so strong. You said you taught before moving."

"Elementary school." A full lie this time. She was a professor at a prestigious witch academy. "I just read a lot, studied a lot. And baked when I could." Camille laughed.

"What is the first thing you are going to bake when you open your bakery?" Willow asked eagerly.

Camille certainly had the sense that Willow had things she was not talking about. An unspoken mutual understanding.

"Apple crisp muffins, I think. I saw the recipe once and never got a chance to make them. I know it should be a fall thing but at least I have the spring and summer to perfect it, right?"

"Oh, that sounds so good. I hope I can try them."

"Of course. I will bring some over after I make the batch this week."

"I can't wait." Willow beamed. "Can I ask you about an enchantment? It seems to be clashing with this lip balm, which I think would be a good seller for summer. There must be an herb I can substitute or a way to not let the oil overpower the scent I want."

"Of course I would be happy to troubleshoot it with you," Camille said, relieved that they could work on their craft together instead of talking about how she fled her coven.

They worked on testing it and Camille took diligent notes. It felt good to use her magic. She could only do so much in the cabin. The range top and oven were so small as were the counters. Plus, she certainly didn't need an entire cake, pie or dozen of anything lying around. She often offered baked goods to the front desk staff and maintenance crew at the cabins.

She glanced over and saw Sitka lounging on the couch. "Oh, Sitka! I'm sorry, is it alright that she is on the couch? I didn't even notice she had gotten up there."

"It's fine. I don't mind." Willow smiled.

They worked on a few more scents, and established when it got busy for Camille, Willow would take Sitka to her shop via the back alley. She was still working on getting the listening aspect down with the cat. Sitka generally responded to Camille's commands, but there was a time limit and Sitka was still a cat. She did what she wanted to.

Chapter 5

The few days slipped by and before she knew it, Camille was getting the final prep done on the bakery for the soft opening.

She had done a few more hikes with Sitka by her side, and found some herbs she hadn't had access to as easily as before. She had sought out Willow to help with shipments of herbs she couldn't find here.

Willow didn't ask too many questions about Camille's past. She had just told her friend it was just a way to cover shipping costs if they split it, and Camille always paid her share. The money was half hers, some of what she had pawned, and some she had stolen before leaving. That guilt gnawed at her. It meant more demands Thornwell could make if they dragged her back.

Every sunset those truths stared right at her as she spent all day living a lie.

She shoved all those thoughts to the back of her mind and set to baking some apple crisp muffins, just to get a feel for the equipment. It was much later than her planned business hours. She figured she could give some to Willow, whose shop was next door, and maybe some of the other businesses nearby. Maybe she could give one to the health inspector that was coming by today.

Sitka climbed up to the top of a shelf where the sun was shining through the window and got comfortable. Camille smiled before she started baking.

The space had been a deli before, and save for a few new pieces of furniture, some paint, and thrifted decor, she hadn't had to do much more than getting some shelves installed and getting some equipment serviced. Luckily, this deli baked their own bread so they had left behind a large stand mixer and plenty of baking equipment.

While making some honey butter as the muffins baked, she glanced at the clock, noting she had a few moments before the inspection and added her enchantment to the butter. She had yet to try it on something that would be refrigerated. Just a small little splash to mix into the butter. The aim was to give it a small boost of creaminess for some added happiness when people tried it. Something to send them home with.

Just as she put the butter in the refrigerator to set, she heard the door rattle as if someone was trying to enter. Without thinking, she hurried out and opened the door.

And standing in the doorway was Reyes, who she hadn't seen since the day of the hike. He wore a blue flannel and jeans, and had been looking down at his clipboard when she took him in again. She hated how attractive she found him, and how many times she had thought about him since that day.

"Hello, may I help you?"

"Camille?" He looked closer at his clipboard then at her with a slack-jawed expression. "Bakewell?" he asked. "You bake...well?"

She cringed at how stupid a choice the name was. Maybe she should change the business name soon. She had panicked when she picked it for her business name, not knowing she would get to name a bakery. It sounded clever in her head but hearing the same thought process spoken aloud by someone was mortifying now.

"Yes. May I help you?" she said, regaining her composure, though she still took him in and felt excitement stirring in her chest. Something about the blue flannel suited him.

"I'm conducting your health inspection?"

She just stared blankly at him, as if he had asked her to recite something in Latin. "You? Why?"

He grimaced and remained staring at her. "I am the county health inspector? This has been scheduled for weeks now."

"I'm sorry, I just—you don't strike me as the type to have that job."

"I was unaware health inspectors had a look. What job do I look like I'd have?"

"Ranch hand? Construction? I don't know?"

Again, he grimaced. "Okay. I mean, I know how to fix things and build stuff, but no, I work for the county at a desk or in the field. Now, may I come in? I have other appointments and paperwork to file."

"Of course. I was just testing equipment out. Would you like an apple crisp muffin? I have butter chilling in the fridge. It might not be set by the time you finish though. I am not sure how long these inspections take," Camille said and stepped aside.

He just continued to stare at her in confusion. "I have never had an apple crisp muffin, but I guess? You know you are not supposed to be selling things until you pass right?" He walked in and looked around.

"No charge. I just wanted to get a feel for equipment. It's always an adjustment." She maintained her assured tone as best she could.

"Fine." He patted himself down before finding his pen behind his ear. "I will just be looking at stuff. I will have questions so it's best to stay near. I am sure you are following code so this should be pretty quick and painless. If anything is not in compliance, you have a few weeks to fix and then I will be back to inspect that," he explained, not looking at her. She thought he seemed nervous for some reason.

It was then she realized that she had no idea how to interact with him.

"Alright," she acknowledged and watched him as he began looking at the entryway and the counter. She packed two muffins up and watched Reyes examine everything. He seemed so focused now as he glanced at his clipboard frequently. A very different Reyes from his concern on the trail. She just figured he was in his zone.

The health inspector zone, she thought then laughed softly to herself. She stilled when he turned and looked at her as though he were caught slightly off guard.

"The front looks good. May I see the back, the kitchen area?" Reyes asked, getting back into the zone.

Camille complied and stood watching as he inspected the machines, sink area, and drainage, before he stopped in front of her office. When he looked at her, he paused for a moment and she wasn't sure what his expression meant.

"This is your office, I assume?" he asked.

"Yes, sir," she replied.

He sighed and looked at her. "Please don't call me *sir*, there is no need for that. Reyes is fine. Mr. Navarro, if the first name basis feels too weird for you, Ms. Bakewell."

She tensed. "Camille is fine. Please. No last names needed really." A nervous laugh slipped out.

He remained staring at her for a moment. "Alright. Camille. Do you mind if I check in the office, just for proper ventilation and window seals? Pests often come in through those loose seals. I know flour and sugar are susceptible to infestations. I see it a lot."

"Yes, whatever you need," she responded.

He continued his inspection and stopped on a chest of thin drawers. One of them was opened with some labels and dried herbs that she had begun to place. "What is this?"

"Just labels I make," she replied calmly.

"With dried flowers?" he asked, confused.

"Yes." Camille took a deep inhale, maintaining her composure. She knew how to cover up what she was as it too had been part of her education, yet this was her first time actually applying it.

"Alright. Everyone has their personal taste but they could have pests in them."

"They don't," Camille responded with sternness. "I know how to dry and press herbs and flowers."

Reyes remained looking at her with a baffling expression. "You bake, dry herbs, and have worked with animals?"

"Yes."

Once more, they fixed on each other. Camille did not flinch. She wondered if her parents would be proud of her Thornwell grit showing? *Probably not. They had never seemed very proud of you.*

"Do you mind showing me the restrooms next?" He checked a few boxes on the paper on the clipboard, seeming awkward once more.

"Of course."

She showed him the bathroom and watched as he proceeded to do his inspection.

"Alright this looks good, I just need a few signatures and I will explain the post inspection procedure," Reyes said, making a few notes.

Camille led him back to the front where Reyes set some papers down and explained that everything looked good. He advised her to be very careful with the flowers in the office. He made note of the glass jars in the window and reminded her that she was registered as a bakery and all ingredients would need to be able to be found easily by customers due to food allergies and dietary restrictions.

He explained all of this while looking at her and then at his papers. If she had to place it, he seemed almost bashful, but she could not fathom why. She herself felt that excitement in her stomach the whole time. When he had walked by her, she took in his cedarwood-like scent.

"So the passing decal will be in the mail within the week. I'll place the temporary one in the window for now. The official one will arrive fairly quickly since the bakery is right next to where they are processed. It'll be sent through certified mail for the paper trail," he concluded.

It all made sense to her though she was slightly perturbed at his ignorance with her herbs. Then again, she knew he was just a human. He couldn't know about how she was a witch that used the dried flowers and herbs to enchant her syrups with. In his case, it was best to smile and nod as she proceeded to sign where he had stuck little yellow sticky flags.

"Thank you, Reyes." She smiled warmly. "Would you like some butter with the muffins? They are still warm, so maybe keep the butter separate from the bag."

"I guess. I'm not a big sweets guy but I will try anything just once," he replied with a small bashful-sounding chuckle.

As he proceeded to look over the forms, Camille rushed back and put some of the butter in a little plastic cup. Reyes would be her first human subject here. It would be extra special if he liked them since he didn't like sweets. She hoped for a critique from him somehow, so she would know if it were too much. The last thing she wanted to do was to cause the enchantment to overpower the flavor. She just had to find the sweet spot for humans as she hadn't had much experience with that yet.

Rushing back out, she handed him the bag with two small plastic containers. "There you are. The butter set nicely but it's still soft and easy to spread. I hope you enjoy it."

"Thanks," Reyes said, putting his pen back behind his ear and tucking his clipboard under his arm before grabbing the bag.

They stood there again, awkwardly smiling at each other. They must've looked like idiots to anyone passing by.

Reyes turned and took a few steps then froze. "What the fuck is that?" he gasped out.

Camille's eyes fixed on Sitka, whose head had popped up. Her heart sank and she didn't know what to say.

"You cannot keep a wild animal and certainly not in a dining establishment. Have you kept it the entire time? You were supposed to call the numbers I gave you!"

"She was free to go as she pleased. Sitka chose to stay with me."

"You named it? You can't keep a bobcat, Camille." He dragged his hand down his face.

"You were done with your inspection. You passed me." Her voice was insistent despite it breaking.

"I didn't think you had a wild animal in here."

"Did you see any evidence of her in here before you saw her? I will ensure she stays in my office when I open. I promise you. Besides, what if mice get in? I have pest control. There are tons of bodega cats and shop dogs and stuff." Camille tried to force her confidence out, her Thornwell grit her parents reminded her she had never had enough of.

"There aren't bakery cats and dogs and this isn't a house cat, it's a bobcat. What if a kid comes and makes noises? Or a bunch of people come in at once and try to pet it? We get too many tourists as it is. It's going to attract attention," Reyes pleaded.

This caused Camille to still. Attracting attention would be bad for her. She looked down with a frown for a moment, realizing how out of touch she had been living on the academy grounds. His sigh caused her to look up at him.

"Look, I'm not trying to make life difficult for you. I can tell you put a lot of work into this place. It's just a liability and it's a wild animal. Keeping exotic pets isn't right. No matter how tame they seem, they are still wild, not domesticated. Call one of the numbers I gave you. I will push this through so you can open but I will be back to ensure the cat is gone. Please don't keep it cooped up. I commend you for helping it, since it looks really healthy but let it go. Otherwise, my buddy has to take it to Trinity," Reyes lamented.

"Thank you," Camille said and felt absolutely dejected. She forced a smile as her mind shifted through the thoughts on what she was going to do next.

"I also can't give you an exact date on when I'm following up."

"Understood. Have a nice day, Mr. Navarro," she replied, still masking her worry. Again, he looked at her with remorse but turned and left without a word more.

Chapter 6

Reyes returned to his desk and set the bag down gently. He tossed his clipboard down, causing it to shift a stack of papers on his desk and knock his pencil cup over. Everyone looked over to see the noise as he slumped down in his seat with a sigh.

So much for any chance with her now.

He heard his coworker and close friend, Evan, laugh at him. "Rough inspection?"

"I feel like I'm the bad guy but I didn't do anything wrong. I did my job."

Evan patted him on the shoulder hard. "My man, Reyes, over here just crushin' hopes and dreams." Evan laughed loudly. "Who was it today?"

"The bakery next door," Reyes mumbled, then leaned back in his seat and pinched the bridge of his nose. "Damn it. The look of absolute dejection in her eyes."

"You crushed the bakery girl?" Evan sputtered out. "Damn, you are an asshole. But, I mean, if she didn't pass inspection, what's the problem?"

"She did pass. Everything was immaculate. Despite her trying to do too much for the aesthetic, everything was fine." He groaned in frustration.

"So then what happened? Are you actually the bad guy?"

"No!" Reyes sat forward in his chair. "She has a bobcat in there. She insists she gave it the option to leave. Like what is even going on?"

Evan looked at him. "A bobcat? Aren't they rather elusive?"

"Yes," Reyes stammered then explained how he had run into Camille a few weeks ago on a hiking trail and how she'd carried it back to her car.

"I mean, it is odd, but she obviously takes it to places, so it has a chance to escape if it wants to," Evan explained.

"It can't be in the bakery. And it's a wild animal," Reyes repeated for what felt like the hundredth time in the last twenty minutes.

"Well, check to see if it's there on the follow up before you have to be the bad guy." Evan shrugged. "What's in the bag you so gingerly set down?"

"Muffins," Reyes grumbled.

"Damn, what an asshole. She gave you muffins and you told her she can't keep her pet? I dunno if I wanna be friends with you anymore."

"Shut up," Reyes said and started filling out his report on the bakery. Then he took out the muffin and spread the butter on it as suggested. He set it down and continued typing before he picked it up to take a bite.

The moan that slipped out of him when he bit into it caused everyone to look at him once more. He felt his ears heat.

Evan bellowed out a laugh, embarrassing him further. "Bro, you are losing it. What did the bakery girl do to you?"

"This is absolutely amazing. Try it. A little of it." Reyes broke a piece off and put it on a napkin for Evan.

A small moan slipped out of Evan. "If you shut her down before she even opens, I will never talk to you again. This is heavenly."

"She called it an apple crisp muffin and made the butter too," Reyes added and promptly finished the other half. "She knows how to bake, I will give her that. But what kind of education would she have if she handles animals, bakes, and does botany stuff?"

"Who knows, but she needs to continue baking. What else does she bake?"

"I don't know, she said she was just baking these to test out the equipment."

"Well, I'm going to go take my break and see if she has any more." Evan laughed and stood up.

"She's not supposed to be selling anything, Evan. She's not even technically open," Reyes shot back. "And there's a bobcat in there."

"Look, if I come back with a bunch of scratches then you can feel like less of a bad guy," Evan said as he hurried out the door.

"Dumbass," Reyes mumbled under his breath and went back to typing.

After Reyes left, Camille sat at one of the tables, staring down at the floor. Sitka came up to her and rubbed against her legs, purring. She reached down and scratched her cheeks.

"It's not your fault, Sitka. I just need to be more careful. I'm not leaving you at the cabin nor am I going to let anyone take you now. You chose me and I am honored." She got up and started packing the muffins up for Willow. "We will just have to be careful when we go next door," Camille affirmed as she pulled the butter out and cut the block in half.

Just when she had finished wrapping it, she heard a tug on the door and let out a disgruntled sigh. "Now what?"

She half expected to see Reyes with the police or something at the door but was surprised to see a different man standing there. He wore a black and red jacket with jeans and boots. His hair was a dirty blond and his eyes were blue. He somewhat looked as though he could have been a cousin to Leland Talbot that had grown up humble and normal.

"May I help you?" she asked, nearly cringing but mentally preparing for what her next possible move might be. Sitka had stayed behind the counter when she last glanced back.

"Hi there, I know this might be a bit rude to ask, but well—" he paused and laughed. "Alright, I work with that absolute grump you just had the joy of meeting, Reyes. My name is Evan and I tried the muffin. I know Reyes said you weren't supposed to sell anything but you passed inspection so you are totally allowed to, and I have cash here. It was just divine and Reyes was being a stingy bastard with his stash," Evan pleaded, giving her a big goofy grin. "Please."

"Oh." Camille blushed. "Um, I wasn't selling this batch. I am happy to give you some. No charge."

"Are you sure? I'm happy to pay. Don't worry. It won't get you in trouble with Reyes. He feels bad about the animal too."

"He told you?" Camille frowned. "I know it's hard to believe but she's not in any harm."

"Hey, I'm sure it's fine. There are all kinds of stories of people befriending ravens and stuff. Don't worry about Reyes either. He isn't a dick, he just has a list of boxes to check. He feels like an asshole but he really isn't. You should have heard the moan that slipped out of him when he tried the muffin. It was dead silent in the office too. I have never seen him so undone before."

This warmed something in Camille. She couldn't help but laugh at the thought. Her mind also wondered what a moan from him would sound like for a moment before catching herself. Her eyes met Evan's, who was grinning.

"Please come in. I will get the muffins packed up. Is three alright?" she said, walking back behind the counter to pack the muffins.

"That is more than alright. I honestly was only expecting one. Are you sure you don't want me to pay you for them?"

"It's alright. I don't have the system up yet. I just hope you enjoy it," Camille said and set about getting the butter wrapped up. She was relieved to unload most of them and not have to worry about having too many sitting in the cabin.

"Oh. It's cute."

Camille froze and looked at Evan, confused. He gazed past her, right at Sitka who was sitting on her chair in the office.

"Sitka!" she fretted. "Not in view of customers." Then the bobcat jumped down and walked behind the door. Camille looked at Evan again and was ready to beg him to not say anything to Reyes. "Please don't mention this to Mr. Navarro."

Evan laughed. "Mr. Navarro? I won't tell him. He will be more upset that you gave me three muffins and him two. I will have to remind him to not be an asshole. He actually is rather horrible with women. I tell him to just relax but I don't know if he has ever heard the word sometimes. Also, Sitka?"

"Like the tree."

"Fitting. Your secret is safe with me. Thanks, Ms. Bakewell."

"Camille is fine, Mr.—" she paused. The name Bakewell now reminded her more of the lies she was living. She had known she would have to lie, but she never imagined it grating on her so much.

"Evan, just Evan is fine, Camille. If you need to butter up Reyes, he is very serious about his coffee. Straight black coffee is his vice. If I see him walk in with a latte, I will assume you worked some kind of divine magic on him." Evan laughed before he left.

After the trying morning she had so far, she packed up the remaining muffins and hurried to Willow's shop. Sitka darted into the open door to Willow's shop from the alley and Camille followed.

"Hey, are those goodies you have?" Willow asked, walking towards her.

"Yes. Apple crisp muffins. I'm hoping you can tell me if it's too much or what. Honest critique. I guess I have two human test subjects already. Word is one thoroughly enjoyed it and was very greedy with sharing." Camille laughed, almost embarrassed.

"Who? I guess you may not know their names—wait! You had your health code inspection. Reyes!" Willow proclaimed.

"Yes, and also his coworker, Evan?" Camille confessed then recounted the morning.

Willow laughed and took one of the muffins. "Reyes honestly could use some sweets in his life. He can be such a grump when I see him walking by. Evan isn't bad on the eyes."

"Oh. You haven't pursued him?" Camille asked curiously.

"He was married for a long time and I guess the divorce isn't going smoothly. He doesn't need that. *I* don't need that."

"I never would have guessed. He seemed so cheery. Unlike Reyes."

"Evan and Reyes act like brothers whenever I see them. They go on fishing trips and stuff from what I gather. I am mutual friends with Evan's now ex-wife." She set the knife down. "So, is that curiosity about Reyes I sense?" Willow teased.

"I don't know. Maybe, but he certainly doesn't like me now, and I don't need him. I'm not getting rid of Sitka."

"Oh absolutely not. Reyes, too, had some bad luck with his ex. The few times I saw them together at gatherings, she would insult him a lot. In public too. I'm not entirely sure why he put up with it. It's best just to let both boys work out their shit." Willow chuckled and bit into the muffin. "Okay, how do you nail this every time? No wonder Reyes moaned in his office."

Camille frowned with that knowledge about Reyes. "Do you think the enchantment is too much?" she asked, steering her thoughts away from him.

"No way! I can sense what the enchantment is doing, but the flavor is really speaking for itself. I bet you could make a batch without the enhancements and it would still make people moan." Willow laughed. "I have been working on figuring out how to make the salves and lip balms last longer. I think I've figured out the candles. Though I'm not sure how long the effect lasts. It's hard for me to tell since I'm so attuned to the enchantments already. Do you think you can test my newest candle out?"

"Yes. Depending on the scent and enchantment I will try it in the bakery. I'm not home too often and I don't want to start a fire. I'm in an older model cabin."

"Oh down in Dunsmuir, right? I know the place. Yeah, I can imagine candles would be bad there," Willow said and brought out a cedar & cinnamon scented candle.

Together, they worked out the enchantment while being mindful of customers that walked in.

Chapter 7

By the following week, she'd brought Sitka to the bakery one morning and she was happy to hang out in the back. Things were going better than expected but she watched and noted every single customer that had walked in. Watching for any witches, or anyone from Thornwell coven. She always kept an ear and eye open, always took in her surroundings as much as she could before fully entering a space.

Then again unless Thornwell wanted to out themselves, they couldn't exactly haul her out of the bakery in broad daylight. *They could just wait for you to leave. They could follow you home or wait until you are alone on a trail,* she reminded herself. *That's why you have Sitka. To warn you.*

The bell rang and she instantly forced her frown into a smile. She grew slightly tense upon seeing Evan walk in. He appeared relaxed.

"Hello, Camille, my favorite baker," he mused.

"Are there many bakers here?"

"No, but even if there were, they would not compare to you." He grinned wide. "A few coworkers put an order in so I'm doing a bakery run today."

"Oh, alright so a large box then, yes?" Camille asked.

"That will do." Evan began to read off the items off the list and Camille tried to offer the best substitutions, apologizing for not having the exact things and noted the popular items. "And, lastly for my boy, Reyes, he asked for an apple crisp muffin if you had any. With some butter."

"Yes, I have some of those left. I am surprised he asked for one. He said he wasn't a big sweets guy. And I haven't seen him since that inspection." She frowned, once again chastising herself for how many times she had thought about him. Never had she felt such an attraction to someone before. His absence in the bakery would lead her to believe he didn't seem to feel the same way. Shaking off the thought she put the muffin in a separate small bag with the butter.

"Would you like to see him again?" Evan's smile grew mischievous.

She couldn't tell what he was really getting at aside from that he found this situation amusing.

"I don't know. I'm sure he is busy."

"Well, I have it on good authority you might see him on Thursday." Evan gave her a wink.

Realization dawned on her that Evan was telling her when the follow-up inspection was. "Oh. Okay! Thank you. I feel like I am not supposed to know that though."

"None of us want to see you shut down, especially not Reyes. Just act surprised." He laughed. "This place will pass. I mean it already did technically and it looks fine."

Evan placed the bag with the muffin and the small container of butter in his jacket pocket before he grabbed the box and headed for the door, pushing it open with his shoulder. He glanced back and gave her a smile then he was gone.

Reyes watched Evan stroll in with the box. The number of times he caught himself thinking about Camille was way more than he cared to admit. He leapt up the second he saw someone go to the box.

"Did she have any muffins?" Reyes asked, then stared blankly at his friend's wide grin.

"She did," he said. Reyes looked down but didn't see it. Evan's expression hadn't changed.

"Did you get me one?"

"Obsessed much?" Evan replied.

"Yes or no?" Reyes sighed, almost annoyed. He wasn't sure why he was craving one. Or why he was acting like a dog with a treat. Just the muffin alone was one of the best things he had tasted.

Reyes felt his heart pick up slightly upon seeing Evan pull a bag out of his jacket pocket, then raced upon seeing the little plastic container with the butter.

"There you are, Mr. Navarro. Enjoy your muffin mastication," Evan replied, still grinning.

Reyes felt his ears heat again. "Shut up," he muttered and snatched the bag from his hands and grabbed the butter. "Thanks though."

Once back at his desk, he eagerly set to prepare the muffin and fought the urge to moan with everything in him. He knew Evan would say something and Reyes did not need any more embarrassment over this.

"Damn this is so good. Where did she study again? Paris or something?" Evan gushed as he sat down. He had some kind of berry Danish from what Reyes could deduce.

"Seattle? I don't think she went to school for baking though. I don't know what she went to school for exactly," Reyes pondered.

"Well, she has a gift for it. Certainly makes the workday better." He smiled wide. "You are not going to shut her down, right? You better not."

"As long as she got rid of the bobcat. If it's there, though, I have to file it." He had a dreadful feeling she hadn't gotten rid of it. It sat heavy in his gut.

"You could just check with animal control?"

"It honestly looked fine. Hopefully she just released it. I cannot imagine it wants to stay cooped up all day. It's got so many miles it could be roaming. A little cabin in Dunsmuir is no place for it," Reyes explained and started typing on his computer.

He took one more bite of the muffin, trying to savor it and fight a moan. *Damn what does she put in this? Magic?* he wondered, laughing silently at the absurd thought.

"You creeped on her personal address?" Evan asked curiously.

"No, you idiot. I would never. She told me she was renting a cabin in Dunsmuir when we found the bobcat. You know exactly where she is staying and no, I don't know the cabin number."

"Sure thing, bud," Evan laughed and went about his work.

Sometime after Reyes had finished the muffin, he mindlessly reached for it again and realized it was gone. He frowned, and for a split second he debated on running over to the bakery.

You could see her again. See that look in her eyes. Maybe it would be that look of wonder she had when she first laid eyes on him. No one had ever looked at him like that before, and it did such weird things to him. She had looked at him after he finished the inspection, before he saw the bobcat. Then she looked at him with fear and worry. *Right, because you are the bearer of bad news. You make people nervous with what you do. You can crush hopes and dreams.*

He frowned at the thought and slumped back into his chair, releasing all the air in his lungs in a big, long sigh. Regardless of what he wanted right now, and what he thought was best, he was going to have to see her on Thursday. He just hoped with everything in him that she had let the bobcat go. Or at the very least leave it outside and be a good liar about releasing it.

Maybe he could let that slide. If he didn't see it.

He hadn't written anything about it on her paperwork. He hadn't wanted to, but how would he explain it if the cat attacked someone and he was asked about it? He had mentioned it in the office already. Yet no one else had mentioned it. Not even Evan on the day of the first inspection when he knew it was still there.

"Hey, Evan, you sure you didn't see the bobcat that first day you went in there?" Reyes asked.

Evan didn't even look up from his computer, but Reyes could see his smirk.

"I don't know what you are talking about. I can't recall ever seeing a bobcat in my life."

"Dude, don't lie, did you see it today? I know it was there the first day."

Evan finally looked up. "No. I didn't see a bobcat."

"You are impossible sometimes," Reyes muttered.

When Thursday rolled around, Reyes couldn't help the lingering worry that he was going to not only crush her but any chance he might've ever had with her as well. Would someone ever look at him like she had again? Would *she* look at him like that again?

At times he felt like half the town hated him. It was not as though he wanted to make life difficult for people—he didn't enjoy seeing restaurants fail health inspections.

After he printed the follow-up inspection form and padded himself down for his badge, a pen, and wallet, Reyes grabbed his clipboard before heading out to the bakery. Catching a quick glimpse of the mountain between buildings, he gave a silent plea to it that the bobcat was not there. His last few steps were slow as he entered the bakery.

There were a number of people inside so he watched her. He noted the way she took such care to talk to everyone and tell them exactly what was in the item they had selected. He noticed her tense up slightly when people said they had come from further away and had heard about it by word of mouth. One customer even said they had driven an hour from Redding to try the bakery.

Camille's nervous tone confused him. Redding was not that far. It wasn't uncommon for people from Redding to come up here to hike or fish and it wasn't uncommon for people here to drive down to Redding. He had done it plenty to get things that stores just didn't have up here since it was a bigger city. It was still a mere fraction of what his hometown had.

His eyes scanned the case for a moment and locked onto the apple crisp muffins. He frantically checked how many people were in front of him and counted four. He just hoped they didn't order the remaining half dozen she had left.

He heard her gasp and his eyes locked with hers. A heat flushed over her cheeks for a moment before she took a deep inhale and looked away, focusing back on the customers.

What was that for? he wondered to himself. His eyes scanned what he could of the bakery, looking atop all the shelves. *No bobcat. Please don't be here, little beast.*

After the customers left, he stepped up to the counter before some people came in behind him, throwing him into a frenzy. Which was dumb because he had done plenty of inspections while restaurants were busy.

"Hello, Mr. Navarro."

"Hi, Camille, I am doing your follow-up inspection today." Reyes couldn't help the tremor in his hands.

"I'm not sure what is expected on follow-up inspections. Am I supposed to just lock the door or..."

"No, operate like normal please. I just need to check the back and the restrooms. I will announce my presence before entering the restrooms, of course, for anyone using it. I assume it is not a public restroom given where it is located?"

"No, sir. It is just for my use."

He glanced up at the ceiling for a moment at the use of *sir*. He hated being called that. Never in his life had he been very dominant—about anything really. He just had to be an ass sometimes because of his job.

"Alright, well, I will announce my presence for any staff that may be in there." He tried his best to smile but he already felt her tension. *Please don't let that cat be in here. Please lie to me, Camille.*

"There is no staff, just me."

The statement caught him off guard. She was running this place by herself? He expected a part-time helper at the very least. The deli that occupied the space prior had at least three people at any time despite a rather frequent turnover rate.

"Alright, well protocol still requires that I announce myself while the business is open."

She nodded and eyed him with determination. "I have dishes in the sink, from this morning. I promise I will clean them before I leave for the day."

"Camille, I don't expect you to not be operating. Dishes are fine as long as they have not been sitting for weeks and have pests on them."

"No, sir, they don't."

His shoulders sagged slightly at the use of the title again. He had a job to do and the quicker this was done, the sooner this awkward interaction would be over.

"May I get one of those apple crisp muffins? With the butter please. I will pay for it on the way out."

"Of course. Anything else?"

"Maybe a coffee if you have any?"

"Yes," she said with an assertion.

"You can relax. I'm really not here to shut you down. I promise," he said quieter this time, trying to ease her tension.

"You better not," someone muttered behind him. Reyes turned to see another restaurant owner who had given him problems in the past. "This guy can be a real asshole."

Reyes sighed. He didn't have any fight left in him, so he held his head low and headed to the kitchen area. He noticed the dishes. A whisk and large metal bowl was hardly anything for her to worry about. Everything else looked really clean. He went to the bathroom next, announcing he was entering. Everything was pristine, as if it hadn't been used today. Then he paused before entering the office.

No bobcat. A smile formed as he looked high and low. Then he noted the herbs were all stowed away in secure containers.

He noticed what appeared to be a large round cast iron pot set in a box under the desk and he wondered what it was for. He hadn't seen anything like it. It wasn't the usual shape for a soup pot. For a moment, he wondered if it was something for bread making to let it rise in.

It was none of his concern. His concern was the bobcat, and it was not here. So he turned and headed back up front. Just as another customer left.

She looked at him, wide-eyed.

She's beautiful, he thought. Then he noticed a blush creeping up on her cheeks again and she chewed on her bottom lip. He forced himself to look anywhere but her lips. *You are being so unprofessional. Stop!*

"Everything looks great. I just need a few signatures. You are all done dealing with me for six months when I will have to perform another random inspection as per county guidelines."

"Understood, sir. Thank you," she said, relieved.

"Please don't call me *sir*. I really don't like that title. Reyes is fine, honestly."

"Alright," she said in a smaller voice than he had heard her use.

She signed in all the spots he had marked. When she was done, she set the pen down and slid it to him with the clipboard. Then she pushed a small brown bag towards him. "Here you are, Reyes." A small bashful smile came to her now, as if she was uneasy saying his name.

He paused for way longer than he should have, suddenly forgetting how to function. *She's bashful? With me? You are too much, Cami.*

His eyes widened in shock that he had just called her Cami. Sure, it was in his mind, but what was happening to him? Evan was right; he was really losing it and he shouldn't be.

"How much do I owe you?" he fumbled with his words, trying to maintain his composure.

"It's on the house. Don't worry about it."

"I can pay, you don't need to give me handouts. You passed with flying colors. I take it the cat was released back out in the wild?"

"Yes," she said, rather quickly. "I just—I want to give you this. I imagine you might not be a food place's favorite person and I'm not trying to make assumptions but what that customer said about you was out of line. I don't think you are an asshole at all."

His mouth fell agape as he felt his ears burn. He had to blink a few times before he spoke. "Thanks. That guy is a restaurant owner in a town north of here. I am not allowed to say anything more." He laughed nervously. "But seriously, let me pay for this."

Another customer walked in and Reyes felt a sudden urge to glare at them for interrupting the moment. If he could have growled, he would have.

"Get it next time. I hope you enjoy it. Have a good day, Mr. Navarro."

Shock hit him again, only this time it hadn't left him feeling all warm and fuzzy like he had a few minutes ago. It felt as though she had been in a hurry to end the conversation.

"I will. Thank you, Ms. Bakewell."

He saw her frown before turning to the customer and all he could do was promptly leave.

As soon as he was outside, he muttered an expletive under his breath. "I need to stop acting so stupid around her. I need to figure myself out or I'm going to go crazy." He felt utterly hopeless now with Camille.

Chapter 8

"Well that was awkward," Camille said to herself as she closed up for the day, thinking about Reyes. "But I'm safe for six months. With any luck, Evan will have my back next time and give me a heads-up."

As she packed up the last few items that she had set aside for herself, Willow, and the cabin staff, she wondered if she would actually see him again. Or not. She wanted to, but she knew she shouldn't. Then again, she shouldn't have bonded with a familiar, but she just couldn't help it. Sitka was choosing her. Much like that mountain obviously was.

She stopped by Willow's shop and set two boxes down on Willow's desk.

"Hey, how was today?" Willow asked and slowly pulled the pink box towards herself.

Camille nodded. "Yes, that one's for you. It was another good day. Not much left at all. I did save some for the front desk staff at the cabins though," Camille explained. It was too warm to leave the pastries in the car though. Not even her enchantments could withstand the heat that came from the area. It was a wonder that it would get so much snow in the winters. She would be prepared for the snow, though. It was April and she could see plenty of it on the mountain. There had even been some snow hanging on in some patches on her hikes if she was at a higher elevation.

"Well I appreciate you thinking of me."

"Of course." She smiled and sat down. "Had my follow-up inspection. Passed and safe for six months." She exhaled a sigh of relief.

"Oh that's good. I doubt Reyes would have really gotten you shut down." Willow laughed. "But he might have been a headache for a bit. Did you leave Sitka near your cabin?"

"Yeah. I have tested it out a few times, and she does pretty well. I'm trying to tell myself to not worry as much."

"Of course. She will be safe," Willow assured and bit into the berry turnover. Her face told Camille it was excellent.

"You haven't found a familiar in your four years here?" Camille asked.

"Nah, that hasn't happened. Besides, the rental doesn't allow pets. I'm sure that applies to familiars." Willow laughed. "I haven't felt the need for the extra alert when I'm out foraging on trails."

"You could just leave a window open for them." Camille laughed. "I actually never gave much thought to a familiar before. My coven didn't often think much of them." She didn't miss Willow's curious expression. "They preferred bigger apex predators."

"Oh. Well I think a bobcat certainly is easier to have in a house or nearby. Mountain lions get big, bears even bigger. Wolves might even be too much. Not that we have any wolves here."

Camille was relieved with the save and the focus on animals. "There were some wolves near Seattle on occasion. Were there any here?"

"I'm sure a long time ago, but no one talks about them or seeing any like they do mountain lions or bears."

Camille nodded and noticed Willow's notebook on the desk, with notes on an energizing scent. "I need to get used to the heat here. My enchantments aren't going to hold up against them if someone leaves their pastries in the car."

"It might not be a bad thing; people might think you are loading them with preservatives."

"That sounds like something Reyes would be upset about." She laughed then tensed when she realized she had brought him up again. A heat crept across her face and it had nothing to do with the temperature outside.

"That sure does sound like something he would look into." Willow chuckled. "Honestly I don't think that guy would know what to do with a girl's attention, especially yours."

"Do you mean, what I am or..." Camille asked, confused.

"I mean someone sweet, kind, and cute. He can't know what we are, of course, but I imagine him stumbling through a conversation with you." Willow laughed.

"Well, he has stumbled through all our conversations. As if I make him nervous. He makes me nervous, but he has a nice smile, and nice eyes and—there I go again. Thinking about him." Camille shook her head in dismay.

"He is single. There's no saying you can't make the first move with him."

"No, it was really awkward today. I called him sir and didn't realize how uncomfortable that made him. Sometimes we give each other these looks like two idiots and I can't—"

"You called him sir? I cannot tell you how badly I want to see these interactions." Willow snickered again.

"Glad you might find them amusing. I have to remind myself not to address people so formally," Camille groaned.

"Did you have to before? Is Bakewell a coven that uses honorifics?"

Camille tensed again, realizing her mistake. She couldn't keep bringing up her past. Of all her lessons at the academy, she thought she had learned to fit in with the non-magic users. For the first time, Camille realized again how she hadn't ever gotten to apply what she learned until now.

"Yes. They preferred that." Camille looked at the open notebook, trying to deflect. "Is that an enchantment for energy? What does it go in?" she asked.

Willow blinked then shifted her gaze to the notebook. "Oh yeah. I put it in a salve." She laughed. "It's getting warmer out with summer coming up. People will be out camping more and stuff so I usually put these out to keep people alert. There is a lot of open land and dispersed camping here. It's not uncommon for people to be out drinking and forgetting to store their food and stuff. We hear about it often, run-ins with wildlife and stuff. Nothing happens luckily. Our wildlife doesn't like loud and that's everyone's first reaction."

"Oh, that makes sense. I wonder what I could put an energy enchantment in. The caffeine seems to do the trick in the coffee drinks."

"That's true." Willow stood up as a customer walked in.

Camille took hers out and started to write some pastries down that might be good for summer. She hadn't been to the farmer's market yet but figured she should go this Monday. The bakery was closed and it was in the afternoon.

"They just bought the energy salve." Willow chuckled.

"You got me thinking now. Have you been to the farmer's market?"

"Yeah, it's small; the good ones are down in Sacramento. We should go some Sunday. Maybe we could do a weekend down there? If you want? Sightsee some stuff. It's about three hours south of us."

"Wouldn't it be hard for Sitka?"

"Oh yeah that's true. There are a lot more people down there. But maybe if we kept her in a carrier and rented something along the river? We could go back to the lodging often?"

"That sounds fun," Camille said.

Willow then went on to invite her to the local bar, saying it was made for great people watching. Cami hadn't been to a proper bar with humans before. Just the one on campus a few times.

"I'll let you know. I should check on Sitka. I'll see you tomorrow."

"Sounds good. See ya, Camille."

She got up and put bags in the car and went to start her car.

It didn't start.

She'd had a lot of lessons at the academy, but none of them had covered automotive stuff aside from driving. She had no idea what to do. She tried again and the car made a horrible sound. She didn't even know who to call.

"Damn it, you should have prepared for this." Camille groaned and leaned on the steering wheel for a moment. It burned her skin slightly. The heat was getting to her. "Maybe Willow knows what to do. One more try and maybe?"

She turned the key—and nothing. With a disgruntled sigh, she got out of the car and jumped at another car door slamming shut nearby.

"Camille? Would you like some help?" Reyes asked, walking around to the back of his truck's tailgate. Camille wasn't surprised to see him since the bakery and city hall shared a lot.

"Umm. I'm not sure what's wrong with it."

"Sounds like a battery problem. I have cables to try to jump it. If not, I'm happy to run and grab a new battery. To pay back for all the muffins," he said with a small smile.

"Oh, I can pay for it. Don't you have to get back to work?"

"I'm on a break. It's fine. I'm sure my boss will understand that I helped the baker next door. He loves your stuff. Pop the hood." He unlocked the tailgate and dug around stuff before he pulled the cables out.

Camille looked at her car. It took a second for her to locate the hood latch. He walked around to his driver's side and popped his hood. He leaned over her car as she came to stand next to him.

"Looks like your connection somehow came loose. They look pretty corroded too. How long have you had this car?"

"I bought it when I moved here, so a few months. I didn't have much so I kind of took the first one I could find. Most of my money went into the bakery."

He looked at her and his mouth fell open again. "You literally just moved here and opened a bakery? From Washington?"

"Yes." She had been staring at his eyes and then his lips. She cut her eyes to his hands, now not sure if the flush was due to their proximity or the temperature.

"Hold tight, I got stuff to fix this. Old truck and by all means I gotta keep it running, but Old Skye here is reliable. She's good to me." He laughed.

Camille looked at him then at the truck. "The truck? Skye with an e?"

"Yes. I named my truck. And yes, with an e. You are the first to ask." With another laugh, he poured some liquid on the connectors.

"Island of the clouds, or winged? Scottish, right?"

He paused and looked at her with that look of awe. "Yes. I'm surprised you know that. I randomly saw it in a magazine once and thought it was fitting since she's blue and all. You know a lot about a lot of things."

"Not cars obviously." She frowned.

He laughed and grabbed some pillars, clamping down the connectors. "That's alright. They aren't everyone's thing. Try to start it."

"Yes, sir." *Shit.* Her eyes shot wide. "Sorry, Reyes."

He sighed. "It's alright. It's usually used in a negative way with me given what I do." He nodded to city hall.

She got in her car and it still struggled.

"That's what I thought. Give me a second."

He hooked the cables up then put them under the hood of his. He jumped in the seat of his truck and started it, prompting the loud roar of the engine to fill the cab of her car. It made her clench her jaw and he looked at her for a moment in confusion.

Reyes rolled his window down. "Alright, try to start it."

She took a deep inhale and did. It struggled to turn over and she groaned.

"Wait," he said and she did. "Okay, try it again."

She did once more and her car started. A huge sigh of relief escaped her. He left his truck running and got out, slamming the door. She jumped once more and caught her breath. She really hated loud sounds like this. Yet she couldn't deny that this behemoth of a truck had saved her. He unhooked the cables and closed his hood. She braced herself, expecting him to slam it but he didn't. He lowered it and dropped it slightly, pushing it down. He did the same to hers but she still tensed up.

"Are you alright?" he asked softly.

"Yes," Camille replied, forcing her shoulders to relax and reminding herself to unclench her jaw.

"You seem tense."

"I-I don't like loud sounds."

He remained fixed on her with a look she couldn't exactly figure out. Concern maybe? *Probably not.*

"Sorry. The truck is loud." He sighed. "You are not the first person to think so. If you have any more problems with it, I'm happy to look over it."

"I should get home. Thank you though, Reyes. I really appreciate it."

"No problem." He smiled and wiped his hands on his jeans. "Happy I could help. Drive safely."

She sat there and stared at him, feeling drawn in as he stood, leaning down and looking at her. The mountain caught her attention in her peripheral. Mt. Shasta sat and watched all of this unfold.

He moved and her eyes shifted to him again.

"Thanks again. I hope the rest of your day goes well," she said with a smile. He backed up and she drove off, heading south.

"I need to stop being so awkward around him. I haven't felt this much attraction to anyone before," she muttered to herself before getting out of the car.

Once inside the cabin, she saw Sitka lying on the bed and gave her a pet before heading out to pawn off the rest of the baked goods to the front desk staff. They all beamed with delight. As she walked back to her cabin, Camille wondered if she should take Willow up on her offer to travel to Sacramento. Then she thought about the bar.

Would it hurt? she wondered. It was more interaction with people, and more interaction to learn how to act human. Then again, it was more chance for her to accidentally slip and say something that might make Willow question more about her past.

She groaned with indecision. Her parents would tell her to not be so indecisive. Thornwell was assertive, not wishy-washy. Going to a bar would be far below Thornwell too.

Chapter 9

The weather was getting warmer as May arrived. Reyes approached the bakery one morning and noticed people inside. Three guys and one woman.

"Well, let me know if you need anything extra in your—" Camille's words abruptly cut off when he entered and she smiled widely at him. Then he noticed the intense gaze of three guys. It definitely made him feel self-conscious.

The shortest one of the guys was the first to avert his intense blue-eyed gaze. He had fair skin and blond hair with an undercut that was brushed to one side. He was slightly taller than the woman who had dark brown, wavy hair and tanned skin that was a hint lighter than his. The one with green eyes and chestnut colored hair pulled her closer, as if Reyes was some kind of threat. The woman only offered a glance and laced her fingers with the guy who looked at her with a smile.

Reyes could see they were crazy about each other. He couldn't help but glance at Camille and wonder what it might feel like to have that with someone again. What if Camille acted like that with him one day?

"Okay, I know what I want," the woman said, breaking Reyes's wandering daydreams. He was almost grateful for the distraction but was bothered he was even thinking that.

He thought this entire interaction was odd. Then he heard someone laugh. The other guy. He was stocky and had at least six inches on Reyes.

He had tawny colored skin like his own, a goatee, and a shaggy buzzcut. Reyes could feel the guy sizing him up with his gaze and smirk.

"Are you in a hurry or can I make their drinks before I take your order?" Camille looked at Reyes.

"Oh, I'm in no hurry, Camille. Tend to all these lovely customers," Reyes said sarcastically.

"Will do. Mr. Navarro. It's so nice to open your own business then acquire a supervisor," Camille replied wryly. The biggest of the three guys laughed loudly.

"Oh, I like her. This place is great already. Good pick, El," he added after he got his laugh out.

Reyes noticed Camille's cheeks redden and felt a bout of jealousy followed by worry. This guy looked like he was in great shape. He obviously worked out. He had the buzz cut—though it was shaggy. What if Camille was attracted to the type of guy that looked like him, but she wanted someone more in shape? Or had a beard? His had grown patchy when he tried to have one and just gave up on having any kind of facial hair. His shoulders slumped with his exhale as he stared at the floor.

She had seemed to be more comfortable over the last few weeks when he walked in to pick up the office order. He volunteered often to do that. Her bright smile and cheery demeanor towards him had become the highlight of his day. She would occasionally offer some witty banter and he would clam up since he wasn't used to it. And she would always make him feel seen or acknowledged before he left. She always packed his stuff separately too.

"You know I couldn't miss out on this place, Q," El responded with a smile.

Q is the guy's name. And El is the girl's name? What weird names if they aren't short for something, Reyes thought.

"There you are. Anything else I can get you all?" Camille said in her usual chipper voice, sliding the bag towards the counter. The green-eyed male paid for the group.

"No, we are all set. Thank you," El responded.

Reyes heard them walk towards the door.

"Oh, do you mind me asking where you heard about Bakewell's?" Camille asked the group.

Reyes sighed. He felt awkward now. He looked up to see the fair-skinned guy now watching Camille with curiosity and a slight grin.

Are you kidding? Reyes thought. *They can't both try for her.*

"I found it online. Best bakeries near McCloud Falls. I really wanted to hike it since it's been a while. This place popped up on a few top ten lists and stuff for the county. The photos on social media looked amazing," El beamed. The green-eyed male smiled at her like an idiot.

At least he doesn't seem interested in Cami.

"Oh, that's nice." The dread was more than apparent in her voice. "Well, enjoy your day. Safe travels to Redding and back to Humboldt."

Reyes wasn't sure why she sounded dreadful about her bakery getting as much attention as it did.

El smiled widely again and walked out. The other two followed but not before Q smirked at Reyes one last time.

"What did the fire marshall say your max occupancy was? Did you check on that?" Reyes stammered out before the door closed, ignoring Q's gaze.

"It's certainly more than five," Q laughed and Reyes sighed in distaste, frowning at him. "I'm with CalFire in Humboldt. Building codes are not my specialty but I know enough of them. Have a nice day, Mr. Navarro." Then Q shut the door and followed the others to a van.

"There is your answer," Camille replied merrily.

"So who were they? Q?" he scoffed then handed her an order list.

She looked at him with confusion. "Just customers, from Humboldt apparently. They had business in Redding, but drove up here." She was nearly fretting over her words now.

"You don't want the attention? Social media posts? Because you are all over it. The entire town will not shut up about your baked goods and drinks." As soon as he said the words, he wanted to take them back. He smacked his forehead with his palm after seeing Camille take a deep breath and brace herself against the counter. "I'm sorry, that came out rude."

"No, it's alright, I just get really busy. It's great for income but, you can see it's a lot when everyone is in and out. I am really happy here though." She feigned a smile and grabbed a pink box after setting his coffee down.

"Hire some help then?" he suggested.

"It's just more paperwork and something to worry about. I enjoy being busy; I just don't care for social media. I'm worried they got something wrong."

"No, none of it is wrong, Camille. I assure you."

"You read it?" she gawked.

"Yes," he replied, looking at her. "Can an apple crisp muffin go in its own bag?"

"I didn't make any apple pastries today," she replied, regaining her composure. "But try an olallieberry scone instead."

She placed various pastries in a box. Then she went to the refrigerator and grabbed a small cup.

"A whatberry?" he asked, confused. "I'm not trying to get all adventurous here."

"It's like a blackberry. Let me prepare one for you," she said, placing it in the toaster oven with tongs. Once it was toasted, she wrapped the scone and scooped a large portion of cream into the small plastic cup.

"Spread some Devonshire cream on it and I guarantee you will love it just as much as the apple crisp muffin," she explained.

"I never said I loved the apple crisp muffins," he grumbled and took the wrapped-up scone, placing it in his jacket pocket before grabbing the box.

"Well, maybe you will find love in the scone? I gave you some extra cream to try in your coffee too. Have a good day, Reyes."

"You didn't charge me for the scone." He groaned and went to take his card out.

"I know." She smiled wide at him. He held her gaze for a few moments until the bell rang once again and Reyes rolled his eyes, shoving his card and wallet back in his back pocket.

"I don't need handouts, Camille. But thanks," he said, disgruntled, and headed towards the door, moving around the new customers walking in.

Just as he was at the door, he saw a bundle of fluff high up on a shelf. His eyes shot wide at the sight of the bobcat. He turned and watched her. Camille was so attentive with the customers and explained what things were with such happiness. She even smiled at how excited the customers were. Camille was in her zone and didn't even realize he had seen the cat. It hardly moved save for its slow steady breathing.

He caught her eye for a moment and she smiled at him before tending to the next customers in line. *Are you really going to shut her down now? After all that?* He supposed the best thing he could do was play dumb at this point. Not one person had mentioned the cat. He'd told her to get rid of it and she lied to him.

Though it looked healthy, calm, and comfortable.

When the next customer entered, he headed back to the office, telling himself he needed to stop staring at her. She was very easy on the eyes. In fact, if he would ever admit it to anyone, he found her very attractive. Especially when she smiled. The fact that she had nursed and tamed a bobcat truly fascinated him. She had to be some kind of forest princess or a cottage witch or something.

Forest princess? Cottage witch? What are you even thinking? Get. A. Grip.

Reyes awkwardly walked into the building next door and headed for the elevator to the third floor. Once he reached the floor, he set the box down on a desk.

"Perfect timing, my man," one of his coworkers said, walking up and opening the box. "This place is great."

"It certainly seems busy," he responded, then grabbed the small cup of cream out of the box.

"Are you taking cream in your coffee now? That bakery owner is sweetening up your grumpy demeanor," another coworker walking up teased.

"No. She insisted I try a blackberry-like scone."

"She's very friendly and is very passionate about her craft."

"There is too much traffic outside. People don't understand the loading zones either. They think they can just park out front and spend hours looking at everything in the bakery then wander into Willow's shop and spend a day shopping."

"So that's Camille's fault? Since when did anyone care how that loading zone was used? Delivery drivers just stop in the middle of the street anyways," she laughed.

"No but it's adding to the problem," he grumbled.

He went to mention the bobcat but realized he didn't want to lose her. He was being unprofessional and he knew it, but she had brought this little ounce of joy to him. How would she act towards him if he raised an issue over the cat now? Shaking his head again, Reyes walked to his desk.

With his coffee set down, he pulled the scone out of his pocket and opened the bag, expecting it to be cold and crumbled. To his surprise it was in the same condition he had seen her package it up in, and the cream was still cold and with a slight firmness he had seen in the container.

"Okay, so how much do I put on this?" He noticed the scone had been cut and to his surprise, it had been buttered too. His mouth was already salivating thinking about it. He eagerly set to opening the cream and dipped his pinky finger in it to taste it. He couldn't remember what she had called the cream.

As soon as it hit his tongue, the faintest moan slipped out of him again and his mind wandered to places it shouldn't be. He wondered what it would be like to lick this off her finger with her seated in his lap. These thoughts had been occurring to him more these days. Nearly every night as of late. He felt ashamed to be thinking of them. Especially her.

"Reyes!" someone called his name. "Are you high? What are you staring at like that?"

Reyes jumped and his ears heated. "Like what? Nothing," he muttered as he stared at Evan.

"Like you are lost in some wistful fantasies about a certain bakery girl." Evan gave him a smug smile before biting into his strawberry croissant. "She *is* pretty amazing, I'm not going to lie. Maybe I should start asking her to package stuff separately for me too."

Reyes glared, feeling a hint of something. Jealousy? Competition? From Evan? He would never. He knew this was just Evan being himself and joking around. He also knew Evan found Willow attractive but was too weighed down to do anything about it. Reyes had no clue where this possessive streak had come from and made a mental note to get it in check. That was just weird.

"She probably wrapped it securely so it would be in perfect condition when I got around to eating it, even a few hours later."

"Ya know now that you mention it, those muffins did stay fresh for far longer than I thought they would. I still scarfed all three down by the next afternoon."

"Ate mine that night. I don't know how she does it. If there is some preservative in it." He groaned. "If she isn't labeling that, it's going to be a problem."

"Relax. Not a single person has gotten sick here from anything, or had a case of food poisoning or an allergic reaction. With how meticulous she is with her labels, I doubt she's not up to code," Evan said, shoving the rest of the pastry in his mouth then sat down at his desk.

Reyes spread some of the cream on the scone and bit into it. He couldn't stop the moan that slipped from him. Evan laughed but didn't look at him. "Fuck, this is amazing. I don't even remember half of what she called it. A something-berry scone with some kind of cream."

"Are you going to ask her out or are you going to just keep having dirty thoughts about her?" Evan asked, finally looking at him.

Reyes felt his face heat and something in his stomach twist. "What? No. I don't have dirty thoughts about her. Evan, we are at work," Reyes chided, clearly embarrassed. He felt as though he had been caught even though he knew his flustered reactions were the damning evidence.

"I told her about your moan, and she looked as though she was having a few curious thoughts of her own."

"What the hell is wrong with you?" He was in full panic mode now. "You told her? And, no, I act like a complete dumbass around her. Why would she like me?"

"So you're telling me she packages your stuff separate from the office order and gives you all the extras because she hates you?"

"It's just customer service."

"Sure thing, buddy." Evan snorted and went back to work. "At least you are right about acting like a dumbass."

Reyes shook his head and went back to work and savored the scone. With a little of the cream and scone left, he debated on putting some in his coffee as she suggested. He didn't care for coffee creamer in his coffee and he only really had heavy cream on hand at home if a recipe called for it in a sauce or something. In fact, he'd never even made whip cream before.

He figured he could try some in his coffee and scooped some on top. When he took the sip, he noticed Evan watching him.

"What?" he asked.

Evan just smirked to himself and went back to work. "Dumbass," he said to himself.

Reyes sighed loudly and took the sip of coffee, promptly adding more and savoring the rest of the buttered scone. She was right, the cream was amazing in coffee.

"Come to the bar with me Saturday night, yeah?" Evan asked.

"Why?"

"I don't know, it's been a while, and it seems like you need to unwind."

"Maybe. I will think about it," Reyes responded and went back to his work. Maybe the bar would do him some good. Not that he wanted to talk to anyone other than her.

Chapter 10

Camille took a long deep inhale and said a minor affirmation in her head before exhaling it out as she stepped through the threshold to the bar. She wasn't exactly sure how to feel about this setting as bars were not a place she frequented. In all reality she probably shouldn't be at one as she knew firsthand what kind of attention being the new person in a small town brought.

But Willow had invited her out and she liked Willow. The fast friends and near sisterly bond with the woman was something she had come to treasure. She scanned the crowd for the familiar witch energy and walked towards it with her head held high. Though she was all too aware of the eyes on her.

Then she caught his eyes—Reyes. He was fixed on her. His gaze caused her to falter yet she wasn't sure what his gaze told her. It didn't strike her as anger or annoyance but assertion maybe?

Unable to decipher that particular expression on him, she quickly followed her intuition towards Willow's energy and found her. A sigh of relief escaped her when she sat down.

"Well that was certainly a charged exchange and he's still looking at you. Did you do something to him?" Willow asked in a soft tone. Music and chatter were drowning out their conversation, and Camille glanced around at anyone nearby who may be listening but no one appeared to be.

"What? No. I'm pretty sure I ruin his entire work week and now, I'm ruining his weekend too," Camielle laughed.

"We both know that's not true. He just didn't expect to see you here. I didn't expect to see him tonight. He usually isn't here," Willow explained.

"So if he's normally not at this bar, what does he do?" Camille asked.

"I honestly don't know. I don't hang out with the guy; we just had some mutual friends. He comes into the shop a few times a year to get his parents and sister gifts. He hangs out with Evan and they do whatever they get up to. Maybe you should ask him?" Willow nudged Camille's boot with hers and laughed.

"No. That would be weird. Then he is going to ask what my hobbies are and it's going to be awkward. Did you know that my bakery has stuff written about it online and that he had read it all?" Camille began to fret.

Willow looked at her then laughed. "What's the problem with any of that?"

"I just want an unassuming life. I don't need fame or glory, it's going to attract more people and ruin Reyes's life more. Plus, why is he reading about me?" Camille groaned.

"Reyes thinks McCloud Falls and the autumn colors ruin his life. People visit this area all the time, we are right off I-5. It's a good place to stop and stretch. You both want a quiet life. Sounds like a great match already."

"But his job is never going to attract attention like my bakery being all over social media."

"Camille, every restaurant, café, bakery, and food truck in the county knows who he is. He certainly doesn't like the attention that comes with being a health inspector, I'm sure."

"I guess I got a little wrapped up in how well everything went with moving here."

"Attention like that is great for business and besides, he doesn't even have to concern himself with your bakery anymore. You have the 'A' grade in your window. He is choosing to." Willow leaned in before she continued, "I know you will continue to be careful with the flavors."

"Of course. Everything gets put away as soon as I'm done," Camille said, as if giving an oath.

They chatted about Sitka, who was off in the forest, but a window in the cabin was opened for her so she could get back to safety should she need to. They talked about how the snow would come and Camille's commute from Dunsmuir would be a bit questionable at parts. She debated on maybe just staying at the bakery on some nights when the weather was really bad.

Camille got herself a drink before she resumed her chatting with Willow as they took to people watching. All the while she had fought the urge to look over to see if Reyes was still watching her, or if he was even still there. She fought the urge to ask. It drove her a bit wild how often he crossed her mind. She always thought of what he looked like when he smiled, the few times she'd seen it. Then wondered what his hands might feel like in hers, on her body.

She hadn't really considered ever being interested in someone like him. In fact, she hadn't ever been with someone like him. Only a handful of experiences with other witches and even less with humans. And she had been reprimanded for that. Her coven leaders insisted none of the partners she had chosen were suitable and she had soiled herself. After a while, she had stopped looking.

Leland flashed in her mind. She could not figure out why her parents had deemed him worthy but no one else. He wasn't even that strong of a witch for being from the Talbot Legacy. He was wealthy, but other than that, he looked like every other well-manicured witch from high society. It never had made sense to her. He hated her. And she had grown to despise him.

This was why she ran. She enjoyed teaching but honestly she had more fun teaching Willow and helping her through experiments. She wished Thornwell Academy admitted students based on academic curiosity instead of wealth and status. She had seen applicants in tears over learning their families didn't hold enough status to be granted admittance.

She had told her students a few times far better things waited for them, and that they would be amazing without Thornwell's teachings. She did, however, stop speaking out so much when she was reprimanded for doing so.

Reprimands usually included a few lashings and a night in the dark, damp lofts of the old underground of the academy. They were originally storehouses or washrooms for the staff to remain hidden in, but now they were used for detentions and discipline.

Camille had already gotten a stigma at Thornwell for spending a few nights in them. And her mother had reminded her how disappointed she was about it too often. Camille never did feel like she was a very good Thornwell. Her parents along with Leland reminded her of it. It honestly made running that much easier.

To have people like her bakery felt good. It was validating in some sort of way, not that she could share that feeling with anyone.

She looked at Willow, who glanced at her with a soft smile.

"What is on your mind?" Willow asked.

"Just a lot, but nothing worth talking about. I like it here." Camille smiled.

"If you need to talk, I'm here. Always."

"Thanks, Willow. I appreciate it."

She took a sip of her drink she had been nursing and settled back into her thoughts. She wanted to be honest with Willow, but she feared putting liability on her. If Thornwell ever found Camille, and knew that

Willow had been hiding her, Willow would be just as guilty and she would not let anyone else take the fall for her actions.

It was Camille's choice to flee. If she had to do it again to protect this place, she would.

As much as it would hurt.

"Are you going to talk to her or just stare at her all night like a creep?"

Reyes sighed. "I don't know, Evan. She's obviously not interested. She hasn't looked back at me once."

"You didn't smile at her. You just looked like you couldn't believe she was here. What do you expect her to do, always offer you muffins?"

"She literally thinks I am an asshole. I know it's my fault but I don't even know what to say to her. I'm terrible at this stuff. I freeze up every time I talk to her."

"When did you last pursue anyone aside from Jodie?"

"I haven't since Jodie worked out oh so well," Reyes muttered and crossed his arms, sitting back in his chair.

"You aren't hung up on her, are you? She's long gone, bro. Sorry to say but it's been over a year. Go pursue bakery girl," Evan encouraged him.

"No, I'm not strung up on Jodie. Her leaving was better for everyone. But Camille is honestly out of my league. I let myself go." Reyes looked down at his stomach.

"That's Jodie still having an effect on you, Reyes. Go on and talk to her. Look around, others certainly are debating on it." Evan patted him on the back.

Reyes did glance around and he could see people looking at Camille and Willow. They didn't belong here. They were both beautiful, but something about Camille just had snagged his attention before he even realized it. Ever since he saw her on the trail and then how well she handled the bobcat. Deep down, a part of him had wanted to pet the bobcat. It just seemed so docile in her arms. This beautiful woman who appeared out of nowhere seemed to be good at everything—hiking, handling animals, and baking. She seemed so simple on the surface level but he knew there had to be more to her and he wanted to learn all about her. She was beautiful in her down-to-earth simplicity. The way her simple retro style dresses always flattered her curvy form so well.

An even deeper part of him had wondered what she might look like in one of his flannels, baking something in his kitchen for them both to enjoy before enjoying each other. He bit his bottom lip at the thought then glanced at her just in time to see someone walk up to her and run his hand along the small of her back.

Reyes watched her spine lock up and her body go rigid. Worry colored her expression when she looked up at the guy. He looked younger than Reyes, likely in his twenties.

"Told you someone would pursue her." Evan smirked and took a sip of his beer.

Reyes then noticed Willow wasn't at the table, and assumed she went to the restroom. He watched the scene play out with disgust. Camille was tense, and the guy kept leaning in as she leaned away. Then he placed a hand on her shoulder and said something. Camille's expression was enough to send Reyes into action. She looked nervous. She didn't even look like that when she picked up the bobcat.

Attention from this guy was not what Camille wanted and maybe she didn't want attention from any guy, or anyone for that matter but he knew if he let this continue, he wouldn't feel good about not offering a hand.

Reyes sat in Willow's empty seat, catching both Camille's and the guy's attention. "Kindly remove your hand from her shoulder, please."

That possessive streak was back in him—some animal rattling in a cage he had only just discovered was trapped inside him.

"We were having a conversation. Who the hell are you anyway?" the guy asked, annoyed.

Camille's attention was fixed on him, and he noticed her take a hard swallow before she spoke.

"Hey, I was wondering when you'd get here."

Her words made him smile slightly. She trusted him and felt safe enough with him. He hoped she continued to, always.

"Sorry, hun. I got pulled into a conversation with a coworker. I'm here now, though, and all yours for the rest of the night," he hummed with a smile. The blush on her skin made his smile widen. The words had just slipped out of him, and he hadn't frozen around her. Her bashful demeanor gave him newfound confidence.

She laughed as if she were slightly embarrassed.

"Whatever, you're obviously an uppity prude," the guy said and removed his hand from her shoulder. The scowl on Camille's face was one Reyes hoped to never cause either. This was far more than her annoyance or anger; this was one that ran deep.

"Hey, how about you stay the fuck away from her," Reyes shot back. The guy scoffed and walked off before Reyes brought his eyes to meet hers. "Sorry."

"For what?" Camille sounded unsure.

"That he was an ass, for inserting myself into Willow's seat. It didn't seem like he was going to get the hint and I don't like guys that act like that, that think it's alright to just touch people and then keep doing it when it's clearly not wanted."

"Thank you. I left a bit of a—bad situation before here and he felt a bit overbearing."

Those words made his gut twist. A need to comfort her and fight someone. She was jumpy and she'd used the word sir a lot. He hoped that situation had not caused that.

"I'm sorry for the situation, I assure you not everyone in Mt. Shasta is like that guy. He is probably passing through anyways. This place isn't bad, so I don't want you to think you moved to a bad place." He stared down at his hands.

"I don't think Mt. Shasta is bad. I like it here actually. A lot." Camille's inflection indicated a smile, causing him to look up. He felt his heartbeat increase when he saw her smile.

"You have a wonderful smile," he said, then slapped his hand over his mouth. "I'm sorry, that slipped out."

She laughed bashfully and her cheeks reddened again. "Was that a compliment from Reyes Navarro? I shall cherish it always."

Now it was his turn to laugh. "I'm not a miserable grump all the time, Cami. I promise."

She paused and looked at him in stunned silence and he wasn't sure why.

"I know, I can see it in your eyes when you look in the bakery case for something you like, and I have noticed your curiosity grow when I suggest something you haven't tried before. There's ways to break into your grumpy demeanor," she cooed, regaining her composure.

"You can tell that just from my face? I didn't think I was that expressive," he asked.

"Your eyes show a lot of emotion. At times I feel like I cause you a lot of grief, but after what you did just now, I think I was wrong."

"I never meant to make you feel that way. It's different is all, a lot different. Bobcats are not exactly something I have encountered on my new case inspections." He laughed. "How is she? What was her name again? Spruce?"

Her face turned to panic. "What?"

"I saw her on the shelf last week. If something happens, I told you. I left it off the first inspection to not raise an alarm. I'm really not trying to shut you down. So, I won't."

She let out an uneasy sigh. "Thank you. It's Sitka, and she's out exploring. I leave the window to my cabin open for her, but I probably shouldn't be telling you this."

"It's fine, but it might make people uneasy if she's in the bakery. Maybe keep her in the back?" he said. Camille nodded but her smile dimmed. "Camille?" he asked.

She looked up at him. "Understood."

He could see stress on her face and for whatever stupid reason, he just blurted out the next words, knowing right now was not the best time for them. But no other time had been good either. "Do you want to go on a date with me sometime? I know this is probably the worst time to ask but we got off on the wrong foot and—"

"Yes," Camille said with a blush returning to her cheeks again. "Yes, Reyes, I would."

He closed his mouth, taking in the light glowing again in her expression. "Alright then. I am looking forward to it," he said and they exchanged numbers.

Then someone walked up to him, and he saw Willow looking at him then over to Camille.

"From ruining his day to getting his number. Good job," Willow praised.

Reyes felt his jaw drop slightly. "We definitely got off on the wrong foot. You have never ruined my day, Camille. Not once." He caught her eyes and was relieved to see her smiling once again.

Willow's laugh made him remember she was still standing because he was in her seat. He glanced over at Evan who was smirking to himself.

"Sorry, I'm in your seat. We guarded your drink. There are some creeps here tonight," he said, getting up hastily. "See you soon, Cami." Then he went back to where he had been sitting and let out the biggest exhale, the adrenaline kick finally fading.

"Was she interested?" Evan laughed and patted him on the back.

"Yes. She thinks she ruins my day. Do I come off as that much of a dick?" Reyes asked.

"Sometimes. I know you better, though. You are scatterbrained. She will learn, I am sure, but also don't fuck this up."

"Do you think it's safe if I ignore the bobcat? It comes and goes from her cabin. Like a house cat but one that goes with her everywhere?" Reyes asked, almost pleading. As if Evan would have the power to change the laws, or somehow make it so nothing ever happened.

"An adventure cat is the term you are looking for, and so what? She obviously knows how to handle it. I think you'd be an ass if you did try to take the cat from her. Camille doesn't seem like the type to keep it locked up, or even put it on a leash. Some people just have the gift of animals."

"She named it Sitka."

"She named it. You can't separate them. It'd be like someone taking Belle from me," Evan declared.

"Belle is a lab, Evan. Two totally different things. You got her as a puppy." Reyes groaned as usual.

"Don't worry about the cat. The girl moved here and got a pet. Unless you want to ruin her day, leave it alone."

"I guess you're right," Reyes lamented.

"I think Sitka should be the ring bearer for your wedding though."

"Stop. I asked her on a date, and didn't even set a time or a place." Reyes shook his head.

"Okay, but when you do set a date for the wedding, I'm just saying."

He glanced up to see Camille and Willow getting up. She smiled at him and gave a little wave. He smiled back and finished his drink before heading home himself.

Chapter 11

One week later, Camille arrived at the trailhead for her first date with Reyes. She had left Sitka near the cabin again because explaining why Sitka was so loyal would be a challenge. As well as why Sitka liked Reyes since technically he had helped her too.

She parked and double checked the pin on the map.

Reyes had sent her the location—a hike to a hidden waterfall he knew about and a picnic. For a moment, she wondered if she should be going on a secluded hike with him. This was what people warned her about. But she didn't think he was that type of person. Just to be safe, she had some pepper spray in her pocket, and an enchantment to make him sick to where he would be vomiting for a bit while she ran back to her car. It was also why she agreed to meet him here instead of being stuck in his truck or him being in her car.

The herbal enchantment would be used as a last resort since it would certainly be harder to explain than pepper spray in this situation.

As foolish as this idea was, she was excited about it. A chance to find a new spot, and see him for more than a few minutes in the bakery juggling between customers.

Then she noticed the warm air in her car and the back of her shirt sticking to her. It reminded her of one of her last interactions with Leland.

"Oh, out hiking again. Covered in sweat and red in the face. Disgusting," Leland had said after she walked back into the courtyard from a hike with a bundle of herbs. She could feel the dirt on her hands. She hadn't known what to say in response as his friends all laughed. He stepped forward and loomed over her. "You embarrass me. Thornwell expects more of you; I expect more of you. Clean up before anyone else sees you."

"It's not like people don't hike, Leland. I'm not yours," she muttered back. She had wanted to say more. She had wanted to comment on how he needed a lot more practice to not embarrass her and Thornwell. But she knew that would likely lead to more humiliation later.

"Yet. You will be a Talbot, and you will stop looking like some feral dirty animal," he seethed then abruptly went back to his circle of friends.

On the entire walk back to her apartment, she felt as though everyone were staring at her. She felt foolish for enjoying things like hiking and baking. Until she shut her door. She only felt free from judgment in her apartment.

That interaction had been a few days before she actually booked her rental car and left. It had been another push to leave. To be here. Still, the words stung.

Reyes had met her on a hike, and he had asked her out on another one.

Why? She was going to look disgusting by the end of this hike. It was four miles roundtrip and while the elevation wasn't bad, the air was warmer than anticipated. *Why did I agree to this?*

He was running late; she could leave and just text him that something came up. If she were late, it would be a reprimand. It was unacceptable when she was teaching lessons.

'If you were efficient, you should be early. You can rest at the end of the day.' That was what her father would say. That was what he expected. Camille had, too, before she was on her own. Now she was learning to hit the snooze button, to just sit down after the lunch rush instead of making more enchantments or going through mail for the bakery.

She oversaw her schedule now. While the rigid schedule of growing up at the academy helped her manage her time, this was entirely foreign to her. Here, she was on a Sunday with nothing to do other than what she wanted.

The rumble of an engine came down the road and the blue truck pulled behind her car. She had been leaning against her car door to let the back of her shirt air off. He got out in a hurry.

"Sorry I'm late. Thought I was leaving on time, then I realized I forgot my day pack," he laughed, clearly embarrassed.

"Oh, it's alright."

"Hopefully it's not too crowded at the falls. It's mostly hidden but obviously word gets around. I have our lunch in my pack."

"Thank you, I brought something for dessert," she said and they were once again awkwardly grinning at each other.

"I can't wait, shall we?" Reyes responded and held his hand out towards the trailhead. "It's about two and half miles to the waterfall. One of my favorites. I take it you have done Hedge Creek and Mossbrae?" They started walking.

"Yes. I'd seen them when researching the area. They are both really neat," she said.

"Did you research anywhere else to move to?" he asked, glancing over at her.

Camille was quiet for a moment. Once again realizing she was going to lie more to these people who she didn't want to lie to. He glanced at her again but she kept her eyes forward.

"A few places." Her reply was short and curt, and she knew it at least it wasn't a lie.

She found an ease in talking with him but also worried about the awkward silence. It felt as though she needed to fill it or he might ask something she hadn't come up with a lie about. So Camille thought of more things to ask, things she would be willing to answer if he asked back.

She discovered he liked to cook, usually smoking or roasting meats. He fished and camped, which was why he wanted an area in the northern part of the state. Siskiyou gave him access to a lot of forest and mountains, and when he wanted he could go to the coast. He lived just outside of the town of Mt. Shasta off an unpaved road but was still only a short drive to work.

"My younger sister lives in Seattle. I try to make it up there once a year but our nearest major airport is a little far so it's a long trip. She lives with her husband and son, or I guess my brother-in-law and nephew. My parents still live in San Jose. I see them once or twice a year." Reyes smiled. "What about you, what's your family like?"

"They are—" she paused, not sure what to say. Not sure what she *wanted* to say. "I'm the youngest of three, two older brothers. They kind of have high expectations for all of us. I'm not sure I was ever built to live up to our parents' standards. My brothers did well though at least." The words dragged her eyes down to her boots and the dirt. She could see the small clouds of dust forming with their steps.

"You don't have to talk about it if you don't want to," Reyes said, bringing her gaze to him.

"Thanks. When did you last go fishing?" she asked abruptly, changing the subject.

He talked about how they had taken his boat out to a lake she hadn't heard of in the area. He and his friend had spent most of the day out there.

"You've met him a few times, Evan. He is my best friend."

"Yes, Evan. He is nice. He seems very carefree."

She glanced over when she heard him sigh. "Yeah. He's generally pretty upbeat. Everybody likes Evan. It's hard not to." She heard the defeat in his laugh too.

Camille wasn't sure what to say. Here she was on a date with Reyes, who she found way more attractive than Evan and they were talking about him. *I really don't know how to be normal do I?*

"If it helps, I like seeing you come into the bakery more than him."

She noticed him stumble slightly as if he'd tripped over something and stopped to look at her in shock.

"You do?"

"Yes." Heat warmed her face.

"Why? I act like a complete idiot around you."

"You didn't at the bar, and you haven't today. You seem down to earth, kind, genuine, and not afraid to get your hands dirty," she explained. He was quiet and appeared as though he was at a loss for words. If she had to lie to people about herself, she could at least be honest with them about them. "And, maybe this is a bold statement, but I'm not sure I'd have believed it if someone told me all that was wrapped up in someone so attractive." She watched his jaw drop.

"I—are you—serious? Me? Attractive?"

She tilted her head in confusion. "Yes. Your warm, amber eyes are beautiful."

"I'm sorry, I have absolutely no idea what to do with such compliments. I'm—not used to them," he stated.

"I mean them, Reyes," she said with her intent directed towards him, hoping he would believe her. It was the truth and he obviously hadn't been told those truths enough in his life.

"I have no doubt you do. You are absolutely beautiful and if I am being honest, I want to learn everything about you. Well, everything you are comfortable sharing."

That blush was back and she became increasingly more aware of the sweat causing her shirt to stick to her. As well as how red her face probably was with her messy hair.

'Out again sweating like a disgusting pig?' Leland's words echoed in her ears.

'Why are you even doing that? Thornwells always look prim and proper. No one will want you if you look like that.' Her mother's words now seared right into her.

"Except right now, I'm sure. I'm not very nice looking," she muttered as the bitter memories came to her.

"Cami? You look beautiful all the time. Even now. I'm the one who looks disgusting. I didn't even think of how unflattering I was going to be; but I wanted to show you this waterfall. You look gorgeous. I can't stop thinking you are just the embodiment of spring wrapped up in this amazing woman who bakes, knows everything about plants, and tamed a bobcat. You look so in your element out here. I bet you'd look even more in your element with your bobcat. Spruce, right?"

Now it was her turn to gawk at him. "Sitka. You aren't mad about her?"

"I'm turning a blind eye and no, I'm really not mad. I never thought I would see one. I'd caught glimpses of two on the trail cameras at my cabin. But you tended to one."

"She does get free time; I don't keep her cooped up. She is off exploring her land."

He laughed and they kept walking, occasionally brushing their hands against the other's.

When they reached the waterfall, she had to stop and take it in. It was a smaller version of Mossbrae with the water almost seeping out of moss-covered rock face. It created a little pool surrounded by lush plants and the tall pine trees provided the perfect amount of shade. The mist from the falls provided a much-needed cooling spray too. Reyes helped her over to a nice patch of rocks and pulled his pack off.

"I made some chorizo sandwiches. My mom always made these for my sister and me growing up and I make them pretty often. I always have chorizo in the fridge. It's usually a little more expensive up here. The demographic and all." He chuckled.

"I don't think I've had it before. It's delicious," she said once she took a bite and smiled, savoring the seasoned pork sausage with roasted red pepper and lettuce. The bun had been toasted and lightly buttered. She took a drink of the water from the hose that came from her day pack and noticed him watching her with a grin.

"This is a lovely view with you in front of the waterfall." Reyes leaned back slightly.

She looked at him and noticed how genuine he seemed. The hike wasn't too hard but they both had worked up a sweat on the incline. His hair was tousled and his shirt had some damp spots. He was wearing cargo shorts and his legs looked as though they had gotten plenty of sun to match the russet skin tone of his arms and face. His hands looked strong and she wondered what they might feel like holding her hand, on her hips, in her hair.

Camille had to take a deep breath and look away bashfully. "It's a lovely waterfall." She took out the dessert, a slice of berry and cream cheese pound cake she had made. She had put the freshness enchantment in it to keep it perfect despite being in her pack.

His chuckle caressed her ears as he took the slice she offered him. A slight moan slipped out of him when he took the first bite and she had no idea what he was doing to her.

Reyes had no detectable magic; he was just a human. One who was one of the good ones. At least she thought he was or wanted him to be. He could very well turn on her, be one of the people who wished to see her burn at the stake.

The very fact of the matter hit her hard right in the heart. All the lessons Thornwell had drilled into her about remaining hidden, the ones she never got to actually test out. She had gotten too close to a human and it was such a terrible idea. Even if for some crazy impossible reason he would stand by her, Thornwell would hunt him alongside her. Reyes didn't deserve that. He didn't deserve her lies.

"Cami," he said quietly and she turned to him.

The nickname made it hard for her to listen to her brain. That someone saw through her lies and didn't care, wouldn't care. *Of course he is going to care that you are a witch. But he's looking the other way with Sitka.*

"I'm not trying to assume I know anything about you, but I hope you find what you are looking for here. They say that the mountain has a lot of magic. I'm not sure I've found everything I'm looking for myself, but I'm confident Shasta will watch over you."

His voice was soft and comforting, which did something to her again. Camille realized he wasn't asking her to share anything. He never had pushed her yet. He seemed to recognize her boundaries even if she didn't know what they were.

"Thank you, Reyes. This was a wonderful date." She beamed. Despite her worries, she hoped he was right and maybe some part of her hoped he would be there when she found it.

"It was. Hopefully we can do this or something else again soon."

"I'd like that," Camille replied.

"Then we will set something up soon."

After taking in the waterfall for a few more moments, they gathered their trash and headed back down the trail. When they got back to the cars, they smiled at each other and she was unsure if he wanted to hug her or kiss her, but he didn't make a move so she didn't either. They had passed a few people on their way down that were heading up to the falls and there were a lot more cars now. When she was in hers, she watched Reyes get into his. This time when he closed his door she didn't jump, nor did she when the engine fired up.

Chapter 12

The following weeks had gone well for Camille. The few dates she'd gone on with Reyes were more than she could have asked for. She was living the life she wanted and yet the fear of being found never fully left her mind. Every time she felt close to telling Reyes that she was a witch, the fear crept back in. If her coven caught up to her somehow, and it was discovered that he knew, he could be in so much danger. The same went for Willow.

Lying to them ate at her because they had become her family, but they could easily be taken from her by her blood relatives and bonded coven. Leland's family could do a lot worse to them both too.

The bell to the door rang and she glanced at the single burner, ensuring it was off. "Stay put, Sitka," she said quietly then left the office door open a crack. Camille hurried out and saw Reyes walk in with an older couple. His expression was bashful.

"Hi, Cami." He sounded hesitant.

"This place looks and smells amazing, Reyes." An older man beamed.

Camille glanced at him and traced the russet skin that was a hint lighter than Reyes's, the salt and pepper hair color, and those warm amber eyes. Then she looked at the woman who had a sun-kissed tan and she could trace Reyes's smile on her, as well as the shape of the nose. Her eyes snapped back to Reyes, who was biting his bottom lip nervously. These were his parents.

"You really run this entire place on your own? Everything looks perfect! Reyes raved about everything he had tried and knew we had to try it," the woman said.

"Hello. Yes, baking has always been a passion of mine. I enjoy it," Camille replied, playing her confidence card. She had gotten better at this over the months. "I am happy to know that Reyes likes it too."

He rolled his eyes and his worried look was replaced with a slight scowl. "Camille, you know I have loved everything you have given me."

"Reyes, I'm kidding. I do have apple crisp muffins, just out of the oven, but what else can I get for you all?"

His dad looked from Camille to Reyes with a smile. "Kid, you need to lighten up, but you should introduce us."

Reyes sighed and Camille couldn't help but laugh a little. "Camille, these are my parents. Mom, Dad, I'd like for you to meet Camille Bakewell."

She had tried to convince herself that it was her name but the lie still grated on her.

"It is an honor to meet you. I can see why Reyes is such a wonderful person." She smiled at them. It was true. She had liked him, and now she liked him even more after the few dates they had gone on. Sure, he was a bit scatterbrained at times, but he always came through for her.

"That is wonderful to hear. We do worry about him up here all alone at times but we are proud of him," his mom said. Reyes scowled again.

"Are you visiting from San Jose?" she asked.

"Yes. Last year got busy for all of us so we didn't get to visit him. His sister is up in Washington, so it's a little easier for us to see her. Plus she's married and with our grandson. The drive up here is long."

"It's hard to settle on and stick to a day sometimes. Though we know our boy has his hands full with a lot of projects." His dad laughed softly and Camille looked at them then to Reyes, who was pinching the bridge of his nose.

"Dad." Reyes groaned. "I just like working on stuff. It helps me focus."

"It's nothing to be ashamed of, Son. We are proud of you and you have built an amazing life for yourself up here."

Something tugged at her heart. This was what a family who supported their children looked like. She didn't need any special abilities to see how loved Reyes was by his parents. Camille could also see his parents were kind, warm, and welcoming people. A pain scratched at her throat but she pushed it down with a hard swallow. Her parents had never supported her hobbies, and yet whatever projects Reyes had going on, his parents were proud of him. She couldn't help but feel a sense of loss all over again.

Thornwells were supposed to have nerves of steel, so why was this moment making her feel so emotional? She had seen tons of families walk in over the past few months. All kinds—parents doting on their children, couples doting on each other. It made her smile, but seeing his parents tugged at her heart.

"Look around. I need to grab a few things; I will be right back." Then she rushed back to the office, taking a deep inhale.

Sitka looked at her with some concern. Familiars were in tune to their bond's emotions. Kneeling down, she pet Sitka's head and took a deep breath, letting the sensation of the soft fur under her fingertips soothe her. No words were said to the cat, just a few deep breaths before she rose once again and regained her composure. As she stood up to walk back out, her phone buzzed.

Reyes: I'm so sorry. I completely forgot they were coming into town. I know it might be a lot to meet my parents right now.

Camille: It's okay. I'm not upset.

She finished typing back and walked back out.

"Sorry about that, I needed to check on the Devonshire Cream. The mixer was set to a timer but I can't be too sure." She laughed, nearly back to her confident self. Thoughts about how disappointed her mother would be in her coiled around her insides. *Thornwells do not falter.* Her mother had said that countless times.

"Oh, for the scones! Reyes mentioned those," his mom praised, then began ordering.

Camille noticed his dad leaning closer to him and nudging him.

"Ask her about tonight," he said quietly. Reyes groaned again and ran his hand down his face. She knew this was his embarrassed response.

"Would you like to come to dinner with my parents and me tonight? Because I'm apparently fifteen or something and they want to know your intentions with their son," Reyes grumbled.

She laughed now and despite the desire to cry at the sense of family she had missed out on, she felt so lucky to have witnessed this. Reyes often exuded a rugged exterior, and he was for the most part, but he had a soft side too.

"I'd like that. Thank you for the offer. I really don't want to intrude at all, though. Family time is important and all."

"We would be delighted. We hardly ever hear about any of his friends up here so it will be nice to share a meal with you."

Camille finished packing up their order and made their drinks. She naturally didn't charge them for everything. Reyes looked at the total, and then at her with a tight-lipped smile. He took the bag and his coffee before his dad stepped closer.

He leaned in and hesitated for a second before speaking. "Do you really have a pet bobcat?"

"What the hell, Dad?" Reyes gawked.

"I'm just curious. You can't tell me she has a bobcat and then expect me to not ask."

Camille looked unsure and went to speak but then realized she didn't know what to say. She glanced between Reyes and his dad for a moment.

"It's fine. I'm not going to say anything. I'm off the clock anyway."

"Promise me you will not hang this over my head later? She isn't going anywhere," she asserted.

"I promise. Dad worked at a wildlife rehabilitation center for a while and with a lot of zoos in the Bay Area."

"Alright. Give me a second," Camille said and walked back to the office. "Sitka, come on." Camille walked around the counter and Sitka trailed right at her side. "She is very docile if you are calm. She is far more than a pet. A sort of familiar if you will."

Camille watched Reyes closely as he eyed her then the bobcat. Then she noticed his mom looked at her with a slight head tilt and her heart stopped. She chastised herself for using the word familiar as his parents both knelt down and pet the cat, who purred softly in response.

"She acts like a house cat. Did you buy her as a kitten or something?"

Camille had to take a deep breath, reminding herself that this was one of the struggles of having a familiar like Sitka. Another reminder that she was not human, but a witch who lied to people.

"No, didn't I tell you I was there when Cami found Sitka?" Reyes groaned. "I swear I told you about it."

His statement did odd things to her insides. She realized this was him defending her and Sitka. And he'd used that nickname again.

"I think the exotic animal trade is horrible," Camille managed to respond.

"I meant no offense, Ms. Bakewell. It's just that bobcats are not known as the most social of the cat kingdom," he explained. "Reyes just mentioned you had one. I would love to hear the story."

"None taken, her wellbeing is extremely important to me. She is free to come and go as she pleases," Camille affirmed.

"Fascinating," his dad marveled.

"I will see you tonight?" Reyes asked with some uncertainty.

For a moment, Camille wasn't sure she should continue anything she had built here, and that she should leave. Not because she didn't want it—in fact, she had never wanted anything more—but she knew she would never be human and fit in here. She had been a fool for trying. The thoughts always gnawed at her very soul.

But the look in his eyes told her to keep fighting for what she wanted, because people like him were out there in the world, and his parents and Willow were out there too.

Then she noticed Sitka circle around Reyes's legs. Camille couldn't even tell him how bonded to him Sitka was or why she seemed to approve of him.

"Of course. I am looking forward to it," she responded despite fighting far too many emotions.

"I am too. I will tell Dad how you found Sitka," he said and looked at Sitka. He had yet to actually pet her. Camille watched as he awkwardly knelt down to scratch her head for a moment before they made arrangements for the night and left.

Chapter 13

"We are going to be late, Reyes," his dad said from downstairs. "She could have met us here and we could have taken our car."

"She would've seen the house," he groaned and looked around. It was a mess. He was always embarrassed at the fact he was never good at putting things away and fixing all the bad habits he had.

"If you're interested in her, she will have to see it someday. We could have picked her up."

"No, this entire thing would be awkward. I'm awkward enough," he said from the closet as he grabbed a flannel. He knew he should have dressed nicer but it was too late now. He wore what he usually wore to work: jeans, a henley, and a flannel. Despite the warm summer days, the nights would get cold. There was little cloud cover these days, which led to all the heat from the sun escaping quickly. The temperatures could drop quickly when the sun went down.

He ran downstairs and realized he forgot socks. "Damn it." He huffed then ran back up the stairs to put them on and rushed to put his boots on. "Alright, let's go," he said, grabbing his keys.

After he locked the front door, he got in his parents' SUV. It had been charging in front of the garage. For a moment, he hoped she didn't run into car trouble. It would be harder to help if he didn't have his truck with him.

Once they arrived, he spotted her car. *Always early and I am always late,* he thought to himself. When they walked in, he saw her smile by the door. Out of habit, he looked down, half expecting to see a bobcat but there wasn't one by her side.

"Hi," he said.

"Hello," she replied with a smile then turned to his parents. "It is so lovely to see you both again. Thank you again for the invitation to dinner tonight, Mr. and Mrs. Navarro." Then she lowered her eyes as if she wasn't supposed to make eye contact.

She was so formal sometimes in her responses. Her mannerisms reminded him of an outdated time when women were to be seen and not heard, and yet she was so well-suited for hiking and foraging for plants. She'd identified nearly everything on their hikes and explained facts he hadn't known. She sometimes told him what the plants could be used for. A few times when she ate a flower or chewed on a leaf, he panicked that it might be poisonous but she never suffered ill effects from ingesting them. He had tried two plants he couldn't remember the names of.

Camille remained an enigma to him.

"Oh it is wonderful to see you again too," his mom said as they made their way to a table. He pulled the seat out for her, realizing if she was going to exude good manners he probably should too. His ex would have laughed at him and said something about being shocked he remembered. He feared hearing any damning comments from Camille; he was sure they were coming soon. It had been nearly two months and they hadn't done much more than brush hands on occasion. He certainly wanted to do more with her.

Reyes had thought about many things he wanted to do with her while he lay in bed. Of course, he would never say those things.

As his parents insisted she get whatever she wanted and that they were paying, Camille of course had excellent manners and offered to pay her share a number of times.

"Camille, we invited you out to dinner, it is really alright," his dad said and she backed down quickly. Reyes watched this interaction in confusion. His dad's tone was soft and inviting, certainly not angry. He knew his dad's angry tone and this was the furthest thing from it. But she didn't even try to speak back to him.

What happened? he wondered. As the four of them chatted, he started to notice increasingly how she interacted with his parents. Every question they asked, she would reply and look down. She hadn't had a problem maintaining eye contact with him or her customers.

Her responses were poised and rigid-sounding and at times, she would deflect and change the subject. The latter response usually came when it had to do with her past or her family—never going into too much detail about her upbringing or schooling. She asked a few questions but let them lead the conversation.

Did her family instill this in her? Or did some poor excuse of a man who insisted on obedience? The mere thought made him clench his fist under the table. That thing inside him he didn't understand was rearing its head. Possessive? Anger? Protectiveness? He had no idea. At any rate, he needed to get it under control.

"How is your car running?" he asked. He hadn't really asked her a question tonight and he wondered how she would respond to him.

"It's been running well. No issues, though sometimes it's a bit jerky on the acceleration, and I'm not getting as good of mileage as I thought I would," she said before lowering her eyes again.

Damn it, don't do this to me now. "Do you want me to take a look at it?"

"Thank you, Reyes. I appreciate that."

"No problem, Cami," he said and slowly placed a hand on her leg.

Reyes watched her glance at his hand and smile, but it looked almost confused at first. *Don't tell me no one's ever done this to her?*

"If it's too much you can tell me. I won't take offense," he said quietly.

"No, it's not. At all." She met his eyes.

"Good."

His hand was on her sage green skirt. His eyes traced upward, noting that her top was a silky white button up with a collar and short sleeves and a goldenrod floral print. It reminded him of the wildflower blooms that took over in late spring in the area.

He loved the way she dressed; she had a soft vintage spring look all the time.

When their food came, they all began to eat but he noticed her wait and watch for a moment before she ate small, controlled bites. He noticed that she always seemed to be excited about food but never acted as though it was anything special. Except for the things he made her. Still, she ate that carefully, too, taking small bites.

Then something in his gut twisted and he seriously hoped no one had made her feel bad for enjoying food, or anything for that matter. He hoped she would relax as time went on. He supposed maybe she was just nervous about being in a new place. She seemed to be close to Willow, and she had Sitka. And him.

She always would even if they didn't go much further than a few dates. Reyes would cherish these dates. She had shown him so much and he hoped he'd shown her something special too.

When the night concluded, he walked her to her car.

"I hope that wasn't too much tonight," Reyes said, taking her hand.

"No, it was nice. I'm glad I got to meet your parents. Tell them I said thank you again." Her tone was soft and sweet.

"I'm glad you got to meet them too. I will see you soon, alright? Text me when you get home?"

"Of course."

He smiled and gave her hand a squeeze but didn't let go. She looked at him, almost hopefully, he realized. *Was she waiting for me to make a move?* Hesitantly, he pulled her close into a hug. For a moment she tensed up but soon relaxed, hugging him tightly and molding herself to him. It felt nice, except he was all too aware of his gut, making it awkward. *Well, there goes her attraction to me.*

He'd barely finished his thought when she hugged him tighter and rested her head on his chest. Slowly exhaling his nerves, he rubbed her back.

They heard footsteps and she instantly pulled away from him and looked to see his parents.

"We will get the car."

"Be there in a second." Reyes groaned. He couldn't help but feel confused and concerned as he gazed at her again. "It's alright, Cami, they wouldn't have said anything if they saw us hugging. I've told them we have gone on a few dates. They were excited to meet you."

"Sorry, I just wasn't sure who was coming." She reached for his hand, giving it a small squeeze.

He squeezed back. "Say hi to Sitka for me."

Then they parted ways and he waited until she left the parking lot before going to his parents' car.

"She's very polite and proper," his mom said.

"I noticed. She grew up near Seattle, but I'm worried something bad happened to her. She is really jumpy at times. Doesn't talk about her past much," Reyes confided. "I really like her."

"Just take it slow with her. If something bad has happened to her, it's the best you can do," his dad advised.

"I know. I will. I don't want to mess this up."

"Well, we already like her a lot more than Jodie. I think she likes you a lot too. I saw the way she smiled at you. Just be your sweet loving self, mijo," his mom complimented.

Once they were back at the cabin, Reyes awaited her text and when it came through, he wished a good night and hoped to see her soon.

When he finally lay down, he stared up at the ceiling and thought of her. As he usually did. He wondered what her life was like growing up, and what her life was like before she left. Was she excited and hopeful to leave? Or was she sad to leave her home? Was she going to leave this place one day?

Then he realized he didn't even know why she decided to leave. Was it just to start new somewhere or did she run away?

The sudden thought struck him and he propped himself up to look at the mountain. His cabin was dark and still, with his parents in the guest room downstairs. The moonlight shone on the crags of Shasta.

"Please keep her safe here," he said softly, though he wasn't even entirely sure what he meant by the words. He just said the prayer to that mountain because it felt right.

Chapter 14

Later the following week, she was exceptionally busy as she needed to make more enchantments. She knew she should do this at the cabin but all the herbs were here and the equipment was set out on the table. She could leave them here instead of getting them in the car and transporting them.

"Alright, as soon as there is a break, or I sell out," she said to herself during a moment between customers being in the bakery.

Reyes had already stopped by earlier and gotten the office order. She had learned the routine by now. There was one day a week someone else would come, usually on a Tuesday or Thursday where she wouldn't see him, but he always sent a good night text without fail.

When she sold the last pastries, she flipped the open sign to 'closed.' Just as she was about to lock the door, she watched the bell fall and break on the floor. Slightly sed, all she could do was stare at the pieces before sighing and picking them up. After setting it on the counter and vowing to fix it tonight at the cabin, she closed the register and let it run its reports.

The herbs had been ground into a fine powder and her cast iron cauldron was on the burner with the water and sugar boiling. Eventually, it would become a reduction and bottled up into a syrup which she used in the baked goods. The remainder of the various powders would be left for beverages. She ground some herbs to be coarser so they could be mixed into the creams and fillings or with a sugar topping.

All the small dishes of various ingredients were set out and she began to make a batch of a happiness enchantment. Her magic would unlock the natural preservation qualities in the herbs too. The next step required her focus and great attention to detail as she needed to set her intention. Slowly, she poured the intent from her fingers as though they were small embers into the mixture. The sensation of the magic flowed through her veins and with each small ember, a bubble full of glowing green smoke would form. The reduction would produce a glowing smoke that would rise up. The physical magic then burned off and the intent was embedded into the syrup.

When she was done with that part, she took a step back, taking a deep inhale and recentering her breathing. She was advanced at this, and with a few deep breaths, the exhaustion would dissipate. She would often talk Willow through these breath relieving exercises to ease the tension and dizziness that came from using their magic. Willow was strong in her intent but she hadn't had the proper recovery training. Camille learned that Willow's coven encouraged a lot of rest and lying down afterwards. Thornwell never accepted anything less than being ready to enchant another batch within fifteen minutes of the last one. So she'd had plenty of deep breathing and quick bouts of meditation work on it. Sure, there were classes on these techniques but it was usually taught while making enchantments. Never before.

However over the last few months, Camille had grown comfortable. She had let her guard down more each day. Her senses were less sharp during her cool down. It was a relief to not have superiors breathing down her neck, and not having an audience every time she performed an enchantment was almost liberating. With a deep exhale and a smile, she admired her work and felt her senses return.

Then her peripheral caught Sitka growing alert and facing the door.

"What is this?" Reyes gasped.

Camille spun around to face him, wide-eyed. He braced himself on the door jamb, looking terrified.

Camille's heart pounded. "Reyes! Leave! What are you doing here? I'm closed!" Her breathing grew frantic and she had to brace herself against the desk, as if preparing for an oncoming tidal wave. Every fear she had for Reyes waiting to crash into them both.

"I-I-I was going to see if you wanted to grab dinner tonight. What are you doing back here?"

"Leave! Now!" she hissed, too stunned and confused to process this moment. She had never anticipated being seen. Of course she hadn't. She hadn't ever enchanted anywhere other than at Thornwell Academy where she was tucked away, a place that humans were prohibited. "Leave."

She wanted to set the intention towards him but she couldn't make herself do it. She had no control over the elements. She was a green witch who worked with herbs, not an elemental.

Without a word more, Reyes ran. Then she heard the door shut along with the bubbling of the syrup in the cauldron. A moment later, she felt Sitka rubbing against her leg.

All Camille could do was drop to her knees with a whimper as she pulled Sitka close. She sat like that until the stench of burning syrup hit her nose.

"Dammit." She leapt up and turned the burner off. An entire batch was ruined and wasted. With a reluctant sigh, she set to cleaning everything up. It would be a long night of trying to remake the enchantments, if she could get her nerves settled down. It would mess with her intentions if she didn't get her emotions under control.

Once everything was finally cleaned up and either put away in a locked cabinet or her car, she triple checked the front door was locked then walked into the back of Willow's shop and slumped on the bench. Sitka remained by her side.

"What's wrong?" Willow exclaimed as Camille wiped her eyes.

Thornwells don't cry, she told herself and fought the tears as much as possible as Willow watched.

Finally pushing it all down, she met her friend's eyes. "Reyes saw me making enchantments. I lost the entire batch too." Camille's voice broke and she hated how it sounded. This was all her fault.

"Fuck the batch; Reyes is the concern. I don't know how he is going to react. You need to go talk to him," Willow urged.

"I didn't know what to do, I just told him to leave. I was so stupid to do this, so careless. I trained better. My parents saw to it."

"They are not the concern; Reyes is. What are they going to do to him?" Willow asked, sitting next to Camille and placing an arm over her shoulder.

Once again, Camille had to fight the emotion back. She knew very well what her parents would do to Reyes. They couldn't find out. She couldn't bring this on him. He had walked in on her being careless. It was entirely on her.

"I won't let them do anything to him. He will not take the fall for my carelessness," she declared. Willow looked at her with some concern.

"How? Coven leaders have their rules. Short of throwing yourself on him, I'm not sure what can be done about it."

"They will not find out. They can't." She felt her eyes well up.

"Then you better talk to him. When they come to visit it's going to be hard to cover up."

Camille squeezed her eyes shut. "They...won't come visit."

"They won't visit you? Why wouldn't they? My parents visit me at least once a year."

"They don't know where I am. It's why I don't want any social media presence. I'm worried they will link it all to me." She felt her throat sting now with a cry that she refused to let out.

"Cami? You left without telling your coven?" Willow asked, caution lined her tone.

Camille looked at Willow. "I'm estranged from my coven," she whispered and looked down.

"Cast out? Did Bakewell vote? Surely their reasoning was wrong? What would get you cast out?" The concern in her voice was too much for her to bear.

She couldn't look at her friend. All her lies were looking right at her. She was pretty sure that mountain was judging her. She hated lying to people. Especially the people here that she was close with.

"There is no Bakewell coven. I made the name up." Camille's voice was barely above a whisper.

"What? Why? You lied to cover up your actual coven name? What coven? Why would you cover it up?" Willow said with some apprehension. "What are they going to do to Reyes? To me?"

Willow hadn't asked to be guilty by association, but Camille had just dug herself a hole and now Willow and Reyes were going to be dragged down. Why had she ever thought she could do this?

"I wanted to protect you; that's why I lied and made up the fake name. I'm the third born and only daughter of Thornwell," Camille replied.

"Thornwell? As in Thornwell Academy? A legacy? You rejected a legacy?" Willow gasped.

"I'm sorry. I will do anything I need to keep you and him safe. Even if I have to leave and hide out. I just...I had my reasons. I had to, Willow."

Willow's hand rubbed her back. "I know as well as you do what the repercussions might be for this. I cannot imagine what would have been worth the stigma of being branded a betrayer amongst witches, but I know you well enough to know that it must have been worth it. Reyes is the concern right now, though. Make sure he understands to keep his mouth shut. He could have told Evan or his coworkers already."

"I know. I will," Camille said, her voice breaking as she turned away to wipe her eyes. "I'm sorry."

"I will keep Sitka with me and take her to your cabin if you are not back before I close. Don't tell him about me though. Please?"

"Never. I will protect you and this entire place even if I have to run. I will sever my bond with Sitka if I need to as well. I'm sorry."

Willow just looked at her, looking somewhat shocked.

Without a word more, Camille headed for the door, not able to look at Willow. Sitka rose up to walk towards Camille.

"Sitka, stay," she insisted and the cat bowed its head and let out a small groan.

Then Camille was back in the bakery where she huddled in the office and let the tears fall freely now. The realization of how alone she was in this moment hit her. She felt each of these threads close to fraying within her.

After some time, Camille finished closing and turned out the lights to the bakery she hoped to return to tomorrow. Otherwise she would be on the run once again. Alone and only with the lessons learned that familiars and loved ones were only going to shatter her bit by bit.

It had never been in her nature to have that iron will Thornwell demanded. Try as she might, she never was able to put it up. All the focus and reprimands never made her into a proper Thornwell.

She walked to the shared parking lot and nervously walked up to Reyes's truck. She knew she should have texted him, but there was so much to process. The fear that he had told someone at work gnawed at her.

"Talk to him. All you can do now is ensure he is safe. That this place is safe." Her eyes glanced towards the massive mountain on the horizon. Shasta watched, steadfast and strong as it had for hundreds of thousands of years, as it would for thousands more. It was the epicenter of so much power and she was but a small pebble standing in its shadow. "I'm sorry. I never meant to be so careless," she said softly to the wind.

As if it heard, a small gentle breeze blew against her face, as if it were pushing her towards the truck.

Camille wasn't sure what to make of Mt. Shasta's message, but she had no doubt it was a message she had to follow.

Chapter 15

The last two hours left Reyes in a daze and when he shut his laptop and stood up, he had no idea what to do. He hadn't said a word to anyone upon returning. It was a small blessing Evan was off today because he wouldn't have known what to even say.

When he walked out to his truck, he stopped in his tracks seeing Camille standing by it, looking nervously at him. Her face was riddled with worry.

"Can we talk?" she asked and bit her lip. He just remained frozen, still at a loss for words, but his eyes were focused on her. He had dreamed about someone like her—this embodiment of spring with her bobcat. "Please?"

He could hear the pleading in her voice. "You told me to leave." The words left his mouth and he could feel his heart shrivel up. Had he always been bound to lose her one way or another? How many more chances was he going to get with her? Then he realized he hoped for at least one more.

"I know, I'm sorry. I was shocked that you saw that." She gestured towards the back of the bakery. "I just, I think we need to clear some things up. It is imperative you understand my error."

Reyes didn't understand what she meant and part of him wasn't sure he wanted to. Yet, she wanted to talk and to help him understand. He let out a deep exhale. "Yes. Where would be best?"

"Somewhere private. I haven't found many places yet and I was hoping maybe you knew somewhere. Or just in your truck? I would suggest the bakery but it might not be the most comfortable for you, all things considered."

His shoulders slumped and he nodded, fumbling for his keys in his jacket pocket. "Let's go." He walked to the passenger side of the truck where he unlocked and opened the door for her. A sigh escaped him as he watched her stare at the seat with papers on it. "Sorry, I'm a trash human being," he grumbled and shoved the papers behind the seat.

There was a tension in her when she got in the truck and he hated it. He noticed she jumped when he pushed the truck door shut. All he could do was sigh once more in defeat and run around the front of the truck to get in the driver's seat. He met her wide and worried eyes.

"I'm sorry; I didn't expect to have anyone in my truck today. I wasn't sure when I imagined you would be in my truck, honestly."

"It's alright. I didn't expect to be in your truck today either." Her tone was filled with apprehension.

"I didn't slam the door shut either. They are just heavy doors. Older truck means it's mostly steel," he began explaining nervously. His door was still open.

"I know. I just don't do well with loud sounds. They look heavy."

"I'm going to close mine," he said, as if asking for permission.

"Okay." She appeared to brace herself with a strain in her jaw and clenched fist.

Once the door was closed, he turned the ignition and the engine roared to life. He headed north to a small park at the edge of town. Once there, he undid his seatbelt and turned slightly to face her, completely unsure how to start the conversation.

"So, you were never supposed to see what you did, but now that you have, you absolutely cannot tell anyone what I am."

"I don't know what I saw. What were you doing? How were you doing it?" Reyes asked, watching her eyes well up.

This situation was going to drive him mad. He hated seeing her so distraught, but he also didn't understand what she had done today. All he saw was a medium-sized rounded cast iron pot and glowing green sparks and green smoke. As if she were a witch making a potion. *A cottage witch,* he recalled the thought from so many months ago. *No.*

"You saw me brewing enchantments. The herbs in the drawers that I dry out are the ingredients for them. I usually make them in the cabin I'm renting, but it is easier at the bakery since that is where I dry the herbs."

Reyes stared at her blankly for a moment. "Enchantments? What?" he asked, trying to wrap his head around what she said. "Enhancements?"

"No. Enchantment. I guess if you really want to define it that way then fine. Yes, my enchantments do enhance the freshness and therefore the flavor of things." Frustration was seeping into her tone now.

"That's a health code violation, Camille. The FDA hardly monitors enhancements as it is. And you are adding that to food people are consuming? My parents ate there." He couldn't help the absurdity in his voice.

"This isn't some kind of synthetic drug! You saw the herbs. That's all they are. Dried lavender and elderberry. And before you want to tell me about how elderberry is poisonous, it's cooked to the correct temperature before use. I know how to handle my herbs and ingredients. I have had extensive training. I taught it too. I was a professor."

His mouth gaped open like a fish a few times, trying to figure out how to even respond.

"What even are you? Animal handler? Baker? Professor?"

Reyes did not miss the seething anger that came out of her, nor the hurt spilling out of her eyes.

"What am I?" Her venomous words shot out at him. "I'm something hunted and feared by pious men for just doing what I was born into.

They would see me drowned or burned at stake. I am an asset to a coven who sees me as little more than a breeding mare for a pedigree bloodline. My mother would say I'm an ungrateful little brat for putting me through such a prestigious program and giving me a professorship until it was time to sell my hand off in a union. That's all I am. Evil to self-righteous humans, and an asset to a corrupt coven."

He could hear the hurt in her words now. But he still didn't understand. Luckily, she continued saving him from floundering through words that eluded him.

"I am a green witch. I am grateful for my education. I worked hard at the academy but it, like most things, gained enough prestige and power to turn rotten. And no one was going to save me, so I fled. Humans and witches can be just as deplorable as those they condemn, my family and coven included. I love to bake. It's what I wanted to do, but was never allowed, never would be allowed. I was there to uphold the legacy and then produce heirs, and I could see the days growing darker with each sunset."

"Witch?" It was the only word that he could muster in his disbelief.

"You know what history tells of us, but the only part that's correct is how we were treated. We don't eat children; we don't steal the souls of men or corrupt women to sin. We help the earth where we need and treat ailments naturally. We care for the animals and the plants we tread on, and thank the earth for all her gifts in gratitude for the magic she gives us."

"Witches aren't real though. It's all just fairy tales," Reyes said in confusion.

With a loud defeated sigh, she undid her seatbelt. He hadn't even realized she still had it on this entire time. She opened the door. "Then just forget I was ever in your truck. Forget I was ever here. The bakery and all my lore will not exist in your life. I'm not real anyway."

His heart seized when she got out of the truck. A second later the door slamming shut sent a shock through him and he jumped out of the truck, running after her.

"Wait! Camille. Stop," he pleaded. She stopped walking but didn't look at him. "I don't understand any of this. I'm so confused, but you don't have to uproot your life and run."

She finally met his eyes and there was no more anger, just hurt. Her bottom lip trembled.

"If you talk, word will spread, and my coven will hear of the occurrence and they will come. Be sure you lie low when they do."

He let out a slow, quiet exhale. He just needed to understand this. He wanted to, because losing her would destroy him. "Don't leave. Don't uproot everything you just built. I just don't understand any of it, but I want to." He reached his hand out.

She looked at his hand then back at him for a moment before turning away. "I made a mistake. The bell broke and I didn't hear you enter. You were never supposed to see that. Now I'm too scared you will be standing with the angry mob, pitchforks and torches in hand. That is what witches warn their children about so they keep their mouths shut."

He moved to stand in front of her. "Cami. I promise you I will not talk about it to anyone, but I need to understand it more. I want to. You wanted to talk to me so let's get back in the truck and keep talking. Please?"

Camille wiped her eyes and looked towards the horizon. "Alright," she said, not looking at him. He noticed her walk back towards the truck with her head hung low, as if she were already walking into the gallows. The overwhelming need to protect and comfort her felt like it was a dog trapped in a cage, eager to get out and run after her.

He didn't want her to feel hurt or fear but he didn't understand anything that was happening right now.

Once Camille was back in the truck, her face burned and she hated it. All she could hear was her mother's disappointed voice. *Thornwells don't cry, and they do not cower down.* She thought she was stronger, but when had she ever encountered humans being a threat? Her training to test her mettle had been extensive enough and she'd passed those tests with flying colors. But she never had to apply it in real life. She'd hardly ever been off the campus and she was seldom ever alone.

What was the point of teaching her how to have an iron will if they had never planned to let her have this kind of life? It wasn't as if she could ever exude this iron will with her coven elders. She wasn't even supposed to take it against Leland. The thought of him made her blood boil.

Camille wiped her eyes again and realized Reyes was watching her, back in the seat of the truck. She had been so angry she hadn't even heard the truck door slam to make her jump.

After a long exhale, she spoke. "Witches have magic given to them by the earth. Some make talismans, write spells, or make elixirs and such. Some make the tools we use and others embed their magic into things like I do. I am a green witch and learned herbal enchantments as a focus." Camille looked at her hands before continuing.

"Baking was always a hobby and so I started to test the herbal enchantments. I excelled at it and it was encouraged at the academy while I was studying but baking is considered trivial. It wasn't useful. 'Anyone can buy a cupcake,' my mother would say. 'Why would you waste your energy enchanting something someone would shit out in a few days,' my dad would say. My parents wanted me to enchant metals, weapons, and talismans. Things people could use." Her tone shifted to spite she could almost taste.

"So anything can be enchanted? Anything living? Or does it have to be made?" he asked.

"Living things are affected by the enchantments I make but not enchanted. So you can't be, the trees can't be, but your truck could be, the pot a sapling might be planted in could. Blades or charms require different enchantments than a muffin does as they are used for different things."

She could see Reyes thinking. "Has everything I've tried from the bakery been enchanted? What if you didn't enchant stuff, would it taste different?"

Camille felt frustration gnaw at her. "I still know how to bake. The enchantments do a few things. I set my intent in the enchantments when they are brewed in my cauldron with concentration and focused thoughts. They keep the baked goods fresh for a longer amount of time. For people who order a bunch to take back home or work. The flavors would remain at their peak freshness for about a day," she explained. "They also offer a small serotonin boost. I can enchant for deeper sleep, to calm, to energize, a lot of things."

He looked down and then back at her. Once again she could tell the wheels in his head were turning. He opened his mouth before he closed it as if he didn't know what to say.

"So, it's like a preservative but for fresh baked goods? But alters mood like a drug?"

She hated how he phrased things sometimes. It reminded her of her parents' disappointment. All of her education just to keep a muffin fresh. But she had to remind herself Reyes didn't mean it like her parents did. He was asking about it instead of shutting it down. That small hope she had was strong enough to grab hold of the chance that he would accept her.

"I want the flavors to be perfect for everyone. It's not a preservative. At least not in the sense of the human world. It's just the herbs doing what they do, with some of my magic. It gives people that serotonin boost they normally get when they eat a muffin, or scone, or cupcake, or when they have a slice of fresh bread." Camille had to let out another sigh, realizing none of this sounded good to a county health code inspector. Especially one who didn't understand magic.

"Think of it like this. You are craving something and you are excited to get it. So you order it for lunch but you're planning to get it to-go and take it back to work. You get back to your desk, and it slides around in transport or you get distracted with your phone and your food gets cold. It's still good, still hits the spot, but it would have been that much better if it were fresh. There is so much going on in the world and in everyone's lives that a baked good just makes the day that much better for people. I want them to have that thing that hits the spot in whatever chaos is going on during the day."

He just stared at her once more. "What if someone has a dietary restriction? Or an allergic reaction? How do you know?"

"They are baked goods. I list everything in them. People can see I used eggs, cream, flours, sugar, and everything any bakery uses. You saw my ingredients listed on the labels. The nutmeg, thyme, lavender, it's all there. Do I need a surgeon general's warning that consuming too much sugar or butter can kill you?"

"No." Reyes looked down. "What about the long-term effects? Does it alter us in any way? If you consume it too often, then what? Nearly everyone in my office eats from the bakery multiple times a week. Me included."

She had to smirk to herself. "No, you don't have a bunch of magic herbs coursing through your veins. You pass it like everything else you consume. Honestly, the sugar or caffeine are probably the things that need the warnings. Not my herbal enchantments."

"What if you didn't enchant stuff?"

"It would still be a bakery, but I need to release my magic somehow. All witches need to exercise it. If I use too much of it, I will grow tired. If I don't use it, I will get too antsy, as though something is going to explode inside me. I have had training on that too."

"Training?" Reyes asked.

Camille let out a sigh and spoke of the academy. She explained the wide array of classes she took and taught. There were classes where she was forced to not use her magic for weeks upon weeks and it was the punishment if she acted out of line. For the next month, they would require her to use it almost nonstop to enchant herbs and other things, making her rise earlier than normal to drain her all over again.

Camille explained the etiquette classes to make her prim and proper and how despite her passing those classes, her mother always reprimanded her for being outside, hiking and digging her hands into the dirt to forage. They had the lesser covens to do those things for them.

It all made her feel such conflicting emotions that she hated feeling. It was always wanting her parents to smile at her, tell her she was proud of her, while hating her name.

She had felt like a pedigree show pony that was to always be sequestered away into the stables until she was bought and then moved to another stable to strengthen the pedigree. Then guilt would always follow—she despised her magic and education at times; even going as far as to hate being born a witch.

Here, she was granted every luxury and security in life even if it had come with chains. Thornwells knew how to hide. She wouldn't have ever been hunted while remaining tucked away in those stables like some smaller covens were, or the ones who remained solitary.

Then she thought about Willow. Here was a witch living her best life, part of a coven of nurturing matriarchs who encouraged their young to spread their wings, but always kept the nest warm if they wanted to return. Willow had wanted to see what was out there and found her slice of heaven in Mt. Shasta. Not far off from Reyes, who had just wanted a slower, quieter life where he could fish and hike but also own a piece of land comfortably.

"The lessons sound more like a strict boot camp and no offense, but it sounds a bit like a cult," Reyes said. Camille snapped her gaze to him, causing him to flinch. "I'm sorry. I don't know much about anything, obviously, but I thought witch covens were smaller, like a little commune or something just living off the land. I always thought the witch trials sounded so horrible, that women had been accused and never allowed to speak for themselves. Even if they did, their words would be twisted and used against them. That one slighted prick could make a comment that would condemn someone else to death."

He didn't wish ill will on things he didn't understand; he just needed someone to be patient and explain it to him. He was a genuinely good and kind soul, and he hadn't condemned her. Reyes had been so gentle with her, and recognized her boundaries before she even knew she was allowed to have them.

At that, Camille felt her heart begin to crack. There was no more fighting her tears so she let them pour.

Chapter 16

Reyes froze when she covered her face with her hands and cried. He could see her entire body tense and tremble. *Comfort her! Do something,* he told himself. She needed someone to just tell her she would be alright even if he didn't know what her coven was capable of.

"Camille." His words were soft as he placed a hand on her shoulder. "I'm sorry."

"I wake here every morning safely tucked in the shadow of Mt. Shasta. This is the freedom and life I want, yet with every single sunset, the lies face me with my back pressed up against the mountain and I can only hope they don't come for me while I sleep."

"That's why you would run? To put distance between them and you?" he asked softly.

"Yes. I was so stupid to choose Bakewell as a name and I feel like leaving is the best thing I can do for you now that you know all of this."

"What would they do to me?"

She looked up at him in defeat. "There are a number of things they might do. If you fought too hard, they might cut out your tongue. They might curse your home, or your truck. It might be getting fired from work. It would be something with a lasting effect, to silence you, or demean your character. No amount of money would satisfy them. The police can't do much either. Thornwell is powerful."

He stilled. "What if I remained silent? If I swore I would?" he asked.

"They would demand something in exchange to prove it. To bind you to your word."

He remained quiet for a few moments. His hand remained on her shoulder.

"If I left, though, they might pass through and search without you being noticed. They would continue searching and have no reason to believe anyone knew. I was merely here and then fled again," she explained.

He now moved his hands to take one of hers in his, lacing their fingers together. She stilled, looking at him with shock. "Don't leave. We will work on a plan if they come. You deserve your freedom. I may not understand it all, but I don't want you to live in constant fear, or have to flee. Maybe it's freedom but it's also a new kind of prison. You said you liked it here and I like this place with you in it."

"Reyes. The bakery has done nothing but give you a headache."

He smirked. "The bakery is not a headache. Headaches are the food trucks and businesses that change 'ownership' by changing the business name. I want to learn more about the enchantments." He gently ran his thumb over her hand. "And I want to continue what we started, Cami."

"You aren't mad that I lied about all this?"

"You didn't lie about anything. You fled for your life. I want you to stay here to find a new life. Maybe part of that makes me selfish that I hope it might be with me, but even if it isn't, this place is pretty magical. I want you to experience it."

She choked out a laugh. "Thank you, Reyes."

"Do you have any plans for the evening? I'm not keeping you, am I?" He rubbed the back of his neck nervously.

"No, just going to make a few more batches. I kinda lost the one you saw me making. I didn't take it off the heat and it burned," she said bashfully.

"I'm sorry. I feel bad." He wanted to spend time with her and learn more about her enchantments but he didn't know how to broach the topic.

"It's alright. I am feeling antsy though since I was mid-casting and didn't finish. I will knock about six more out tonight. Maybe I can stretch it to eight before the fatigue sets in. Thornwell had me doing at least twelve after lessons."

His eyes shot wide. "Twelve? No. Don't. Don't exhaust yourself."

She smiled at him again. "I am not going to. But I need to get the energy out and replenish some of my stash."

"I don't want to keep you, but can I bring you dinner? To make up for the lost batch?"

She looked at him as if she were reading a book. He didn't mind. He hoped he was on full display. He wanted her to see past his faults and somehow see *him*.

"You really want to learn about what I'm doing?" she asked.

"Yes. If you don't mind teaching a clueless moron. I don't have magic obviously and I promise I won't tell anyone about it. I just want to understand it. If I do, then it will ease my worry. The last thing I want is for the bakery to get shut down."

She took an inhale and looked down. "Alright." Then she met his eyes and he felt his smile grow as she bit her bottom lip. "Want to come to my cabin?"

"Yes. I will drop you off at your car and grab dinner. Is Mexican food okay?"

"Yes. I will text you my address. It might be a little hard to get parking, since it's a cabin rental."

"I think I know the place, a little down from Hedge Creek Falls?"

"Yes. Did you get that off the bakery paperwork?"

"I didn't even think to look, but you mentioned Dunsmuir and there aren't exactly a lot of hotels there. My parents stayed there once shortly after I bought the land for my place." He gave her hand a squeeze.

She looked at him longingly and he felt like the luckiest man alive. He put on his seat belt and started the engine. She put hers on, too, and when he drove back to the bakery, he glanced at her lips then at her. Reyes knew he would never tire of her bashful smiles.

Camille had to exhale all of her nerves and excitement. As she drove home, she thought about how sincere he seemed. He wanted to learn from her; he wanted her. Even with the danger, he wanted to fight for her. She could sense he was nervous; she was, too, but she also got the sense he didn't expect anything. Sure, he had his wants and desires, she had them as well, but she was not above simply exploring what they had started.

And now he was coming over to her place. Another nervous exhale escaped her. She had no idea where the night would end up, but it would end up somewhere. Curiosity would get the best of her too.

As soon as she parked her car, she bolted inside to clean as much stuff as she could. They would likely be sitting at the small table or her bed. That thought got her a bit riled up but it was far too soon for that. They hadn't even kissed yet.

She heard a pawing at the door and promptly opened it for Sitka.

Kneeling down, she gave her a pet, relieved to see her. Sitka purred loudly, likely just as relieved.

"Okay, Sitka, we are having a guest tonight. So let's hope he finally understands," Camille pleaded to no one in particular. She realized she hadn't explained the familiar bond but she supposed it would be a good time to. If he wanted to learn, he was about to learn a whole lot.

As she was setting out the herbs she had packed up for the day, she heard a knock and rushed to the door to see Reyes. He smiled widely once again. It always made her feel warm upon seeing it.

"Hey."

"Hi, come in. Sorry it's a little small. And probably awkward. I've actually never had anyone over here."

"I've actually never seen the inside of the rustic cabins. My parents stayed in the modern ones."

"Makes sense. These were cheaper. Even with a monthly rate."

"Isn't this costing you a lot?" Reyes asked as he followed her into the kitchen area.

"Kind of but I'm not sure what my alternative is," she explained.

"Guess you're right. I can imagine you want your privacy." He set down the food and took hers out along with a cup of red liquid. "I got us some drinks, too, if you wanted some. It's Agua de Jamaica. One of my favorites. The people at this place rolled their eyes when I walked in." He laughed, sounding a bit embarrassed.

"It's actually been a while since I've had hibiscus tea." She watched him jump and look down. Sitka was rubbing against his legs.

"Oh, right. Sitka." He held his hand out.

Camille chuckled softly.

"Never thought I would interact so much with a bobcat. It really just stays with you?"

"Yes. Like I said, I gave her the option, I set the intent towards her. She stayed with me through the night. So the next morning, I opened my bond to her as a familiar and named her Sitka. It felt right."

"Oh right, your kind has familiars. What exactly does that mean?"

"She looks out for me, and I look out for her. It is a give and take. If I am hiking or there is danger nearby, she will alert me, if not protect me.

I'm not about to let her go up against a mountain lion or even a coyote but she will guide me back to the car or the cabin if something is lurking nearby, even a human with bad intentions. In turn, she gets a warm bed to sleep in and easy meals. Plus, lots of attention."

"I take it she approves of me then?"

"Yes, she does. She knows you helped her and me. So she is as much in your debt as she is in mine."

"I didn't do much other than help you back to the car though. You had no intention of calling either number, did you?" He smirked.

Camille smiled but she felt somewhat tense. "No. I knew I could help her and send her on her way. I had intended to, but Sitka chose me. So I chose her," she stated, feeling the intent in her words. She would protect this place.

Reyes let out a sigh then grinned wide. "Alright. You have a bobcat. Evan told me to ignore it. Said it was no different than someone who befriends a raven or his dog. I didn't exactly agree that it was the same as him getting Belle as a puppy, but again, what do I know? That's why I am here tonight, to learn."

Camille smiled and they began to eat while she explained the basics and named the herbs she had laid out. With the mortar and pestle, she put some herbs into it and asked if he wanted to grind it up. He did and she learned while he cooked a lot, he'd never tried baking. He enjoyed cooking a lot of meat and fish with whatever sides that complimented them. He got a bit bashful when he admitted at times he got too distracted and overcooked things, but he usually tried to focus as much as possible.

"I can't remember half of what these herbs are when they are all ground up."

"The importance of labels, right Mr. Health Inspector?" she mused.

"Yes. Also so the health inspector can check all the appropriate boxes." He laughed then sighed in defeat. "I don't know if you have figured it out yet, but I have ADHD. I manage it, but obviously not always."

"I had a feeling it was something like that. A lot of students at the academy had it. We had our herbal medications that would be prescribed. But it's really nothing to be ashamed of, Reyes. You've come through for me so many times."

He grimaced and looked down. "You really aren't annoyed I've been late? Or have called your bobcat the wrong name a few times?"

"I just told you I'm essentially hiding out from a powerful cult-like coven. Being a little late is tolerable," she said, setting the cauldron on the stove top.

She really wasn't sure why he was so self-conscious of having ADHD, but she figured asking him why would likely make it more uncomfortable for him.

When she began to make the enchantments into syrups, he watched in awe this time at her abilities. He mentioned he could almost feel her intention just being near it and he was fascinated by it. Camille had realized how good it felt to teach again, and how much joy it gave her to see his awe.

At one point during an enchantment, she asked him to hold her hands with his fingers on her palms. He came around behind her and placed his hands on hers, gently holding her hands in his and she couldn't help but feel a warmth brewing in her unlike any she had ever felt before.

Sure, she'd had partners in the past. Leland was simply there for a business exchange arranged by their families. They'd never held love or affection for each other, and they never would.

Yet she felt so connected to Reyes right now. And how she wanted him. How she knew it was so unwise to be this invested in another soul, given everything she had fled in the middle of the night, but feelings were hard things to stop.

Camille wondered if she had always been destined to flee Thornwell, if she would be a shamed legacy. A betrayer. That's what it would look like on Thornwell's part. Her two older brothers were going to carry the name on; she was the daughter to be married off.

"That was amazing," Reyes said softly in her ear.

She snapped back to the moment and was grateful she had finished the enchantment. It surely would have been wasted with that thought process and what if Reyes had felt he was the one who messed it up because he had been touching her? He was likely what saved it; his sense of wonder and curiosity made this batch something new.

"Did you feel anything?"

"I felt your hands warm, and I could see the glow on mine. As though your magic was connecting to my very core."

Camille could hear the smile in his voice. She turned and looked at him, taking in his smile.

Then she came up to her tip toes and pulled his flannel down to meet his lips. She felt him tense for a second but he quickly relaxed into her lead and wrapped his arms around her.

She felt his tongue beg for entry and obliged. In fact, she quickly handed the lead over to him when he tipped her back.

Reyes pulled back and gazed into her eyes now. "I will never get enough of that."

"I am not sure I will either." She smiled.

"I have wanted to kiss you for months." He leaned in to kiss her again.

They laughed bashfully and got to talking about various things as she cleaned out the cauldron. He'd mentioned that he was going camping with Evan over the weekend.

"I can make you a safety enchantment. You can drop some of it in your water, or coffee. I can give it a vanilla or brown sugar taste or maybe a citrus if you put it in your water?"

"Alright." He smiled. "Is there anything I can do to help?"

"Try measuring out the herbs I say in the mortar."

He nodded and did an impressive job of identifying most of the herbs correctly. She only had to correct him on one of them. Again, she had him place his hands on hers and she released her magic intentions outward, creating the citrus flavored syrup.

"What if Evan has some?" he asked, looking at a small amber colored vial with the dropper top.

"It will keep danger away from him too. Animals will steer clear but maybe don't push it by leaving food out and stuff."

"Of course not. We will have my truck to store stuff. Evan has the red truck you may have seen, so we usually take mine since it's bigger," Reyes explained.

"Well I hope you have fun."

"We usually do. I will call you when I can. We are leaving Friday, but I will definitely stop in tomorrow during work and before we head out the next day."

She nodded and set to bottling up his enchantment. "Remember, just three drops max. More might upset your stomach."

"Three drops. Got it. No lasting effects otherwise, though?"

"No. It will likely be out of your system by Monday or Tuesday depending on how hydrated you are."

After he helped her clean up, he glanced at her. "Hey, Cami?"

"Yeah?"

"Have you done any love spells? Do you do any?"

Her heart came to a screeching halt just before she felt it start to crack. "Is that what you think I did to you?"

His body demeanor changed. He grew tense and his mouth gaped open again. Panic crossed his expression. "I've just never felt like this before."

"Ask yourself how long you've felt that way. Does Evan feel the way you do? Any of your coworkers? And when would I have had time to target you?"

"I certainly hope not and I don't know. It's just that women tend to glaze over me and go for Evan anyways. So I guess I'm just not used to this. All of this."

"I don't know any of those enchantments, and I don't know how to put spells on people. Look through my notebooks, none of it is for a love enchantment."

"Okay. I'm sorry I asked."

"Do you believe me?" She crossed her arms and he remained silent, too long for her liking. Camille should have known. What could this ever become if he questioned what he felt for her? She knew what she felt for him. It was typical that it wouldn't be reciprocated. It never was. She was such a fool.

"Whatever we started should end. If you question what you feel, then I can't waste the time trying to convince you otherwise. I don't want to have to." Her voice broke on the words.

"Cami—" He took a step towards her.

"And stop with the nicknames. It hurts too much. I know what I feel. Just go." She looked away and felt her face burn as the tears formed.

"No. I'm sorry." He moved closer. "I don't want this to end. I just don't understand it and it's all new to me. If you say you didn't, I believe you." He held his hand out. "Please. It was a stupid question. I've felt this way for a while. The fact that you do, too, isn't something I'm used to. It's new and different. Admittedly, it's hard to believe you want me."

She finally looked at him, the pain and sincerity in his voice pulling her gaze. She recalled both Willow and Evan saying he didn't have the best luck with partners. He'd been hurt and it clearly left an impression on him. The monsters from her past certainly had left their mark on her.

"They are stupid if they overlook you. You are way more attractive than Evan," she muttered with her arms crossed but looked away to wipe her eyes. She heard a slight chuckle slip out of him.

"I will go if you really want me to, but I am truly sorry I asked. I'm sorry for fucking this up. I don't want this to end. I want it to keep going."

She sighed in defeat, realizing how honest the question was. He had no idea about the hierarchy of magic. Witches casting spells was the extent of his knowledge. He'd felt her magic tonight and was in awe of it.

Finally, she took his hand and his relief was palpable. He pulled her close and rested his forehead against hers. "I'm sorry. I know what I feel and I want to keep feeling it. I want you to feel it too."

"No one's ever given me a nickname before. My parents said those were stupid, and legacies were above such trivial things. So the first time you said it, it made me feel accepted."

"Can I still use it?"

"Yes." She hugged him tightly and buried her face in his chest. It was toned; his stomach was soft and his arms were strong as he pressed her into him. Camille knew it would be so hard to leave if she had to. She knew she never wanted to leave. She had stopped being a Thornwell so long ago; she didn't belong with them. She wanted to belong here, with Reyes.

"Cami. Thank you for showing me what you have tonight. I hope you will teach me more some other time."

"I'd like that, Reyes," she whispered and looked at him.

He looked at her and pulled her into a deep kiss again, which led to another makeout session but neither one made a move to go further.

Camille was fine with that. There would be time.

When Reyes found out what time she had to be up for the bakery, he panicked again and insisted she get some sleep. It still didn't stop one last makeout session and she could have sworn she felt another hard part of him before he rushed out in a hurry, promising he'd see her tomorrow. She could guess he would be up at least a little longer after he got home.

A smirk came to her when she finally lay down. Sitka had gone out of the window a little before they made the last batch so she was alone. She stayed up a little longer, thinking about him and his hard parts.

Chapter 17

The next morning on his break, Reyes walked into Willow's shop. He had known the two were friends and he wondered if Willow knew her secret. He wouldn't tell Willow but he wanted to encourage them to hang out this weekend. Cami needed a support system. Maybe it was overstepping but he wanted to try to help her. He'd known Willow for a few years but always thought of her as Jodie and Sophia's friend. He never did talk much to her. But now she was Cami's friend. It was not lost on him that his best friend had a crush on Willow too. Maybe, just maybe, he could help both Cami and Evan out.

Once inside, he took in the scents that usually hit him as soon as he entered. Then he looked around and realized she called it The Apothecary. He hadn't actually used much from here, but his mom and sister raved about every gift he had bought them from here. Much like everyone raved about Cami's bakery.

Enchantments. The thought flashed in his mind. *Is Willow a witch too? This entire time? Is that why they are so close?*

Willow came rushing out of the back. "Sorry. How may I help—" Her words cut off abruptly and he couldn't help but wonder if she had been doing the same thing he had seen Camille doing. "Hello, Reyes," she said with obvious tension.

"Hello, Willow."

They watched each other for a moment before he looked away.

"This isn't your usual time for gift shopping."

"No, it's not," he said, unable to hide the curiosity in his tone. Glancing around, he spotted a candle with a bergamot and aloe scent. The label said 'Energy.' He picked it up and smelled it. It did smell good. Then he realized he was feeling energized. Not exactly what he needed right now. He saw one next to it that said 'Calm.' It had a lavender and sandalwood scent. Sure enough, when he took in the scent, he felt a calm wash over him.

"These candles certainly do what the label says," Reyes noted then looked at lip balm. It didn't claim to do anything, just said 'Honey Lemon.' "Does this do anything else?"

"What do you mean, does it do anything else? It soothes chapped lips."

"Would it leave you feeling any type of way?"

Willow narrowed her eyes. "Reyes. Why are you asking?"

"I'm just curious. We are both close to Cami and she needs a solid support system. I'm going to be whatever Cami needs me to be. But you and I should actually be friends now. I want to be," he said softly with a smile. Then he realized Willow was not smiling; she was tense.

"So you two obviously talked last night about what you saw yesterday. Did she tell you? About me?" Willow gawked.

"You are one too?" he asked, somewhat baffled. "No! She didn't. She only told me what she was last night. She showed me how she enchants. I felt it. Now that I am aware of what her enchantments are doing, I feel like your stuff is doing the same. She never mentioned your name. I promise I'm not going to tell anyone. I won't tell Evan either."

"I don't think you fully understand what her being here means. If Thornwell tracks her down, there will be absolute hell to pay," Willow explained. "Knowing puts both you and me at a huge risk."

Something rattled deep within Reyes. Something he couldn't recall feeling before. This was deeper than anger or rage, he couldn't pinpoint it. Couldn't wrangle it back before the words spewed out.

"They would have taken everything from her, belittled her, and made her feel less than. I'm not letting them take this place from her too." That feeling he didn't fully understand stirred wildly again. He clenched his hands into fists before he released them.

"Reyes." Willow sounded stunned. "I don't know where this side of you came from but you cannot do anything against a legacy coven, especially if it's her parents that show up. You are a mere human. This is literally the first time I have ever seen you be this irate. You need to understand that."

"So what? Are you going to distance yourself from her? Just like that? That woman deserves a life of freedom, not a damn cult that tries to keep her obedient and subservient to their wants. I know you see it when she avoids eye contact and acts so formally. It makes me so angry for her."

"I don't know what Thornwell did to her, but I imagine if she fled it was worth the repercussions. You nor I can stop that. There are ruling councils for our kind. And it's so much bigger than her simply going back or leaving. She involved us."

"Hear her out; be there for her. Be a coven or however that works for her. I want her to be happy and safe. Sitka, me, you. She needs us. I know it sounds soon but I feel like I'd do anything for her. She needs a friend. Please do not shun her," Reyes asserted. "I will stand by you, too, if needed, any day, any time, Willow."

They remained fixed on each other. Never had he ever said this many words to Willow. Now he felt as though there was little more he could say to her. So he left and went back to the bakery.

"Hi, Reyes," Camille said with a smile. Instantly, whatever tension he had felt vanished upon seeing her.

"Hello, beautiful," he hummed, then smiled widely when her face flushed a hint of pink. Something in him now warmed at the sight. Reyes wanted to be everything for this woman and he didn't understand why he felt this so soon, or why he didn't care.

"Are you alright?" Camille asked. Worry cascaded over her expression.

"Yeah, long day." He laughed nervously then glanced at the case of pastries. "May I get two apple crisp muffins? With the butter?"

"Of course. A coffee as well?"

"Yeah. Can you...add something to the coffee?" he asked, unsure.

She paused for a moment, eyeing him. She was growing cautious and he didn't want her to. He felt as though she would flee at a moment's notice.

"Whatever you think will make the day feel less long?" He eyed her, hoping what he was not saying was obvious. "Also, do you have anything not uhh...ya know."

Again she paused, unsure, and he knew he needed to soothe her. He had all these urges in him.

"Cami, seeing is believing. I know we had last night, but I just want to see it in use. Please don't be scared."

"Alright," she said with her eyes shifting to the counter. "I have a blackberry croissant that I didn't bring enough for."

"That sounds lovely. One of those, two muffins, and whatever you want to put in the coffee, please?"

"Alright," Camille responded and set to getting everything packaged together. "I will add some vanilla cold foam to your coffee?"

Reyes nodded and saw the total, knowing once again she hadn't charged him for something. With a shake of his head and grimace, he made up the difference in a tip then glanced at her. She looked at him with a pensive smile.

"We are alright, Cami. Still continuing what we started as long as you want to, of course. You needn't worry," he said softly and offered his hand across the counter.

She looked at it before she placed her hand in his. He laced their fingers together and gave her hand a little squeeze. She smiled and squeezed his back.

"See you soon," he said softly and took a sip of the coffee. It was perfect. Doing exactly what she had said it would with a dopamine rush that pulled a light moan out of him and he tensed, seeing her watching him. "Sorry."

"It's alright. Nice to know you like it enough for that reaction."

"Oh, there is plenty about you that merits such a reaction from me." He laughed. Again, where was this side of him coming from? Never in his life would he have made such an innuendo to someone. Certainly not someone he hadn't made it official with yet. Though, her eyes traveling down to his lips as she bit hers told him they both knew what they wanted.

Once he was back at his desk, he took a seat.

"Damn, are you sharing any of that? Plus, you were gone for a long time," Evan said, grinning.

"Had some things I needed to take care of, and I have plans for the rest of this." Reyes took another sip of the coffee then remembered he had experiments to do with it.

"I don't even want to know what those plans might be." Evan smirked.

"What kind of response is that?" Reyes looked at him, baffled as he took the muffin out.

He knew he needed two because he did not have the willpower to not scarf one down immediately, but he wanted to know how long something would maintain its freshness. So he also made himself refrain from drinking his coffee too. Just to see how long it would last.

Sure enough, the coffee maintained its flavor until the end of the day. He was able to easily play off pouring himself the office coffee, which now tasted horrible to him, as merely being distracted. After eating half the croissant now, for control purposes of course, he would check on the texture after dinner. As for the other muffin, he would leave it out and eat it for breakfast. There would be plenty of hiking this weekend to make up for how much he was going to eat.

On that evening in her cabin, Camille bottled up her fourth batch of enchantments. Explaining it to Reyes had been enjoyable but it also was a slow process. Her professor demeanor took over that night and she'd explained a lot to him. If she were still at Thornwell Academy, four more would be expected from her within the hour.

She loved this place and the fact that she may have to leave it upset her. Of course there were other places she could go. Maybe to Humboldt, that place those three shifters and the girl were from.

Maybe they would keep her safe. Then again, fae seldom ever got involved with the witches' dealings. They had their hands full maintaining the lands and environment. It was common knowledge to her that the fae were just as prevalent among humans as witches were. Often holding county and state positions of governance. The three she'd met were all the heirs and that girl with them was special indeed to have them be so protective of her.

Camille thought back to how bonded the mountain lion and the girl were. How they interacted and part of her felt slightly envious. At the time, she'd still thought Reyes didn't like her. She couldn't have been more wrong. He was really sweet and they were becoming something.

They'd made out pretty passionately before he left. His embrace was so strong and safe when he wrapped his arms around her. The flannel he wore was soft under her fingertips and smelled so much like him. She could get lost in his cedarwood scent, as she often did with thoughts of him.

Part of her wanted to ask him to stay that night and lay with her but she wouldn't ask. He hadn't either. His hands had slid down to her waist but he didn't push. Of course, that didn't stop her from thinking about it once she was in bed and she wondered if he'd thought about her in his bed too.

It wasn't just that she found him attractive both physically and mentally, it was also that mutual curiosity about each other that had been forming. Something she had never experienced with anyone before. He was curious about a lot, and he wasn't afraid to admit when he didn't know something.

He had nothing to prove to anyone when it came to his intelligence, but he was smart in his own way. Camille recalled how he had fixed the battery issue on her car flawlessly as though he'd done it countless times. But of course he had, with a truck like his. He was made for a place like this. The way he looked at her and smiled at her, as though he simply wanted to explore his curiosity with her. As much as she wanted to explore hers with him.

Reyes hadn't shied away from her being a witch. He hadn't seen her as some pedigree either. She felt as though he saw her as a person. She couldn't recall a time when she had felt seen like that.

The faint buzzing of her phone pulled her back from her thoughts. "Getting ahead of myself," she admitted to Sitka, who was curled up in a throw blanket on the bed as she grabbed her phone.

> **Willow:** Would you like to have dinner at my place tonight?

It wasn't that the message was out of the ordinary. They often met up at least once a week to work on things over dinner, but yesterday had been a lot for Camille. Though she knew she owed it to Willow to tell her the truth—all of it. Even the parts she had left out for Reyes. Some part of her couldn't bear to tell him about the betrothal to Leland.

Her worries got the better of her that maybe Willow had contacted someone and was ready to hand her over. She couldn't blame her for that. But she trusted Willow and valued their friendship. Camille didn't think Willow would do that.

She knew, deep down, if leaving kept Reyes and Willow safe, she would do it, regardless of the means. That much had always been cemented in her mind. Still, that didn't stop Camille from impulsively texting Reyes as she cleaned up her supplies.

> Camille: How is your evening?

> Reyes: Good. Just getting stuff out of the garage for the camping trip this weekend. Yours?

Relief came over her. He was fine. Safe and sound a mere twenty minutes north of her.

> Camille: Good. Just cleaning up and going to have dinner with Willow.

> Reyes: I'm glad. Let me know how it goes and when you are home.

Another thing he did that she wasn't used to was ensuring she was safe. The check-in text was simply because it was dark out here at night, and accidents happen. It comforted her to know at least one person was there for her. Maybe two depending on how this talk with Willow went. With that revelation, she and Sitka headed out to her car and made their way to Willow's house.

She knocked on the door as she held a grocery bag, Sitka by her side. Her heart thundered when she heard the lock turn and the door open.

Willow looked at her and offered a small smile before stepping back. "Come in."

"I grabbed some wine and salad stuff. And I have a loaf of brioche for you. Not sure what we are having," Camille replied. She maintained her neutral tone but her body certainly felt tense.

"Oh, thanks. It will pair nicely with the chicken primavera. It's just about ready," Willow replied. They finished prepping and plating the food in silence and Camille was growing uneasy. The silence continued and Camille was doubting everything in her life. She forced a few bites of food down. It tasted amazing but her stomach was in knots.

"I'm sorry," she offered, not able to stand the silence.

"I'm sorry too. I grew up hearing about how horrible leaving a coven was, and how prestigious a legacy is, especially Thornwell. My younger cousin is hoping to apply soon. That aside, I suppose I need to know why you left. Reyes damn near demanded it of me." Willow blew out a sigh.

Camille looked worried. "You talked to him?"

"He came into the shop today," Willow explained. "So I guess I outed myself. Something was different in him though. I have never known him to have such a dominant streak."

"I'm sorry, I didn't think he would do that," she fretted.

"I don't think he did either and it's not your fault anyways, nothing to apologize for. He looked confused after. As though he didn't realize what came over him." Willow sighed then sat forward and took a bite of food. "Well I'm ready to listen, Camille."

"I fled. I didn't know what else to do." Camille began to tear up, but she managed to tell the story once again. In the end she still felt horrible, the fear still lingered and now, instead of having a weight lifted off her shoulders, she had just damned Reyes and Willow. Judgment would be passed and she would have to atone for it one way or another. "I will not let anything happen to you, him, or this place. I meant it yesterday, if I need to flee, I will. Just, look after him and Sitka please," Camille begged. Sitka rubbed against her legs.

"I didn't realize they were so strict. You weren't encouraged to pursue baking? Weren't you given a choice? They didn't even encourage you to at least venture out? Even if it were temporary?"

"It was a waste of the bloodline. They acted as though I was already a waste." She frowned.

"Reyes knows all of this?"

"Yes. I didn't go into detail about my betrothal. Leland and I had no interest in each other." Camille scoffed. "I was never able to please him during the coupling nights."

"Coupling nights?"

Camille gulped. "Yes. It is an old practice. Traditions are important to Thornwell, though. Essentially when betrothals are announced, the pairing-to-be had one night a month where they get to know each other, and are encouraged to get to know each other in all aspects. Like I said, we hated each other and I never understood why him. I just tried to be grateful. I tried to get to know him, and he put minimal effort in. Eventually came the intimacy part and it wasn't great either. I tried to be attentive to him, yet he never reciprocated anything. I was left feeling like I did something wrong and that neither one of us enjoyed it very much."

"I'm sorry. I see why you fled and why Reyes is protective of you now. He really does care for you," Willow soothed.

"Reyes is so...I just can't put it into words. I've never met anyone like him. He is so sweet and attractive yet he gets so flustered." She laughed, finally thinking about him and forcing Leland out of her mind. "As if any partner isn't lucky as hell to have him."

"Look at that pink on your cheeks. You two are good for each other. His ex really did a number on him and his self-esteem. But he smiles now. I think you are helping him."

"I promise you I will not let anything happen to this place," Camille assured.

"You will be safe, Camille. You took your precautions," Willow said, taking a sip of her wine. "I remember coven members working so hard at Thornwell Academy. They would come back in tears having passed the entrance exams and trials only to be denied admittance with no explanation. My cousin is convinced she will get in. She is so talented too. She has her own perfume line."

"I saw so many gifted witches pass through. They were so hopeful and eager, so determined and exuded so much talent and skill. Then they would leave in tears or anger. I wondered how many turned bad from that experience. It always came down to money and what Thornwell thought of the coven name. I never felt I belonged there, but bloodlines kept my spot."

"Your enchantments are flawless though and you are so strong and talented. The magic appears to come naturally to you. Then again, I suppose in a place like that, it's hard to ever be seen."

"I am so enamored with your life, your coven—they encouraged you to go off on your own if you wanted to. Even seeing Reyes's parents hurt a bit. That's what parents should do, this is what covens should do. Support and encourage their young. I never got that."

"Calarook isn't without flaws. I certainly have my reasons for being here. You are home though, Camille. Stay," Willow urged. "I think Reyes would really hurt if you fled. He would understand, but I wonder if part of him wouldn't. He tends to blame himself a lot."

"I told him it wasn't his fault, that it was mine," Camille said.

As the two continued to talk, Camille felt like she had at least two friends that made this place feel like home. In some ways, she felt better about everything, in other ways, it made things that much harder.

Chapter 18

On Friday morning, Reyes got up and made breakfast then set to loading up the truck. He admired how organized it was and knew full well it would be a complete mess on Sunday when they packed it back up.

After he cleaned the kitchen and looked over the house, all that was left was to wait for Evan and load his stuff. It wasn't a long drive over to Trinity Alps, so he wasn't in a hurry to leave. Their camp site was already reserved and they would be meeting up with his friend, Seth, who worked at the wildlife refuge there. They'd gone to high school together in San Jose and it would be Evan's first time meeting him.

Part of him was tense about Camille or Sitka being brought up. The last thing he wanted was for her to lose Sitka because of him or his connections. He had already upset her too much this week and he couldn't possibly fathom her giving him another chance regardless of what she felt. So he swore he would do whatever he needed to do to keep her. Even if he had to fight off some witches with his bare hands.

As he leaned back on the couch and stared up at the high-peaked ceiling, he thought about how much he wanted her, all to himself, in every way. He wanted her hand in hand with him, wanted to come home to her every evening, and kneel before her every night in his bed.

He wanted her to feel safe, not as though she was merely biding her time until hell reigned down.

Reyes brought his hand over his face and sighed. "Fuck, what is wrong with me?" he asked himself in the silence of his cabin. His gaze came to rest on the mountain. Shasta watched him. Just as it watched her, though she was tucked away on her ledge above the river in Dunsmuir.

Suddenly the thought struck him, what if something happened to her this weekend, when he was two hours southwest deep in another mountain range with little cell reception? *What if she took this time to leave? Would she leave?*

"No," he said to himself. "She can't do that." What could he even do if he was here this weekend? It was not as though he kept tabs on her whereabouts. He saw her during the week, and they had gone on a few dates, never spending more than a few hours together.

He focused on the mountain again. "Keep her safe. She belongs here," he pleaded. With a long exhale, he stood up just as his phone alerted him someone was arriving on the property. When he opened the app, he saw Evan's truck pulling up in front of the garage.

He grabbed his keys and hurried outside. "Hey, there should be plenty of room in the back, I organized it this time," he said then opened the top hatch and the tailgate.

"Impressive. You got the stove top loaded?"

"Yep," Reyes responded.

"I grabbed some extra mini propane tanks in case you forgot." Evan smiled.

"Got those too."

"Fishing poles?"

"Yep. Cookware, food, clothes. Checked three times."

"Backup battery for the cell phone?"

"Yep and the fully charged backup generator. Coffee, sleeping bag, tent. All set." Reyes rolled his eyes. "Prescriptions and my toothbrush too."

Evan laughed. "I'm impressed. You must be ready to get out of Dodge for a while."

Something twisted in his gut and he glanced at the mountain again. *Look out for her, please,* he pleaded and wasn't even sure why.

"Just trying to stay on top of things," Reyes responded with a tight-lipped smile.

"Organized too. Who are you and what did you do with Reyes?" Evan chuckled and tossed his bag and tent bundle in the back before heading back for the cooler. Reyes grabbed Evan's fishing gear.

"Need anything out of the house? Water? Bathroom?"

"Nah, I'm good for now," Evan said, putting his water bottle and cell phone in the front seat.

"We gotta stop in town before we hit the road. Seth will meet us at the campsite. He's just in Weaverville, so not far."

"Sounds good." Evan grabbed the last of his stuff and locked his truck. Reyes hurried off to double check things in the kitchen and that his house was locked up. Then padded himself down for his phone, wallet, and keys too. His usual onceover check system before he left.

When he parked in the lot, Evan looked at him. "Forget something at the office?"

"No, not going to the office," he said and got out. Evan got out too and followed him.

"Oh, I should have known. Gotta say bye to your bakery girl?"

"I want to get stuff for the road, and the trip, but yes," Reyes huffed, and pulled the door open. Evan just laughed.

He smiled when he saw her walk out from the back.

"Reyes, hi!" She beamed at him with a wide smile then glanced at Evan. "Hello, Evan."

"Well, now I have to know what Reyes did to merit such a bright welcome," Evan mused.

"Nothing," Reyes hurried out. "Order whatever, it's on me."

"Aww thanks, sweetheart," Evan joked.

Camille couldn't help but laugh as she grabbed a tray. "Should I package this separately?" she asked.

"Together is fine. Hopefully this asshole doesn't eat everything on the way to the campsite." Reyes rolled his eyes.

Once he ordered his iced coffee with some cold foam on top, Evan chuckled to himself.

Camille finished getting their order and drinks, ringing them up and meeting his eyes. Reyes saw the amount then looked at the menu and prices. Again, he made up the difference with a tip and then some. They smiled at each other like idiots for a moment before she walked around to the counter.

Evan cleared his throat and glanced at Reyes then back at Camille. "Can I, uh, pet the bobcat?" he asked.

Camille panicked and looked back towards her office to see Sitka sitting back on her haunches in the doorway.

"Sitka." Camille frowned and looked at Reyes.

He smiled at her. "It's fine, Cami. If she scratches him or bites him it'd probably be his fault anyways."

She nodded and called Sitka over. "You should come over here so she doesn't have to be in view of the windows as much. Let her sniff you first."

Evan walked over and scratched Sitka's head, meriting a purr from her.

"Let's grab dinner when I'm back, yeah?" Reyes asked her as he took the box from Camille.

"Alright. Be safe this weekend."

Reyes looked at her and reached for her, giving her hand a bit of a squeeze. "I will be." He gave her a wink. "Be safe as well." Then he leaned in and gave her a kiss.

She pulled back and smiled widely at him again.

"Okay, obviously I missed something if you two are kissing now." Evan laughed and stood up. Sitka sat back.

"Well, you have a drive to Trinity coming up, you two should get going. I don't want to keep you any longer," Camille said.

"It's like two and half hours away," Evan retorted.

"Grab your drink and let's go, Evan," Reyes said, grabbing his coffee.

He gave Camille one last smile and walked out to his truck, giving the mountain a glance, and repeating his silent plea.

Then they were on the road, taking them south after Reyes had scarfed his apple crisp muffin down. He could feel the serotonin kicking in, and he also noticed the coffee had maintained its taste and the cold foam had a delightful, sweet cream flavor to it.

"So, are you going to tell me how that all happened? Last I heard you went to dinner with her and your parents and didn't want to talk about the details."

"There aren't a lot of details to share. We've gone to dinner and hiked a few times; we talk, have talked a lot. She's—" He paused, not sure how to broach any subject. "She is estranged from her family and worried they might track her down."

Evan looked at him with shock. "What?"

"I don't want to go into details. I probably shouldn't have said that. I just, I don't want her to hate me. She likes me, and I'm such an idiot I don't know what I'm supposed to do with someone like her. She's kind, and smart, and just...I like her, a lot."

"When did you two make it official?" Evan inquired, glancing over at him.

"We haven't exactly. We just started something?"

"Like last night?" Evan asked.

"We kissed for the first time on Wednesday evening, and then we may have made out a lot, in her cabin. But it didn't go beyond that. I swear. I want to, but I mean look at me, I'm a total slob." Reyes groaned.

"Relax, the way she looks at you, smiles at you, tells me she likes you. I'm pretty sure she's just as crazy about you as you are about her. But I can't imagine her talking to Willow like this."

"I just don't want to mess it up with her." He sighed, knowing Evan was likely right. Cami did like him, he was just so worried she was going to find things she didn't like about him. While he knew no one was perfect, he recalled all the things Jodie had grown to loathe about him.

"If those looks told me anything, I think you are safe." Evan shook his head and took another sip of his coffee.

"Don't mention Sitka to Seth, please. I just don't want to open a can of worms."

"Alright I won't. Are you getting attached to the cat?"

"No." Reyes grumbled then sighed. "Maybe. Cami would be devastated if anything happened to her."

Camille officially sold out of things by the time it was around two in the afternoon. Of course, she had a few items packed aside for Willow and the front desk staff at her cabin rental. Just as she reached for the tip jar, someone walked in.

The man looked to be in a rush. He wore a long sleeve button-up shirt, jeans, and had a mustache. He also appeared to be red in the face and sweating though she could assume it was due to the long sleeve shirt. These late summer months were definitely something she was adjusting to. It was much warmer here than it had ever been near Seattle.

"Hello, Ms. Bakewell," he called out, walking to the counter.

"Yes." Her entire body tensed at his demeanor and she was grateful she had closed the door to leave Sitka out of view.

"Pardon my barging in here. I have a rather urgent and large request."

"Okay." Camille was unsure about this interaction.

"Next weekend is the fireman's ball and we would love to request if you could bake an assortment of things. We usually have a bakery we get things from but well, we wanted to try yours and the committee took so long to approve the order. It is over in McCloud, but we consider the area part of the community. I know it's short notice but we will pay generously and of course we won't turn donations down. The event operates as a fundraiser."

"Alright, what sorts of things would you like?" she asked, grabbing an order form.

"What would you recommend? I have only tried the fruit tart and it was delicious," he beamed.

"I can make mini tarts if the spread is going to be more finger foods or buffet style." She began to think of what fruit was in season.

"Yes, that would be perfect."

Camille went on to recommend a few more items and when everything was agreed upon, she realized how much work this would be. Then again, she could get a lot of made the night before with the preservation enchantment.

After he left, she went back to closing up, ensuring she locked the door. Once her closing routine was finished, she grabbed the baked goods she had pulled aside for Willow and headed next door with Sitka trailing behind her.

"Hey," Willow said with a smile. "How was today? Sorry I didn't stop in."

"It's alright, it was busy. I guess there is a fireman's ball next weekend. In McCloud?" Camille asked, setting the wrapped pastries down on the counter and glancing at the herbs Willow had out. Enchantments for Willow worked entirely differently since there were so many different ones she could use. She could use things like actual pine needles whereas Camille couldn't. Willow's operated by scent, Camille's worked by taste.

"Oh yeah! It's an annual fundraiser. Everyone goes. I go, Reyes goes, Evan, pretty much the whole town. Everyone gets dressed up and it's a good time."

"Oh." Camille frowned, unsure why she felt as though she might miss out. She hadn't really wanted to go at first, being uneasy with the attention and all the people, but if she baked things, people were obviously going to talk about it. She chewed on her lip for a moment, debating if she should get a ticket to go.

"I have an extra ticket if you want to go. I usually buy two and pawn it off on someone who waited too long. Although Reyes might ask you. You should mention the order and see if it jogs his memory, since he probably forgot. He usually gets tickets early."

"No, I don't want to assume, and if he bought two tickets, he probably had someone in mind to take."

"Yeah. You." Willow chuckled. "He certainly isn't taking his ex."

"He's in Trinity until Sunday with Evan. I'm not sure when I will talk to him next."

"What?" Willow looked perplexed for a moment.

"Yeah, he mentioned it to me on Wednesday night." Camille paused. "I made him a protection enchantment for his water."

"Well obviously I saw Reyes yesterday, but he didn't mention a weekend trip. Hopefully they have fun," Willow said with a smile.

"You don't talk to Evan much?" Camille asked.

"Nope. He doesn't exactly have gatherings at his house anymore. That was all his ex-wife's doing. Evan lives closer to town but still has a pretty nice house. It's an older Victorian. Actually, Reyes has a really nice house. Great for entertaining but I have only been there a few times for his ex's birthday and stuff."

"Were you here when Evan got married?" Camille asked curiously.

"Yes, I was on the bride's side. I met Sophia when she worked at the wellness center in town, teaching yoga and pilates and stuff. She would come in often and buy a lot of the candles and oils. She still orders once a month, and claims I have scents she can't find in Chicago." Willow laughed.

"Was Reyes at the wedding?" Camille asked with curiosity.

"Evan's best man."

"Oh." Camille thought about what it must have been like.

She learned that Evan and Sophia had met in college but hadn't started to date until shortly before he had gotten the job in Siskiyou County. Willow explained that civil service usually took sometime to actually get hired from the application date and the strain of long distance put likely put pressure on Sophia to move before they actually had established enough of a foundation. Evan bought the house and she moved shortly after.

Jodie had moved here three years ago as a dental hygienist and became fast friends with Sophia. Since Jodie and Reyes were around each other so much, they just started dating. At first everything seemed fine, but Willow had always sensed a disconnect between the two. They didn't seem to mesh well. Jodie wanted someone who wasn't Reyes. He was way too quiet for her and she had such a bold personality. At times, she would literally drag Reyes around. Willow never understood why he let her do that since he always looked slightly humiliated by it.

Camille also learned Sophia and Jodie never were fond of the fishing or camping trips Reyes and Evan liked to go on, and they never wanted to go so the guys just stopped going on the trips for a bit.

"You said Trinity County? Good for them." Willow laughed and gave Sitka a pet.

"Yeah." Camille sighed then looked at Willow. She knew she shouldn't be divulging things between them but Evan certainly had been curious. She didn't mind him knowing they had kissed, but she did mind Evan knowing she was a witch. Something she would have to ask Reyes about on Sunday, if he did call her.

"He told me he isn't used to someone liking him back. He asked if I put a love spell or something on him. I know it's an honest question after what he saw me do, but it still hurt."

"I'm sorry. I couldn't imagine how that felt. I know you like him. Jodie insulted him a lot—told him he was lazy, needed to lose weight, and he should really take one of Sophia's classes, then she talked about how she wished Reyes would sell the cabin. Like I said, he was miserable and so was she. The only problem was Jodie wanted to fight with him about stuff and Reyes doesn't do that. He just took it all and then would shut down. Although when it comes to you, he seems to want to fight for it." Willow laughed softly.

Camille thought about that too. He certainly didn't shut down the other night. "I kind of lost my cool with him a few times on Wednesday." Camille recounted what had happened.

"I think he really likes you too. He fights for you, he wants to ensure you are well," Willow said and started putting some of her herbs away. "Did something more happen on Wednesday night? If he was at your place?"

"No. Aside from a fair amount of making out." Camille giggled.

"He will ask you, but I will save the extra ticket just in case." Willow gave her a knowing grin. "Anyway, I can't seem to get this enchantment right. I actually don't have one for sleep. I have been too scared to try it. I have no one that can check over my enchantment and never had a chance to try before moving here."

"Oh, yeah, you do want to be careful you get the mixture just right. I usually don't put them in my baked goods or even infuse them into tea. I only really do it for myself. I can help you if you like though."

"That would be great, a few people have asked for them and I'm a bit worried about making a candle so I was thinking of a salve or a spray or something."

"Ah that would be good, obviously the mixture would be a bit different depending on the application. I usually make syrups as you know, but yours would be an oil."

They agreed the shop wasn't a good place to try that out so they agreed to do it tonight after a short golden hour hike.

Once again, Camille was sweating by the time they made it back to Willow's car. Camille was relieved she had packed a change of clothes and toiletries for a shower at Willow's house. Everything could affect one's intentions, including feeling gross or uncomfortable.

Chapter 19

That night as he sat around the fire with Evan and Seth, Reyes thought about her. He'd tried to send her a text but it was not going through. Evan and Seth got along great; he knew they would, and much to his relief, Evan hadn't mentioned Sitka once. He looked at the stars and hoped she wouldn't be upset with him. *It's just until Sunday; she's not going anywhere.*

A weird sensation had started to creep into him. A stirring in his gut had formed and his heart rate increased. He looked at the beer and figured he should drop drinking, despite only having had two tonight.

He got up and pawed through his truck for his water flask and slumped back down with a sigh.

"You seem extra glum all of a sudden," Seth noted.

"I'm fine," Reyes responded.

Evan smirked. "He's missing his bakery girl."

"His what?" Seth sat up.

"He started seeing the new bakery owner in town, as of like two nights ago," Evan said with a smug grin.

"We aren't official or anything yet. It's not a big deal." Reyes took a long swig of water.

"They just make out a lot and he stops by the bakery three times a week for the office runs. Her stuff is great. We stopped before we headed down here to stock up and so he could make out with her," Evan laughed.

"We didn't make out today. It was a small kiss."

"Oh right, the make out sessions are saved for her place."

"Wow, good job man, what's she look like?" Seth asked, sounding happy for his friend.

"Gorgeous," Reyes blurted out. "Like some embodiment of spring. She wears the cutest dresses, and is so passionate about her bakery and animals." Reyes beamed but quickly caught himself.

"She's pretty amazing. I actually think her friend Willow is pretty attractive but he and I tried dating friends and it ended pretty miserably," Evan followed up.

"It's different though with Willow and Camille. They both run their businesses in Mt. Shasta. I guess they could open up their shops in another city, but Willow has been there for a few years. And Camille..." he trailed off for a moment, thinking about her staying with him. "She wants to stay, and I'm going to do whatever needs to be done to ensure she can stay as long as she wants." His fist had clenched just thinking about anyone belittling her. She was so strong but felt she was mere seconds from getting all of this taken away from her. *Bastards.*

"Where did this side of you come from? You have always been so quiet and reserved," Seth asked.

Reyes looked at him, feeling a bit embarrassed at how crazy he must look. The last thing he wanted to do was to look like some territorial dog. He couldn't exactly tell them the story. "I don't know. She just—her family wasn't very good to her. I don't want to go into details."

"Fair enough."

"Yeah, you two are definitely good for each other," Evan said, finishing his beer off.

"You should talk to Willow more," Reyes urged. "You told me to go for Cami. Try with Willow."

"The divorce isn't finalized and it feels weird. Besides, she doesn't need to be involved with this mess. She is still friends with Sophia or something." Evan rolled his eyes.

"Suit yourself. Someone will come and snatch her up. Or she will leave." Reyes shrugged, knowing that both women had heavy burdens they shared with keeping their magic hidden.

"Are you trying to tell me to date her for my sake or Camille's?" Evan jested.

"Come on, you know I'm looking out for you," Reyes said. "But also maybe I want Cami to have a friend too. It's a win-win really."

"I guess you're right." Evan sighed and got up to tend to dinner.

Seth and Reyes stood up to help too.

Reyes stuck mostly with water though he did take a shot with the guys when they finished the meal. Then they set to cleaning up and getting ready for bed after they planned to hike out to a lake tomorrow.

At some point in the night, Reyes awoke to a pain in his stomach. He groggily reached for his phone and saw it was two in the morning. He could hear snoring and deep breathing nearby from his friends.

A sigh escaped him as he rolled on his back. Then the realization that all the water he had drunk certainly needed to pass through him. The pain started back up, dragging a groan out of him. He sat up and hastily fumbled for his flannel. It was brisk this late at night out here. He had on sweats and a T-shirt but the flannel would help. The next step was to shove his boots on and walk a short distance away from their tents. He grabbed his head lamp, too, knowing the cell phone light would be useless. However once he got out, he noticed how bright it was.

When he looked up, he could see the full and bright moon. The pain hit him harder right in his stomach and pulsed through his chest. "Fuck," he huffed out and clutching the headlamp in his hand, Reyes hurried off away into some bushes. The pain subsided when he relieved himself.

However, that relief was short-lived. After he had taken a few steps back towards the tent, the pain came back like a punch to the gut. He had to brace himself on a tree.

"Fuck, I'm going to die out here," he heaved. When he fell to his knees, a bunch of horrible images came to his mind.

Of Seth and Evan finding him dead. Of Camille learning the news and being sad. Her leaving Shasta. Of someone else doing the annual health inspection, finding Sitka, and taking her away from Camille.

"No," he groaned and tried to take another step. He was sweating despite the freezing night air.

An awful spasm hit his abs and brought him to his hands and knees. "No." He forced himself back on his haunches and padded himself down for his cell phone. Not that it would do any good with the lack of signal. He stupidly left the spot tracker in the truck. Then he realized he had forgotten to even charge the damn thing.

Of course he forgot something. He always did.

Despair ripped a whimper from him when he realized he left the cell phone in his tent; he had only brought the headlamp, which he had dropped by the tree in his pain.

However his hands brushed the vial she had made him.

The safety enchantment.

Reyes didn't know if it would be a pain reliever, too, but he was out of options. He held it up and tried to ignore the pain clawing at him.

He squeezed way more than three drops in his mouth.

After he swallowed it, the pain subsided. His body temperature went back to normal and his breathing leveled out.

"Cami, you brilliant, gorgeous woman. I think I love you," he whispered and kissed the bottle after he screwed the lid back on.

Slowly, Reyes stood up and backtracked to grab the headlamp then hurried back to his tent. He nearly scoffed at his friends' tents. They hadn't even roused while he could have died. Then again how would he explain the magical enchantment to them?

Once back in his tent, he took the flannel off and was sure to be so careful with the bottle. "I need to keep this on me, at all times," he whispered as he kicked his boots off and crawled back into his sleeping bag.

Comfortable once again, sleep came on fast. That ordeal exhausted him for some reason. Fighting sleep, he typed out a text to Camille.

> Reyes: You have no idea how spectacular you are.

Just as he hit send, sleep won its battle over him.

Chapter 20

On Sunday afternoon Camille sat in Willow's car, both tired from the hike in Castle Crags State Park. It was located just south of Camille's cabin but due to the snow at heavier elevations, she hadn't had a chance to hike there until now. The hike had been a challenge. And Sitka was sleeping in Willow's backseat, content as usual. Her buzzing phone caught her off guard.

Heat rushed over her cheeks upon seeing it was a message from Reyes.

"I take it, that's Reyes?" Willow laughed.

"Yes. He said I have no idea how spectacular I am."

"Spectacular?" Willow laughed. "He is smitten with you."

"I swear I didn't put a love spell on him," Camille fretted.

"I know you didn't. It's cute watching you bond with each other. Did you hear from him all weekend?" Willow asked.

"No. He said he may not have a cell signal," Camille said then set to replying to Reyes.

Camille: Thanks? I take it, the pastries hit the spot?

Reyes: They always do, but I sent that two nights ago.

Camille set her phone down and looked at Willow. "Do you think it's wise for me to be so involved with him? I'm pretty much a fugitive in hiding."

Willow glanced over with some irritation in her expression. Camille had to look away in shame.

"You are, but ask yourself how you are going to feel if you leave him. His feelings aside. What is it going to do to you? Not only that, but how long do you plan on running? How far? I thought about it after dinner the other night. Reyes is right, you fled for freedom, but is it really freedom if you can't ever find comfort and stability?"

Camille thought about what Willow was saying. They both knew Reyes would hurt but Camille would be left to pick up pieces in a new place, after Mt. Shasta, and then again somewhere else, and it would be a series of failed endeavor after failed endeavor. The only problem was she would continue to put people in danger everywhere she went.

"You could keep running, sure. But look at what you have here. A loyal familiar, Reyes, the bakery, me. It's hard to deny how smoothly things fell into place for you here. Maybe that mountain wants you here," Willow noted.

"I don't know why it would if I'm a danger to everything."

"Do you have a plan if you did leave? A place in mind?"

"No," Camille said quietly. "Get a rental car, break the bond with Sitka and release her. Find somewhere new, likely out of state?" The sadness crept into her voice.

"You know it would hurt Sitka. She chose you. Forgive my bluntness but Thornwell did you an immense disservice in how to actually be normal. If anything, they should commend you for applying what they taught you so well. They wanted you to remain hidden, but had no intention of actually letting you live. Deplorable," Willow muttered.

"I hated Leland. He hated me. I tried. I did try to be obedient, it's what my mother said my name meant, to serve others. Like that was all my parents saw my education as. Not to give me any kind of skills but to make me more marketable for a suitor. And even then, I wasn't enough for Leland. Not that either of us had a choice." Camille had to wipe her eyes.

"Leland doesn't sound like the type that thinks anyone is good enough. But you are more than enough for Reyes. Maybe there is something else out in the world for you, but I just think it would be hard to find more than this place. I would like to think it would be hard to replace us all."

"I don't think I could. I hate thinking about it. But I also hate thinking about what could happen to you all. If I left, my parents might pass through but they wouldn't know any of you had anything to do with me. If I was gone, they would know and move on to track me down."

"Camille, I get your reasoning, but I just don't think it's any way for you to live. You need a support system, and you found one. Don't toss it aside in the name of safety. If you think it's an admirable sacrifice for our safety, just know it's going to hurt all of us. You are my friend, one of my best. There has to be a way you can gain your freedom."

Willow pulled into an open parking spot up the road from Camille's rental. The two looked at each other.

"I don't know what my parents or coven might ask."

"They didn't ask you to be an asset, they just took the liberty to treat you as one. Covens don't treat their own that way. I know covens, like any type of family, aren't perfect. But the way yours treated you is absurd. Let's find a way for you to gain your freedom. Join mine; I am sure if they knew what really happened with Thornwell, they would welcome you."

"That would be such a huge mess between councils and covens. When really, it was my actions that caused it," she responded, and thought about joining Willow's coven. Close knit, by the ocean, cooler, damp air, with fog. It sounded so alluring but Reyes wouldn't be there. That mountain wouldn't be there.

"I know, but if you wanted a new coven, they would take you in."

"I'd have to leave this place, at least for a time to live with them."

"I'd go with you," Willow said. Camille didn't miss the tension in her friend's eyes.

"Evan and Reyes wouldn't, though," Camille lamented.

"I know, but it's an option. They would be safe. You would be safe. But if the thought of that option makes you sad, then I think you have your answer on bonding with Reyes. You don't want to leave. So do you spend your time finding a way to keep this, or spend it running?"

Camille forced a smile, despite how much was warring in her against the hope she wanted to feel. "Thanks, Willow."

"See ya, Cami. Let me know if you want to come over tomorrow."

The two girls gave each other a hug before Camille got out of the car. She opened the back seat, watching Sitka stare at her. Camille checked to see how many cars and people were around. A few more than she would like. "Use stealth, Sitka."

The cat gave a small chuff and hopped out, frolicking off into the brush and out of sight.

Camille walked back to her cabin and her phone buzzed again just as she unlocked it.

> Reyes: Can we have dinner? I'm about an hour out still but maybe around four or five? I need to tell you why you are spectacular.

That certainly made Camille pause for a moment until Sitka pawed at the door. She rushed over to let her in and closed it. She had no idea what to make of his text.

Camille was greeted at her door with Reyes standing there, smiling wide. His hair appeared damp as though he had just showered.

"Hey there, beautiful," he said.

She felt the butterflies in her stomach flutter wildly at the sight of him and the sound of his words. While she knew that maybe somewhere else out there someone else could make her feel the way Reyes did, she wanted him. She had him here and now. He was a part of this place.

"Hi. Sitka is fine to hang back in the cabin. She got plenty of nature earlier today. I left a window open for her," Camille said and locked the door.

When she turned around, Reyes pulled her into a deep hug and kissed her before they headed to his truck. She could get lost in his cedarwood scent.

They had decided to get takeout and watch the sunset from the back of his truck since he said he needed to talk to her privately. Camille still wasn't sure what to make of that but she was getting anxious. The worry of something happening to him this weekend began to plague those butterflies.

He drove them to a perfect spot on the west side of the mountain. The setting summer sun was creating brilliant colors and shapes against a rocky canvas. There was a blanket, pillows, and some other camping gear in the back of the truck. Reyes had told her he usually kept some basics in the back.

"I know we should be facing west for the sunset, but the summer sunsets are amazing against the mountain."

"It's beautiful," she said, finishing her food.

"Sometimes I find myself saying silent prayers to Shasta. I'm not really religious by any means but I don't know. It feels like it's listening."

"It's not foolish at all. It does listen." She glanced over at him. "I looked at it that day you found me making enchantments, and I apologized to it for putting you in danger. I vowed I would leave if I needed to, but as I stood there, I felt a gentle breeze push me towards your truck. So I definitely took that as a sign."

Reyes smiled and placed his hand on her leg. "I asked the mountain to keep you safe this weekend. Not knowing what it could do. I was worried about not being here, not even sure what I could do if I was and something happened to you. I guess there is a lot I don't know about this world."

She placed her hand over his. *No, this would be impossible to replace.*

"I was safe this weekend. Willow gave me some eye-opening insight to my situation on our way back from Castle Crags today. I need to find a way to make sure I'm safe here. I feel like, or at least I want to believe, that mountain wants me here."

"We will find a way. I think that mountain wants you here too. Or at least that's what I want to believe, because I want you here, too, Cami."

She couldn't help but lean into him and feel so much when his arm came around her. This was what she would have missed out on if she had stayed with Thornwell. Leland would have never done this; he didn't even drive himself anywhere when he left the grounds. He'd never be caught dead in a big truck with faded paint.

The only compliment Leland had even given her was about her chest. She was pretty sure Reyes had glanced a few times, but he'd never once acted as though he was entitled to any part of her. That was one of the things that set him worlds apart from Leland. Reyes respected her. He always had.

Camille realized she was going to lose Thornwell one way or another. If not as a betrayer, then as a Talbot. Now that she sat in the shadow of the mountain, she wondered if being the betrayer was worse. Every witch she encountered would know she betrayed a coven, and she'd obviously be kicked out of Thornwell permanently. But was that all worse than being shackled to Talbot?

"Two nights ago," Reyes began, once again pulling Camille up from drowning in a sea of damning thoughts. She looked up at him, listening to him speak of the horrible pain in his abdomen—how it had brought him to his knees doubled over in pain and he really thought he might die. Then he took more than the instructed three drops but he felt better, and once he could breathe normally, he was able to get up and get back to the tent.

Camille had forgotten all about Thornwell at that moment. She had never known the safety enchantment to work like that. All her books and studies said it was for warding off external dangers. It wasn't a healing serum or a sedative. Her eyes fixed on him closely, trying to detect if he in fact had any magic in him that might have caused some reaction to the enchantment. She never sensed anything in him but she could not deny he was changing ever so slightly. His appearance was mostly the same but he did stand a little taller since she had first met him. Willow noted his dominant side showing too.

"Do you have any family history of anything? I don't think it was a heart attack if it started in your abdomen. But maybe? You should go to the doctor," she said, gripping his hands.

"How do I explain what stopped it? I was going to call out to Evan and Seth but I didn't know what they could do. The spot tracker wasn't charged and an airlift would have been my only option. If they even got there in time. When I brushed the safety enchantment, something told me you were there with me and I was so grateful you came into my life. I didn't mention it to them the next morning. Those assholes didn't even wake up anyway but I was so careful to not say anything about you. I told Evan to not even mention Sitka to Seth. He's my buddy in Trinity."

"The one I was supposed to call?" she asked.

"Yeah. I would never forgive myself if she was taken from you because of me. I know Seth wouldn't hurt her, he loves animals, but still."

"Thank you, for keeping me safe."

"Thank you for keeping me safe too," he said softly then leaned in and kissed her. "I don't think I will ever get tired of kissing you."

"You know how you said you aren't used to this feeling?" she asked and he nodded. "I'm not either. There is something about you that I never realized I was missing too."

"I hope I always am," Reyes said. "Lie down with me?" he asked and scooted himself back on the thin mattress on the truck bed. Camille crawled in next to him and they lay there, watching the remainder of the sunset.

She had never done this before but something about being in this truck with Reyes felt right.

They remained laying there for another hour after the sunset, watching the stars form behind the mountain. He held her close and she rested her head on his chest.

And when he dropped her off at the cabin, they kissed before parting ways, letting all the unspoken wants and fears alike pass between them.

Chapter 21

By Tuesday, Reyes was definitely ready to see Camille again. It had only been a day since the bakery was closed on Mondays but he never felt as though he had enough time with her. A few of his coworkers had mentioned the fireman's ball coming up and he'd completely blanked on it. He was ready to ask Camille and got excited thinking about being there with her. So he headed into the bakery and saw Camille glance at him with a smile. He smiled back. There were two women at the display case and one laughed.

It sounded vaguely familiar.

"Hi, Reyes. Want me to get something started for you?"

"I can wait, Cami."

He glanced at the case then fixed on who was grinning at him. He had almost forgotten that grating laugh. Almost.

"Reyes, long time no see," Jodie hummed out then looked at Camille. Sophia was giving him a smug expression as well. "I will get one of these Danishes and an iced latte."

Camille looked unsure but nodded before starting the order. Reyes just scowled and crossed his arms as Sophia ordered as well. Jodie approached him and he tensed, taking a step back. "Stop. We have nothing left to say to each other."

"Obviously distance didn't make your heart grow fonder. The months certainly have not been very good to you either. No shocker if you are on a first name basis with the baker."

Then Jodie patted his stomach and his insides shriveled up.

He didn't want Camille to see this or to be around Jodie. In truth, he was ashamed of himself, and he was in better shape for Jodie, but he wanted Camille. He was so nervous for that first time that Camille might find him repulsive. Despite how she looked at him, he was scared for when—or if—she saw all of him.

"Please don't touch him or harass my customers." Camille's voice held more venom than he had thought possible. When he looked at her, he could have sworn lightning flashed in her eyes. He supposed she might have that power, too, though he hadn't even thought to ask.

"Oh I used to do this to him all the time. We have a history together, don't we, sweetie?" Jodie looked at him and batted her lashes, and all he could do was shake his head. This was his worst nightmare.

"Then stop making him uncomfortable. You obviously don't know him that well."

Reyes was shocked to hear Camille stand up for him. He didn't hate it but he also didn't want her to get into it with Jodie.

"Just get your order and leave, Jodie. What are you even doing here? You hate this entire town," he said, finding his voice.

"You remembered that much at least. I'm helping Sophia get the last of her stuff from Evan's house. At least he tried to put some effort into himself. You are still wearing these stupid flannels?"

"Your order is ready," Camille said with the same resentment as before.

Jodie turned towards Camille. Reyes watched as Camille fixed on Jodie, but Jodie just eyed Camille up and down. For a moment he wasn't sure if his heart was beating.

"Thanks," Jodie said after a few moments of tense silence then she walked to the counter and paid.

Reyes remained where he was, watching Camille's narrowed eyes that were still on Jodie before they shifted to Sophia. Never once did Camille back down. He wondered if that was the Thornwell in her.

"A word of advice, if you think he's going to be very attentive, he won't be. He can hardly pick up after himself half the time and his house is a total mess. Like him," Jodie scoffed.

Reyes almost ran out of the bakery without a word. If Jodie and Sophia hadn't headed for the door first, he might have. Instead, he remained where he was looking at the ground as Jodie laughed again. The bell chimed and then the only sounds that could be heard were the sound of the refrigerators.

He swallowed hard and went to walk out the door. Embarrassment engulfed him.

"Reyes," Camille said softly.

All he could do was sigh. "I'm sorry. It's been almost a year since I last spoke to her. When she left me."

"I can see why. She is pretty rude to say the least."

"We broke up and it wasn't a smooth split. I shut down a lot when she was expressing her concerns, and she's right. I'm not very attentive; I get distracted easily."

"I don't think you are. Was attentiveness the only issue?"

"No. She thought I should tone up, have more of a buzzcut, and my truck was an eyesore. She also thought I should move to a bigger city and rent my cabin out. I have an open loft for a master bedroom and she hated that too. I said some less than savory things in retort but I did get a buzz cut and started working out more the next day. I debated on selling the truck, too, but it's reliable, and I can fix most things on it when it breaks. I like working on it. ADHD and all, but working with my hands keeps me focused."

He went on to explain that even after he started changing himself, she still found more things she wanted him to change. He would always shut down for the night and start changing things the next day until he would fall off track with working out, or looking for a property management company.

"Eventually, she started talking about kids and admittedly I didn't tell her that I had gotten the snip a year before I met her." He explained how he had always been on the fence about having kids and then most of his effort went into his house when he bought the land. The house wasn't very kid friendly and he was happy being an uncle, but he didn't want to be a dad.

"I finally broke the news to her a few months after she started to ask about them. I wasn't even sure I was going to propose to her. Jodie called me every terrible thing you can imagine then left. I came home and all of her stuff was gone. She told me it was over and that I was a massive waste of time and space. I sat there alone in the quiet but messy house, since she certainly hadn't been tidy about taking her things either. And I couldn't help but feel it was my fault it didn't work out. If I had just told her I had ADHD, or that I wasn't going to have kids."

He looked at Camille, who was wide-eyed now and saw her reach her hand up hesitantly.

"Can I take your hand? I don't want to assume you are alright with touch after what she did."

Reyes took her hand. "You don't touch me to demean me or point out my flaws. I honestly had forgotten what it felt like to be touched by someone kind and passionate."

"She is out of her mind to not find you attractive, Reyes. I love your flannels too. They're so soft and suit you far better than anything else I could imagine you would wear. I also like that you are not afraid to get your hands dirty to fix a problem. Maybe your truck is a little loud but you need something like that here and it helped get mine started again."

Reyes felt his heart warm with her words and touch. "Thanks, Cami. I've always been a little self-conscious and she's right, I did let myself go after she left. I'm terrified you are going to find something you don't like in me. People always do."

"You are fine just the way you are, Reyes. Unless you start setting animal traps or chopping down trees for no reason, or take Sitka away from me. The things she thinks are flaws are the things that make you, *you*. They aren't flaws at all."

"Thank you. I promise, I will never do any of those things. Ever." He pressed his forehead to hers.

"I take it your parents didn't like her much."

Reyes laughed. "No, they were polite of course, but I know their tells when they are not fans of people. When she left, I guess she stayed with Sophia and Evan. He hates her. He would say, 'Sorry I'm not sorry she finally moved away.'"

Camille wrapped her arms around him for a moment then pulled away. "Let me get your order. You are on your break, yes?"

Reyes exhaled and followed her to the counter. "Yeah. It's fine. My boss isn't checking." He handed her the list of things and she set to getting the items boxed up.

"What about you? Apple crisp muffin? Olallieberry scone?"

"Just a coffee please," he lamented, dropping his eyes to the counter.

"Are you sure?" Camille asked. Reyes could hear the concern in her voice.

"Yeah."

"I can enchant it with something to boost your mood, if you like? Maybe just an extra boost of serotonin in your coffee?" she offered.

"It's alright, thanks though." He pulled out his wallet.

"Alright. Will you text me later when you are home then?"

"Of course. Be careful if you go out for a hike or something."

"I will," Camille said. He looked up to see her warm smile. "I know words can hurt and you are allowed to feel them, Reyes. But you are amazing just the way you are now. Remember that. I like this thing we started and I like you."

"Thanks, Cami. I like you too. A lot." He smiled then gave her hand a squeeze before walking outside. He kept his head down and rushed inside back to his section of the office where he set the box down. Then he slumped down at his desk and stared at the cup of coffee. He hadn't wanted her to enchant it. Not because he didn't find it incredible with what she could do with herbs—in fact he was eager to learn more about it all.

However, he felt as though he was asking too much of her despite her offering. He recalled her saying she needed to release the magic somehow and the most productive way she could was through something she loved—baking. Yet he didn't feel as though he deserved any of the things that made her, *her*. Who was he to share in this glorious thing she had created so easily?

But she liked him. *For now. What happens when she gets your shirt off? When you are late to pick her up? When she sees your truck is still a mess? When she sees how you live in a cabin that looks photo worthy but isn't clean on the inside?* All these damning thoughts that he knew were insecurities clouded his mind. He knew it was Jodie's words all coming back to him. *Clean it. Clean the cabin, clean the truck. Go for a run tonight. Be something worth her affection.* He leaned back in the chair and dragged his hands over his face.

"What the hell happened now?" Evan asked. "I haven't seen you so disgruntled since your bakery girl's first inspection." Reyes snapped his eyes up to see Evan with half a Danish in his hand. "Damn, she makes the best pastries." He moaned in delight.

"You didn't think to mention Sophia was back in town, with Jodie?" Reyes accused.

Evan gave him a look of shock. "Oh, you ran into them?"

"Yeah, I did. She basically embarrassed me and insulted me right in front of Cami."

"It was a rough night for me too. Trust me. I wanted them out of my house as soon as possible, then I just took a few shots and went to bed."

"And yet you act like you always do. Chipper as can be."

"Well, the pastry certainly helps. Tell Cami I said thanks for the pick-me-up, or I guess I will." He smiled. "What was her response to Jodie?"

Reyes sighed and told him the rest of the encounter and by the end of the tale, he was smiling to himself. He truly wasn't sure he deserved anything from her.

"You got yourself a keeper, Reyes. That girl wants nothing more than to see you happy," Evan reminded him. "You are taking her to the ball, right?"

"Crap! I meant to ask her and I completely forgot," Reyes huffed out.

"You got time, just ask her tonight or something. I'm sure she'll say yes."

"I hope so. I would love to walk into that dance hall with her on my arm," Reyes said with a sense of wonder in his voice.

Evan smirked and finished his Danish off. "Well enjoy the night, I'm sitting out this year, I guess."

Reyes gawked at him. "What? Why?"

"Sophia has the tickets and unless I want to contact her, which I don't, I don't have a ticket. It's fine. I will go next year."

"You have to go. And is she going? With Jodie." Reyes groaned. "They are just going to have it out for us. Or me."

"I don't know why they would go; they could hardly be bothered with it the last time they went."

"Don't remind me. Jodie drank way too much and I took care of her all night and the next day. Then she claimed I ruined her night somehow. You have to go. You can't leave Cami and me to deal with them."

"They are sold out of tickets by now, you know how this event goes. It's like the biggest thing in the area."

"Ask Willow?" Reyes suggested.

Evan let out an absurd laugh. "Right, 'Hey Willow, want to go to the ball? By the way do you have an extra ticket? Your buddy Sophia took mine.' Come on, I'm not going to do that."

"Think about it. It's not going to feel right if you aren't there."

Camille had watched Reyes walk outside. He carried a weight on his shoulders and she wanted to help lift it off. But when she looked at the apple crisp muffins, she knew it wasn't her place to do that. All she could do was be there for him when he needed support.

The bell rang and she felt a giddy hope he had come back. However it was a woman and her daughter, who had come in before. She put a smile on and gathered their order. They got an apple crisp muffin and she thought about how he hadn't gotten anything for himself aside from coffee. If it were anyone else, she may not think much of it, but she knew him.

The thoughts plagued her as she tended to customers.

Jodie had hurt him, had hurt him before, and she still held enough power over him to make him feel less than. Anger seethed through her at Jodie.

As the day went on the lunch rush came and went. She was plenty busy and she frowned every time someone bought a muffin. Until there was one left. It slowed down finally and she would be closing in two hours. Camille wasn't yet sure what to call Reyes. He was certainly more than a friend, but they hadn't said they were an item. Though their kisses did.

Now she feared he would close off from her. But he'd said he usually set to fixing things the next day. Not that there was anything to fix.

"Why am I dwelling on that so much?" she asked herself. Sitka trotted up to her and rubbed against her leg as she mindlessly set to wrapping the muffin up to save for Reyes. "I can't numb him from negative feelings, but I don't like seeing him feel so beaten down," she fretted.

Then she looked at the muffin, not even sure how to get it to him. It would be too much to walk into his work, as it wasn't a public office. She supposed she could leave it on his truck but the birds or some other critter were more likely to get it. For a brief moment, an image came to mind of her trying to open his doors but she figured that might not be the best look.

Jodie had come back to help Sophia get stuff from Evan's place. Camille recalled Willow saying Evan and Sophia had a messy divorce. Evan had gotten married, and Reyes had been the best man. Something tugged at her, a sort of deep-seated want and longing. Evan and Reyes were close friends. She had only seen them interact once aside from the bar, but they were close. Their partners had also been close. They had formed their own little informal coven that took care of each other. To an extent.

What if she had that with Reyes, and Evan could be a friend too? Then she looked at the common wall she shared with Willow's shop and recalled that Willow liked Evan. What if this could be her home? This place with people who looked out for her and she for them. She could almost see it. Her and Reyes. Willow and Evan. Planning to surprise one of them for their birthdays, holiday gatherings, camping trips, and town events.

A soft laugh of joy slipped out of her but it was short-lived. Sore spots and bad blood obviously remained and she couldn't erase that. Certainly not with the assumption to take that spot for Reyes. Maybe she could help. If nothing else, maybe she could help Reyes make words sting less.

This place as her future could very well vanish in the blank of an eye. She had to remember that. All she could do was help in the ways she could and prepare for a worst-case scenario. Embrace the freedom as long as she could.

Sitka rubbed her head again and that too tugged at her. If she was taken, she would have to sever the bond with Sitka. It would only drain both of them and it wasn't fair to Sitka to take her from this place. Sitka had chosen Camille but she also deserved her home, not to have it disrupted or taken away from it.

As she scratched the fluffy cheeks of the bobcat, Camille couldn't help but see the parallels between it and Reyes. She had entered both of their lives and inserted herself in such a dominant way. Mt. Shasta had watched all of this too. Just some outsider, possibly here to hurt two of its own.

"What is wrong with me? Thornwells don't dwell on such stupid thoughts." She wondered how she let Jodie ruin her day too? "Easy, I want Reyes and I want this place. I don't want either one hurt. Yet it feels inevitable that I might just end up doing so."

With a long drawn-out exhale, Camille set to putting things away for the day. The bell rang and she hurried out to the front to see Reyes. As if all her lamenting had summoned him.

"Hi," she said instantly, feeling giddy but nervous at the same time.

"I...this morning when I stopped by, I meant to ask you something and of course I got distracted." He sighed and looked down as his hand rubbed the back of his neck.

"Oh. It's alright. I'm not hard to find." She laughed.

He looked up and smiled at her. "Do you have plans on Saturday evening?"

"No. I just have a large order to fulfill that morning. I will be here late on Friday too."

"I think I can guess who the order is for. Would you like to attend the fireman's ball in McCloud with me? As my date?" he asked as though she would say no. As if he wasn't sure where they stood despite everything. Being there for him was the best way to help him. Not only that but she wanted to be there for him.

"Yes," she said, smiling wide. "I'd love to."

"I can pick you up or you can meet me at my place? I will drive us there."

"I will meet you at your house?" The thought of seeing his place made her excited. She wasn't sure why but she was curious about who he was outside of work. It was the only place they really saw each other regularly so far.

She shook the thought from her head. "Willow said you might ask me; she said she had an extra ticket but wasn't going to give it to me until the day of if you hadn't asked." A flush of heat burned her cheeks.

"Cami, that ticket had your name on it a long time ago." He laughed. "You talk to Willow about me?"

"Sometimes. Usually it's us working on enchantments, but that doesn't mean we don't talk over dinner too."

"Hopefully it's good talk."

"It is. Though she talks about Evan a lot."

"I knew it! Encourage her to ask him if he wants the ticket. There might be two loathsome guests attending too," Reyes groaned.

Camille raised her eyes and learned who that might exactly entail. She reassured him that it would be fine and that she would talk to Willow. Before he left, she shoved the muffin in his hands. With a grin and a kiss, he bid her farewell.

Chapter 22

It wasn't long before Saturday evening had arrived. Camille drove down the street with Sitka in the back seat, noticing the road was rougher than the main highway, as though it hadn't been paved in some time.

Her eyes glanced at the map and the signal was fading but the pin remained, all the way at the end of the long road. The houses she passed were few and far away from each other. This was certainly outside of the town of Mt. Shasta. There were so many trees and all the while the mountain appeared to be getting closer, looming on the horizon.

Finally, a dark wooden A-frame cabin came into view, the small mimic to the mountain it sat in front of.

She noticed his truck was parked parallel, as if it had been backed into its perch facing the castle. His text had told her to pull in front of one of the garages. So she did.

She glanced at the backpack with a change of clothes as she certainly was not above where the night could end up. She knew she wanted it, but she would not push nor assume she could invade his space. Her cabin was a rental; it would never really be hers. This place was his claim though and it would remain that way as long as he wanted it to.

Camille got out and planted her feet on the ground. She chose green pumps to go with her dress. Her outfit was a cream collared short sleeve dress with a cinched waist and a sage green knee-length pleated skirt. Her hair was tied back with a silky green scarf. A simple clutch was her main accessory.

She let Sitka out and knelt down to rub her cheeks.

"Be safe tonight, I will be back in a few hours. Don't wander too far from this cabin," she said softly, feeling the cat purr in understanding. When she stood up, she watched Sitka wander off towards the trees. The door opening had her turn around to see Reyes hurry out.

"Hey, sorry, I was just cleaning up a little bit." He laughed and gazed at her as she stepped towards him.

She watched his eyes take in her outfit and his jaw fell slightly agape. It made her heart race. It was not the gaze of a man who wanted to take as some others had done at the academy. Reyes, however, had a look of wonder, and she could see the faint blush form on his cheeks. This was the gaze of someone who was ready to kneel for her and she wasn't sure what to do with that.

He wore jeans and a navy long sleeve button up with dark boots. The shirt was tucked in and while his attire was what she had seen plenty of men wear at the bar, something about seeing him dressed up sent her heart racing too.

"I didn't quite finish cleaning. But let me show the inside of the cabin." He held his hand out to help her up the steps on the deck.

Her eyes took in the cabin, the peak of the A-frame was high up in the air, and the large windows made two triangles at the top. She imagined the morning and late golden hour light to be amazing. A railing indicated there was second level and the deck she stood on now jetted out far, providing a large space for entertainment. There were not many low windows facing her and she imagined the other side facing the mountain to be the main feature.

"This is me," Reyes said with a grin, opening the door for her.

Her jaw dropped upon confirming the star of the show. The windows nearly made up the entire wall facing Mt. Shasta. The furniture was plush and there were plenty of blue accents. A throw blanket draped over the couch, with a large fireplace and big TV mounted off to the side. A laptop was on the coffee table.

The kitchen was spacious, taking up a large part of the lower level with a dark stone slab for the island. Her eyes fixed on the high-end double oven and all the counter space. She couldn't help but imagine the amount of things she could bake in this kitchen, and all the herbs and enchantments she could tend to.

The stairway led to the open loft he mentioned and she wanted to ask to see it, but thought that was overstepping. Instead, she turned to him.

"Reyes, this is a dream." Camille beamed in awe.

"I bought the plot of land and had it built a few years ago. Four acres but honestly, I'm only using about half an acre for living, the rest I just let the forest do its thing. My way of protecting what I can. There are trails out there that feed into federal land, though I do have my property line clearly marked. I get deer, bears, mountain lions, coyotes, and all kinds of animals passing through. The trail cameras pick up a lot. The garages were basically a small one bedroom house. I added on to those after I had the cabin built. It was a glorious day when I finally got to move into this place," he said. "Admittedly the garages are kind of chaotic, but I can get the boat and the trailer out easily. I actually set to organizing some of it the day we met." He laughed and rubbed the back of his head.

"This is amazing. Never sell it. Even if you decide to move," she said. "I can't believe Jodie even thought to ask you to move."

He laughed again. "Every time I thought about it I felt a pool of dread in my gut. I knew she wanted a big city and something like this would be impossible. Even if I had a smaller plot of land, it wouldn't have a view like this."

"There are some large A-frames outside of Seattle, but they cost a fortune, and they are closer together."

He walked closer to her and wrapped an arm around her waist.

"Are you familiar with all the lore around Mt. Shasta?"

"It is said to have a hidden city inside of it, or contain a portal." She looked at the mountain.

"I should have known you'd do your research before coming here." Reyes chuckled. "There is also a Klamath legend that a spirit chief from the heavens fought with the spirit of the below world of Mount Mazama, which is now Crater Lake."

"Crater Lake is not far, right? I remember seeing signs for it on the drive down here."

"About two hours. We should go sometime." He rubbed her back.

"Mt. Shasta has so much power. I know the mountain watches me. But I don't feel as though it's judging me. It feels almost safe in some weird sort of way," Camille said.

Reyes took her hands in his and turned her to look at him. "Stay, Cami. We fight for this, whatever or whoever may come. This is your home as long as you want it to be." His words were nearly a proclamation and she wondered if he meant the town or this cabin they stood in.

She remained quiet, looking into his soft amber eyes. "I want to stay, as long as you and this place are safe. We will fight for this but I will do whatever I need to ensure you are safe. I owe it to that mountain to keep its own safe."

"I'm not from here either. I'm not one of its own. I guess I'm one of Santa Clara County's own." He laughed softly. "So, by that logic you belong here as much as me."

She leaned into him and hugged him tightly. "You built a small castle here, and you watch over a small patch of forest."

"You could, too, Cami." He embraced her just as tightly and if this thing blooming between them was a tangible thing, she knew it would be love growing strong. "Let's head out. Not that I don't want to stay at this moment, but we can resume it after the ball."

"I'd like that, Reyes." A slight soreness crept into her cheeks from smiling so much. She couldn't recall a time when she felt the same before.

Reyes offered his arm and she took it, letting him lead her towards the door and eventually the truck. He closed the door as softly as he could, and she didn't jump this time.

The drive to McCloud was a short twenty minutes, southeast from Mt. Shasta, not that the actual mountain couldn't be seen from here too.

Reyes got out of the truck and opened the door for her. He offered his arm and Camille felt almost embarrassed she had never been treated like this before. She loved it, and if she wasn't more guarded with her past, she might have told herself she loved him. But she wasn't going to say it, certainly not tonight.

An old fire truck was parked out front as people made their way towards the entrance. Reyes handed over their tickets where they were punched.

Camille took in the venue and the merriment of everyone. It was everything she expected for a small-town event. The building was old and the wood created a warm ambiance. Everyone was dressed in a range of clothes from semi-formal to formal and most of the men wore jeans and button-up shirts like Reyes. Though a few sported cowboy hats for whatever reason.

People greeted Reyes, seeming almost surprised to see her with him.

They all raved about her baked goods and she certainly wasn't sure how to feel about the praise. She knew they were good, but she'd never felt like she was worth the praise. Some people even asked about Sitka, saying how neat it was that she was so well-behaved. It was surprising considering how they hardly noticed her half the time when she was on top of the shelf. She noticed Reyes just smirked and shook his head.

"Want to dance?" Reyes asked.

"Sure, but I'm not very good at it. Those were some of the lessons I didn't do very well. My parents naturally liked to point out how I should be better at that."

He pulled her close. "If you don't want to, we don't have to. I just want to give you a break from all the attention. I know you don't like being in the spotlight."

"How could anyone think you are less than perfect, Reyes?" she asked, hugging him and feeling the gentle vibration of his laugh.

"I'm not perfect, Cami. But I want to be as near perfect as I can for you."

"Let's dance," she responded and let him lead her onto the dance floor.

He was good at dancing and led her through the steps of a swing dance she hadn't practiced much. Occasionally, she and her classmates would watch videos and try the moves out but none of them really had any idea if they were doing them right. Her dance lessons were more formal, with more practiced steps to assess your partner or get a read on others' intentions.

Sure enough, she fumbled and messed up a few of the steps but found she was able to laugh. The fear of being reprimanded for messing up steps was not looming over her anymore.

When the slow dance came on, he held her close and they gazed into each other's eyes.

"I like being so close to you," she said softly.

He smiled and pulled her closer, giving her a little squeeze. "Cami," was all he said before he kissed her softly as the song ended.

They headed over for a refreshment and Camille felt a familiar energy approaching. She turned towards the door and stared in shock.

"Look at that," Reyes laughed and placed a hand on her back.

Willow arrived with her arm linked through Evan's. He wore a dark red button-up shirt with dark jeans. She wore a sleeveless lavender maxi dress with a plunging neckline and high slit. It looked amazing on her umber skin tone.

Camille noticed the stark difference between Willow and Sophia. Sophia had dark brown hair and fair skin; Willow, on the other hand, looked like a daughter of a sun goddess. She certainly thought between the two, Evan was the lucky one to be next to Willow. And she herself felt lucky to be next to Reyes. Then again, Willow and Evan had the personality to compliment each other. They were both outgoing and bright. Everything she hesitated to be despite her trying.

"I told her about how Sophia took the tickets from him and dropped the hint," she said quietly. "Hopefully they don't show up. I can't imagine it will go well."

"Honestly if it keeps the attention off you and me then that's fine. Both Willow and Evan know how to deal with them."

Their friends greeted them, and both Evan and Willow seemed slightly smug about their arrival together, but Camille got the sense there was a lot they weren't saying. Hopefully, she would hear about it soon, since her and Reyes were no longer a secret.

She had accepted the fact that leaving this place was an absolutely dire circumstance last resort.

A short time later, she heard Evan groan and Camille looked at him. "Brace yourself. The drama has arrived. Don't worry, the three of us will protect you."

Camille glanced over to see Jodie and Sophia enter, looking very smug. Their outfits didn't look very formal either.

"I imagine Evan and I here together will be the main point of contention for them. Jodie has no right to say anything to you or Reyes," Willow said with a sigh.

"Doesn't mean she isn't going to try. It felt like insulting me was her favorite pastime near the end. Given our recent encounter, it still is," Reyes added and gripped Camille's hand tighter. "They are not staying with you, are they?" He glanced at Evan.

"No way. They said they got a hotel room down in Redding."

Reyes let out an absurd laugh and shook his head. "Best avoid eye contact."

They went back to their night and tried their best to avoid the recent arrivals. However, Camille certainly had heard some of Sophia's vitriol.

"Willow? You're here with him?"

"Yes. I am," Willow stated and Camille felt envious of Willow. She didn't back down or look away. She just brushed Sophia off.

"I should have known. Well, enjoy my sloppy seconds, girl. He is such an asshole, can't be bothered with anything and will be drunk by the time you leave."

"Right. Just ignore the fact that I tried, Sophia. I suggested counseling. I'm aware of your browsing even before you moved out," Evan replied.

"Whatever. You certainly had fun after I left too. Words travel fast in small towns. Let's see who else is here, Jodie." She linked her arm with Jodie's.

Camille felt Reyes tense. "I think we should go look at that firetruck now," he urged lightly, pulling her hand towards the door. Camille obliged and followed him outside. There was a photographer who offered to take their photo and Camille felt nervous. *This is a photo that could be used to trace me back here. But it seems like such a basic thing for couples to do. To have.* The war inside her rages but her curiosity won. Her selfish wants won. To just build a life here with him.

When Reyes put his hand around her waist and stood close for the photo, she knew she had a flush on her cheeks in it. She felt so giddy to be doing something so normal.

They walked around to the other side to look at the firetruck closer.

"How are you liking small-town life?" Reyes asked softly.

"It's nice." Camille didn't have much to compare it to. "I didn't spend a lot of time in Seattle actually. I mostly just stayed at the academy."

He looked at her in shock then a sadness cascaded over him. "I'm sorry, I didn't realize. You probably want to experience a bigger city. I could see you thriving anywhere in the Bay Area or Sacramento."

"I like it here, though. Big cities usually mean more noise. More people that would know who I am and what I did."

"You didn't do anything wrong," he insisted. "If you ever want to travel to a big city, we can go. If you want to go on your own or with Willow, I will be here. I promise. And I am sure my parents would love it if you and I came for a visit."

"Traveling together sounds fun but I am content here, with you all for now."

She reached up to kiss him. He placed his hands on her waist to steady her as he kissed back.

They smiled at each other like they normally did for a moment before hearing footsteps.

"Seriously, girl, you are much better off finding someone else. You look so put together and he looks like every other average lackluster dude here," Jodie laughed.

Reyes visibly deflated with his sigh. He looked as though he had been cut down and Camille hated seeing him like this. Why had anyone ever made him feel this way? How was he still so genuine and kind, after all the lies she had told him? She supposed he might have some ulterior motive, but she could see any fight dwindling in him.

Camille glanced at Jodie and Sophia, who looked like they had accomplished something. As though they had come tonight just to make their exes miserable, as if to remind them they still could, months or years later. That Thornwell grit sparked a fire in her veins.

"I think you see only what you want to justify your actions. I think you know he is anything but average or lackluster and how dare you try to convince that he is. Move on with your life, we certainly are," Camille said and took his hand.

"If he needs a little baker to speak for him, take it as a hint about his averageness," Jodie retorted.

Camille heard Reyes inhale and pull her hand closer. "I told you we were done. I'm not what you want. Move on," he said and put his hand on her waist again, leading her back inside. As they passed them, he glanced back. "Enjoy your evening, I'm going to prove my bakery girl right."

Chapter 23

As the night grew to a close, they said their farewells to Willow and Evan before Camille took Reyes's hand as they walked to his truck.

"So do you think Willow and Evan are going to start something like us?" she asked once they were on the road.

"Hopefully they do. I wasn't blind to their looks at gatherings. Part of me wonders if he had met her first, what might have happened," Reyes said.

He went on to talk about how Evan showed up at his cabin in tears one night about a month after Sophia left, as though the pressure had gotten to him. Reyes had, of course, opened his door and let him stay.

"After a few shots, Evan confessed he had thought about Willow. I'm sure that makes him sound like a sleaze, but Sophia was traveling more and pressuring him to move. I guess Jodie had found a really great place in Chicago of all places. I'm sure it's fine but compared to here? Like how much different could you get? It was like she and Jodie had this narrative in their heads about dragging the boys along with them to a big city, but Evan and I like it here. He nor I wanted big city life. We both left big cities to come here."

Camille watched the trees pass on the highway. Her peripheral caught the skipping of reflectors in the center divider line. The highway they were on was a two lane until they would turn right on I-5 where it would widen by a lane on both sides.

"I never asked why he didn't pursue Willow, at least not until recently. I told him he should last weekend."

"She talks about him, but says she doesn't want to get mixed in all his baggage. She told me a bit of how Jodie treated you and I despise her."

Reyes laughed softly and placed a hand on her leg.

"No one's really defended me like you did. Honestly, the other day in the bakery was like my worst nightmare, seeing you two size each other up. Thanks for defending me. It was such a simple fact you told her and it never occurred to me she didn't acknowledge my feelings much."

"Like I said, I know words can hurt. My parents and...others said some things about me that I still struggle with. How unladylike I looked after hiking and foraging, all sweaty with dirt under my nails. How I was nearing the end of my prime for bloodlines and stuff."

"No. That's not true. Your parents said that to you? Bloodlines and stuff as in, kids?" he asked, confused.

"Yeah. Witches generally have a longer 'prime' if you will, given our magic and the herbs we take. So they didn't push as much in the beginning but once I became a professor, they told me I would be expected to wed soon." She stared at her lap.

"Was that final push what got you to run?" he asked softly.

"Yes. I always thought I would have kids because it was expected of me, but once my betrothal had been announced, I felt each day grow darker and darker."

She heard him gasp and look at her before turning the wheel back to steady the truck. "Arranged? Betrothal. You were going to be forced to marry someone? Have kids with them?" Reyes sounded panicked.

"I guess it was how my entire family came to be. How I came to be. His name is Leland. And I despise him." Camille went on to tell him why.

"Bastard. He won't get anywhere near you," Reyes seethed, gripping the steering wheel tight. Camille watched and almost felt a shift in him she couldn't pinpoint. That thing that her and Willow noticed changing in him was there again and she couldn't figure out what it was.

He blew out a deep exhale. "Do you think you do want kids?" he asked.

"No. I don't. Sitka is as much as I want to handle. Even if I wasn't trying to run the bakery and hiding out?" Camille shook her head.

He turned his hand to cup hers. "Hey, you're here and safe. I will see to it."

Camille felt so warm and loved in this moment. She never wanted to let him go.

Once they parked and headed towards her car, they stopped walking but he didn't let go of her hand. "Would you like to come in?" he asked somewhat nervously. "I'm not in any hurry for this night to end."

"Yes." Her voice was soft. "I just want to grab my bag out of the car," she said somewhat bashfully herself.

"You came prepared." He laughed.

"I wanted to be just in case." She grabbed her bag and they headed into the house.

"You can set that upstairs if you'd like. Of course if that's too forward, the guestroom is just past the kitchen," he offered.

"I was curious what your loft bedroom looked like. I just didn't want to impose."

"You wouldn't have imposed, but honestly we may not have made it tonight." He chuckled and led her upstairs.

Camille took in the space. A dividing wall split the floor up. In the middle of the bedroom was a plush king-sized bed, unmade. One of his flannels and a towel draped on the edge of the bed. Two bedside tables sat on either side. The high-peaked roof stood tall overhead but it created a cozy space. A dresser rested against one side. On the other side of the wall was the master bathroom with a large shower and tub. The windows were much higher on this side. Dark granite countertops and white tile with a stone-like appearance reflected the mountain.

"I can't believe this is your house. It's amazing," she said, looking at him.

He smiled. "You are always welcome here, Cami," he said, then leaned in and kissed her passionately.

Camille felt all of him as he pressed against her. His arms felt so strong and secure. They felt like a place she always wanted to be. She hugged him back and ran her hand up his back to his neck and hair.

Slowly, he began to nip at her neck, feeling the bit of scruff. His large, strong hands trailed up and down her ribs and stopped on her hips. He dug his fingers into the sides of her rear.

"You are gorgeous," he breathed out heavily, kissing up to her ear. His hand was now lightly squeezing her rear.

"Reyes," she moaned.

"Yes, I have dreamed of hearing you moan my name."

"Reyes," she moaned again. "I love feeling your hands on me." She pressed into him as her fingers trailed through his hair.

"I don't want to fuck up this chance with you, but I want you so badly," he groaned.

"I've thought about you a lot, when I'm alone in my bed. I think about what this might be like tonight and tomorrow with you. If you want me to stay."

"Can I show you how badly I want you to stay? What tonight could be like and the morning after, every morning after," he groaned into her ear.

"Yes, Reyes." Her words were full of lust as she squeezed his bicep and tugged his hair ever so slightly.

Anticipation built in her core when he slowly undid the buttons on the front of her dress. As she maneuvered out of it, he kissed her neck hungrily and his hands pushed down, letting the dress fall off her hips. Then he unhooked her bra.

"Is this okay?" he asked, looping his fingers around the straps.

"Yes," she breathed out heavily.

He removed it and took a step back, raking his gaze over her. She felt exposed in just her underwear but his eyes did something to her.

"Fuck," he exhaled slowly. "May I?" He glanced at her exposed chest. The cold air made her all too aware of their increasing sensitivity.

"You don't need to ask, Reyes. Show me what you have thought about," she purred.

"Good thing the bakery is closed tomorrow. I'm going to show you exactly what this could be well into tomorrow," Reyes cooed then began to rub and massage her chest lightly. It became less gentle and more intentional with his palming and pinching then he brought his mouth into play. One hand slid down to her backside where he squeezed while the other supported her as he leaned her back for a better access.

Soft moans slipped from her lips. When he moved to the other side, she felt the cold air filling the absence of his warm mouth.

"Reyes." She reached for his collar. "I want to see you. May I?"

He pulled back and took a deep inhale. "Alright."

She could see how defeated he looked and pulled him close into a hug, pressing herself into him. "I like what I see so far."

"It's only fair I suppose." He laughed, wrapping his arms around her tightly and gently running his nails along her exposed back. She began to undo the buttons on his dress shirt and pushed the sleeves back, almost eagerly. Liking the sight in front of her, she pulled off his undershirt and took a step back once it was on the floor.

While he had muscle tone, he was not hard lines and rippling abs. He carried extra weight in his stomach, but she knew his core was solid strength. She took in his chest that was dusted with some hair and her eyes followed the thin line of black hair down to where it vanished into his pants. He looked so real, so human, exposed and bearing himself to her.

Her eyes traveled up to meet his eyes and she could have cried at how utterly perfect he was in all his imperfections. How real he was with the obvious shirt tan and stretch marks in places. The years showed on his skin and held every story in who he was in this body that helped shape him.

"You're staring at me like you're seeing a Greek statue, why? I'm the furthest thing from that."

"Because, Reyes, you are perfect. Everything about you is the purest, most real thing I've seen. You are everything I love about this place. Every real and beautiful thing in the earth and the trees, the soil, and the water here." She stepped forward and took his hand.

He laughed and she could tell he was self-conscious. "No one's ever had that reaction to seeing me shirtless." He kissed her again and walked her back to the bed. His fingers trailed down her stomach and started sliding down her underwear. "Tell me to stop."

"Keep going," she said, locking eyes with him. Then she carefully reached for his pants, watching him, letting him take charge if he wanted. She never wanted him to think he was not good enough again.

"Keep going, Camille." His hand had stopped, as if waiting to see if she would proceed.

She slid her hand into the band of his boxer briefs and watched his eyes grow heavy when she took him in her hand. As she began to stroke him, he let out a moan before he quickly resumed removing the rest of her garments. She did the same to him and he stepped out of them.

There they stood, drinking in the sight of each other fully exposed, and she could feel herself longing to feel his weight on top of her. She also knew the look in his eyes was of someone who had never been more aware of what he wanted.

Camille held her hand out to him and a moment later he took it, pulling her into him again. Feeling their exposed bodies pressed together made them both moan.

Her hand resumed stroking him as his fingers found the wetness between her legs.

"Camille, can I show you what I've really thought about doing to you for many, many nights, on this very bed?" His voice was low and his words were nearly moaning.

Her lips found his ear and she gave a gentle tug with her teeth. "Yes. I want to know."

Within seconds, he seated her on the bed and laid her down before kneeling between her legs and tasted her. He licked repeatedly before throwing her legs over his shoulders and licking more, savoring everything.

"Reyes," she moaned while tugging his hair. Every movement of his tongue and mouth sent a sensation of ecstasy through her. "*Reyes*," she cried out louder.

Never had someone feasted on her so passionately as he was. She could hardly keep her breathing steady with how good it felt. Squeezing her eyes shut tight, she bucked under him. It proved useless as he held her there, even as she convulsed in pleasure and the stars burst behind her eyes. "Reyes," she panted out heavily.

As his licking slowed and became light, sending mini convulsions through her entire body, he slowly and gently pulled away.

"Absolutely divine. That was even more intoxicating than I ever thought possible."

All she could do was lay there, slowly letting her breathing and senses return to her.

"I'm going to do that every night you let me," he murmured softly.

Finally, she pushed herself up to sit and saw him sitting back on his haunches, lightly stroking himself to the sight of her. She watched him and bit her bottom lip.

"Stand up," she instructed and he did. Reaching her hand out, she took his and pulled him closer as she came to kneel in front of him.

Slowly, she took over where his hand was and slid part of his length into her mouth. She would have to work up to taking all of him in her mouth. He certainly was well-endowed. The sensation of his fingertips bracing her jaw sent an odd sense of submission through her, a sensation she was more than willing to explore with him. He was not forceful; he'd been so careful with her tonight and she knew he would continue to be even when he was near exploding. She trusted him.

"Cami. Yes. Yes. This feels so good." He thrusted gently, cupping her jaw with both hands for a few more moments before he pulled back. She remained kneeling as she looked up at him.

"Get on the bed. On your back. Now," he said through gritted teeth.

She gave him one more long, slow lick from the base to the tip then stood. The next thing she knew was him embracing her and pushing her back onto the bed. He leaned over and kissed her as he reached into the drawer on the nightstand. Camille heard the faint sound of a condom being opened as he pulled away and sat back on his knees. She watched him put it on.

"Cami," he heaved out, holding her hips. She met his eyes. "I don't have anything, I have the notice on my phone, and obviously you know about the vasectomy."

"Negative for anything as well, and I'm on a birth control tonic, but I appreciate you being proactive," she said.

"Will you tell me if I do something you don't like, or if it hurts?" he asked, sounding almost nervous.

She sat up and cupped his jaw in her hands. "I will, Reyes. Now, let me feel you." Then Camille pulled him towards her.

"Anything for you." With that, he eased into her and they moaned in unison as they felt her adjust to accommodate him.

He pulled back and pushed deeper into her on a forward thrust where he repeated the motion, eventually leaning forward and kissing her neck.

The embrace he pulled her into felt so secure and his body heat left her wanting more. His scent engulfed her and she couldn't help but melt into him as his arms wrapped around her.

"Reyes." She hugged him tight as if she would never let him go and brought her teeth to the nape of his neck, giving a light bite.

"Cami, fuck yes." He groaned and picked up his pace until he was slamming into her hard. Every thrust forward forced a whimper from her and he watched in complete awe.

Then with one last thrust, he groaned and trembled, going limp on top of her.

She felt his final push send him over the edge, as well as his heavy breathing. Now she felt his heaviness on her and the thin layer of sweat that he had worked up.

Her fingers trailed up and down his spine and traced his shoulder blades while he twitched and caught his breath. His hand reached up to run his fingers through her hair.

"Camille?"

"Yes?"

"I was serious, I will do that every single night if you want me too. I don't know what we are, but I want you to be my girl, if you want to be of course."

She laughed lazily. "Sitka stays."

It was his turn to laugh. "Of course she does."

"Sounds like you have yourself a girlfriend, Mr. Navarro." She smiled widely.

He laughed and kissed her hard.

They cleaned up and got back into bed, talking softly as he held her close.

Camille savored the safety she felt with him. Yet she could not shake the nagging fear that she would lose this one day but she refused to dwell on it. Letting those fears in right now would ruin this night and she wouldn't let that happen. Just as she wouldn't let anything happen to Reyes.

Chapter 24

The next morning Reyes woke up with his body snugly curled around Camille's. He nuzzled into her hair and pulled her closer.

"Morning," she murmured and wrapped her arms around his.

"Good morning," he said, giving the nape of her neck a kiss. "How long have you been awake?"

"Not long. I usually don't sleep in this late."

"It's seven in the morning on a Sunday. It is not late by any means. Especially if we are staying local."

Camille laughed. He moved his legs and bumped something pressed up against him. He looked up to see Sitka reaching a paw out in a stretch from the ball she had been curled up into.

"Why am I not surprised there is a bobcat in my bed?" He smiled.

"I might have opened a window for her. She doesn't go far from me, but she's certainly welcome to."

"Sitka is very bonded to you. Was she here all night?"

"Most of the night. She has her ways of finding me." Camille wiggled around to face him and it sent a heat through them both, feeling their bodies pressed against each other. "I'm going to freshen up; I want to make some coffee."

"I will be down in a moment," he said, kissing her lightly. "You are absolutely stunning in the morning. Not that I had a doubt you wouldn't be."

Camille smiled at him. "You are lovely to wake next to as well, Reyes." She got out of bed and grabbed her bag then went into the bathroom. He watched her as she walked in then grinned at seeing her walk out in one of his flannels. She looked at him with an endearing smile before heading towards the stairs, but she paused to take in the view.

The image of her looking through the windows at Mt. Shasta in his flannel left him yearning for her.

At that moment, Reyes was certain this was who he wanted to marry. Something deep within him told him there was nothing truer than that. He couldn't place it, not a thought, and it was more than a feeling. He knew he was going to do whatever he needed to be able to see this image every day. She was everything his life had been missing and if she wasn't, she would help him find whatever else he needed out there.

"I can't believe this is your view every day," she said, turning to him.

"The view is especially nice this morning," he replied, still staring at her.

Camille let out a bashful laugh and looked at him as if she felt everything he did. His cheeks heated and he wasn't sure anyone had ever reacted that way to his compliments like that before.

She went downstairs and his eyes moved to the bobcat. Carefully, he reached out towards the bobcat who was now loafed up on the bed. It turned towards him and watched him.

"Easy, Sitka, you are on my bed." Then he scratched the bobcat's head and as it purred, he moved to scratching its fluffy cheeks and he felt a sense that it would all be alright. That this would be his future, with a witch and her bobcat.

He had never dreamed of having this, but now he never wanted anything more.

Getting up, he put on the nearest pair of sweatpants and a flannel he didn't button up then headed downstairs himself. When he got there, he saw her whisking some cream together.

The sight got him riled up.

Reyes leaned against the counter next to her and scooped a bit of the cream up on his finger to taste it. The urges in him were growing. He wanted to take her again so badly.

"How's it taste?" she asked.

"Perfect." He pulled her hips to meet him. He kissed her deeply and brought his hands to unbutton the flannel.

"Reyes," she moaned as his hands came to his hips.

"I love hearing you moan my name." His kisses trailed down to her chest and his hands slid down to her rear. Eventually as he came to kneel before her, he slid her underwear down slowly and began to lick her again.

"Reyes," she moaned again and braced herself against the counter.

"The only better sound than hearing you moan my name is hearing you scream it," he groaned as he brought his hands to her hips and licked faster.

He felt her convulse as she cried out his name. Her cheeks were flushed and she was panting while bracing herself on the counter.

"This, too, is a beautiful sight," he said, looking up at her.

Her breathing evened out.

"You seem to like doing that." She laughed, finally pushing herself up right. He came to stand behind her.

"I do. A lot," he said and lowered his sweats. "I'm not being too overbearing, am I?" he asked softly, not touching her. Assertiveness was pouring out of him faster than he could comprehend. It felt like more than newfound confidence, but he wasn't going to fight it. He would be fighting other urges all day.

She turned around and he tensed since his pants were hardly covering him.

"I trust you, Reyes. I feel safe with you."

"I hope you always do. I will always keep you safe," he said, letting his sweats fall to the ground. "Turn back around."

She did and then Reyes positioned to take her from behind, pushing deep inside her.

He leaned over and kissed her shoulders. "You liked nipping me last night, may I return the favor?"

"Yes," she moaned softly.

He gently used his teeth. He'd never really done this before but he enjoyed it with her. His witch. His bakery girl. Camille was his girlfriend and he could not feel close enough to her. Reyes bit a little harder as he rocked his hips back and forth slowly. He wanted to claim her. The sounds of her moans, the way she breathed out his name did something to him that he had never felt before.

"Mine," he growled between bites.

"Reyes," she heaved out in lust.

After he felt his release, he eased his grip and held her, gently kissing where he had bitten. He pulled back slightly and was horrified at how red her neck and shoulders were. He could see teeth marks fading on her.

"Shit. Did I hurt you? I don't know what came over me. I just, I don't know that I have ever slipped into a moment like that before. I didn't even use a condom! Camille!" He panicked and went to pull away until her hands came over his hands.

"I trust you, Reyes. I've never had a partner do that, it felt good. You didn't hurt me, it just feels hot right there. A cold compress should ease it down, plus I have a salve for that in my bag. Yours. I am yours and you are mine."

He let out a slow exhale in relief. "You are amazing." He gave her a little squeeze then leaned over more to grab the paper towels on the counter. He tried to rip one off but struggled until she helped. "Gravity is going to do its thing," he laughed, handing her a few.

"I know. I will clean up."

With a quick kiss on her shoulders again, he pulled out and watched her head off to the restroom nearby. Reyes got an ice pack for her and wrapped that in a dishtowel.

Once they were seated with a light breakfast, Reyes watched her, still in his flannel that was now buttoned up. He had been thinking about how no one had claimed her in that way. While he was grateful, he also hoped they had been good to her. That she hadn't been hurt. *Until my hand was bartered off in a betrothal.* Her words played back for him. *She ran. She fled. Leland, that bastard.* Anger made him clench his fist.

"Cami?" he asked, not sure what he could do about anything, but he had to know. "Did he ever hurt you?"

She looked at him, somewhat stunned. "Before the official ceremony to join in a union, we had one night a month. Coupling as it's called in the older practices where we spend a night together getting to know each other in more intimate ways. He sometimes bit too hard. He usually never reciprocated what I liked, though I often did everything he wanted," she explained and his stomach was in knots.

"He usually didn't even stay the night either, which was never a good sign to learn you weren't enough to keep your future spouse with you for a night. At least that's what my mother would tell me when she learned I would leave the room too. It wasn't so much all that hurt but more what he said. That I was too thick; he said I was dirty and made him look bad because I would get gross from hikes. And the insults went on. He insulted me our entire lives. I never understood why my parents chose him. He wasn't that strong of a witch. Talbot is powerful and wealthy but Leland wasn't."

She looked down and away from him again.

Reyes felt so many emotions boil in him. He leapt out of his seat and knelt in front of her, taking her hands in his. "Never change, not unless you want to. Even if you and I don't work out, never think you are anything less than a goddess. The moment you looked up at me on that trail, I knew I'd never be able to forget your face. I won't let him take you. He is an absolute dumbass for not worshiping you," he proclaimed, holding her hands gently.

Camille laughed but it held no joy. "I have two older brothers who will continue the name on. I am the youngest of three so I figured they didn't lose much when I left. I pawned my ring off somewhere in Oregon along with some other things that connected me to Thornwell. I ditched my phone on a semi in case they tracked me that way and used the money to get a burner phone and a new rental car."

"I'm sorry, I shouldn't have said so much this morning. You really didn't find it overbearing?" He was so worried. "Please be honest, Camille."

She cupped his jaw and looked into his eyes. "No. I feel safe with you. You haven't pushed me to do anything. You have looked out for me and even when you were a grump, you were always polite and respectful. And it's why I know how much people like Jodie can still have an effect on you. You are perfect, Reyes."

He laughed and then he rose and kissed her. "You are perfect too. I am yours as long as you will have me. I hope it's forever."

"I hope the same."

They set to finishing up breakfast and went on a short hike. It was the first time he was hiking with her and Sitka, and he loved the glimpse of this future with her.

Chapter 25

A few weeks later as the summer heat was beginning to waver and the trees nestled between the conifers were getting hints of yellow, they went on their first camping trip. She hadn't really been camping for fun but was eager to be with him. They stayed local in Siskiyou County, not going too far out. They had headed out in Reyes's truck with Sitka in tow on Saturday afternoon after she closed the bakery. Reyes had taken Monday off work since the bakery was closed that day.

He had the bed set up with extra blankets for them to sleep in the truck. They didn't bother with a tent.

"I think the clouds will clear up and we will get to see the moon," Camille said watching Reyes stoke the flames on the campfire.

They had just finished eating and she was cleaning up for the night. The campsite was one of the tucked away ones with no others nearby on federal land. Reyes had explained that was another reason he liked it up here much more than San Jose where he had grown up. The camping was much more dispersed and while he did love redwoods, the firs and sugar pines that would open up to valleys and wide-open skies were what he craved. Plus the view of Mt. Shasta was magnificent at every angle.

"I think so too," Reyes said, sitting in the seat near her. "I love it out here." He leaned in and gave her a kiss.

"It is beautiful. It's got a quiet stillness to it. Like parts of Olympic National Park, or Mt. Rainier." She went on to talk fondly of the parks.

"Do you miss it?" Reyes asked. He seemed relaxed as he glanced over at her.

Camille felt herself frown and looked down. "I don't really know. It's lovely and I have good memories, but I can't go back. I don't want to go back."

He took her hands in his and she looked up to meet his eyes. "Then stay here. I hope Shasta can be just as good to you."

"It has been, Reyes. For the first time, I feel like I found the life I want, the life I dreamed of."

He smiled again and let out a soft laugh.

As they talked, she noticed Sitka begin to pace with her ears flattened. Her eyes followed the cat, watching her look around as though a predator was just beyond the light.

Camille sat up straighter and looked around, trying to sense where the animal was. But Sitka clearly didn't know either, and she was looking everywhere.

"What is it?" Reyes asked slowly, getting up. He had left his knife on the cooler.

"I don't know. Sitka isn't sure. Something is near but she hasn't focused on anything..." Camille trailed off, focusing on Sitka.

A low growl slipped out of the bobcat again. Camille watched the animal continue to pace and look around, trying to find the intrusion. Things got brighter and Camille realized it was the moon emerging from the clouds.

Surely it's not the full moon having an effect on Sitka. I have experienced plenty with her. What is out there? Camille asked herself. The thud of the knife hitting the dirt snapped her attention as well as Sitka's.

Reyes was heaving. A groan slipped out of him as he clenched his stomach.

"Reyes? What's wrong?" Camille got up and rushed over to him but Sitka instantly latched onto the flannel of his she was wearing and tugging her back. "Sitka?" Then Reyes fell to his knees.

"Cami." His voice was hoarse and strained. "I feel weird. It's happening again."

"Reyes!" she rasped and took a step closer, halting in her tracks at what she saw happening.

His entire body was twitching and a second later, something was ripping itself out from inside him. His hands started to change and hair began to cover him. The trembling mass that had been Reyes doubled in size as his clothes ripped to tatters, falling to the ground around him. His entire skull was changing shape and yet, Camille could not look away.

A part of her knew she should run, jump into the truck, or hide. Another part of her knew she should be horrified at what she was witnessing. His skull shape change was just as grotesque as the rest of him was. Two pointed ears sat atop his head and he had a snout, a very long one. He no longer stood on two feet but four giant paws and his tail was fluffy. His fur was brindle brown and tan. His eyes were still the rich warm amber they had always been only now, his pupils were much more dilated.

The witch part of her knew exactly what had happened to Reyes, but she did not understand how it had happened.

Reyes Navarro was a wolf shifter and judging from the slow transformation, and his agonizing cries, he had just shifted for the very first time. His wolf was in charge of this hulking mass of a body now, not Reyes. He was likely buried deep inside the wolf.

"Reyes." She took a step back, trying her best to remain calm. Camille hadn't been around that many shifters, and certainly not any new to shifting shifters. "Reyes," she repeated again.

He snapped out a snarl as he stalked towards her.

Sitka ran in front of Camille and arched its back with a hiss.

"Sitka! No," she yelped as Reyes snapped again. "Please, Reyes, listen to me, scent me, or something. I know you are still you," she pleaded. He lunged towards Camille and Sitka lunged for Reyes. Effortlessly, Reyes threw Sitka back by the scruff. She landed on her feet but it still made Camille's heart seize.

Reyes would never forgive himself if he hurt Sitka. It would hurt Camille.

He lunged again and Camille stumbled back over a rock. The impact of her head hitting the back of the truck stunned her and before she realized it, she was on the ground. Claws scratched down from her clavicle as he stood right over her, his fangs drawing closer. She could see the drool drip from his maw.

"Reyes! Please. You are going to wake up in the morning. Please let me help you through this. Connect with me," she pleaded once more, setting her intent to form the mindlink with him. Links connected two parts, though, and right now he was not willing to connect with her. She wasn't even sure he could hear her.

She tried to kick him and get away but he had her pinned.

Sitka jumped on his back and scruffed him. He growled in shock. A bobcat was no match for a massive wolf, but Sitka had the agility and ability to climb. He rolled off Camille and lunged for the bobcat.

Sitka ran and the wolf followed.

"No!" Camille cried out. She quickly pushed herself up and swayed back against the truck from the dizziness. As she braced herself, she crawled into the back. Her eyes welled up as she shut the tailgate and top hatch of the camper shell. She curled up on the bed with the blankets that smelled like him. "Reyes."

After what felt like way too long of her just crying, she slowly sat up. Her head throbbed but she wasn't dizzy. Silence was all she heard. Nothing but a stillness loomed in the air and it was heavy. Sitka had defended her and led Reyes away from her.

She wiped her eyes but the tears kept coming. He looked like he was in so much pain. How far would he run? Would his wolf know to avoid traps? Farmers' land? Gunshots? Roads? Were the wolf and his mind connected enough?

"Please keep him safe. Please," she begged the mountain looming on the horizon. They were far from it but she could still see it.

As swiftly as she could, she put the fire out and threw the food in the airtight receptacle in the cooler to stash back in the passenger seat of the truck. Then she rustled through the shreds of his clothes for his keys and stared at the truck.

She had never driven it. It was his and she couldn't leave him out there either. He'd shift back with the break of dawn. She would have to track him down if he didn't return. After crawling into the truck once again, she inspected her wounds, finding he had broken the skin and the blood made her shirt stick to her skin. She set to work on rummaging through the first aid kit and tended to her wounds.

Camille had no idea Reyes had this ability. He obviously didn't either. She thought back to last month on his last camping trip. It had been a full moon. His wolf was trying to emerge. The safety enchantment suppressed it. But he said he never experienced anything like that before.

Her mind raced through all the things she had read on shifters, how their feral form and human form needed to find a balance. Usually it was easy when they were kids, since everything was so new to them as a child or cub. She had never heard of an adult having to learn it.

It had to run in his family somewhere. But would his parents never help him learn this? Would he not have seen them shift? What if they couldn't? It wasn't uncommon for the shifting trait to become so diluted that it skipped generations. *So what had triggered Reyes to shift?*

She had no answers and very little service out here. Her first resource was Willow but she also knew she would have to talk to his parents. They would find out what she was.

She had to find him but she couldn't go now. Sitka and him probably had covered miles and elevation she couldn't even begin to navigate in the dark. When she found him, what state would he be in?

Something thudded on the hood of the truck and she jumped. Sitka stood then jumped down. Camille promptly opened the top hatch and gritted her teeth at the motion with her injuries. As soon as Sitka was back inside, she locked the truck back up and pulled Sitka close.

"Tell me he's alive? Please. Please. Tell me he is alright?"

All Sitka did was purr and nudge her head.

After setting her alarm to a little before dawn, Camille curled under the blankets and wept into Sitka, praying to anything out there he was safe.

Chapter 26

When Reyes roused, his head was pounding. His stomach felt as though it was going to cave in on itself from hunger, his muscles screamed with exhaustion, and he was freezing. He reached over for the blankets but found his palms scraped against dirt. It scratched his chest, stomach and side of his face. The realization set in that he didn't have any clothes on either.

Opening his eyes did little to ease his headache, in fact making everything worse. It also kicked his heart rate up. He was outside. In the forest. Alone. The early blue light of dawn was far too bright already.

"What happened?" he asked the air as if it would respond. He couldn't get up nor did he want to. It was a wonder he hadn't frozen to death out here. Had it been two months from now, he likely would not have woken up at all.

Scanning for any of his clothes nearby, his thoughts began to come back to him. He hadn't known what was happening. There was a bobcat that ran, then climbed a tree. He had chased it but he didn't know why. There wasn't even a trail nearby that he could see. The deeper he ran, the more distracted he had become by the scents getting so strong all over the forest. The sounds were near deafening and before he realized it, his senses were overwhelmed.

The screams that tore out of him. They did not sound like screams. They were frantic whimpers. Almost animal-like in his ears. He recalled his hands feeling different. His body was different. He had been trailing the bobcat until he had started running but he recalled its scent nearby as if watching him, tracking him.

"The bobcat? Sitka?" Then as soon as he had said her name, everything came crashing back into him. Camille screamed his name while looking right into his eyes. His hands—no, paws—were pinning her. She was screaming for him to stop. He had scared her, hurt her? "No." He curled in on himself more. "No," he cried out.

Something had changed in him and he didn't understand any of it. It had driven him mad and led him to hurt Camille and chase Sitka.

He came to his knees and hunched over, feeling the dirt dig into his knees and feet. Was it hair or fur covering his entire body last night? Now he had his hands and skin. Hunger and fear overwhelmed him, but what scared him more was what he may have done to Sitka or Camille.

"No," he whimpered. As he glanced around, thoughts began to swirl in a panic in his mind. What was he going to do? Stay out here and become some legend of the Siskiyou wilds? What had happened to Camille? Was she alright? He remembered they had been camping, and the full moon. Some werewolf campfire story and he had turned into the thing of nightmares. Dropping his head into his hands again, he sobbed softly, completely unable to move.

Steps approached and he grew fearful. He didn't want to be found like this yet he couldn't move. They came closer then stopped and he could feel someone's gaze but was too ashamed to look up. Mortification gripped him and he lowered his hand to cover himself, not sure what exactly was visible, still keeping his other hand over his face. Pain was digging into his knees and feet from the dirt.

"Reyes," Camille said softly.

His heart leapt at the sound of her voice and oh how he wanted to hug her and kiss her and nuzzle up against her for warmth but instead he turned away, still unable to look at her.

"I'm sorry." His voice broke and embarrassment gripped him tight. "I'm sorry," he repeated, just as broken.

"I'm going to set some warm food down and put a blanket over you, alright? Just remain still. It's cold and I'm not well versed with shifters, especially ones new to it all. I assume that was your first time?"

He shook his head. "I'm sorry. I don't know what happened. I'm sorry." The words pained him to repeat. "I don't deserve your kindness."

"Shh, it's going to be alright. Just remain where you are," she said and took a soft step closer. His ears took in the sound of the pack sliding off her shoulders and touching the ground. His senses felt amplified now. The scent of food made his mouth salivate and his stomach groan. "There's clean clothes for you and your boots survived the shift."

He remained still as she draped the blanket over his shoulders. Her touch was gentle and the blanket offered him a shield from the cold air. An overwhelming bout of despair sent a tremor through his body.

"I suppose I should have brought a towel so you could rinse off in the lake."

His heart tried to push himself towards her but he still couldn't make himself move or even look at her.

"I'm sorry," he whimpered again, trying to bury himself in the blanket. The warmth felt good despite his scratchy and dirty skin.

"Eat, please. I think you burned a lot of calories. I recall reading shifters having a bigger appetite."

"Shifter? What does that even mean? What happened? I attacked you," he cried out, turning his head even more.

"Well, it means you have a feral form, and something triggered it. I think it's hereditary."

"My mom or my dad?"

"Yes."

"My sister? My nephew?" Reyes started to plead.

"They likely have the trait. In some cases it gets so diluted over the generations your nephew may never change, maybe your parents and sister can't shift but you were exposed—" Her words cut off and instinct brought his head up to meet her worried expression.

He took in the bruises and scrapes on her neck, which disappeared under her tank top and his flannel. That was his doing. He had hurt her. Once again he cut his eyes away and whimpered out another apology.

"I spent time reading up on shifters when I had my flora and fauna communication courses. The wolf is part of you now. You just need to learn how to balance them. I know there's a way to form a mindlink with shifters in their feral form, but you are going to need to learn that too. The ones I have talked to, just linked to my mind."

"I have to learn how to be a wolf?" he asked, terrified.

"Yes. It will likely happen during the full moon, something we will need to be mindful of. The cabin might be chaotic the first few times, but I will help you. I can make a calming tincture and we will work on it." Her voice was almost pleading.

"No. I don't want you near me when I become that monster. I don't even know why you're near me now. You made me food and found me?" Reyes whimpered.

"Sitka must have led you to a safe place. She likely knows this whole county better than anyone. It is her home, and why I didn't want your friend to take her to Trinity. Maybe she had roamed that far but this is where she belongs."

He looked at Sitka. He examined the bobcat who looked fine. "Did I hurt her?"

"No. She's probably had her share of run-ins with much bigger apex predators. Coyotes and mountain lions and such. She was alright and came back to the truck a few hours after running off with you."

"She saved your life and I chased her. I'm so sorry, both of you."

"I'm not mad, and Sitka is still loyal to you. I'm not afraid of you either, Reyes. Let me help you. I am scared of you pushing me away or running off, honestly." Her tone told him she was frowning.

"What if I hurt you again? Or Sitka, or someone else? I feel so alone right now, like I can't even go back into civilization ever again, but I don't know if I can bear the thought of you walking away right now." He wiped his eyes.

He heard her move and sit next to him but he still couldn't look at her.

"I'm not going to leave you here, Reyes. Let me help you. I want to. At least come back to the campsite." She placed a hand on his shoulder. "I will make some more food and you can rest in the truck. We will stay out here as planned then head back tomorrow."

"I don't want to hurt you again. I can't," he whimpered, then cried harder when she moved closer to him and wrapped an arm around him.

"You won't. I know what to expect, I will read up on it, and we can work through it. Together. Willow can help, maybe she knows someone?"

"Alright, but you have to promise me, if I shift again, you will run with Sitka. Please just take the keys and my truck and go. I will show you where I keep the shotgun and bullets in the cabin."

"Reyes!" she scolded. "I'm not going to do that, ever. Do not ask me to. I will take cover but I will never do that." She squeezed him tighter then placed the food in front of him.

"I don't want to do that again."

"Eat something please. We can head back to camp when you feel ready. I'm here."

With a sniff, he finally reached for the foil wrapped provision in front of him. It was a breakfast burrito and he felt ravenous for sustenance. He was starving.

"Sorry I didn't bring coffee. I should have." She laughed as he took the last bite, setting the water bottle in front of him.

Reyes wanted to laugh, and smile at her but he was so overcome with emotions he couldn't. "I don't deserve this. Or you." His voice broke again as he drank the water in large gulps. The food and water were so refreshing.

"Now we fully know what each other is. Stay with me, please," she asked, holding her hand out.

Reyes took it and gave her hand a squeeze.

"I fear I might have triggered this dormancy in you," she said quietly.

"What?" he exclaimed and looked at her again. "No. You didn't do anything wrong. If this is hereditary, how could you possibly have any hand in it?" he asked, tightening his grip on her hands.

She went on to further explain her thoughts.

"So, you think it was a combination of being around your magic, and consuming your enchantments that did this?" he asked, thinking about it.

"I think so. If neither of your parents are able to shift, or even know, then it might have been diluted. Witches and other types of magic can bring out the magic in others that have it, but if your parents hadn't had the exposure to enough magic, then it might have gone dormant. Maybe if it went dormant in them, they figured it was dormant in their kids too. Or maybe they just don't know. And didn't wolves recently find their way back into California? That too might have an effect when paired with my magic."

"Would it be both of my parents or just one? Is it more dominant in one or the other?" he asked, recalling his dad's obsession with wolves.

"From what I recall, shifting is usually always based on what the mother is. If two shifters of different species have offspring, it would be what the mother is, if say the father is but the mother doesn't have a shifting ability, the trait might get passed down but isn't a guarantee," Camille explained.

"So it's my mom then?" He glanced at her.

"It could very well be just your dad. But my theory is it's both of them."

Reyes looked at her with an inquisitive gaze. "What leads you to that theory?"

"Well, it would be hard to hide it from a spouse and kids. Which leads me to believe, neither one of your parents has shifted. A shifter could tell what I am." She went on to mention the slight glance his mom had given her at the use of *familiar* and how in turn Camille could see a shifter's animal inside. She could see his wolf now, just as exhausted as he was.

As Reyes continued to listen, he realized how likely it was that both his parents had the dormant ability. If it was dormant in his parents due to a dilution, that meant he had as much as they did. So did his sister. Camille's presence had broken it free.

"What does this mean for us?" he asked. "Are there rules for this sort of thing?"

Chapter 27

Camille pondered his question then looked at him.

"No. No rules banning the bonds between different beings. Each type of bond has its own unique challenges. Thornwell thinks humans are beneath them. They also want to stick to their bloodlines and dislike the idea of hybrids or crossbreeding. Witches keep to their own. Fae and other folk are different, though high fae have their purity things too. It's a whole other hierarchy with them and witches tend to keep their distance. Though, some fae shifters have passed through," she explained as he pulled his clothes on.

"They have?" Reyes asked, confused.

"Yes. They obviously just keep it hidden for humans."

"But what does this mean for you and I?" he asked.

Camille looked at him and again recalled how it worked for shifters. "We will figure it out. I don't think we have to worry about offspring. I don't want them; you don't want them. Witches normally take their lovers as they choose, and should they find one they love, they marry by the traditions important to them. They can have multiple lovers or just one. Usually free to choose, unless you are a legacy of course. Though plenty of legacies just produce heirs as expected and have other lovers. Coupling when they need to then tolerating each other for the responsibility. "

She could see the dread in his eyes and hated it because she too felt dread in the pit of her stomach. She explained the dynamic of shifters and how they generally had a lifemate. Naturally, that was due to not only the bond with each other but also for bloodlines. It also meant more to a wolf shifter as wolves generally only had one mate. Some part of her felt saddened that maybe he did have a lifemate out there, a female wolf shifter. It saddened her that they might never meet, but it saddened her more that they might one day cross paths and he would choose his lifemate.

Camille hated thinking like that, it was a glorious thing to find one's mate and she wasn't sure if they would ever feel the same type of bond with each other.

She had been so lost in the thought that she hadn't noticed him walk up to her until he cupped her chin.

"Then you are my lifemate. I'm sure that's overbearing as hell right now, but my human side wants you and has for so long. I think my wolf side will realize that as soon as I figure it out."

She smiled at him, feeling some relief. "I'm happy to hear that, Reyes. I'd choose you for a lifemate too. I'm not sure how the bond feels for you or works for you now. So if you cross paths with another wolf shifter, don't pass them up, okay? Wolf shifters are rare here and they can teach you better than I can." She could feel her throat start to sting with the pain of fighting a cry.

"The way I feel about you tells me I'm looking at my lifemate. I'm choosing you. The way you look at me, like you want me, like you can't keep your hands off me in the bedroom. No one would have come for me this morning. I'd be a fool to even think someone else like you existed out there and that I'd be made for them."

"Reyes," she breathed out and hugged him tightly.

"Let's get back to camp," he said, hugging her back. She nodded and went for the backpack. "Let me take it."

She looked at him with big eyes then dug around for a moment, pulling out a small silver container before handing him the pack. Once he had it on, she opened the container. The scents of some kind of mint hit filled the air.

"This will help with your soreness. A little on the temples and behind the ears will do the trick. May I?" she asked, holding it up. He nodded and watched her take some on her fingers, offering to hold it while she applied it.

Camille watched his eyes grow heavy with the sensation as she rubbed the salve into his temples, then he did the same when she rubbed it behind his ears. The faintest moan slipped out, causing him to snap out of his daze and look at her in embarrassment.

Smiling, she took his hand in his. "We have shown a lot to each other. I'm honored to call you mine."

"Thank you, Camille, I am honored to call you mine as well."

After one more kiss, they walked back to camp where Reyes rinsed off and started a fire to make more food. They would not have much for the morning before heading back but they would leave earlier than planned. Camille informed him that he may be lethargic for a time but should be recovered by Tuesday when they went back to work..

Instead of the hike they had planned to do, she napped with him as he slept in the truck, and when he woke up, he insisted on cooking dinner for them.

When the next morning came, they took it slow before driving back to his cabin.

"Stay with me tonight, please? I'm close to the bakery."

"Alright. I will stay with you. I have enough enchantments for the week."

"I completely forgot to keep the safety enchantment on me," he sighed.

"I don't think you should suppress this now. It might make it worse."

"I don't want to hurt you again, Cami," he whined.

"We will work on it. Let's talk to your parents tonight, then meet up with Willow this week." Camille placed her hand on his leg this time. He nodded and continued driving home.

"They are going to call me," Reyes lamented and slumped back on the couch, grabbing the remote to cast the video call to the screen.

Camille sat next to him and ran her fingers through his hair. "It will be alright. We will figure this out. Let me tell them about me though. I do not want that liability on you."

He looked at her then leaned in to kiss her. "I do not deserve you. I'm so glad you are still here." He pressed the remote to turn on the TV to display the laptop and receive the incoming call.

"Hi, mijo, and it's so nice to see you, Camille." His mom beamed.

"Hello, Mrs. Navarro. Mr. Navarro. I hope you are doing well." She caught her rigid tone and posture and forced herself to relax. These were not people examining her every move at the academy. Nor was her mother there ready to criticize her. These were two parents who loved their son and had wanted the best for him, despite keeping a major secret from him.

"Oh, we are fine. Just finished up some errands. You're off on a Monday?" his dad asked, confused.

"Yes." Reyes's voice sounded nervous. "Cami and I went camping. Saturday afternoon to this morning. Bakery is closed on Sundays and Mondays and all."

"Oh that sounds fun," his mom chimed in.

Camille watched the two and tried to sense any sort of magic or wolf in them but it was no use through a screen. She could see Reyes fidgeting nervously with the hem of his shirt, so she grabbed the nearest fidget toy on the coffee table and placed it in his hand.

"It's alright," she said softly.

Reyes let out a deep exhale and nodded. "Is there anything either of you have kept from Andi and me? Is Andi my full sister? Half-sister?" he asked, finally looking at the screen. Camille could hear the hurt in his words and placed a hand on his knee.

"What? What are you talking about? Of course Andi and you are fully related. We have two kids. What's wrong, Son?" his dad asked in confusion.

"There was a full moon last night." Reyes's voice broke. "I hurt her, and chased Sitka! Andi needs to know what could happen, what could happen to Weylyn."

Camille stilled and looked at Reyes in shock. She knew what that name meant. "That sure is a convenient choice of name for your nephew." Her eyes wandered back to the screen seeing the shock on their faces.

"What? Andi said they picked it because it was an old Celtic name or something. For whatever reason, I don't know." Reyes groaned.

Camille swallowed hard and nodded glancing at him. "It is, it means son of the wolf."

"Can she already shift? Did you tell her and not me?" Reyes growled and glared at the screen. His parents looked shocked.

"What are you saying, Son?"

"I changed or shifted or whatever into a fucking wolf. Some rabid beast thing out of a legend and it was horrible. I lost all control and lunged for Cami. What are we? Which one of you has this? And why wouldn't you tell me?" Reyes demanded.

His parents remained silent and looked at each other for a moment.

Camille took his hand in hers and rubbed the back. She wanted to soothe his worries, to let him know it would be alright. She read about it before—the more one fought against their magic the harder on them it would be.

"I'm terrified I'm going to hurt her again," he whimpered.

Camille finally spoke up. "I-I have studied a lot before moving to the area and have had some exposure to shifters, but never any new to shifting. It was my first time witnessing someone's first shift. I have natural ways of calming him when he shifts but if you have any information, it would be greatly appreciated. I want you to know, though, I will not leave him. I will watch over him as best I can. Sitka will too. She shares a bond with him as well."

His mom smiled with affection. "Thank you, Camille. You are truly a blessing."

Camille felt her insides shrivel up at everything that made her the opposite.

"The fact of the matter is, there are legends in both my family tree and your father's of wolf shifting. My grandmother was the last I saw do it, but I was young. My mother spoke of the stories while I was growing up but she never shifted."

"And it was the same on my side; it had been two generations on both sides of the family. We didn't even tell each other until we laid you down to sleep for the very first night at home. I was worried your mother would think I was crazy. Until she told me the same. Pointed out pictures in the photo albums. We agreed there was no need to continue these legends. The magic had been so diluted in us we just simply let it die out. We talked about it as you got older, how you struggled with focus and routines at times, that maybe it had something to do with that. But once you got the ADHD diagnosis, we figured it was fine for you to manage it. It never felt right to tell you or Andi with you two being so active in your teenage years. Then you both moved away. We debated maybe relocating to be closer to you or Andi, but moving closer to one made it harder to get to the other with Mt. Shasta being far from a large airport," his dad explained.

Camille could hear the remorse in his tone and see it in his body language.

"I hurt her," Reyes said. "I woke up alone in the middle of the forest because her familiar is so loyal and led me away from the campsite."

She smiled and looked at the camera again. His mom tilted her head and Camille could see the word forming on her lips.

"I do not mean this to be offensive, but normally humans have pets. Witches have familiars."

Camille lifted her head and held it high as she looked at the screen. "I am. I fear that I may have triggered something in him." She explained herself and apologized profusely for lying to them. She left out all the parts of her upbringing and Thornwell. She still feared they would call her a betrayer if they knew of witches.

"We are glad our boy will have someone looking out for him and we will keep your secret safe," his mom said and went on to explain what little they knew. They said they would send what they could find of his great-grandparents on shifting.

For the remainder of the evening, they made dinner and searched what they could on his laptop. All the while she assured him he would be alright. She also set reminders on his phone for the full moons and told him to remember to request the days off.

"Why not put a shock collar on me that limits how far I can go?" he asked, half joking and half defeated, as they laid in bed.

"Reyes," she scolded. "No, that is going to drive you insane. The more you fight it the more the wolf will fight you."

He sighed in acceptance and hugged her, resting his head on her waist since she was sitting up. Her injuries had nearly healed with some herbal ointments she made.

Chapter 28

Reyes dropped his head into his hands as Camille told Willow what happened on the camping trip.

"What? I never sensed any magic in him. A wolf shifter. This entire time? And that was the first time you shifted?" Willow marveled.

"Yes." He glanced at Camille. "I'm sorry. I'm so fucking unstable."

Camille took his hand. "Shhh, Reyes. I'm here."

"Guess that explains your agression when you came into my shop."

"I'm sorry. It's just not fair how she was treated. You can't tell me you think she's in the wrong," he said with spite.

"No, I don't. And I am sorry, stigmas are hard to erase and I had no idea Thornwell was like that. We see Thornwell as prim and proper, strong and desirable. Well, I didn't see them as the last thing. I knew I'd never be prim or proper enough for them or the academy. Obviously I wouldn't have, being mostly self-taught. And now I have the best tutor in the world," Willow said.

The two women smiled at each other.

"But you are changing, Reyes, and people are going to notice. They did notice at the ball. Let me send you home with some candles that can calm you down. Camille can handle your food, and we can both make you salves. I knew a few shifters, some even married into my coven, but they were all pretty advanced at shifting. Still, maybe they can help."

"Thank you," he grumbled. "I imagine a puppy is a lot less to handle than some hulking monster."

Camille brought his hand to her lap and held it with both of hers. It was so soft and he knew he had calluses on his. He imagined his pads would be rough.

"I guess this explains my possessive streak with Cami too." He slowly brought his eyes to meet her.

"What?" Cami asked.

"I felt it in the bar when that prick touched you and when I learned about Leland—he still infuriates me. A bunch of other times too."

"That morning after the ball? You were a bit bitey," Cami mentioned then realized what she insinuated and blushed, glancing at Willow then back down. Willow just laughed.

"Fuck, all I thought was *mine*. My witch, my bakery girl. I'm not some possessive asshole. I swear."

"It's expected. Shifters are always a little rowdy." Willow laughed.

"Can you maybe ask them about the mindlink thing? I tried to set my intent to connect with him, but links connect two things." Cami laced her fingers through his.

He groaned again. "I remember you screaming my name and for Sitka, but I didn't know what was happening."

"What do you remember from being the wolf?" Willow asked, grabbing one of her notebooks to take notes.

He looked down at it then glanced at Camille. "Do all witches keep a lot of notebooks on everything?"

"Well, for me, my books and tomes are kind of all I have. I can't exactly access Thornwell's library anymore, so any knowledge I gained is going to be my library. I am teaching myself, too, now. I imagine since Willow is a bit far from her coven, her books are her knowledge base too."

"Sometimes I ask them to send me some books and I usually always swap some out when I visit. But, yes, similar situation to Camille. Now, what do you remember when you were the wolf? I know what happened when you woke up."

"My bones literally broke, and my muscles tore and reshaped themselves. All I could recall was that I couldn't move. I was so tired. I didn't feel the pain and I was warm. I felt like I was nodding off to sleep. Then I heard Cami screaming. Telling me I was going to wake up. To scent her, connect with her. I heard her but I couldn't move, I couldn't respond. Then I started to panic, I felt my heart rate pick up and then I was running, chasing Sitka, stumbling over everything. I'm not a good runner; I hate running. Obviously." He patted his gut. "Then the sounds and smells got too overwhelming. I couldn't focus on anything. I lost Sitka, and I finally was so tired with no idea what was happening. Then all I remember was scenting the bobcat—the faintest scent of pear and honey—before I passed out. I woke up, well, you know how Camille found me."

Willow noted all of that. "So it sounds as though you are somewhat aware until panic sets in, then you, the wolf, takes over you, the human. That's a start." She looked at Camille. "I wonder what would happen if you gave him a lot of calming or a sedative before the moon rises."

"Worth a shot?" Camille asked. "I just don't want to prevent his shift."

"I'd rather you did," Reyes said. "The safety enchantment works."

"Wait what?" Willow asked.

"I told you I made him a safety enchantment but this was ready to rip out of him when he went camping in Trinity. I never knew it would suppress a shift, though," Camille noted.

"I thought it just warded animals away and provided a buffer for bad weather?"

"When I took it, the pain went away and my body temperature went back to normal. My heart rate slowed down too."

He noticed Camille tilted her head as she stared off at nothing. "I think it did work, exactly as it needed to," she said then tensed and bit her lip sheepishly.

"How? Was he going to have a heart attack? I'm not sure I would consider that an external danger," Willow pondered.

"Think about it, he was with Evan and Seth. If his wolf ripped out of him on that trip, they wouldn't have known what to do. He wouldn't have had Sitka to lead him to safety or lead anyone to him."

Reyes deflated and slumped back in his chair. "So I was the danger. It protected them." He ran his hand down his face in despair. "Cami, you have to let me take it next month. Please?"

"I told you the more you suppress it now the more it's going to fight you. You have to learn how to balance it."

"That's true. The shifters in my coven spoke of their kind that fought their shifts for whatever reason. The animal got more aggressive. It made them aggressive, and it would always come out eventually. The only problem is it would suppress their human form longer and longer and eventually they lost their ability to shift back entirely, remaining in feral form," Willow explained.

"I don't want this," he whimpered. "I never asked for it."

"I'm sorry, Reyes. I...I didn't even realize how much damage I was doing," Camille sighed.

"For fuck's sake. Don't start that, Camille. You are not leaving and you still need to release your magic. I could have contributed to him shifting too," Willow said with clear annoyance. "You are staying put and you are going to continue running that bakery."

"You aren't really still thinking of leaving, are you?" Reyes asked worriedly. "This isn't your fault. What if after so many trips to Willow's shop, years from now, it happened when I was old. Alone. You'd really leave, after what you are to me?"

He noticed Willow sit back and cross her arms.

"And what is that?" she asked with a smug grin.

Reyes took Camille's hand again. She had let it go when she apologized. "My lifemate. Wolves mate for life."

They both looked at Camille. He felt her squeeze his hand. "If it keeps you safe," she said, not looking at either of them.

"It isn't going to keep him safe at all. He's going to follow you. This is your home. Stay. Now onto the next full moon, why not try at the cabin? Reyes has a bunch of land."

"I'm scared I'm too close to people, and I doubt my wolf knows what the property markers are. What if I run into town?"

"Well you obviously can't be out in the middle of nowhere by yourself. And you can't just take Sitka," Willow stated.

"What might happen if Camille took the safety enchantment on a full moon?" he asked.

"That is something to try I suppose," Willow suggested. "I can go camping with you I guess if you'd like next month. You should try at your cabin eventually. Let your wolf find it's den."

"I just don't want to hurt anyone. And I feel like Evan should be there but I don't want him to know. I don't want him to know I'm a monster or hurt him."

"I am a little hesitant of him knowing what I am, I take it he doesn't know what you are? You'd have told me, right?" Camille asked.

Willow uncrossed her arms. "No, he doesn't know what any of us are. He can't really be bothered with me anyways, it seems."

"What?" Reyes said, perplexed. "You guys went to the ball together. Sophia and Jodie certainly had some choice words to say about both him and me."

"Yeah well they had choice words about me too. At least Cami seemed safe from their annoyance. He apologized for Sophia's behavior and for ruining a friendship. I told him I wasn't really close with Sophia since she had moved and it didn't surprise me she moved halfway across the country. She only talked to me when she ordered from me. He hasn't said a word to me since the ball. As if he doesn't want me around either." Annoyance lined her tone.

Reyes went to tell Willow that Evan liked her and that Evan was being stupid, and that he didn't know how to play wingman like Evan did. But he stopped himself from speaking.

"Yes, I like Evan, I have since before he and Sophia split. Sorry if that makes me a shitty person. No I'd never have pursued him if she was still here."

"No. I...I wasn't going to say that. I don't think that. I noticed the gazes you two gave the other when the other wasn't looking. I may be an idiot when it comes to my own interests but I'm not blind. I had no idea he hasn't talked to you since then."

"How did the night end up?" Camille asked.

"After he apologized, he didn't say anything else. We drove in silence and when we got to my house, he wouldn't look at me. I asked if he was alright and of course he gave his bullshit smile saying he was fine. Said good night then unlocked the door. I took that as a hint and left. So he can stew in whatever he wants to."

Camille glanced at him. "Why would he do that? He isn't hung up on Sophia, is he? Willow looked stunning that night; he was lucky to be there with her."

"Cami, you and Willow had the entire room's attention. I couldn't believe I was the one you were with. But you are right, Evan was lucky as hell to walk in with Willow. I don't know why he did that. He isn't strung up on Sophia, I know that, he was actually relieved when the divorce papers came in. He talked about how he wouldn't have to hear about moving ever again. I don't know what's gotten into him."

"Well it doesn't matter what got into him, I don't need his dumb baggage. It's better this way. Honestly Reyes, I'm proud of you for getting her. You better smother her and not let her go. As disgustingly cute as you two are together."

He felt Cami tighten her grip on his hand. "I would love to," he replied.

"Good. Now, I am going to figure out what I can about shifting. I'm going to suggest a plan and Camille, please tell me your thoughts and suggestions. She and I will compile notes since this is new for both of us and we are building our libraries."

Reyes groaned as he listened to Willow's plans and when Camille had agreed to most of it, he felt as though he had no other choice. He could push back all night but he knew they were his best resource for now.

Chapter 29

Over the course of the month, Reyes and Camille spent a lot of time with each other. He helped her measure out enchantments and watched her make them. He would feel something stirring in him but it never did turn into that pain. She would stay at his place on some evenings and they would simply have dinner in his truck on others. Sometimes they would spend the evening separately but they always texted each other good night.

Camille knew he was nervous about shifting again, but they had made plans to camp on the full moon. She knew how to read the lunar phases and normally stayed on top of them. Since this full moon fell at the end of the week, Reyes requested the Thursday and Friday off and Camille closed the bakery. They checked in with Willow before they left and she sent them off with a sedation salve. Camille, too, had made sure to have more of the safety enchantment, as well as a lot of simple syrups to help Reyes before and after.

She had decided to get a small harness and pack for Sitka to at least offer Reyes clothes if he woke up like he did last time.

She clipped the pack on and Sitka let out a small sigh.

"You are going to need to adjust that in the winter. Bobcats plump up a lot," Reyes said, looking at the cat.

"We are going to need to make sure you can get back to the cabin. Or I need to get her a bigger pack. There is no way you can be out here in the snow."

He blew out a huge exhale. "Maybe the shock collar is going to be the best option then."

"You will just rip it off anyways."

"I know. Let's sit outside. May as well not destroy everything in this house," he groaned. They walked outside. "Keep the door open until I start to shift then run inside and lock it."

"Alright. Want to help me set up the calming circle?"

"Sure." He walked to an open spot in the yard. The house was similar to his and fed out onto federal land. No fence to get in the way, not that many would give him trouble.

Camille drew a large circle around them with a stick and they set about arranging some stones with rose petals, lemon balm, and stinging nettle spread between. All the while Camille set her intent as she dropped the petals and buds. She also had some mimosa flowers she had dried out from the spring. She watched as Reyes sprinkled the simple syrup of lavender on top of the petals.

Sitka sat nearby but remained outside of the circle.

Once they were seated facing each other, Camille began to massage a salve into his temples that Willow had made with valerian root and skullcap. She could see him exhale slowly and his eyes grow heavy. When she was done, she placed the lid back on the tin and set it down. Placing her hands on the crook of his neck, she pressed her forehead to him and set her intention outward silently.

"Come back to me tonight, Reyes," she spoke softly.

"I want to. I want to, so badly." His voice was low and held a hint of tension. "I imagine something like this would make a pretty wedding circle, with flowers in your hair." His voice held a longing.

"Come back to me, to this circle. I want to curl up with my wolf under the stars next summer. In the shadow of the mountain," she whispered softly.

"We will. My lifemate," he said.

She pressed her lips to his and he pressed into her.

His body grew tense and she opened her eyes, seeing the moonlight form around them. He pushed her away.

"Go. Inside." His voice was strained.

She sat there for a moment longer until he growled it out and glared at her.

"Come back to me," she said one more time then got up. When she was on the deck, she watched him strain and groan once more. It looked just as painful as before but it was faster.

It took him far less time to get to his paws and growl. He spun around and snarled at her. Yet as the wolf heaved in air, it didn't leave the circle. Though after a few moments, he did take a step forward and his paws broke the circle.

This time his growl was nearly a bark as he snapped his maw towards her. Camille slid the door shut and watched in horror once more as Sitka jumped on his back and scruffed him. Before he could roll her off, she jumped and ran towards the forest. The wolf bounded after the bobcat.

"Please. Please keep them safe," she begged and wiped her eyes as she sank to her knees. Eventually, she picked herself back up and opened the kitchen window for Sitka. Camille wouldn't have minded if she stayed all night with Reyes. She really didn't like the thought of him out there by himself in either form.

She made herself some chai and after adding two drops of a calming enchantment, she sat on the couch and stared into her tea for a while, not even taking a sip. *Let them be safe,* she whispered a silent prayer in her head. She was just so desperate for him to come back, to not have to endure a night like last time. Her eyes took in the house they rented. It was all foreign. Plenty of people have passed through here before. There was no familiar scent or affects of Reyes or herself here. Her familiar was not here either. She was alone.

It would be like this if you left. It would be worse for them if Thornwell came for you. If your lifemate fought for you. She finally took a sip of the tea, feeling the enchantment working. "It would be worse for him to do this alone." Sitka might not bond to him. It wasn't Willow's responsibility. Was it hers, though?

"Of course it's your responsibility," she muttered to herself. "You chose this place." She took another sip and looked out at the sliding glass door. It was dark, and she watched her reflection. "And this place sure as hell chose you. Keep him safe."

With a deep breath in and out, she grabbed her notebook and started writing down what had happened. How part of her hoped that her scent would linger with his wolf, that maybe, just maybe he would find his way back to the circle. That he would find his way back to the yard. What she really wanted to see was the wolf sitting outside, calm and ready to try to communicate with her.

But she knew that was all wishful thinking. It was going to take time. She would recount his words tomorrow. So, she set her pen and notebook down and finished her tea, pleading again that they would be safe.

Tiredness hit her hard and before she realized it, she passed out on the couch, not even making it to the bedroom or pulling the blanket higher than her waist.

She woke up the next morning and saw the light through the windows. Sitka slept on top of the couch cushion. It took Camille a moment to comprehend she was on a couch in an unfamiliar home. The moment the recollection hit her, she shot up, startling Sitka. She saw that Sitka didn't have the harness on.

"Where is he?" she pleaded. Sitka purred and Camille looked to the window to see Reyes face down on the circle. He was wearing a shirt and athletic shorts.

She rushed outside, not even bothering to put shoes on.

"Reyes!" she cried out.

"I hurt." His body shivered with his whimper of words. He finally opened his eyes and looked at her.

"Come inside. I will make food then you can shower and sleep. Or just sleep."

Reyes pushed himself up and went to stand up with her but hissed and fell hard on his knees. "My feet. I changed and walked back part way. I dunno how many miles. Sitka led me back. I woke up with her next to me just as the morning light was breaking."

Camille looked down and saw the bottom of his feet. His boots were too heavy and clunky for Sitka to run with. "Should I tend to them out here and bring your boots?"

With a frustrated sigh, he pushed himself up once more. "Not in the dirt."

"At least rinse them outside. The hose is there. I will get your boots and you can go into the bathroom or the kitchen."

All he could do was nod and wince with every painful step as he leaned on her. When he finally arrived in the bathroom, he nearly collapsed in the shower. "I hate that you are even doing this. But I'm so grateful for you," he muttered as she began to shampoo his hair.

"I want to though."

"I know. Thank you. Did you sleep? You are in the same clothes as yesterday."

"I think all the calming tinctures made me tired. I passed out on the couch."

"Was it comfortable?" he asked.

Watching the soapy water run into the drain, Camille moved the detachable shower head across his shoulders and chest.

"Kind of."

He laughed. "Nap with me?"

"I will after you eat," she said, and began to gently tend to his feet.

Reyes headed back to work on Monday after the long weekend. His feet were still sore and had small cuts. Getting up to his room at home had proven troublesome the first day back.

"Why are you limping?" Evan asked near the end of the day.

"Overdid it this weekend," he muttered.

"Doing what? Trekking to the top of Shasta?"

"Sure." Reyes didn't want to have this conversation. He didn't know how to cover it up. Not only that but he felt bad for excluding Evan. Willow had come over to his place on Saturday when they got back to compare notes. Her coven didn't have much other than confirming it was the worst thing possible for a shifter to suppress their feral form.

It didn't help that her coven was now asking if she had a shifter she was talking to. He got the sense her coven meant well but could hover a lot. He couldn't blame them. She had been by herself here, until Cami had showed up.

He wondered if Evan would even care if the three of them had hung out.

"You went camping this weekend?" Evan asked.

"Yeah. Marble Mountain area. Cami hadn't been."

"Cool. Was she alright?" Evan asked, taking a sip of his coffee.

"Yes. Luckily. She tended to my injuries," Reyes replied, not looking up from his computer.

"Did you overdo it on a hike? Or what happened?"

"Yes."

"Well, lucky guy to have her take care of you."

Reyes looked up at Evan now and took in his same carefree attitude. He shook his head in frustration. "What are you doing?"

"What?" Evan asked.

"Why haven't you talked to Willow?"

Evan sighed. "This again?"

"Yes, this again. You two were the talk of the night and you just left her hanging. Come on. You thought I was a dumb ass for not pursuing Camille and honestly she's so far out of my league, but you and Willow? Sophia is gone. Willow said they hardly talked after she moved. They clearly were not best friends."

"How do you know so much about Willow all of a sudden? You make it sound like you are hanging out with her."

"Maybe I am?" Reyes said, not missing Evan's glare for a second before he relaxed.

"Because of Cami."

"Maybe I will see if she wants to go camping with Cami and me next time." Reyes knew he wouldn't, he wouldn't dare put Willow in that position, nor did he want her to see him like that, ever. He already felt embarrassed enough the morning after the full moon.

"Shut up. Whatever you are trying to insinuate, I know you, Reyes. You had all year to pursue Willow yet you never did, then Cami showed up and you're obsessed with her."

"You're right. I'd do anything for Cami. But I don't know why you are not pursuing Willow."

"Because I'm not going to end up in another situation like I'm in now. Sophia gets half my retirement. I'm still fighting for the house that I bought and put so much work into. You put work into it," Evan said.

"You think Willow is going to do half of what Sophia did? It's not like you have to ask her to marry you. Just talk to her at least. What is your hold up? Mine was that I'm a disgusting slob who can't pick up after himself. Cami is like this perfect little spring nymph. That's why I was scared to pursue her. You know Willow though. She knows you," Reyes urged.

"Yeah and I don't want to fuck it up with Willow, because then it's awkward for Cami and you. You never wanted to come over when Jodie was staying with us, and I get it. The fireman's ball felt too good to be true. Willow was gorgeous in that dress. But she's Willow, the strong single bombshell that screams independent. Plus, Sophia is already making the divorce hell. I don't want Willow getting more mixed up in it, no thanks." Evan groaned and put his hands over his face, leaning back in his chair.

"Did it ever occur to you that she doesn't want to remain single forever? And she can still be independent while in a relationship. She runs her own business, just like Cami. They both do it all on their own."

"I'm just not ready. I don't want to mess anything up."

"That's fine if you aren't ready but tell her that. Don't leave her hanging. You are messing it up by not talking to her. Camille isn't Jodie and Willow isn't Sophia. They are different."

"You are different, too, you know. You sit up straighter, you are more assertive. More confident. I guess getting laid by a cute little thing like Cami will do that for a guy."

Reyes felt something in him stir and his eyes narrowed on Evan. Something in his head screamed *mine* like some animal. Like a dog with food aggression had been given a treat. His lifemate. Of course Reyes was acting like a territorial dog. He was one.

"Yeah, you have definitely changed. I will make an attempt to talk to Willow." Evan sighed and held his hand out. "Truce?"

Reyes sighed and took his friend's hand in a firm shake. "Truce. You can be a real dick sometimes, ya know?"

"Apparently you can, too, now."

They laughed at that, but Reyes wondered if anyone else noticed the change. One more thing he would have to ask Cami and Willow about.

Chapter 30

Two weeks later, Reyes checked his daily tasks on his dashboard. He scrolled through it like normal. The name near the bottom of the case list caught his eye.

Bakewell's.

It was in a red font, which only meant one thing.

He gasped and leaned closer to the screen, reading the closure notice.

"No," he said as he clicked on frantically and saw the image of the notice and the scan of the form. Yet the signature wasn't anyone's he recognized. He read the reasoning. Nearly every offense. Noticeable pests, unsanitary bathrooms, food contamination risks, overall the establishment appeared dirty. "What the fuck is this?" he rasped out. He had just been there yesterday. He had been going in nearly every business day. He had seen none of those things and knew Camille was doing what she needed to.

Yet there was no mention of Sitka. No mention of a bobcat, and that couldn't be considered a pest by the county standards anyways.

"No. No. No!" He started to panic, trying to fight it. His co-workers looked over at him with concern.

"What's wrong?" Evan asked, looking up from his computer.

"Fuck!" he cried out and leaped out of his seat. Reyes stormed right into his boss's office. "Open up the closure notices now!"

"Reyes? What has gotten into you?"

"There's been a huge mistake."

His boss stared at him for a moment, then looked at the computer. His head tilted to the side.

"Oh. The bakery. Is there a conflict of interest? You two are quite the pair, but if it impedes your job, I might have to take you off that account."

"There is no conflict of interest! I'm there nearly every day, it's immaculate. I was in there yesterday and you mean to tell me she let it go to absolute shit in less than twenty-four hours, when she was with me for a portion of them? Go in there and see for yourself," Reyes demanded.

"Calm down," his boss insisted. "I will have to get Josh to do an inspection, I guess. You can't separate yourself from it now."

"Whose signature is that? What kind of ID code even is that? Seven zeroes? It's supposed to be eight characters. Three numbers, the letter S, three numbers and either a J or R for Josh or me. Who did this inspection and when?" Reyes was nearly hyperventilating.

His boss looked at it and squinted his eyes in confusion. "Huh, I don't recognize that signature, the code must have been a glitch," he explained, picking up the phone to call Josh in the office.

Reyes looked back and saw everyone staring at him through the door he hadn't shut. When Josh walked in, Reyes got right in his face, causing him to stumble back. "Did you do that?"

"Whoa, calm down. Do what?"

"Get Cami's bakery shut down?" Reyes was breathing hard and he could feel his wolf rattling in the cage of bones it remained locked in.

"What? No, it's your account to handle. I was there last weekend with my son. It looked fine. I didn't even see the bobcat, which my son was pretty bummed about by the way," Josh said.

"Reyes, sit down or I'm going to have to take disciplinary action! We will figure it out. What has gotten into you?"

"Cami worked way too hard to get that bakery, she deserves to keep it. She wants to stay here. If she doesn't have the bakery..." he trailed off, feeling his eyes well up.

"Just reverse the closure," Josh said. "It must have been a glitch. Our system is ancient, maybe someone typed an account number wrong? And you really think you aren't worth her staying?" Josh asked, somewhat shocked.

Reyes cut his eyes down, not wanting to admit the truth. He had never thought about it until now but why would she stay in here if she couldn't run the bakery? She might even leave the state.

"This form is filled out for Bakewell's. And the notice went out already," his boss noted.

"No!" Reyes cried out. "Reverse it! Please. Evan can tell you how clean the place is. Anyone else can. Give Josh the account and let him do the inspection, I don't care. Just reverse it!" Reyes was nearly pleading.

"It's going to take a few days. We have to figure out how this even got submitted. This is a security risk. What if our payroll system or other offices are compromised? The folks down in Sacramento would have a fit," his boss explained.

"Just reverse it. Let me print the letter so I can at least give her proof if she's opened the letter. If not, I will shred it and no harm no foul," Reyes urged.

"I can't just bend the rules like that. I have to get clearance for that. The notice went out. It's hard to just reverse once that letter has gone out. You know these things, Reyes."

"Please!"

His boss sighed. "Alright, let me make a few phone calls and I will let you know when the notice is drafted and this is reversed. Josh, the account is on your workload now. Go take your break, Reyes. You need to calm down."

Reyes jumped up and ran out of the office, bursting through the doors to the stairs. Never before had he reached the bottom of them so fast. He ran to her bakery and pushed the door open.

"Camille!" he called out then heard her whimper in her office. Knowing she was in distress sent him running right for her.

"You? You didn't do this, did you?" she cried, clutching the paper.

He could see the big letters across the top, saying notice in all caps on the crumbled paper in her hand. "No," he said with reverence then closed the distance between them and pulled her into a tight hug. "I promise you I didn't. I nearly tackled the other health inspector in the office, but the form doesn't have either one of our signatures."

He began to explain the exchange he just had in the office. "My boss is reversing it. I promise you I will get that letter as proof. You are not shut down. Please, Cami, don't leave. Please stay," he begged as he pressed his lips to her head and held her tightly as if she would run away.

"I want to."

"Stay. It will take about two days max to get the letter. In the meantime, stay with me, hell, move in with me. Please?" he urged. He wasn't sure why his wolf was feeling so anxious, or maybe it was him making the wolf anxious.

"I can't stay open?" she asked and he could hear the tremor in her voice.

"The city got the notice too. I don't want them to fine you. Admittedly, I made a big scene in the office when I saw Bakewell's on the list of closures. Please stay with me." He was hurt that she hadn't accepted his offer. What if she didn't, what if she left in two days? The reversal letter would come and she would be gone.

They hadn't said they loved each other yet. Reyes was too nervous to, and she hadn't for her own reasons that he didn't understand but would not push. But they had shown it plenty, he knew they had. He had said she was his lifemate, and she had done so much to help him with this wolf shifting. She had taken care of him. He knew he loved her.

"Cami, we will work this out, I promise." His heart was thundering in his chest and he had no doubt she could feel it. *Now or never, you dumbass, say it.* "I love you."

She let out another whimper then grabbed him tight. Reyes wanted to hear her say it. It made him more nervous that she hadn't. He would never push her or prod but why hadn't she said it back? What if she didn't love him? What if she didn't believe him?

"Say something. Please."

"I-I need some time," she said and he gripped her tighter.

"Please stay. This will all be alright, two days tops. I promise. Please?"

"That's a big step. I might not have income," she whimpered.

"I'm ready for that step and this will save you money. I can understand if you aren't ready but at least stay with me until you can reopen," he pleaded and rubbed her back.

"Reyes," she cried and buried her face into his chest.

"Please, let me fix this for you. I know the bakery is your livelihood, I want it to be forever. But I want to be something you'd stay for too. I want you to stay."

She pulled back and he was reluctant to give her any space but did. He met her glossy eyes.

"Is that what you are afraid of, that I am only staying for the bakery?"

"And Willow, and that you like it here. You have a million reasons to stay, but I want to be one of them too."

"You're a major reason this place feels like home, but if I'm not running the bakery, then, I will fret too much. How am I going to release my magic?"

"Make more enchantments, bake in my kitchen. Work with Willow. What did you do before the bakery opened?"

She took a deep inhale. "Alright."

"Alright?" He looked at her curiously.

"I will stay with you. Tonight. I need to think about tomorrow night and I need to think about moving in with you."

It wasn't the answer he had hoped for, but he would take it for now. "Take as long as you need to think about it, just don't leave. Take my keys and let yourself into my cabin. Bring as much or as little as you want. As soon as I have the proof of reversal, I will give it to you."

"Alright." She sniffed and wiped her eyes. "Can Sitka stay?"

"Of course she can. You know this by now. I can take the rest of the day off. I'm sure my boss would prefer I did." A small frantic chuckle escaped him.

"Don't. I'm going to pack some of my books and the enchantment stuff up then I will go to your place."

"Thank you." He kissed her, pressing hard in case it was his last one. "You believe me right? That I had nothing to do with this?"

"Yes."

"Good. Make yourself at home. Order whatever you want for food. I will text you my laptop password."

"Alright. Thank you, Reyes."

He kissed her one more time because he could not deny that while she said she would be there when he got home, she hadn't said it back and she could still use the next few hours to pack up and leave. The thought of it hurt him. Losing his lifemate would hurt him. With an exhale, he pulled away, realizing how overbearing he was being. It was absurd. Smothering her was not what he wanted to do. Especially not right now. However, what he would do was get the bakery back open.

Chapter 31

After Reyes left, all she could do was stand there for a moment.

Closed. She had to close the bakery. No one knew how that form ended up in the system yet Camille had a bad feeling. *It can't be Thornwell.*

Her eyes wandered to the clock on the wall. It was two hours earlier than she would be closing. The lunch rush had just finished and she had a moment to look at the mail. The feeling in her heart ached deeply when she had read the notice. Then as if he was summoned by her distress, Reyes was there.

He loved her. He said he loved her and she hadn't said it back.

She wanted to. So badly. Hearing him say it sent a sense of warmth through her she had never imagined feeling. So she had gripped him tighter because saying it back would only doom him later.

"Stupid. Stupid, stupid girl. It hurt him to not say it. You got in too deep with him, and if you have to leave, it's going to rip his heart out," she muttered to herself. She knew how deeply he loved, especially with his wolf now. He declared it and it would take more force than Mt. Shasta had to break it. She needed to say it back to him but how could she? The intent was so strong between them. The words meant little to them but it meant everything to this place. It put it into existence for every tree, star, animal, and rock around them. The earth could feel their bond, no doubt Mt. Shasta had watched the entire thing unfold. But saying it spoke it to the wind and the currents.

Camille knew all of this, but she was still clinging to hope that he would be safe if anyone came for her. So she hadn't said it back. She had made a choice for him. Let him question her feelings or let him risk Thornwell's wrath.

She wiped her eyes, pressing hard enough to leave her skin red and heated.

Finally with a step forward, she forced herself to lock the door and flip the closed sign over. She grabbed a box and put her books in it and the small cauldron. These were the items that would be the most difficult to replace if she lost them. Her books were everything now.

Betrayer. The damning thought repeated in her head. Her eyes welled up again and it was getting too overwhelming.

Betrayer. Outcast. Wasteful wretched little girl.

She sank to her knees and wiped her eyes again. Soft fur brushed against her arm and Camille sobbed again, pulling Sitka into a hug.

"I'm so sorry, Sitka. I'm so sorry I put you all in this position."

The small rumble of Sitka's purr prompted her to take a deep breath. It gave her some reassurance that it would be alright. That Willow, Reyes, and Sitka would be there for her.

That thought too made her almost angry. She didn't deserve any of them.

She could sit here for hours until Reyes carried her to the cabin, or she could give him that small reassurance she was alright. Even if she was terrified.

Camille forced herself up and got the box loaded into the car. There were still things that would go bad if left out. Probably attract those pests and make the whole place unsanitary but she just didn't have it in her right now to handle it. She walked into Willow's shop and hung out in the back until the customers left before she made herself known.

Willow walked back to the office and looked at her.

Camille's throat hurt as she wiped her eyes.

"What's wrong?" Willow asked slowly, walking forward.

"The bakery got shut down. Health code violations."

"What? No! How? Reyes knows you follow the rules, he can't possibly have a problem with Sitka now? Hell, he is a violation now too."

"He says he didn't do it; he's trying everything he can to reverse it." Camille met Willow's eyes. "He...he told me he loved me, asked me to move in with him and I'm scared for him."

Willow pulled Camille into a hug and sat her down on a bench. "Shhh, it will be alright. He wants to help. Let him."

"I didn't say it back to him."

"I cannot imagine the amount of pressure you feel given everything, but let him take care of you. He wants to fight for you."

"It's only going to hurt him."

"It's only going to hurt him if you reject him and I know you don't want to. I know how you feel about him. It's clear as day. Say the words back to him. Relax at the cabin; call me if you need anything. But if I know Reyes, he is going to be there too," Willow said.

Camille nodded and clutched his key. After one more hug from Willow, she and Sitka were on their way to the cabin.

It was her first time being over here without him and it felt weird. She unlocked the door and pushed it open, letting Sitka trot in first. Instantly, the familiar woodsy scent of this place reached her, drawing her eyes to the mountain.

Home. The thought made tears well up all over again and just as she was going to crumble back to her knees at how overwhelmed she felt, her phone buzzed.

Reyes: Thank you, Cami, just relax. I'm doing everything I can, and making my boss do everything he can. I will be home in two hours.

Moments later, another text came through.

> Reyes: I'm not watching you btw, I hope you don't think I am. I just got the notification that the front door opened and deactivated the alarm system for you.

Camille smiled and wiped her eyes again at Reyes's text. How could she not have said it to him? She knew she did. Everyone and everything out there knew it. Except for him, he would question it. That was what past demons did, they made you fret that the most obvious things weren't real.

Her past demons wanted to rip her away from this place. Someone wanted to rip the bakery away from her. Just as her mind went to who it could be, she felt another vibration from her phone.

> Reyes: I hope you are alright. Laptop password is the same as the network. 7ruckD4ddy@5hasta

> Reyes: I will explain later.

A laugh slipped out of Camille at seeing the password. That was the last thing she expected from him.

> Camille: That password. And thank you, Reyes. I feel safe here.

She let her eyes roam the cabin. It was quiet. Small piles of things had been left out, the kind of clutter she was used to seeing. The microwave door had been left open. And the lid was left off the jar of peanut butter. She wondered if he had been in a hurry this morning or if this was normal for him. He'd always said he made attempts to clean before she came over.

Anxiousness was getting the best of her and she started to clean the kitchen. She grabbed the box from her car and tried to find a space for the things but felt really weird about putting things here, so she ended up setting it down in a corner, out of the way. Eventually, she turned the TV on and zoned out, getting lost in her anxiousness. The tears came between fitful naps.

Camille was curled up on the couch, staring at the floor, running her hand along Sitka's soft fur when she heard the door open. She hadn't even heard the truck. Realization dawned on her—she hadn't changed out of her dress; she didn't even have clothes. She hadn't been in the habit of leaving any here. *How did that make him feel? Your lifemate. If you stay in this cabin at least you will be hidden?*

Tears welled up in her eyes again.

"Cami?" Reyes asked. She heard his keys being tossed down then his hurried steps. Before she knew it, he was kneeling in front of her. "Talk to me please? I didn't want to keep texting you and sound overbearing, but I'm home now and all yours for the night."

"I feel so overwhelmed and it's hurting you, but I don't know what to do. I'm scared," she wept, looking away.

She felt him sit next to her and pull her into a hug. Much like she had done for him after his first shift.

"It will be alright. You are safe, and I'm working on getting the bakery open again. My boss pulled me off your account but my coworker is cool. He loves that place too. As soon as the reversal goes through, Josh will do a new inspection and you will pass and all will go back to normal," he comforted her while rubbing her back.

"I...I didn't know where to put my things, and I didn't even have a change of clothes."

"Wear mine. I have plenty of things you can wear. Put your things anywhere you like. I will clear some shelf space. I need to clear it off anyways."

"Okay, I can help, if you like. I felt anxious and cleaned the kitchen up."

"I saw. Thank you, but please don't ever feel as though you have to. I'm going to try my damndest to be better about that. Especially if you are here."

"I want to be, Reyes." She grabbed him tightly, grasping onto his flannel.

"Then you should." He pressed a kiss to her head. "I'm never going to force you into anything. Not even this lifemate thing if you don't want it. But just know I meant everything I said today. I hope you continue to feel the same about me as you always have."

"When I moved here, I had the bakery to prepare for. Finding the location, the renovations, the permits, the health inspection. Going hiking or tutoring Willow was a nice distraction. It felt good to decompress that way, but now, I just feel lost. And it feels like such a shitty thing to say because you and Willow want to be there for me, but I lied to you both for so long. I bonded with Sitka and she could be hurt too. You're all here for me and I'm just a betrayer, a wretched little spoiled brat."

"Camille." Reyes pulled away. "You fled for your life. Your freedom. You made something of yourself. That's not being spoiled, that's being successful, for having a dream and going for it. You didn't lie either. Between Bakewell and Thornwell, Bakewell sounds a little more inviting for a bakery, no offense."

"You won't offend me by saying anything about Thornwell. I did lie though."

"You followed the rules to protect yourself. People omit things all the time and you had a valid reason to keep your magic secret. We all chose you. Willow, Sitka, and I. Even after learning the truth, which you admitted to, we still choose you. So stay, please. You can be scared. I'm still scared shitless of the wolf and every full moon. But I know I have you here and I feel safer. I'm glad you feel safe in the cabin. If you want it to be, it's your home. Contribute however you can."

"Thank you." Camille wiped her eyes with her hand and finally met his concerned gaze. "I will inform the leasing office tomorrow and pack up my cabin. I need to clean the bakery up too. I tried today but I just couldn't look at it anymore."

"Would you like help? That sounds like a lot. I can go in late or leave early tomorrow?"

"No, I will be alright. I think I need closure. I want to be ready to take this to the next level. We started something and now, I think, I'm ready to let it thrive."

Reyes smiled wide. "I'm so happy to hear that, Camille. Welcome home. You will be able to sleep in a little later. Like I said, Josh is a good guy and he knows your bakery is an easy account to manage. It's still my account until it is opened again, so I'm pouring everything I have into it."

"Thank you, Reyes," Camille said, letting out a big exhale and releasing all the tension she had been holding onto.

"Have you eaten?"

"No," she lamented.

"Let's go upstairs and get into something comfortable. Whatever you like, even if it's naked. I will turn the heat up if I have to." He laughed. "I will get some cleaning done, and then start on dinner, alright?"

She laughed, too, and kissed him before nodding. They got changed and she felt ridiculous in a pair of his athletic shorts, T-shirt, and flannel but it was comfortable.

Camille finally felt she could relax as she and Reyes set to clearing space for her books before cooking dinner together. The dread still sat with her about the future of everyone's safety but she wanted this place so badly. Tonight was a glimpse into a future she could have, with Reyes, in his cabin. Their cabin. Her lifemate.

"Your password is the last thing I would have expected from you," Camille noted. It was the first piece of random conversation she had said all day.

Reyes let out a chuckle. "It was a randomly generated one before. When Jodie moved out, I changed everything. I set it to everything she hated about me. I'm not getting rid of the truck or leaving Shasta without a real good reason." He glanced over at her.

"Well, then I suppose it is a very fitting password. I'm not a good reason to do those things either. I don't want you to do those things," she stated then put the last of her notebooks on the shelf.

"I know, it's why I know you are a good reason if it ever needed to happen."

"Reyes." She frowned.

He walked over to her and she felt his arms wrap around her waist. "This is our home though. You are safe. Whoever filled out that form will have hell to pay. It's not just a threat against you, it's a security risk for the county, maybe even the state."

"So your office doesn't have any idea how it got there?" Camille asked, sliding her fingers under his shirt.

"No. That ID code has us all confused. It's not even enough digits to be a placeholder. We don't do those. My first inspection when I started had my code on it. I wondered if it was the deli owner before, but he left town a year before you submitted the application for the bakery. Someone tried to open a bar in that spot six months ago but it fell through. So I doubt it was a previous tenant. I had Evan look that up. He's ready to throw down right alongside me too." He laughed.

Camille hugged him tightly. "I guess I can't expect everyone to like my stuff." She tried to laugh but again her throat hurt.

"That doesn't give anyone the authority to get your business shut down or hack into the county system. It will be open in one day. I'm confident the letter will go through tomorrow and you can reopen the next. Like I said, I will print it and give it to you as soon as it hits our system, but it will be mailed for a paper trail of course. The city will see it as soon as it publishes to our system."

"Alright, thank you for working so hard on this, Reyes."

"I'm just glad I can be of use for once. You have done so much to help me. I want to help you. Let's get some rest. I want to take care of you." Reyes pulled her closer into him and started kissing her neck. "If you want me to, of course."

"I'd like that, Reyes."

Chapter 32

As Camille went about her day, she couldn't shake the lingering tension.

Reyes had asked if she was sure she was alright to take care of stuff today. He had offered again to leave early or go in late, and have his boss call him when the account was cleared and he had the reinstatement letter in hand.

But she declined. She wanted to do this, wanted to be ready. The leasing office wouldn't open for a few more hours and she really didn't have much to pack in the cabin. Clothes and some books and small things. She would clean the cabin as best she could too.

Since she had time to kill, she set to cleaning up after breakfast and straightening up around the house. It still felt weird that she would be living here with him now. Some sort of anxious tension simmered inside her, but she was also excited about it. He wanted to build a life with her. He wanted his lifemate here. He was her lifemate.

She recalled the conversation they had this morning before he left.

"You don't have to jump right back into opening back up, but I imagine you are antsy. Call me at any point if you decide you need help, alright? If you need any money to cover the remainder of the cabin, let me know and I will get it."

"I will be fine. You offering me a place to stay is more than enough."

She tensed for a moment upon hearing him sigh. "Cami, this isn't me offering you a charity case. This is me asking you to move in with me, to build a life together. I'm ready to pursue it with you. I want to."

She took his hand and looked at him. "I know, I want to too. I want to be ready to embrace it fully, to say it."

He grinned. "Then I will see you this evening. Where I will really claim you as mine, lifemate." Reyes kissed her and eventually she saw him off. After his truck was out of view, she felt sadness creep in and she wasn't sure why.

Should I have said it? He could have gone to work hearing it. I will say it tonight over dinner. She had decided it last night as she lay there awake next to him. It had taken her a while to fall asleep as she went over everything she needed to do. She needed to clean the cabin out, and the bakery.

Now though as she thought about it, maybe she didn't need to reopen tomorrow. She could reopen for the weekend. Or even the following week. They could spend time putting her things away here. There would be time.

So she started cleaning up the kitchen and doing things around his cabin. After changing back into her dress and closing the door for Sitka, who was in the back seat, she drove to Duinsmuir and packed her things.

Since it had taken some time for her to actually get started, she had just barely made it into the leasing office in time to inform them she was moving out and the place had been emptied of everything.

They wished her well and she took care of the final bill, not wanting to ask Reyes for any help with it. She would just put in more time at the bakery. Maybe she would be open on Sunday or Monday to make up for it. Not wanting to leave all her stuff in the car since she knew she would be bringing home some things from the bakery, she went back to Reyes's cabin and unpacked her clothes. He insisted on giving her closet and drawer space so she decided if this was home, she should settle in. When Reyes came home, she realized how late it was. She had tried baking something and reorganizing the counter while things were in the oven.

Her mind had just been so anxious that she wanted to focus on something. It had been the first time she hadn't made any enchantments in nearly two days. The last time was when she moved here and she had the road to focus on.

She froze. "Oh, I just realized the time. I got distracted."

"It's alright, there's time," he said, giving her a hug and a kiss.

"I need to clean the bakery out. Stuff is spoiling. It looks horrible and the enchantments aren't going to last till tomorrow. And if I'm getting another inspection—"

"Hey, it will be alright. Take care of it tomorrow. Unfortunately, we didn't manage to get the account reinstated. The tech department can't figure out how the notice even got in the system so it's now elevated to a security risk." He frowned and pulled her close. "I pretty much demanded my boss to reverse it and he said he would push it through first thing in the morning. I'm sorry. I did everything I could today short of forging documents."

"I believe you, Reyes," she said, hugging him tighter. "I still want to go tonight. There's things I don't want left there any longer."

"You don't have to go tonight. It will be safe."

"I'd feel better if I just took care of it. I didn't want to leave a bunch of stuff sitting in my car so I came back here after leaving the cabin. Can I just go take care of it?"

"You don't need to ask me to go do stuff. Can I go with you?"

"It isn't going to be long. I just need to toss things and grab stuff out of the office. You have worked hard all day."

"You aren't going to leave, are you?" He looked her in the eyes.

"No I'm not. I don't want to. It just feels like the closure I need. I will take care of it then we can make dinner?" she asked, feeling good about the future. She was ready to do this.

"How long do you need tonight?" Reyes sounded apprehensive.

"Maybe an hour or two at most."

"If you are not back in two hours, I'm driving to the bakery. I'm not going to relax until you are back here."

"Two hours tops. I will be back before then."

Camille felt good about things. The intention to begin the next chapter, and a place she wanted to call home.

Once she reached town, she parked on the street in front of the bakery since everything on Main Street was closed. It was after dark and hardly any cars were around. She got out and Sitka followed on her heels, remaining close. Once inside, she began the process of figuring out what was salvageable and tossing what wasn't in a trash bag she would dump out back.

Then she noticed Sitka start to pace and had a bad gut feeling about it.

Just grab what you need and go, she told herself, dropping the bag and turning towards the office. Hastily, she took her phone out in case she needed to call Reyes.

Just as she had his number pulled up, Sitka's growl snared her attention to the front and the windows to the bakery shattered into thousands of small pieces as a shockwave hit them. Sitka fled back towards Camille and arched her back with a hiss.

Camille saw the four cloaked figures walk in. The wave of energy they sent throughout the shop shook everything and pushed her and Sitka back into the desk, knocking all the vials down onto them both.

"Stop!" she cried out.

Then she heard the ringing and noticed her fingers had hit the call button. She gasped in terror and stared at the four familiar cloaks walking towards her. "No!" she screamed.

It hardly rang before he picked up. "Cami?" His voice was panicked.

She couldn't speak when she saw the figures part, revealing her parents standing there with anger burning in their eyes.

"Stupid little insolate waste," her mother seethed.

"Please. I'm sorry," Camille cried, forgetting entirely about Reyes at the sight of them.

"Destroy this. All of it," her father said with nonchalance.

"Cami?" Reyes asked through the phone, sounding worried.

Then the four coven officials began knocking down the cases, pulling the shelves down.

"Please," Camille begged. "Please stop."

"It's time you return home. We need to see if you're salvageable still," her mother hissed and approached her.

As she went to grab her, Sitka leapt and bit her hand. Camille dropped her phone, forgetting all about it.

Camille watched in horror as her mother slammed Sitka against the case of thin drawers for drying herbs and the cat fell limp to the ground. The screech of pain ripped a cry from her lips. "Sitka," she sobbed and dropped the phone and knelt beside her. "No. No. Please. Stop."

"Your familiar is equally as pathetic as you," her father said then looked over at the other officials. "Ensure it's dead."

"Please don't! I will go with you, just leave Sitka alone. Please. Please! I will break the bond."

Camille noticed the light on the phone go off. The call had ended and something in her heart shattered. She knew he was probably firing up his truck right now. She had to leave before he got here.

She screamed out a cry and grabbed a shard of glass. Sitka's eyes were nearly pleading with her to not break their bond but she was out of time.

Reyes would be here and she had known it would come to this. She had always known it.

She sliced her palm open and dripped blood over Sitka's blood. The bobcat hissed in defiance.

"I'm so sorry. Keep him safe please," she said softly then she dragged her fingers through the blood, breaking the bond and causing her and Sitka to cry out in pain.

With tears in her eyes, she stood and looked at her parents. "We have to leave before the alarm company sends someone," Camille stated through tears.

"At least you're not completely stupid," her mother hissed out. "Grab her and let's go." Camille got out and walked behind her mother so the men would not grab her. They followed close behind.

With every step she took, thoughts of what her life would be like now came to her. She hadn't told Reyes she loved him. She hadn't realized she lied to him tonight. She was leaving, leaving this place that chose her. These souls that chose her. She was leaving her familiar and her lifemate.

Only it wasn't what she wanted. She didn't want to leave. She was going to lose Thornwell either as a Talbot or a betrayer.

Leland would be waiting for her. The academy would be waiting for her, full of wealth and elitism that she would have to teach if she had a job. She realized she wouldn't be going back to a teaching job. She would be scorned, ridiculed. Her mother had already started that with the insults and destroying the bakery. She would never see Mt. Shasta again. She knew it was waiting for her; it was watching Reyes drive over here.

Fear struck her right in the spine and the impulse to run scratched at her. So she did. She fled through the streets and towards the mountain. The moment she ran, she felt the breeze against her back as if it were pushing her towards the mountain. The mountain that chose her, that was her home.

As soon as she was in a meadow, she was tackled down by one of the officials. Setting her intent and staring at that mountain, she took a deep inhale and pulled what she could from the soil and broke free from her captor. Until she felt a suffocating force engulf her.

"Let her go!" Reyes growled.

She watched the mountain stare back at her and in that moment, she gave up the fight. There was nothing left she could do other than go. Her lifemate had come for her, just as he always would and now she had to save him.

Chapter 33

Reyes watched as Camille turned around and looked at him with tears streaming down her cheeks.

"Seize her. I doubt she will run again. Because she had to go and make things difficult with this filthy human."

"No. He's not!" she screamed back.

"We gave you everything. A professorship at the academy, a legacy, and arranged a marriage to one of the prominent families in the community. But no, you had to pursue baking in a drab eyesore of a building? It needed to be shut down. And are you involved in this? An ordinary human male?" her father snapped and walked towards Reyes.

"You shut her bakery down! You were behind this." He held his ground and willed his wolf to come out. It wouldn't budge, because they were still weeks off from a full moon and he had fought it the last two times. Why would it listen to him now? *Damn it!* "You never gave her a choice. She isn't your property!" He clenched his fist, nearly snarling with anger, still trying to rouse the wolf.

Her mother snapped her head to Camille. "You are an absolute disgrace. He knows about what we are." Her mother then looked at Reyes. "She has expectations of her. They do not concern you."

"Everything to do with her is my concern!"

The woman stepped forward. "She stole from us and has a very heavy debt to pay. It will not be settled here. She will come with us to face her trial and settle her debt. I give you the choice, you can remain here and live out your life as you should have before she disrupted it, or you come with us and rot in the cell. We kept our abilities secret and Camille didn't. She has consequences to face."

"Reyes, let me settle the debt. Stay here. Please take care of Sitka. Please be safe," Camille cried.

Reyes felt his heart break. "No. Don't do this, Cami." He looked back to her mother. "I need her help. I need her."

He watched the woman's eyes bear into him with a murderous gaze. "A disgusting wolf shifter? Whose wolf isn't even fighting for you? Typical. You soiled yourself for nothing."

"That is not true!" Reyes yelled, begging the wolf to show itself. He didn't care how horrific it looked.

"I will go with you willingly, I promise. Leave him alone. You cannot take him from this place nor can you leave him at Thornwell. It will cause unrest. Let me settle the debt," Camille pleaded.

"You can't take her." He growled again. "My wolf already chose her."

"Stupid boy," her father said. "I suppose I can give the fool one small mercy. He is obviously ignorant and unaware." Her dad's tone indicated he was bored with all of this.

"She's your daughter and you're letting people grab her like that?" Reyes spat.

"She was my daughter. Now she is a disgrace."

"I didn't mean for you to see any of this, I didn't mean to disrupt your life, town, commute, any of it," Camille sobbed.

"Cami, I can only pray you continue to disrupt everything I know every single day." His sob came out as an erratic laugh.

"Reyes. Be safe. I need you to be safe. Help Sitka, please." Camille looked at him as if she were trying to say more.

He flashed a glare at her parents. "Let me speak with my lifemate," he proclaimed.

Her mother sighed. "Very well, make it quick."

Reyes walked up to Camille and kissed her hard. "Come back to me. Promise me! Come back to me. I will take care of Sitka. We need you. I need you."

"Just take care of yourselves. Sitka is free; not mine anymore," she cried and kissed him back. "I'm sorry."

"Promise me!" He pulled her close but the men holding her tugged her back. "Promise me you will not marry whatever pompous asshole they think is better for you. Just come back home."

"I promise," she said softly, for his ears only.

Two other men came up to either side of him and effortlessly pulled him back despite his struggle.

"Listen very closely, Reyes Navarro," her mother said, placing a hand on his bicep under his sleeve. He gasped, feeling the immense heat form. It was near scalding. "You will carry this curse until she returns, if she does. Tell no one what she is or what happened tonight. If you try, your words will vanish. The more you try, the more you will forget. Walk this line very carefully. If you are bonded to her, you are better off forgetting her. So consider this a mercy."

He felt the burning on his arm stop then the wind was stolen from his lungs as he was released, falling hard on his knees. He willed the wolf to respond, angry that he was not faster or stronger. He should be able to help her. This was his lifemate and he couldn't stop her from being taken. She was sacrificing everything she had built for him and he cried in frustration at being too stunned to move as they hauled her towards a van.

"Reyes! Look at your arm," Camille rasped out before being muffled and with that, Reyes pushed himself up to his knees but he was exhausted. He managed to lift his sleeve where the burning sensation had been to see a scar. A perfect circle with lines going through it, forming an x.

"What? What is this?" Reyes pointed out.

"Silencing evocation. Now go," her mother hissed. He could hardly push himself up as he watched Camille be thrown roughly in the van. She looked at him, still crying.

"Come back. You promised me," he cried out then dropped his head.

"I love you." Her words were soft but painful, and he looked up just as the van door slammed shut.

"No!" he cried, still trying to gather his strength. Before he could even get back to his feet, the van was gone.

Camille was gone.

"Please," he rasped out and looked up at the sky. The stars were framed by the sugar pines and firs peering down on him. She would probably say the trees and stars were watching him, too, just like that mountain was. "Bring her back!"

It was silent, as it usually was here. The silence he had grown so used to only left him empty now.

He pushed himself back up to his feet and glared hard at Mt. Shasta. He set his intent and spoke it for the mountain and everything else that made this place his home. Almost everything. Camille wouldn't hear it, but she had promised she would come back. He would hold her to it.

"She will settle the debt. She's going to come home. I will rebuild the bakery and see to it that Sitka has a perch in the damned window," he declared.

Finally, he brushed the dirt off him, then ran back to the bakery. The back door was broken open and he could see Sitka breathing hard. He hurried inside and found a large cardboard box.

"I'm sorry, girl, this is going to hurt. But I need to get you to Willow."

The cat remained where she was, watching him as he slid the box just under her, hearing the scrapping of glass. Blood smeared on the box. With a deep exhale, he swiftly slid Sitka into the box, narrowly avoiding her fangs as she screeched out in pain.

His truck was still in the street right next to her car with the door opened so he hastily made his way to it. He set the box on the passenger seat and got in. He lifted his sleeve up and looked at the scar again, wondering how this all worked. He certainly hadn't forgotten anything yet. He needed to get to Willow.

Reyes gently pet Sitka's head

"It's going to be alright. She's going to come back, but I have to get you better. I have a lot of work ahead of me but I'm not letting either of you down." That painful sting engulfed his throat as he rubbed the bobcat's head.

Sirens wailed and lights flashed and his heart seized. What was he going to do? Was he going to be pinned for this? He looked at Sitka, who was breathing far too fast. The wounds on her looked horrible. "Please hold on," he begged her, then got out of the truck, sobbing.

"Reyes?" An officer walked up as crews entered the bakery.

Reyes just fell to his knees and sobbed again. "Please." He wasn't sure what he was begging for. If he was begging that mountain for a way out of this or if he was begging the police to find her and that van.

"What happened?"

"Someone took—" His words died on his tongue. He suddenly forgot what he was saying. The crunching of glass under the officer's boots brought his eyes to the bakery. It was absolutely destroyed. "The bakery is destroyed. She's—" His words were so rushed through his labored breathing as the thought fled his mind once again. Tears dripped down his face.

"Can we get a medic assist, stat?" the sheriff called out then looked back at Reyes. "Take a deep breath."

Reyes realized he wasn't sure why he was here or what had happened; flashing red and blue lights were pulsing, striking a pounding sensation to his head. Once again, he looked at the business with the blown-out windows and the wreckage inside. Her bakery. His bakery witch. She had been taken from him. A sob tore through him. He had forgotten her, that easily? That fast? This evocation on him, it couldn't be removed until she returned.

"Sir, can we assess you for injuries?"

Reyes just stared at the bakery through blurry eyes.

"Can you state your name and age?" the medic asked.

"Reyes Navarro. Thirty-five." His voice broke as he just stared at the rubble.

"Where are you?"

"Mt. Shasta."

"What happened?"

Reyes looked at the medic then at the bakery. Officers moved in and out but all he could focus on was the lights flashing on the wreckage and his pounding headache.

"I pulled up and saw that. How? How did that happen? The glass?" he pleaded.

"May I take your vitals?"

Reyes nodded and felt his pulse being monitored. He reacted as instructed when the stroke assessment was done by making a fist, raising his eyebrows, and following the medic's finger. He responded that he didn't have any injuries nor hit his head. When he was asked about the dirt on his clothes, he explained he ran towards the meadow but tripped. He may not be able to talk about what really happened, but he could lie about it.

When they asked why he ran to the meadow, he heard a scream. He saw a van and then his words were cut off once again. Every time his memory grew fuzzy, he would look at that bakery and cry again.

"Sarg, we found a cell phone and are getting surveillance footage from across the street. The camera should show what happened."

He was asked what happened before he drove over here, to his relief he was able to explain how Camille was staying with him, how the bakery had somehow gotten shut down due to a health code violation and she was here to clean it in case she could reopen, for the new inspection. He had gotten a call and rushed down here to find the bakery like this.

Reyes watched the screen in horror as the van pulled up and the figures got out. They merely stood there as the windows shattered then they rushed in and a few minutes later, Camille's parents walked out, following her, then the cloaked figures. She ran and some followed while others got in the van and drove off. Minutes following that, Reyes pulled up, hastily parking and ran out. A short time later, he ran back with a box and that was when he discovered Sitka. Her breathing had slowed and she was lethargic.

"Please. Let me take her somewhere. Please find Cami," he begged.

It was clear someone took her. The officers deemed him innocent of having taken her and would investigate. They had sent officers to the meadow where it appeared there were signs of struggle but little more. Reyes claimed he didn't see anything at the meadow, knowing he would dig himself into a grave if he tried.

"It's illegal to have a bobcat, Reyes," the officer said with some hesitation.

"I know. But let me get her help, please. I have land to release her. She's dying," he begged through his sobs. "I can't lose her. Find Cami. Please."

"I can imagine this is traumatic for you. You and Camille were quite the sight at the ball in McCloud. Promise me you will get some paperwork on the cat. Also promise me you will get checked out at a hospital or at least your primary care. I know you are a good guy, Reyes. Take care of yourself."

"Yes, sir. I will make an appointment with my doctor in the morning and get paperwork on Sitka," Reyes said, still sobbing. It was half an act, half not. His heart was breaking but he was grateful for a small town where everyone knew everyone. The officers had an abduction and the bakery's destruction; one bobcat was not their concern.

"You are free to go. Good luck," the officer told him.

Reyes got in the truck and drove to Willow's house. He picked up the box gently then kicked Willow's front door since his hands were full.

Chapter 34

Willow opened the door and her jaw dropped when she took in the scene.

"What happened?" she asked, stepping aside so Reyes could set the box down on the table. "Where is Camille?"

"They—" The words died on his tongue and he forgot for a moment what he was saying or doing. *Camille is gone.* "She's—" The words left him. He heard an animal groan and looked over towards the box on the coffee table. *Sitka.* "They destroyed—" He rushed the words out then forgot them once again. He looked around at where he was and then at Willow. "Willow?"

"What is wrong with you?" Willow asked. "Where is Cami? A witch doesn't leave her familiar in this condition!"

Reyes pondered for a moment. He didn't know what was happening. The bobcat groaned again. *Sitka. Your arm. The memory thing. Thornwell. Camille.* It was happening again. He was forgetting. He could talk about what had happened before she was taken, but not what had actually happened. It had been the only way to explain to the police. He could say there was a van, but not who was driving the van. It was an abduction.

"I can't talk about it. My—" The words died out once more as he lifted his arm and he was once more confused. "Willow? Why is there an injured bobcat in your house?" he asked, baffled all over again.

Willow's jaw dropped and then she glared at him. "You brought Sitka over here and you still haven't told me where Camille is."

"Who?" he asked and the bobcat groaned again.

"Leave! I will take care of Sitka. How dare you come over here and ask who," she snapped and carefully picked up the box, easing Sitka out. She cried out in pain and he could see Willow's eyes well up. She looked at him. "Where is she?"

All Reyes could do was stand there in shock at what he was seeing. The cat groaned again. A bobcat. *The more you try, the more you will forget.* His eyes welled up. He was trying to tell Willow because he needed to. He had needed to be careful with the police and medics, but not with Willow. This was proof of the evocation taking effect.

"I don't know what to do. Help Sitka." He looked at Willow.

"You remember Sitka but not Camille, your lifemate. Your girlfriend. The one who helps you with your wolf?"

There had to be a way, something the rules didn't apply to. Camille being taken from him was his worst nightmare. It wasn't Camille and Jodie getting into it; it wasn't even Jodie humiliating him in front of everyone he was close to. He would volunteer to experience that if it meant Cami's family never found her.

And what was her family going to do to her? Force her into a marriage with a man that insulted her? That didn't even realize how amazing she was? That expected things from her. Heirs. *No!*

"Forgot," he cried out, then pointed to his arm. "Please." He whimpered. Willow just stared at him.

Her head tilted to the side slightly and her eyes narrowed. "Forgot?" she asked.

With hesitancy, Reyes nodded.

Willow closed the distance between them and lifted both of his sleeves up. Then her eyes shot wide.

"The memory wipe!" She pressed her palm flat against it for a moment then removed it. "Tell me exactly what happened. Where is she?"

"They took her. Her parents found her and took her! They destroyed the bakery and nearly killed Sitka. I heard it all," he heaved out quickly. Then he looked at Willow, stunned. "I was able to speak it. To talk about it."

Willow walked back over to Sitka and started tending to her wounds, leaving Reyes standing there, speechless for a moment.

"I know what that mark is. As long as it is explained to someone, and that person touches the mark, they are immune to it. That's the catch though, how do you tell someone about something that messes with your memories? My coven did it to a few people when I was young. So I know all about it. I just had to touch yours. Tell me what happened?" Stress lined her voice as she worked.

Reyes nodded and recounted the night as Willow cleaned and assessed Sitka's wounds. He spoke of how he'd answered her call and heard the sound of glass breaking, Camille screaming, her parents ordering Sitka be killed, and how Camille broke the bond with her. He spoke of the interaction with the police and what he realized was happening. "I didn't want her to go there tonight, Willow! I knew I should have gone with her and I didn't. She told me she loved me; she was ready to start a life with me. And they took her," he sobbed.

"I'm sorry, Reyes. I know this hurts you. It's hurting me too. You didn't deserve this."

He glared despite his teary eyes. "I don't deserve her but she wanted me, damn it, and I want her. I will drive my truck straight up to Seattle tonight and get her back."

"Deep breath." She lit a candle. "You couldn't have fought any of Thornwell Coven. Certainly not its leaders. Six against one would have been a death wish tonight. Your wolf knows this and it's why it didn't emerge. It just proves it has far more control of you than you do over it."

She walked over to a shelf and pulled a book out. When she set it down, it was open to a page with steps to make a numbing salve.

"You can either sit down and take a breather or you can help Sitka by grinding out the correct amount of herbs. My enchantments work a little differently than Camille's since I use oils. I add a light olive oil or something and enchant after adding the herbs to make my salves," she explained. "I need to stitch up some of these wounds on her and bandage them. I've cleaned most of them but I need Sitka calm to do this. The candle was more for you than her."

Reyes sniffed and wiped his eyes before he began to gather the herbs. He repeated the quantity and herb names and grabbed one, measured it, then put it away, taking great care to focus on this task. Reminding himself he owed it to Camille and Sitka to not mess this up.

After he had the mixture ready, he watched Willow enchant it, and glowing purple light came out from the cauldron. The salve was applied gently to Sitka's injuries and forehead before she set to stitching the injuries up.

"So they got the bakery shut down somehow. They had planned this all along. I didn't even sense their presence. They're good at masking themselves. They left? All of them?"

"All six got in the van with her. She didn't mention your name. She told me to run, to help Sitka. I made her promise to come back to me. Just like she told me about the last full moon." He paused. "What am I going to do, when is the next one?"

Willow sighed loudly as she tied the thread off and cut it. Seamlessly, she set to tending to the next one. "I don't know. You haven't tried it at your cabin?"

"No. We rented one far out in the middle of nowhere. I'm too scared to be this close to town. I did make it back to the circle she made though. I think if Sitka is there, I can get back but it's still overwhelming when I first change."

"This is going to be really difficult. I think Evan would be your biggest help when you are at work. I will keep Sitka until she is on the mend. It might not be wise for me to open the shop tomorrow anyway in case anyone is still watching. I am sure they knew that the apothecary was owned by a witch," Willow deliberated.

"Evan will be liable too. That was why Camille never wanted to tell us about her life. Willow, I don't know how much she told you but they treated her horribly, they arranged a marriage to an absolute asshole. He doesn't love her. He sounded terrible to her." His throat constricted at the thought.

"She told me enough. She also told me how much she cared for you. How you, and I, and this place showed her everything she had been missing in her life. I will reach out to some sources and see what I can find about her status. But I need to be careful how I go about it. I need Evan's help and do not want anything coming down on him. So for now, I need you to have faith in your lifemate that she will fight her way back here."

Reyes let out a big exhale. "Has he talked to you?" he asked, sitting back in the chair and wiping his eyes. He didn't know what else to say.

"He texted me and apologized for how he acted after the ball. He said he is in a weird place mentally and wanted to figure it out. I told him that was fine and that even though he was a dumbass after the ball, I still had a great time with him. It was amusing to see the look of shock on Sophia's face." She began stitching the last large wound on Sitka's leg.

Reyes hoped like hell she would heal fine. That she wouldn't be hindered in any way. He wondered if she would still help him when he was the wolf now that she wasn't tied to Cami anymore.

Willow continued again, breaking Reyes from his thoughts. "I hated that Sophia tried to take that house from Evan. She started prowling for hookups real quick after she served him the papers too. It was like she and Jodie thought they owned this place with no remorse for anyone's feelings. And I wasn't sure what to say to Evan. I didn't want to be a rebound or a one and done with him so I stayed away."

"I'm glad he finally stopped acting stupid. He's such a hypocrite."

"He was being a wingman. I guess he and I were both trying to do right by you and Camille." She smirked then began to bandage Sitka's wounds.

"So we tell Evan?" Reyes asked and they set to making a plan. "I am going to get the paperwork to keep Sitka. I have a friend with Fish and Wildlife in Trinity County. I am sure he knows a way I can keep her with the amount of land I have. But the officers want to see paperwork."

"Then we have a lot to take care of. I don't want to be dragged into questioning any more than you do. Thornwell is obviously messy and careless. I wonder if it's because they assume they have so much power and wealth that their councils will cover up their messes. They involved an entire town in another state with this. Of course they will try to pin it on Camille."

"It's not her fault! The councils or whoever they are have to know that she was a victim of Thornwell's shitty ways. She's not a fucking breeding mare. Do witches not get choices? What is your coven going to demand of you?"

"I am sure my coven will have something to request of me. It's one reason I'm not pursuing Evan. Cami and I have burdens we carry. This is what all witches who don't remain in the confines of their coven have to do. With any luck, though, this will shed light on how Thornwell is behaving to the Washington council. They are not bad, but not good. They want the wellbeing witches, but also the greater good, so she will have a trial," Willow explained.

"Wait, you aren't going to leave, are you?" Reyes asked, looking at her. "You can't."

"One day I might have to, but I plan on sticking around for a while. Don't worry, we will both see Camille return and you will master this wolf shift."

Reyes felt relieved at the reassurance. Nothing was going to be easy going forward. He had known it wouldn't be but Cami had made it easier. Now he was going to have to do all of this without her. He would because in his eyes there was no other option. Camille was his lifemate, she had to return, and he had to be someone worth returning to.

"Stay here. There's a guest room. It's small but you shouldn't be alone. Sitka will want you near too." Willow's voice broke him from his thoughts.

"I'm not sure that's a good idea. My truck outside your house? It's going to look suspicious."

"She is my friend too. The entire town is going to see the damage. We know the story; we tell the story to cover up that we don't know who took her. You commit a script to memory and we will tell Evan everything tomorrow."

He remained quiet.

"Sitka seems to be doing better. I gave her a sedative to help her sleep. Rest will be her best medicine tonight." Willow spoke softly, carrying the cat to a bundle of blankets on the floor in the living room. "The sun will hit her in the morning."

"Can I have some?" Reyes asked quietly.

"Of the sedative?" Willow asked. He nodded. "Alright, I'm not sure what effect it will have on you. But I will give you some," she said, and passed him a glass of water.

"Thanks." He chugged the water before he slunk down to the hall to the guest room and wept himself to sleep.

Chapter 35

Camille awoke sore and cold. She was on the floor in a dark room. It was moving though. She shot up and a cloaked figure pulled her back by her hoodie.

"Do anything stupid and we will sedate you," he growled. "We are stopping to change drivers out. We are just south of Portland. Do you need to relieve yourself? If so, I will drag you in there myself. Or the current driver will."

"No." Camille's voice was small.

"Good. I don't want to be around a betrayer any more than I have to. If you didn't owe Thornwell for what you did, I'd throw you out of the van myself."

"That's enough," her mother said.

Camille flinched and felt her eyes well up. She felt so alone and so scared. Her mother was watching all of this too. Her parents had said they disowned her and that, too, was a loss to her. The loss of Reyes and Sitka hurt her more though.

"I'm sorry," she whimpered.

"So much wasted potential in you. I thought I was molding you into a Thornwell. Not a hopeless sap. Honestly. A bobcat and a pathetic heap of a failed wolf shifter?"

"He's not pathetic! And he didn't fail. He was right; you never gave me a choice, a chance to be like you."

"You shouldn't have needed the chance, you should have just done it. I honestly don't know what's left for you. Talbot, especially Leland, is going to be disgusted when he hears about who you were bedding."

"Leland was looking for an out from me before I left. He hates me," she snapped back. The hurt of her parents disowning her was shedding off her.

"It's your job to appease him. Your father and I were arranged, and we run that academy."

"So you'd have handed it over to Leland to run into the ground. You have to know this. Everyone knows it. He is weak." Camille felt as though she wanted to claw her way out of this hole they shoved her into.

"His family is wealthy and we all know your eldest brother will take over. Talbot knows Leland is weak, why do you think they wanted you and offered a large dowry for your hand?"

Camille didn't even fight the sob now, despite the anger she felt at the truth coming out. She was just a barter to them. She never had her parents' approval. She never would.

So many emotions racked through her body.

"Thornwells do not cry."

"I'm not a Thornwell! I was never going to remain one. You sold me off to Talbot." she sobbed out.

"You gave everything up. For what? That piddly little town? Talbot would have been your name. I suppose the council will have to decide how you can best pay back the money you stole."

"You burned it all when you destroyed my bakery." Her vitriol was back.

The van stopped and as her mother got out, another official climbed in—before the other one followed her mother, who turned back to look at her.

"That wolf will likely get himself killed by the next full moon."

"No." Camille shook her head and collapsed back down. All the fears of Reyes getting shot or lost out there crippled her. The lifemate bond. He must be hurting so badly. And Sitka. And Willow.

She had felt some kind of bond with all of them. That mountain had wanted her there. She had no idea how she was going to get back. *Why didn't I listen to him? Why didn't I just stay with him tonight? The bakery could have rotted, but at least it wouldn't have been destroyed.*

Eventually, Camille cried herself to sleep once more.

When she awoke, she was being hauled into a small cell. She knew it was located under the academy, used for storage or detentions.

She curled up on the bed and continued to weep.

Reyes awoke way too soon to his phone ringing. With a groan, he answered it without even looking at who it was.

"What the hell happened? The bakery is in shambles. Is Cami alright? Are you? The letter is posted; the bakery could reopen if it didn't look like a bomb went off. It's all roped off."

Reyes just started to weep instantly.

"Reyes?"

"Come over to Willow's as soon as possible."

"What the hell are you doing there? Did you spend the night there? Where is Cami?" Evan gawked.

"Gone." Reyes wept.

"What? As in, she left?"

"Please. Just come over."

"Fine," Evan muttered before hanging up.

With a groan, he stumbled out of bed to search for pants. Then he stumbled in a groggy daze to the kitchen.

"Why are you awake?" Willow yelped. She was tending to Sitka in a pile of blankets she had bundled her in on the floor.

Willow's phone rang. Reyes watched as she checked it then looked at him worriedly as she held it to her ear. "Evan?"

Reyes could hear his friend's voice but he couldn't make out the words.

"Come over. I need to explain a lot to you and Reyes needs you," Willow said, annoyed. Reyes couldn't really make out Evan's response. "You really think he's going to make a move on me now? You and I both know him better than that and I would never do that to Camille."

Willow was silent when Evan replied with something before she snapped her gaze to Reyes. "You are both so fucking stupid with your pissing matches," she seethed.

Evan responded again and Willow let out a huge exhale. "He slept in the guest room. Leaving him alone was not wise; Sitka is badly injured and I owe it to Camille to keep them both safe. You owe it to Reyes. Please. I need your help. I want your help," Willow pleaded.

After a few minutes, she sighed and tossed the phone down.

Reyes realized it was the first time he heard Willow show that side of her. She was always in control and confident. He'd seen her cry last night, and now he was watching her nearly beg. "I'm sorry. I will go."

"You can't drive with that sedative still in your system. You told him you'd take me camping? What the fuck?"

Reyes lightly bumped his palm against his forehead. "Yeah. I gave him shit after I heard he was ghosting you. I said I would take Cami and you. That asshole had some really douchey things to say about Cami anyways."

"Well he's on his way. So we're going to have a little chat about how you boys need to stop being children and act like adults," she hissed then walked back to the kitchen to make coffee.

He took a cup and sat down at the kitchen table, realizing it didn't taste like Cami's. He almost asked for sweet cream.

Pounding on the door made Reyes nearly choke on his coffee. He was still groggy after he'd only gotten three hours of sleep.

When Willow opened the door, Evan stood there, furious. "Morning coffee with the two of you, how cute. Start explaining please. Where is Camille?"

"Evan, just sit next to Reyes."

"I will sit on the couch." He rolled his eyes.

"It's really better if you sit with him," Willow encouraged.

"Where is she?" Evan asked, then slumped into a seat at the table.

"She was—" Reyes forgot the words he was going to say. *Cami. Say her name.* "Cam—" The thought escaped him and he suddenly forgot what he was saying. He looked at the unfamiliar table. Then the cup in his hands and back at Evan, who was seething at him while Willow looked at him, wide eyed. "Evan?"

He took in the house. It wasn't his or Evan's. It was Willow's. He leapt up from the table. "What's going on? Why am I here?"

"What's wrong with you? Where is Cami? You just asked her to move in with you, and she did move in with you! What are you doing over here?"

"Who? Cam—"

Reyes heard an animal groan and snapped his eyes around, seeing the injured bobcat. His eyes shot wide. "Where did that come from?"

He noticed Evan tilt his head and look at him. Following his eyes, he saw the cat and gasped. "What happened to her?" He spun to Willow. "She followed Cami everywhere. Was she in the bakery last night? What happened to Camille?" Evan looked at Reyes.

"Evan, what we are going to tell you cannot leave this house. We both need your help. Cami needs a home to return to. She promised Reyes she would and I have no doubt she is going to fight her way through hell to do it. Be angry at both of us but do not hold it against her."

"What are you talking about?" Evan asked.

Reyes watched him then looked at Willow.

"Reyes and I are not what we appear, Camille isn't either. Reyes is new to this, but Cami and I aren't. Roll up your sleeve, Reyes." He did as he was told and watched as Evan fixed on the mark. "Place your palm on it and we will tell you everything."

Evan looked at Willow then back at Reyes and finally complied. Reyes didn't feel anything; he hadn't when Willow touched his arm last night.

"Evan, promise us both you will not speak of what we tell you."

"I promise. Just tell me what is going on. Why is Sitka so injured? Is she going to be okay?"

"She will be, but she needs rest. I'm going to keep her for another day then I will leave it up to Reyes. Camille severed her familiar bond with Sitka in an effort to save her, so that's what Reyes and I are going to do. Camille and I are witches."

As Reyes listened to Willow tell Evan what that meant exactly, it started to come back to him and his eyes brimmed with tears.

"Reyes?" Evan said. "She was abducted? You saw it?"

All he could do was nod and let the tears fall. "She told me she loved me before they slammed the van door shut. She is my lifemate."

"Tell him what that means, tell him what you are, Reyes," Willow urged.

"Two months ago, when Cami and I went camping for the first time—" Reyes paused and dropped his head. A quick exhale later, he told Evan he was a wolf shifter. And how grueling it had been and how Sitka had led him away after he hurt Camille, then he told him about last month and the calming circle. "It's terrible. She took such good care of me and I couldn't save her. I'm some ravenous beast when the full moon rolls around. And now she's gone. It hurts." Reyes put his head down on the table. A hand came to his back.

"I'm sorry. Both of you. Witches and werewolves are real? You've kept this from me this entire time?" he asked.

"Reyes only found out two months ago. Neither Cami nor I ever sensed it before. She and I knew what each other was the moment we looked at each other. Witches are not supposed to tell anyone—we are hunted, especially as the lone witch. Why do you think I never was really close to anyone until Cami? I had to lie to everyone to some degree."

She explained the enchantments and how they worked while Reyes watched the shock and disbelief cascade over Evan.

"Camille had to lie a lot at first and I hate that she was taken by the very people who handed her off to be some breeding mare." Reyes clenched his fist as a wave of anger shot through him.

"At any rate, Reyes can't be left alone on a full moon until he gets full control over his wolf. So I need your help. The three of us and Sitka will need to go camping. He wants to remain far away from town, and my plan is to try at his cabin after a few shifts. I think it would be a good place. Familiar, but with lots of land."

"I'm worried about shifting at home. I can cover a lot of miles as a wolf very quickly and I'm not that far from town."

As the day progressed, they continued to talk about what the days would be like going forward as a hollowing sensation lingered in Reyes's heart. While he knew Willow and Sitka would be there, he hoped Evan would uphold his promise. He also hoped he would not hurt anyone and that Evan would still be there after the next full moon.

All he could do was hope.

The Next Full Moon...

Chapter 36

Images of that night played in Camille's head. Reyes in the dirt heaving for breath hit her like a splash of cold water and her tears formed, ripping a cry out of her. She clutched the thin blanket.

It had been a few weeks since she had been taken back to Thornwell Academy. She hadn't left the grounds or the building once since she arrived. Her parents met with her once to tell her she would be doing remedial tasks. Cleaning up after lessons, washing linens and dishes in the mornings, and then she would be making ten enchantments a day under supervision. She would have a small break for lunch then teach a lesson three days a week to a small group of first years, also under supervision. On the days she was not teaching, she would be grading and reviewing papers. If she proved she could function as a Thornwell should they ease the supervision, she wouldn't have her hearing for two more months.

She would be working to pay her debt off. The only problem was, her parents refused to tell her how much they would claim. She would have to fight for her freedom at the hearing. Countless emotions coursed through her when she was awake.

The anger at being back here, the sorrow for hurting Sitka and Reyes, and the longing for them and that town.

As Camille sat on the small bed, she thought about her bed in her cabin in Dunsmuir. She had built a life there. She had just moved into that castle in the shape of a gorgeous A-frame that Reyes had built. His mighty steed in the form of a loud truck perched and standing guard. He had asked her to share it with him and she had left the safety of it.

Tears welled up in her eyes when she remembered Sitka. She missed her familiar, but Sitka wasn't hers anymore. She had cut the bond.

"Please," she whispered. *Please let her live.*

The bakery was gone too. She missed seeing people get excited for what was in the cases. The cases that had been shattered and knocked over. She missed seeing Reyes walk in, grumpy and unsure at first, then smiling at her and giving her hand a squeeze.

He had made her promise to come back to him. That was the small tendril she had to hang onto. Unless she stayed here and broke her promise to him. *No.*

How long would he wait though? she asked herself. The look in his eyes in that meadow told her forever, but her gut told her a year, maybe? Then what? What if he left? What if something happened to him?

What would she return to? The bakery was trashed. The town surely would think she was long gone. Just some girl who got abducted in a van, and Reyes might forget about her with the evocation. How would they even cover this all up if she did go back?

This was her parents' way to make her life hell if she left. Rip the home she made for herself away.

I just want to go back to Mt. Shasta. Back home. Even if it was to nothing and bid Shasta farewell. Please don't forget about me, Reyes.

A clatter on the cell doors made her jump. She still wasn't used to the guards even though they did the same thing on their assigned days.

Two different guards would alternate days and she figured they both hated being stuck watching her. She hated being here. But once again, her parents didn't give her the choice either. Just like they didn't really give either guard the choice.

"Get up." The gruff tone from one of the guards always made her heart sink. This one hardly acknowledged her when he escorted her to the areas where she did her morning tasks. He would escort her to her enchantments then back to her quarters for her break. He would walk next to her, likely so he could grab her if she ran, but he seldom looked at her. He never touched her either. Yet every time he was about to speak to her or let her know it was time for a task, lesson, or meal, he would hit the door to her cell, causing her to jump.

The other guard was the opposite. He watched her a lot with a grin that made her sick.

When he would escort her back to her chambers, he would wait until they were in the dimly lit corridor where his hand would land on the small of her back, just low enough to press his fingers into her rear. He would tell her to wash up real good and watch while she was in the bathing area, then watch her eat dinner and eventually he would leave. All the while tears would well up in her eyes.

"Aww don't cry, sweetcheeks. You may be a filthy betrayer, but you are easy on the eyes at least."

Reyes. She wanted to cry out for him, but she never wanted this guard to say his name. Never wanted to hear it used in that tone he used while he was objectifying her.

As she wiped her eyes after he left for the night, different footsteps approached. This stride sounded different, lighter, not as clunky as the guards.

"Deplorable," a grating pompous voice spit out.

Leland.

Her eyes roved over him. He had long, silken, sandy blond hair—lighter than hers—blue eyes, and a fair complexion as though he never bothered to be outside long. No, he always had his nose in a book and always rolled his eyes whenever she talked about hiking and tending to drying out herbs. He let the first-year students do that for him and insisted legacies were above getting their hands dirty. She honestly wondered if he just liked his wealth more than his actual magic. His family was also prestigious. For some reason Evan flashed in her mind. How he looked like a normal humbled version of Leland who spent his days outside, fishing, hiking, or with his arms deep under the hood of a blue pickup truck, helping Reyes with something.

Reyes. Her mind always went back to his laugh, his scowl, and hidden smile underneath. She thought of his short, black hair and calloused warm hands, the dirty boots, the soft worn flannels, and how gentle he was with her, how he never failed to drop to his knees in front of her.

"You can keep ogling me but it doesn't change the fact you tainted yourself with a pathetic wolf shifter who can't even shift. I heard all about the weak trembling mass running after you. You probably rolled in the dirt right alongside his grubby mitts. You certainly look like it. You gained weight too. The bakery, the absurdity."

"He's not pathetic." Her voice broke. The words stung and she swallowed them back. "He knew how to love. He knew to worship me."

Leland laughed. "And you think he's going to wait for you? You were easy; you are nothing to him now."

The words hurt but she knew it wasn't true. Reyes was her lifemate. *He chose you. He made you promise.*

A fire lit inside her. Something fierce. "He has more passion and grit than you will ever know."

"Passion and grit for a desk job in some small town. And you know what? He will forget all about you. You were simply something new in his mundane pathetic life. A shiny pretty new toy he will forget about."

"That's not true." Camille's words faltered.

"Enjoy the rest of your lonely existence, Camille," Leland snorted out with a laugh then flung his ring through the bars towards her. She had sold hers somewhere in Oregon and used the cash for the burner phone and a down payment on a used car.

Hopefully no one would ask about his ring. She figured she would need it to sell it to get back, because she was going back. She just had to remember that was her goal. She could not give into her doubts or any of the words they wanted to tell her. The rings were the acceptance of the arrangement, not yet made official until they both enchanted the other's rings. It was one more reason she had taken hers and sold it as soon as possible. For this exact situation she was in and so Leland could not enchant her ring while she was forced to enchant his.

"You sure this is a good idea?" Reyes asked with a frown standing near his truck.

"Yes. We're both here for you," Willow said.

"What if I hurt one of you? I don't want to." Reyes panicked. "Fuck, it's humiliating the next morning too. It's going to be hard without her." The burn in his throat brought his eyes to tears.

"We are here, and she wouldn't want you alone for it," Willow responded.

"Evan, the shotgun is in the back of the truck. If I attack either of you or Sitka, I need you to be ready."

"What the fuck? Take it out of the truck," Evan demanded.

"No. I don't know what's going to happen." Reyes had to wipe his eyes.

"Give Evan the keys; he will put it back in the house. We're not taking it," Willow said.

"Neither of you understand though," he pleaded, not reaching for his keys.

"I have seen shifters shift. I understand plenty," Willow insisted.

"Just tell me what you need and I will do what I can. I'm here, too, man. I promise." Evan placed a hand on his shoulder.

Reyes looked at him. "I don't want either of you to see it."

"You are safe, Reyes," Willow said.

Evan held his hand out. "Give me your keys. I'm driving. Willow, take my truck?"

She nodded.

"You can't do this every month," Reyes fretted. "It's not realistic that we go camping every full moon."

"You and I have a responsibility to give Camille something to return to. Evan has a responsibility to you. We are in this together."

He finally relented and handed Evan his keys.

"Get in the truck, Reyes," Evan said, walking to the back and opening it to take the gun inside. "The absurdity of asking me to do that," he scoffed.

With Evan heading back into Reyes's cabin, Willow placed her hand lightly on his arm. "You will be alright, Reyes. I have plenty of calming tinctures, and Sitka will lead us to you, just as she has every other time. Get in the truck."

After a few more moments, Reyes composed himself and then they were on the road west towards the Marble Mountain Wilderness. Evan had found a cabin to rent, far enough away from anyone else or the Pacific Crest Trail. He was a danger to everyone.

Once they reached the cabin, Reyes remained quiet as they settled in. The place had about four bedrooms, though he knew he wasn't likely going to need one tonight.

Now he wasn't sure what kind of mental state he or the wolf would be in and he was terrified. Camille had told him that his human emotions would fuel the wolf and Willow had explained that for shifters, their human emotions were a lot for their feral form. Animals felt things differently, they processed them differently than humans.

Reyes hadn't said more than a few words.

Sitka had never left his side. He was relieved that the bobcat had made a full recovery.

The police as well had ruled out any foul play on his part. They did however deem him unstable and his boss encouraged him to see a therapist to process the grief.

"I've seen enough werewolf movies, but what is this going to look like?" Evan asked.

"Well, it's been a while since I have seen a new shifter and they were kids, it's different of course as it usually is learning things as a kid versus an adult. Especially one who only recently was exposed to magic," Willow responded. Reyes listened but didn't say anything.

"Is it going to happen when the moon is seen or reaches its peak or what?" Evan asked.

"When it starts to brighten things around me is usually when the shift happens," Reyes said anxiously, bouncing his leg. "Don't leave any doors open after I leave. Just a small window open for Sitka." He clipped a pack to Sitka's harness that had some of his clothes and removed his boots.

"Are you going to walk barefoot?" Evan asked, shocked.

"I'm going to attempt to make the wolf come back here, at least to the yard." He glanced at the sky as he took deeper breaths.

"It will be alright," Evan offered.

"I just wish she was here. I don't know what's going to happen." He rubbed his hand down his face.

"You're alright, Reyes," Willow soothed, watching him closely. Sitka too had been watching him.

He nodded then went to sit down in the circle they had all helped in making. It just made him miss Cami even more as he went to rub the calming salve on his temples. Only he didn't get very much on him when he noticed it got brighter out and the immense cramping in his gut began. It made him double over. Willow stood up from the seat and Evan followed, placing arm in front of her.

"Fuck," Reyes cried out, feeling his muscles tense and bones strain against themselves. His cries eventually changed into animal-like sounds of distress. His vision shifted to mostly blues and grays, and he saw the fear in both Evan's and Willow's eyes.

Cami. I want you back so badly, he cried out in his head as he looked at the stars. He was too deep in the mountains to see Mt. Shasta, but knew if he were higher up, he would scream at it. Then the wolf took over and snapped at his friends.

A bobcat arched its back, looking right at him. Sage green eyes peered back at him. So similar to Cami's.

He wanted her back.

As soon as the bobcat ran, he let out a growl of frustration and chased it, hearing the people on the deck call out for Reyes. It sounded familiar to him but he didn't stop. He just knew he couldn't lose that bobcat.

Too many scents, sounds, and shadows slammed into his head too fast and he couldn't focus on any of it. He was losing the bobcat's scent and he couldn't hear or see it.

After running for miles across a jagged heavily forested landscape, exhaustion brought him to the ground where he slept.

Some hours later the wolf woke up. The bobcat's scent was strong overhead and he met its gaze as it rested on a branch.

Follow me, it seemed to say. A nonverbal method of communication he understood but couldn't explain. But once it was on the ground and started walking again, he followed it, retracing all the ground they had covered until they reached a cabin. It looked warm inside but he approached slowly, not sensing any movement.

The early blue light of dawn began to break and so began his shift back. He forced himself to get to the deck before the pain radiated too far out of his core where he collapsed with a grunt on the deck.

"Shit! Reyes!" A male voice brought the freezing cold air crashing down on his body.

"Here," a female said and he heard feet shuffling.

As soon as a blanket came over him, he buried his face once more and let out a sob.

"I want her back," he cried out. "Cami."

"Come on, let's get inside. Get cleaned up, eat, then go back to sleep," Willow advised.

He only thanked them but did not look at them until he woke up that afternoon, still sore.

The Next Full Moon...

Chapter 37

When Camille woke up to the clatter on the door, her tears formed. She looked at the calendar and saw it was a full moon. *Please let him be alright.* It was a prayer to any great force out there that Reyes would be safe during the full moon.

Oftentimes in the last few weeks, she thought about Willow, and Sitka, about the town and hoped that all was well, yet no one occupied her mind as much as Reyes. He had chosen her as his lifemate and wanted her despite all the pain she caused him and the lies she had met him under. He hadn't run even when he learned the truth and he stood face to face with her parents.

Camille knew it had been a small mercy that they had only put the silencing evocation on him. It would be absolute hell for him to pick up those pieces and her mother had been right, forgetting Camille would be the best thing for Reyes to be able to resume his life.

Yet she knew he wouldn't. The wolf wouldn't let him, he had chosen her, and now it would be a living nightmare of memory lapses on top of trying to shift until she upheld that promise to him to return.

With a deep breath, she made her affirmation that she did every morning to the wind, in hopes it would travel to him. Across state lines and mountains. "I will."

She went off to her tasks and her lessons. They had gone horribly last month. At least this time they were doing the assignments she gave them.

"My lessons still count. Fail them and show Thornwell you are nothing. Is that what you want? Then again, it's not as though they care much about your talent or skills anyways." Anger coiled in her gut.

"That's not true, I passed my entrance exam with flying colors. Perfect on everything," one student bragged. Her name was Roxie and she was a gifted witch who was learning sight-based enchantments using light reflections.

"We weren't given a handout like you were," another sneered.

She wanted to cry and scream. The guard watched her. The one who usually ignored her was now looking at her. She figured he was going to reprimand her if she said anything.

She didn't care.

"They gave me a lot. I am grateful. It helped make me what I am today. Despite all that, they still bartered me off. Do you think they will not do that to you? Wait till you learn of your own dowry, or the one your family is to receive," she muttered, feeling the tears. No one said anything. She didn't bother looking at them; instead she looked at the clock. Watching the seconds tick down until the guard slammed his baton against the chalkboard, causing her to jump.

"Class dismissed," he scoffed and opened the door. He was angry for some reason. She didn't care; he wasn't her concern. He could just go back to ignoring her.

As she ate, her eyes were fixed on the tray. Two sets of footsteps came down the corridor.

One set of footsteps was confident. Not her parents, not Leland. Another set was small and graceful.

"You are relieved of your duties for the night. Be gone," a woman instructed. Camille didn't look up.

"I'm stuck watching her. Orders say for a few more hours," the silent guard muttered and crossed his arms.

He was very muscular, with short, light brown, wavy hair and hazel green eyes. He could be attractive if he wasn't such a brute. Usually he was busy reading and taking notes when she glanced over. He would be so absorbed in them he wouldn't even notice her at times.

"I believe the orders are to follow your superiors. Now you can see on my uniform, I'm a bit higher rank than you, cadet."

"Bitch," he growled and took a step towards her, looking down at her.

"I am ordering you to leave." The smaller figure removed her hood. Camille's eyes widened. It was Paige Talbot. Leland's aunt. She was always quiet. Not as strong as her sister and brother-in-law, but definitely stronger than Leland. Her children were not as bad as Leland; she had two girls. They had not been betrothed yet. They had never been mean to her but hadn't offered more than a smile here and there. They often rolled their eyes at Leland during dinners she had to attend with the Talbot family.

When the guard took a step forward, the other woman with a stocky build slammed him against the wall.

"Go, this does not concern you. Orders."

The two stared at each other for a moment before he stormed off with his books in hand.

Camille looked down when they turned to her.

"Would you say the wolf was worth it?" Paige asked softly.

Camille felt her eyes water but she forced out a response. "Yes."

"Did you unlock his shifting abilities? Through your pastries?" Paige's voice didn't sound condescending; in fact, it sounded more curious. Camille still didn't look up.

"Yes. I think that's what happened. He was in the bakery often. He watched me enchant herbs, and I showed him how to measure and grind them up. His hands held mine as I enchanted sometimes. His parents never told him about the lineage since they couldn't change" Her voice broke at the memories.

"He's good to you, I take it?" she asked and finally Camille looked at Paige.

She nodded and the tears came. "Yes. Never forceful, he was protective. He called me beautiful, even after we hiked and camped together. He held me close throughout the night." She wiped her eyes.

"Your hearing is coming up. I take it, will you reject this place for him?" Paige asked.

Camille looked at her. "Are you going to tell Leland that's what I chose? Tell Talbot? My parents? Leland made it clear he doesn't want me."

"I know Leland is absolutely vile. I'm not blind to it. I'm not telling anyone. I am telling you to get back to your wolf shifter," Paige stated as though it should have been obvious. Camille didn't know why Paige would be telling her to betray Talbot.

"The only way to do that is accept the mark of betrayer, and even if I do, I don't know how long I have to be here." Camille's voice broke.

"Is the mark so bad? Does your wolf care? Does anyone else you met in that place care? The only ones who care are here and you haven't wanted this place for some time."

Camille looked down and noticed she was fidgeting with her shirt. How much she missed Reyes right now. She always missed him.

The guard with Paige stepped forward and looked at her. "You know what your salary was here, you know what money was yours, what you took. Thornwell received the dowry the day they announced the betrothal. It was one of the stipulations. Tell the council to honor it. Work to pay back the amount you took, then be done with this place."

"They had Leland's dowry the entire time?" Camille asked, confused.

"Your parents wouldn't hand you over without receiving something in return. You had a taste of freedom, Camille. You just said it was worth it. So they label you as a betrayer, then you'll build your own coven, where you bake, and camp with your wolf," Paige said. Her smile had grown ever so slightly.

"Talbot bought me as a promise? For Leland."

"Tell the council the dowry is not your responsibility to pay back. Demand they honor that," Paige's guard said.

Camille brought her eyes to Paige when she began to tell her story. "About forty years ago, I snuck off the grounds like so many do. I was at a bar in Tacoma; I met a human. He was handsome. Rugged and strong yet so gentle and soft spoken. We had both been drinking and we spent the entire night together."

Camille listened in shock as Paige recounted how she had gotten pregnant from a one-night stand. Talbot had told her to get rid of the half witch, and they wouldn't accept anything less. They gave her two options for getting rid of it. She chose to give the baby up and tracked down the boy's father, leaving him with money and urged him to move far away, to leave the state if possible because she never wanted Talbot to find the boy. To prevent any other witches from getting the sense, she had put an evocation on the boy that blocked his magic. She never knew what happened to him, but it was one of her biggest regrets.

"I love my girls, and I couldn't imagine my life without them, but I wonder what life would have been like with my son, and maybe his father if I had just accepted the betrayers' mark. So I'm telling you, accept it. Go back to your wolf. I don't want to see you lose your light here, Camille."

She watched the two women leave. Paige leaned into the guard she arrived with as they walked off, very much like how she imagined she might with Reyes.

Her mind shifted to thoughts about what she had learned tonight. She had no doubt Talbot had their skeletons in the closet. Thornwell had plenty and now she would be another one. They had literally used her hand to gain the dowry long before any officiating had even occurred.

It was no dowry despite everyone calling it that too. It was literally a monetary exchange for a good.

Now she was soiled as they called her. *Good*, she thought. Let them discard the spoiled goods then. She'd drag herself back to Shasta if she had to.

Reyes got to packing things he would need for another horrible trip. They were heading to a cabin that was slightly closer to town this time. Willow was trying to convince him to try at his cabin and he knew he would need to, but he was still worried.

With a sigh, he looked at Sitka. "Maybe next month we will stay here and try," he said and shoved some clothes in his backpack. "I bet you have all four acres of this place explored and marked by now." He chuckled to himself and scratched Sitka's head. "I'm talking to you like you will respond. Maybe if I got control of my wolf."

His shoulders slumped as he walked into the closet to grab a few more items. He saw her dresses hanging up and the box he put her head scarves in and frowned. His heart ached that she wasn't here. They hadn't even gotten to start this chapter in their lives. It had been ripped away from them mere seconds before it could even start.

Reyes walked to the railing on the loft and looked at the mountain facing him.

"I hate not knowing anything. It's like she just vanished into thin air, except her things are here, her familiar is here, and this hollow in my heart is here. But she isn't. Just bring her back. Please," he begged the mountain as if it would respond to him too.

His phone started to buzz and he figured it was Evan or Willow but when he checked, it was his mom. With a reluctant sigh, he answered it.

"Hey," he said.

"Reyes, how are you?" his mom asked.

"Okay I guess."

"I'm sorry. I know this is hard for you."

Reyes remained quiet. They didn't know all the details of what had happened. It was too difficult to explain it to them. They had called a few weeks after Camille had been taken and he tried his best to explain but the memory lapses were horrible. He had kicked Sitka out of the house, thinking she was a wild animal. He sobbed so hard and hugged her when he remembered. Ever loyal Sitka had waited nearby and came when he ran out crying out her name.

He knew he could not lose her. It was his only connection to Camille despite her not being her familiar anymore.

"I take it the police haven't found anything?" his mom asked. All he could do was sigh. He didn't want to try to say no for fear he would forget. "I know it's hard to talk about, Reyes, but we are here. We know you're under a lot of stress, especially with trying to fix the bakery up."

Reyes needed to change the subject. He hated giving his parents the silent treatment and he knew it was making them worry even more.

"I'm going camping tonight. Be back in two days," he blurted out.

"With Evan?"

"Yes."

"Is the shift getting easier?" she asked, sounding remorseful.

"I can make it back to the cabin. I didn't dress myself last time, though. I'm going to try this time, maybe make it inside at least."

"Should we come up for the next one?" she asked.

"No! Not until I have this under control."

"I'm sorry we didn't tell you before. We really thought it was too diluted."

"Have you told Andi? She lives in Seattle. There are a lot of magic users there," he muttered with distaste.

"No, we haven't. We aren't sure how to. What does living in Seattle have to do with it? There could be magic users here and it didn't unlock ours."

"I don't know." He knew trying to mention that her family lived there would send him into a memory lapse.

"Maybe you can tell her? We just don't want to scare Weylan or her husband," his mom said hesitantly. "We got lucky Cami was what she was."

"I don't know what I'm doing," he groaned, thinking about her.

"Your father and I will discuss it. Be safe tonight. Call us tomorrow or when you get back?" she asked.

"Fine. Love you, Mom," he sighed.

"Love you too, Mijo."

He tossed the phone down and went into the closet to grab more clothes and looked at her dresses. He paused on the one she wore to the fireman's ball.

"Come back! I can't keep doing this," he cried and collapsed to the ground. Sitka approached and gave a purr. Once again, he pulled her into a hug and cried on her.

Eventually, he found himself at the cabin, sitting alone in a circle of calming herbs he had set up mostly on his own this time. His back was to the cabin but he knew Evan and Willow sat outside. Sitka had her harness and pack on.

Reyes was silently begging in his shead. He wasn't begging for tonight to be easy, he was begging for Camille to come back.

As expected, the full moon rose and he felt the bone splitting and muscle tearing pain and just gave into it. He cried out in pain, not putting up any fight, and his wolf took over faster than ever. He turned and looked at the two terrified people on the deck. The man blocking the witch. As if he was a barrier.

Reyes could see the aura around both of them. The witch's purple aura was much brighter than the man's dull red aura. His was so faint, hardly there as if it were muted.

His wolf was in full control now and neither of these people were his concern despite smelling familiar. He growled at them then turned back around and fled, silent and swift. A bobcat was trailing him but he didn't care. He just ran until everything inside him felt too heavy.

Camille, he said in his mind before he collapsed. The bobcat purred softly from up above a tree.

A male voice woke him up, making him aware of his pounding headache and sore muscles. "Reyes. Come inside, Willow is already cooking. Shame I didn't get to see your ass again, but good job getting clothes on."

Reyes pushed himself up with a whimper and dragged himself to the table, stuffed himself full, then crashed in the first open bedroom he saw.

The Next Full Moon...

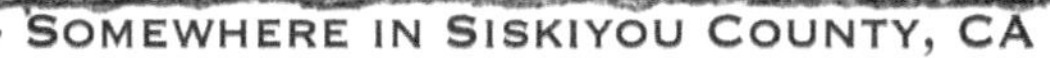

Chapter 38

The clatter of a baton on the bars roused Camille from her sleep. Just as it had every day for months. Another full moon was upon them tonight.

"Please let him be safe," she said in her affirmation.

"Get up. You have the hearing in an hour. So eat, bathe, then beg the council and your parents for forgiveness. Maybe they will let you out of this cell and I can stop having to watch you."

"Request a different post then."

"This is the job I was given," The silent guard muttered and crossed his muscular arms, leaning against the wall and staring down the corridor.

She could at least tolerate him. The long periods of isolation were wearing on her but she would take his hatred over the other one's sick fascination with her.

That one tried to be sly about it. She would look away when she was in the shower but she knew he was always watching. His hands would be on her back and rear; they would grip her arm and he would chuckle in the dark corridors, far too close to her ear. He was stocky but didn't appear to be in as good a shape as the silent one.

She much preferred the silent one. Camille didn't want to exist in this place and the silent one treated her that way. The other one certainly was far too aware of her existence.

Camille looked at the guard as she finished her meal of eggs and toast with water. At least it was balanced, if not bland. Maybe it was the routine of it all that made her finally snap back.

"Just an obedient little sheep to Thornwell. Doing whatever they bid for you."

He snapped his gaze to her. "Shut up."

"Your talent is overlooked, isn't it?" she asked.

"I'm looking over a Thornwell, aren't I?"

"One who doesn't fight back, one who wouldn't stand a chance against you in a physical altercation. You seem plenty strong; you should be teaching the guard, not wasting your day walking me places."

He stepped forward and dragged his baton over the bars, causing her to clench her jaw and squeeze her eyes shut. She wanted to cover her ears but instead clenched her fists.

"Poor little sensitive baby gets scared of loud noises. At least I know how to shut you up."

She took a deep inhale and opened her eyes. She braced herself for what was to come, for she knew something would follow her next words.

"I know you have more skills than being loud and taunting sensitive little babies. I know you are better than this and that's what makes you so angry, isn't it? None of them bother to see it," she hissed.

He picked up an empty tray nearby and went to slam it against the bars. Camille took deep breaths, prepping for the noise but it didn't come.

"Let's go," he muttered and tossed the tray down. She flinched slightly at the sound but it wasn't as loud as she expected.

As they walked, she thought real hard about what she was going to request, and about what she was going to say. What she learned from Paige left her reeling. Part of her had hoped her parents would offer some sort of plea for her. They had sons, though, so what use was the youngest daughter to them? Paige had a son that she obviously never stopped thinking about but she never had tracked him down. He could be a short drive away in Seattle or Tacoma. Maybe he was across the country, or a different country. Yet Paige had known to stay away.

Camille obviously hadn't learned that lesson. Of all the things her parents taught her about being a Thornwell, she had never learned the things that were most important.

Willow's words came back to her after their hike in Castle Crags.

Thornwell did you an immense disservice in how to actually be normal. If anything, they should commend you for applying what they taught you so well. They wanted you to remain hidden, yet had no intention of actually letting you live.

She had fled, built a bakery, and helped Sitka. She'd given Willow a chance to not be so lonely. Her baked goods awoke a wolf shifter who opened up his own little castle and land to her.

Camille had built a life for herself. Thornwell never let her do that.

She sniffed back any remaining tears and held her head high as she stepped before the council of witches. They were all from Washington. She had met with them a number of times, back when she was trying her damndest to be an obedient Thornwell. There were also a few she didn't recognize.

"Hello. We are here to determine the title to best suit you going forward. Thornwell, Talbot, or betrayer," one said. Camille felt her face burn. She looked around to see her parents and brothers. Their wives and kids were absent. The Talbot family was here as well, Paige and Leland included.

Camille did not expect so many people to be here. She supposed she had impacted a lot of people, though. One decision to run had done this.

"We are joined by the Northern California witch council as you certainly left a mark in that small mountain town."

"Then Thornwell destroyed it," she spat.

"We wouldn't have had to if you hadn't left," her dad seethed.

"Where was this Thornwell grit before?" her mother asked.

Camille took a deep inhale. "Where was it when I was told to be obedient and serve Thornwell? Then to serve Talbot? When I had no use for it?"

"Seems as though this will be a quick hearing. Camille seems to be telling us what title she is choosing," a Washington council witch said.

She glanced at the California witches who sat back, as if interested in a show. She couldn't recall a time when they had ever visited the academy. She had met the Oregon ones before and some from Vancouver too. Each area had a council to oversee the witches and covens in the area. They were usually responsible for dishing out punishments to witches who broke rules and left messes. Like herself.

"Let us hear the desired outcomes from each affected party," the witch continued. "Talbot?"

"She is soiled. A waste of a dowry. A waste of a union to Thornwell. We promised our boy greatness and she robbed him of it," they said with distaste.

Camille rolled her eyes. The audacity of them. Paige was a good professor, her daughters were strong, her guard—or lover—was nearby, but so was her betrothed. He remained quiet, watching with curiosity. It didn't affect them; they were merely here by association alone. Camille wondered how strong her son would have been. She wondered if Talbot or Thornwell would've taught him. How much would he have learned on top of being born with the connection?

"Thornwell?" the witch asked.

"She pays back everything she stole from us, everything we were owed. We might find a job for her, but she is not to be a Thornwell again. I let Washington and California decide what happens to her after."

Typical. They wouldn't mention that they already had gained so much. Yet she wondered why Talbot hadn't mentioned they were basically robbed on a promise. Camille wasn't sure if they were robbed by Thornwell or herself, but regardless they had been robbed of a dowry. Leland, however, had been given a free out. He didn't look upset at all.

"The California council?"

"We'd like to hear what she requests specifically. She made an impact in the Shasta Region. Siskiyou had been busy on a few fronts as of late. Yet the witch side is proving very interesting. Go on, Ms.—Bakewell? Or is it Mrs. Navarro?" The smile in the witch's tone was obvious.

That title made her gasp and her heart skipped a beat. *Reyes.* Did they have information on him? Was he safe? He had to be if they said that.

"Speak. Tell us the desired outcome."

She swallowed hard. "I will continue to work as I have been—labor, enchantments, lessons, and grading—to pay back the money I stole. But only that. I did not rob anyone of a dowry. Ask Thornwell about the dowry they already received for me. Nor did I rob the oh-so-dainty Leland of a bright future shackled to someone he hated long before I 'soiled' myself. Ask him yourselves. The work I have done counts towards paying off my debt to Thornwell just after three full moons from now. At which point, brand me as a betrayer and I will never be an issue to Thornwell, Talbot, or Washington again."

She heard the collective insults muttered from both Thornwell and Talbot. She did not miss the glares they shot towards each other. *Good. Let them destroy each other.* Paige's guard, who she learned went by the name of Wren leaned against the wall with a smirk.

She turned to the California witches who watched her with glee. "I beg you to let me return. Even if the town despises me. Let me say farewell to the place that has only ever been a home. I built it on my own, but what I had there will not be replaced. I ask you to let me see it one more time. If you wish to be rid of me, too, then I will go." Her throat hurt from trying to keep her voice level.

"As you may or may not know, many of the various councils of Northern California take their territories' wellbeing very seriously. You unknowingly created a very unique development. Wolves have only recently found their way back into the region. To have a shifter in Siskiyou again will prove essential for our conservation efforts. We are in talks with the shifter council, but he is not ready to stand before them. While he is well and getting help from two he is close with and your former familiar, he struggles greatly. The evocation hinders his efforts mentally and therefore his physical efforts." They glanced in her parents' direction. "We are not here to make demands, so we ask you to break the evocation when you can. To assist him when you return. Thornwell's betrayer is an asset for us. We wish for her to return to us under stipulations, of course."

Her heart was thundering. Reyes was alright, Sitka was alright and with him. Willow was helping. Evan too? "What are the stipulations?"

"You are to report to us, either in Redding or Sacramento, alone, once a month, to work with us and monitor new enchantments that are submitted for use. Should the shifter council request it, you are to report when Mr. Navarro is summoned to stand before them. Otherwise, he is to report alone and do what is asked of him."

"Agreed," Camille blurted out.

"Thornwell? Talbot?"

"She pays back the debt owed to us and to Talbot. She wasted the dowry," her father demanded.

Her heart sank. It was far more than she stole. That was Thornwell being greedy.

"We never see the betrayer again, but Thornwell pays back the dowry we paid for her. They demanded it in exchange for her hand. Then placed an evocation on Talbot that we couldn't speak it to anyone until a Thornwell spoke it first. So maybe Thornwell ought to keep better tabs on their records."

Camille realized that was why Paige's guard told her about it, not Paige. Paige couldn't speak it. Until a Thornwell did and Camille was still a Thornwell until she bore that mark.

The Washington Council glanced at each other before each wrote something. The one speaking read over each of the papers, he declared.

"Thornwell is under investigation for abuse of power. The betrayer will be marked and stripped of her coven name after she pays off the remainder of her debt. The remainder of what she stole. In three full moons. At which point she shall promptly pack any remaining affects and leave Washington, to report to a designated place by the California council."

"The betrayer is to report to the former site of Bakewell's bakery. She is to remain in Mt. Shasta until summoned." They stood with a grin.

"Noted. From here forth, your title is betrayer. With a drop of blood in the binding sands, consider this our bargain to be fulfilled when we, the presiding council members, crush the pearl."

Camille felt the weight lift off her. However, as she drew near to the dagger next to a large vessel of sand, a new weight crept over her. *Where will they put the mark?* Every witch she would encounter, would know she was a betrayer. Not of who, but that she had rejected her coven. Willow would see it.

What is the other option? Beg all your life for them to make choices for you?

Once again with her head held high, she looked right at the council and pricked her finger with the dagger. Her eyes followed the one drop of blood she squeezed out to fall to the sand. As soon as the blood hit the sand, a small red spark created a crimson pearl. A nearby guard fished it out with a small net and walked it over to the council where they placed it in a glass vial.

Everyone left the room with mere sighs and looks of disappointment. Paige and her guard however offered her a smile before leaving. Then the guard took her to her first task of the day.

Sitting around a rented cabin that night, Reyes sighed and groaned. "I don't want to do this again. You can't keep closing up the shop for a few days."

"Well I did and we are here. So we are going to do this. Head out to the circle," Willow said.

"Besides, short work weeks are always fun. Consider this making up for all the camping and fishing trips Jodie and Sophia never let us take." Evan grinned.

"We aren't camping or fishing, though. You're babysitting me," Reyes mumbled. Willow's letters to the council hadn't been answered and that irritated Reyes to no end.

"To the circle, Reyes. It's almost time."

Begrudgingly, he went and sat in the circle to wait.

A stabbing in his rib started the transition this time. He didn't fight it. He just said her name. Begged everything to bring her back.

Then he ran, the bobcat once again trailing him. Miles flew by under his paws and he felt for once he was getting the hang of the wolf's body. Until an unfamiliar energy hooked his attention, causing him to trip over his own paws and slamming snout first into the dirt. His wolf growled and it was a battle to hang onto it. Exhaustion encased him for a short while and when he woke up, he realized he was still the wolf. The moon was still out yet the air felt calm. He felt calm.

This way.

Some nonverbal source seemed to say. When he followed it he looked up to see a bobcat in a tree.

Sitka?

The cat jumped down and ran off. He immediately followed it this time, not wanting to lose her.

Reyes realized he was back at the house. The lights were on. He saw Willow sitting on the couch, holding a mug in her hands.

Evan sat at the bar seating with a beer in hand. The two talked occasionally, smiling at each other. He realized he had no idea how their courtship was going. *Courtship? What the hell? Why did I think that?* he asked himself. He hadn't asked either of them how it was going.

Slowly, he walked up to the deck. Willow locked eyes with him immediately. Evan looked over and jumped, knocking his beer over.

Reyes sat back on his haunches and bowed his head down, trying to submit. He wasn't sure how he felt about rolling on his back to show his belly to them.

Willow opened the window in the nearby dining area.

"You're back?" she asked, surprised.

He still didn't know how to talk to them. Sitka walked next to him and pawed at the door. Reyes watched her then looked at Willow.

"Holy shit, are we going to let him in?" Evan asked.

"I think so. He's calm." She opened the door. "You're learning it, Reyes." Willow smiled.

He felt his tail wag slightly. He wasn't sure why but he felt embarrassed. It felt as though the wolf handed over the reins to him and he had no clue what to do with this new body.

Then he noticed Evan walk up to him and carefully hold his hand up. Reyes watched closely. Evan went to pet his head.

The wolf took over him and growled at Evan, who backed up. He wasn't Evan's dog, Belle. Though he did wonder how Camille's hand would feel petting him.

He walked over to the living room and lay down, not sure what else to do. For now, he was calm as the wolf for the first time ever.

The Next Full Moon...

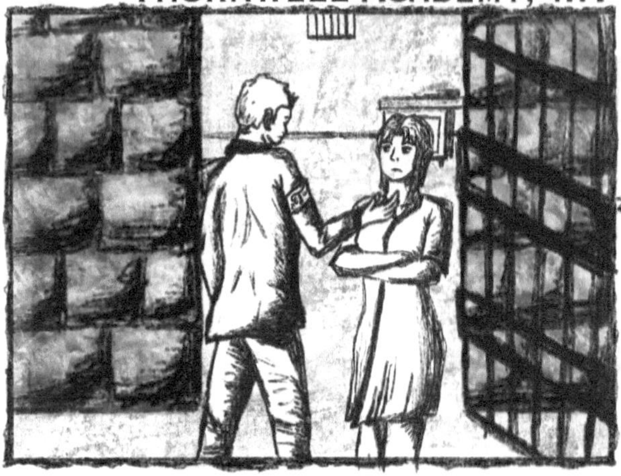

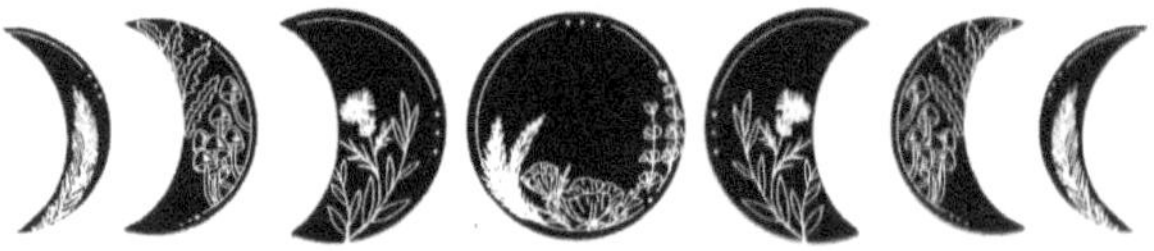

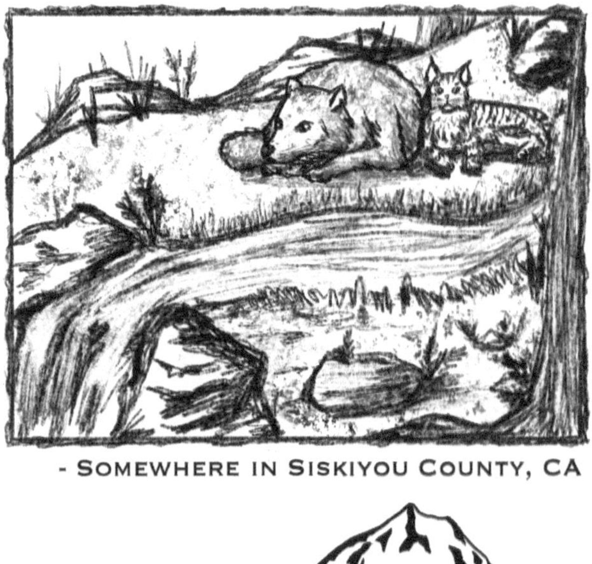

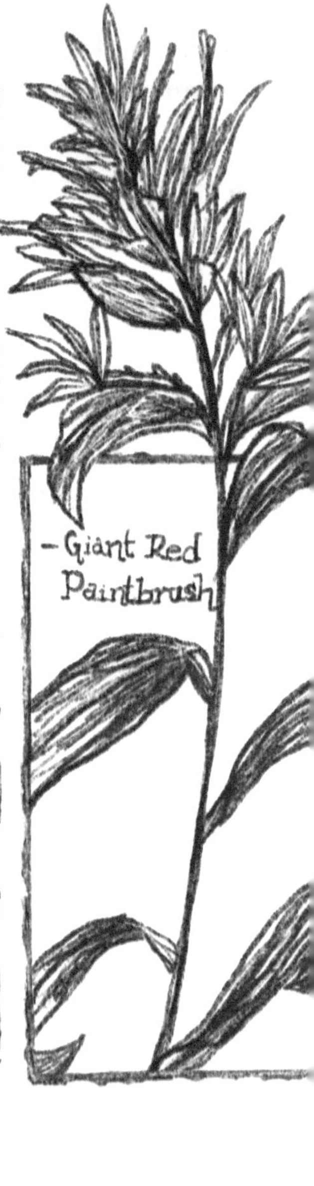

Chapter 39

"Get ready for your morning tasks," the creepy guard said.

Camille felt she should learn their names but it made no difference to her. She was counting down the days to be away from this one's gaze and touch.

She had already begged once more that Reyes would be alright tonight, knowing another full moon was upon her. After tonight, she had two more until her debt payoff.

The silent guard merely spoke to her now instead of rattling the bars on her cage. He hadn't done anything to make loud noises but he still didn't acknowledge her as much. She knew tomorrow would be much the same with him.

If only this guard would ignore her. She went through the motions once more, cleaning and setting up various lecture halls for lessons. No one spoke to her and she didn't speak much.

As she made the enchantments, she wished she was brave enough to curse all of it, but in the end, she knew that wasn't her. She was still the obedient, ready-to-serve Camille. Even as a betrayer. They would figure out she had botched the enchantments anyway and likely tell the California council. They were expecting her in two more months. Where she might get to see Reyes again. Any wrong move now might hinder that.

She sat in her cell on her break, staring at the floor, wishing she was free of all this right now. It was within her reach.

"There is the little betrayer. Off we go to your lessons," the guard cooed. She exhaled in disgust and glared at him.

"Enjoy the stigma of drooling over a betrayer," she said, walking out of the cell. Her insides twisted as his hand came right to her rear and hip.

"I'll do a lot more than drool over you."

"Don't you fucking dare," she hissed then hurried out of the corridor into the main area where she stood waiting in view of others.

As soon as the guard was behind her, she walked to the classroom and closed the door before he could enter.

Her students had grown to look at her with disgust the last month and she didn't care. She just taught them what she could. However, Roxie, the sight enchanter, raised her hand.

"When do you know if tradition is more important than skill? Shouldn't the tradition of the academy encourage us to improve? To strive for improvement?"

This question caught her off guard. She thought this student hadn't seemed like her usual self.

"Well, you should always want to improve," Camille replied, thinking about all she had learned at the bakery. All the times she and Willow worked through troubleshooting enchantments. She had improved her calming enchantments for Reyes too.

"But what if your accomplishments are all overlooked?"

Camille wasn't sure how to respond. That statement had always been obvious to her. It was why she fled after all. Her parents seldom ever cared about her accomplishments. They just said there was always more that could be done.

"There are times when our accomplishments will be overlooked. They may be overlooked by many and those we want to impress very badly." Camille felt stupid for stating the obvious.

"Every time though?" she asked, almost defeated. The other students looked at her.

"It feels like that at times." Camille paused, still not sure why she needed to state the obvious. Had these first years really been so brainwashed by their superiors? "Tradition cares little for your hopes and dreams."

They all gasped. This was not a response she expected from the collective.

"They deemed you a betrayer," another student said.

She looked at him and realized this was the scrutiny she was going to face going forward. There was no going back on it without losing all of Shasta.

"Yes. I accept it willingly. Traditions sometimes do not encourage improvement regardless of how they are worded. Traditions can hinder us sometimes."

"I was told today that I was to be betrothed to someone of higher rank than me but not of higher skill. My parents knew that but they said it would save my coven's rank. They said status was more important than skill and I felt the situation was similar to yours but you accepted the betrayers' mark? Willingly? Why? What might be out there for me? My coven is all I know," Roxie pleaded.

Camille remained quiet, still unsure what to say. "I can't tell you that more is out there for you than this. I can only say I got lucky that the mountain chose me for whatever reason. It chose me for that place, and him." Camille recalled Willow's words once again. "I took a risk that I could survive. I don't know what I might return to, but it's a risk worth taking for me. Staying here obviously isn't any better guarantee. At least out there, I know what I could have. Whether anything there has changed is a risk I will take."

"Isn't the bloodline important to you? This place, your family? Security from people who want to hunt our kind?" another asked.

"They were important to me. This place was all I knew. But I didn't understand why I was nothing more than an asset. Why I couldn't choose simple things that brought me happiness. Why was I expected to just serve someone else? Why are *you* expected to do that? Would your coven do that for you? Would you do that to your children?"

They all remained silent and Camille could see they were all thinking. It was the first time she had seen such a conflict on their faces and she wondered if she was actually opening their eyes to change. To break tradition.

"Ask yourselves what kind of future you want. The ability to use your talent and skills for yourselves, or to simply become more marketable to benefit a coven line? I cannot deny that the loss of such a large coven isn't going to hurt me, that I never will know what a family feels like. But the ragtag coven I formed in that place showed me more than I could ever have hoped for. To see parents who want the very best for their son, watching from nearby as he finds his way. Seeing a coven that was close knit with love encouragement for one of their own to pursue her dreams. To gain a companion so sweet and loyal that would throw herself in front of me every time and asked for nothing more than a warm place to sleep in return. Ask yourselves what you have and what else is out there."

They looked at her and she wanted to know what they saw. She wondered if they saw someone strong, or a dirty betrayer. She wouldn't ask. It didn't matter what they saw, because she wasn't sure what she thought of herself. Her identity was changing and she didn't know what the new her would look like yet.

The door opened and the voice made her stomach drop.

"Aye, sweetcheeks, let's get you cleaned up. Not that it will do a filthy betrayer any good."

Her eyes welled up but she fought it back. "You all have your assignments due the next session," she said then turned to leave, balling her fist as the guard placed a hand on her shoulder and squeezed.

He watched as she showered.

"You get off on watching filth?" she asked, glaring right at him as she washed her hair.

"A body is a body. You fit my type."

"And how often do you get your type?" she asked.

"How often did you let the pathetic shifter bed you?"

An audible gust of air escaped through her nose. Word had obviously gotten around. She didn't care what this place thought of her now. "Every time he or I wanted it. Because he had no issues kneeling before me. I wanted him and he wanted me. How many want you? Especially if you want a filthy betrayer?"

"Finish up and shut your mouth."

"Is that your angle? You think you are entitled to me because I'm stuck here? I'm the one thing you think you have control over? Because Thornwell is never going to give you any more control than watching betrayers?"

"Your shifter should have fought harder for you. We all know Thornwell knew you were nothing more than a body, after all. Leland was far above you. I see who he's flirting with now. Far more attractive and actually into him."

"Talbot doesn't care for you and Leland cares for no one," Camille hissed out and dried off, putting her robe on.

She walked past him to her cell and when she was just outside of it, he pressed her against the bars with his body. She was frozen in fear.

"I don't care who wants me; I take what I want. I was going to wait until just before you were out of my sight but game's over," he growled in her ear and pressed his lips to her neck.

"No!" she screamed.

"Release her now!" A new male she hadn't even heard walked up. Rainier, her oldest brother. The guard stepped away instantly.

"Sir, I was simply ensuring she complied getting back into her quarters. She ran from me earlier. I was told to watch her."

Her brother restrained him. "Watch her, not touch her. You are dismissed! I'm in charge of Thornwell during the investigation," he hissed. The guard nodded and quickly walked off.

Camille didn't know what to say. She hadn't been close to either of her brothers. They often didn't have time to bond while being in different classes.

"How long has that been going on?" he asked. "You aren't supposed to change in the cells."

"It's the first time he did that, but he always had his hands on my backside in the corridor, releasing it when we got into the main hall since he was assigned the post. He's always watched me bathe and eat and made me change in the cells." She felt her eyes well up pulling the robe tighter around her.

"You didn't tell anyone?"

Heat hit her face with anger as her eyes welled up. "I sent requests and they went unanswered! I figured Mom and Dad wanted to test my iron grit or whatever would make me a Thornwell, sorry, a Talbot," she scoffed.

"Camille." He sighed. "I didn't know. They never told me nor did I see the missives. I also told them I didn't think Leland was a good pick for you. That you'd benefit someone else."

"That's the fucking problem, Rainier," she spat out. "You, and Mom, and Dad and this entire place think I'm only here to serve them. That I don't deserve to do anything for myself."

"We maintain our strength this way. I know Mom didn't give you fair treatment like she gave Galen and me, and I know Dad was complacent in it. But you could have had your way with Leland. He doesn't fight back. Mom wanted you to mold him. That was what she told me."

"Leland belittled me. He doesn't fight for me. He never cared for me nor was he going to listen to me," she seethed. She was so angry.

Her brother sighed. "Right, not like your wolf?"

She bore into him with her fists clenched tight. "Reyes did fight for me. He kept me safe and never once expected anything. He is a good man and he works hard. I'd willingly serve him for an eternity but you know what? He never asked me to, he never expected me to. That's the difference between him and this entire wretched academy. Reyes never thought he was better than anyone. Never felt he could even ask anything of me and when he finally found the courage to, he held onto me until Mom and Dad ripped me away from him!"

Her brother watched her before speaking. "You really chose a life of hiding, lying, and trying to control a rabid possessive dog?"

"I never got to choose anything here!"

"My kids ask where you are. They cry asking where Aunt Camille is. I just tell them you are away. They fear for you, and now their classmates whisper about a betrayer."

"Then tell them the truth. I chose Shasta. I chose Reyes and my bakery. Tell them that they don't get to choose things their grandparents deem silly."

"You really are turning your back on us? If I'm in charge; I can get your name reinstated. I can negotiate for you to teach at the academy again. Talbot won't expect anything of you. You can choose another coven, or keep Thornwell. Someone can join ours. Please, Camille? I'm sorry I was complacent. You can teach baking classes; you can bake. If I remain in charge, it will be different for you. I promise. I just want to have a bond with you, I want my kids to have an aunt around. You should have your own kids that are strong."

"Not mixed wolf pups, right? And you want me around so your kids have a babysitter who is family. And I still shouldn't have my freedom with people I chose, right?" Camille sneered. "No. He's neutered anyways."

He sighed again. "You're really leaving?"

"As soon as I can."

"Alright. I'm sorry. For not doing more."

"If you want a bond with me, then make an effort after I leave. I will never come back. Reyes chose me as his lifemate; I will go where he goes. I have a future with him. Start by granting me one request for the remainder of my time. Remove that guard from the watch. Let me walk myself back here to bathe, eat, and sleep, and spare me my dignity if you care."

"I can arrange that," he said.

She showed herself into her cell and closed the door, letting it auto lock.

Her brother turned and walked away.

Camille was fighting for her freedom. She had help in places she didn't expect, so she wasn't going to curl up and rot.

Chapter 40

For the next full moon, Reyes finally agreed to try shifting at his cabin. Evan agreed to sleep on the couch, and Willow would be in the guest room. Reyes offered his bed but both of his friends declined.

They all sat in the living room and talked about how the renovations on the bakery were coming along. It was nearly finished. Willow had helped with the decor and Evan had certainly become the backup on phone calls with contractors.

"How are things going with the contractor calls at work?" Willow asked.

"I usually keep an eye on Reyes when they call and take the phone. Luckily the big stuff is done. It's just minor things now," Evan responded.

Reyes nodded. "People just mention how quiet I've gotten. It's easier to not try to talk, but it's hard seeing their looks of concern. They all say I'm holding onto false hope. How it's so unfortunate what happens to pretty girls that get abducted and thrown in vans. At times I think that's what happened and I can't bear the thought of it happening to her." Reyes looked at Willow. "They wouldn't do that, right? Her coven wouldn't let that happen to her?" He was beginning to panic.

"No. I don't think there is a coven around that would do that to their own regardless of the punishment. The councils wouldn't let a coven go unpunished for that, even putting a witch in that position. She's fighting with everything in her for you, Reyes. I know she is," Willow replied.

"It would be nice if they give you any kind of status update," Reyes scoffed.

"I agree, but last I heard they were checking on it. I will write them again to request updates. But I am a bit relieved they haven't found out about Evan's knowledge of us. At least they haven't mentioned it."

"I'd rather they don't know about me. I'm a bit terrified based on what you've told me they can do." Evan rubbed the back of his neck. "Is there a werewolf council?" Evan asked curiously.

Reyes glanced at Willow, now worried.

"There is, like anything else, the council might have fae, witch, vampire, nymph, or whatever on it, since shifters are a bit more diverse than say witches. Witches are usually not shifters but they are out there, centuries of cross breeding and all."

"Do they know I exist?" Reyes asked.

"I'm not sure."

"I thought I sensed an unfamiliar presence last month but it distracted me and I tripped, ending up with my snout in the dirt. I still suck in my wolf body."

"You will get the hang of it. Was the presence any of the ones that took Camille?" Willow asked.

"No. It was totally new."

"Interesting." Willow glanced at the time. "Do you want to go to the calming circle? Or no? It's nearing the moon's rise."

"Yes. Let's go." Reyes sighed and got up. He walked outside, barefoot with shorts and a shirt on.

He had gone through clothes too fast and kept cheaper clothes on hand for the shift. Willow had also found more information that as the shifts grew more controlled, clothing could shift with the body. She hadn't ever seen any shifter that shifted back naked. It was almost as though the animal ripped out of the body too quickly and didn't allow for much to adjust. It explained the breaking bones and torn muscles Reyes felt and if the shift could be balanced between both forms, then less pain would occur. Clothing could also remain on the animal or feral form. When they shifted back to their human form, their clothes would remain intact.

Sitting with his back to the house, he rubbed the salve into his temples and slowed his breathing. His mind always wandered to Camille in these moments. How the last time she had held him close, even knowing the danger she was in. She had never been afraid of him. She had been afraid *for* him, and sacrificed herself.

Cami. I need you. I'm trying to do this but I want you here. I need my lifemate.

He saw the bright moonlight through his closed eyes. Seconds later, the pain started in his abs but he fought the cry. It traveled through his ribs, reshaping them. His breathing was becoming labored but he forced himself to be calm. Suddenly, pain pulsed from his core and shot out, forcing him to fall on his side with a groan. The terrible transformation took over him yet this time it was over in ten labored deep breaths and the wolf stood, locking eyes with Sitka.

Sounds and scents assaulted his senses. Slowly, he turned and looked at the two on the deck.

Willow and Evan. They stood, watching him tensely. He noted the bright purple aura on Willow and the faint red glow around Evan. He couldn't understand what that meant and he had forgotten to mention it last time.

He was balanced with the wolf this time, able to sync both forms up.

Until a low growl slipped out of him and he realized his wolf was restless.

So he turned and looked at the bobcat.

Sitka, he said to himself.

Yes

She somehow responded. He couldn't explain it. *I want to run.*

Then run this way. Not towards town.

The bobcat ran ahead.

He followed, thinking about Cami. He imagined her out here beyond his property line with her bobcat and her wolf. A perfect little spring princess of Siskiyou that was kind and gentle. Brave and wise. He imagined her looking at the mountain, often smiling for the safety its shadow provided her in the day, and at night, she would have her wolf by her side.

Before he realized it, Sitka had stopped running and he was at a waterfall. One he had never seen before. It was peaceful here. He lay down on the ground and Sitka sat near him but kept her distance. Bobcats and wolves were natural enemies, after all. *You can sit by me if you want. I'm not going to hurt you.*

I know. Just get used to this form.

Reyes couldn't help but feel like Sitka was channeling Willow right now. *Will you become Cami's familiar again?* he asked.

I would like to. She is a kind soul. She may not ask it of me, though. I am not sure who she will be when she returns.

I hope you will remain with us. With me, Reyes said.

I will.

Sitka now leaned against his side and the two sat in silence, listening to the waterfall.

After an hour or so, Reyes decided to head back to his cabin. He led as Sitka followed. He knew his way home from here on scent alone. He missed the pear and honey scent of her. It hadn't had a chance to settle long enough.

When he approached the cabin, the door was closed but he saw Evan and Willow talking on the couch. He always forgot to ask how it was going; they never showed any signs of it progressing when he was around them.

He walked up to the door and sat back. Willow instantly got up and opened the door.

He looked at them and then strode up the stairs, stumbling slightly since he wasn't used to the uniformity of them in his wolf form. Evan laughed slightly and Reyes let out a snarl but disappeared to his loft.

"Don't laugh at him. He's getting better," Willow chastised.

"I know I know. I laugh at Belle when she stumbles. I know I'm an ass," Evan said. Sitka joined him a little later. Ever loyal to him.

"How are you feeling about everything? I haven't asked in a while." Willow asked.

"I don't know. I mean everything I am learning is amazing, but it's so hard to see him like this. He's my best friend and I feel like I can't do anything for him. I haven't done anything for him. I wish I could." Evan sighed. Reyes heard him take a sip of his beer. He could smell it when he walked by.

"You are here, that means a lot to him. It means a lot to me, too, and I know Cami will be so grateful."

"Do you think the council or whoever knows what happened to her? I can't imagine what he's going through."

"I don't know. It takes a certain kind of smart ass to be on a council. They have their ways of doing things. They honestly might see it as Washington's problem now."

"Were you upset with her? She kept the Thornwell name from you both, right?"

"At first, I felt a need to distance myself from her, knowing she could be deemed a betrayer. There is such a stigma to witches who leave their covens like she did. Just fleeing in the middle of night without blessings. A legacy coven's daughter at that. I know why she lied, though, given how they treated her. I'd still be lying to you and Reyes if she hadn't moved here. I think Cami holds a lot of that generational trauma, too, because she didn't even want to defend herself. She just accepted she would leave right then and there. She left Sitka behind with me. As though she didn't deserve anything she had worked for and once I learned the entire story, Reyes was right. He had every right to be upset at me. She needed someone to tell her it was alright and I wasn't the one to do that for her. He was."

"I'm glad he and I got to be such good friends. Honestly, I thought he and Jodie would balance each other out. But obviously they didn't."

Reyes listened to Evan talk about how he felt he did Reyes a disservice by remaining neutral with Jodie. He never encouraged him to stand up for himself because Evan knew it would cause more discourse with Sophia. But it all backfired when Jodie moved in with them for a month. He couldn't stand the two of them together. It was like a completely different side of them emerged. The divorce did hurt Evan. He wanted it to work out with Sophia, but after the way she acted towards him—when he would hear people talk about her flirting with other guys even before she moved out—he was ready for the divorce papers.

"Honestly. I felt like trash after my random hookups. They served their purpose, I guess, to get it out of my system but I figured word would get back to you eventually and you'd think I was trash since you were still friends with Sophia. It was a relief when Reyes suggested we go camping again. I don't deserve him. When he started to deny his feelings for Cami, I knew I couldn't let him fuck it up with her. She blushed whenever I mentioned him too. Talk about two idiots in love."

Willow laughed. "I knew she liked him early on. Honestly, he's perfect for her. Jodie never deserved all he's willing to give. She never appreciated him. But Cami will."

Reyes heard one of them shift on the couch and one exhaled out nervously. "I thought about you, too, you know. Even before Sophia left. Our friendship never was that deep. I feel like she was friends with me because I was here and near her age. I guess that makes me trash too."

"Willow, you aren't trash." Evan sighed. "There's so much going on with the divorce and I'm scared to do this again right now. I don't want Reyes to see it either." His tone grew quieter.

"Reyes isn't blind to it though. He knows."

"I just want him to be alright because I see it weighing on him. I know he's getting stronger with the wolf, but I don't like how quiet he gets. How little he smiles. He doesn't want us near him. I'd feel like an ass if he saw us right now. You leaning against me like this, but damn have I wanted to be this close to you for a while. When the divorce is finalized, or Cami comes back, I promise I will have my shit figured out then."

Reyes looked up to where the beams met on his ceiling. *Stop making excuses, you dumbass. Just go for it,* he said in his head.

Evan gasped and there was movement on the couch below.

"What?" Willow asked.

"I-I don't know. I'm going to sound crazy."

Reyes lifted his head.

"Honestly Evan? What?" Willow asked.

"A voice in my head. Not a thought of mine."

Did you hear me? Reyes asked, shocked.

"Reyes?" Evan gawked.

He got off the bed and walked to the railing, looking down. Evan was standing and both him and Willow were looking up.

Yes.

"You were able to mind link with him? Wait, were you listening the whole time?" Her eyes went wide.

Yes, he said to Willow. *You both holding off on the inevitable on my account makes me feel bad. Just pursue your courtship—relationship. I don't care. Sorry for eavesdropping.* Then he slunk back onto the bed and burrowed under the covers, letting sleep take over.

The Next Full Moon...

Chapter 41

Camille woke up and ate the meal that was served. It was cold and made her stomach churn. It was five months of the same things. Today's breakfast was overnight oats, cold bacon, and fruit.

She glanced at the window then at the calendar. "Please let him be well," she said softly. *One more month,* she reminded herself.

"Get dressed and ready. Council requested your audience," the silent guard said, his journal and book under his arm.

"What? Why?"

"I am merely escorting. It's not my business."

Her heart raced. She had looked over her calculations and she still had a month or maybe even more to make up. She was growing tired from the six days of work and grading. Then she feared her parents had been reinstated and negotiated some worse punishment for her. Or they were not going to pay the money back to Talbot and she would have to. Her brother hadn't been back to visit but he had delivered on her request, and now she only had the silent guard every other day. Despite the isolation wearing on her, she certainly wasn't going to risk a worse guard being stuck watching her.

She walked into the council room, which was much more empty than last time. In fact, no one was there except the Washington council. No Talbot, not her parents, or her brothers. Just her.

"Betrayer. Upon review and request, your debt to Thornwell Coven and the academy has been paid. Tuesday will be your last lesson and on Wednesday, you will pack your belongings, then report to us where we will finalize your title. Once you wear the betrayer mark, you will vacate the premises and report to the designated spot the California council requested of you. Should you ever return to Washington, know that you are banned from approaching the academy. You will need to contact us to make any enchantments anywhere in the state. Do you understand and agree with the findings?"

"Yes!"

"Then it is settled."

"You can't go back on this? No one can make other demands?" Camille stated as if this were too good to be true. She had two more nights until she was free. Until she could return to Mt. Shasta.

"Those are the rules. We requested your presence due to a forgiveness granted. May you not forget that Thornwell and the council can show you some grace. May you do good things as a betrayer," they said and turned to leave.

She sniffed back tears of happiness.

She was going home soon.

Camille felt a weird combination of exhaustion and restlessness after her enchantments were done.

When her last lesson with the students rolled around, she looked at them. It felt bittersweet for some reason that she wouldn't ever be an academy professor again. Not that she had been since she left but she would never have access to this place again.

"This concludes our lessons. Take what you have learned here and of your own futures then decide for yourself what is right. You choose what risks are worth it and what aren't. Security, or a chance at freedom. It never gets easier the older you get. Thornwell will offer you a great beginning, but it doesn't have to be your end," she said, and they all looked at her stunned.

"You're leaving?" one student asked.

"Tomorrow."

"How far is the drive?" Roxie asked.

"Eight to nine hours. The California council requested me to report to a specific place."

"What are they going to ask of you?" Roxie asked inquisitively

"I am to report to them once a month to review newly submitted enchantments. I am to assist the wolf shifter when needed."

"That doesn't sound like a bad outcome for a betrayer," another student said.

"No, it doesn't, but I can't guarantee that anyone after me will be granted what I was. The loss of this place, of the knowledge in these walls, the coven, it will hurt. I will need to find my way again. I'm not sure if I will be welcomed back to my old life. Unfortunately, I don't know if I will be able to rebuild a bakery there or elsewhere and I am truly starting with nothing, and the very basics in securities are now gone. It's all a risk that I'm willing to take because that mountain chose to show me what is out there. So I choose it, if it will have me back. I wish you luck."

They said farewell and thanked her before she was off to finish grading any remaining papers she had. If she planted any seeds of change, she didn't know and she didn't care to stick around to find out.

When Wednesday finally came, she was released. The silent guard escorted her to a storage room where the things she had left behind had been shoved into boxes. Clothing she had left behind and small trinkets from her childhood. He stood at the end of the row letting her search and pack her items in private.

She hurried to change out of the drab gray linen tunic and pants into leggings and a hoodie—all too big on her since she had hardly moved much in the last five months.

Is Reyes going to still find you attractive? What if you can't hike far with him now? Her mind raced then she took a deep breath.

"He will want you. You are his lifemate. Work back up to hiking with him, just like before," she told herself and went back to packing. She wasn't taking much. A few dresses she hadn't wanted to part with, more books, and her first cauldron. She was leaving everything else behind.

"Are you nervous about the blood pearl? Receiving the mark?" someone asked from behind her. She turned again to see both of her brothers standing in the doorway.

"No. I'm ready. I just thought I had another month. They agreed though, they can't go back on it."

"I know. I waived the debt owed for last month after our last conversation. I thought a lot about what you said, and we both talked about it. We felt it was the least we could do," Rainier said.

"You're letting me go? Just like that? Not going to try to convince me to stay?"

"Do you want us to? You seem pretty set on Mt. Shasta, and the California council gave you a pretty good deal. I guess I can't say I'm not curious how this is going to go," her other brother, Galen, noted.

"Shasta is my home. With people who asked me to stay time and time again. Not because of tradition or because they expected me to serve them, but because they like me."

"Are you nervous about what you might return to?" Galen asked.

She looked down and thought about it for a moment. She knew she was anxious and the mark of the betrayer would sit heavy on her. But maybe, she could bear it a little easier with her life in Shasta, or at least find closure from it. She would choose a new last name. She would have to. It was expected of betrayers to file the paperwork after all.

"Yes." Her voice was small.

"And what if you return to nothing?" he asked.

"Then I say farewell to the mountain, thank it for its wisdom, and move on."

"Give us a hug. We hope you will at least write to us. Maybe we can visit, or arrange for you to visit, off grounds of course."

She sighed and gave them a hug. Then followed the silent guard down the hall. Her things would be loaded into a rental car since she would be expected to leave immediately following her final meeting with the council.

She saw her sisters-in-law and nieces and nephews. The kids looked scared and it tugged at Camille. They would never know their aunt if her brothers willed it.

What can you do, though?

So she walked on and with her head held high, ignoring the looks from those she passed by and stood before the council. They held her blood pearl up and spoke the words to unbind her from her debt by dropping it on the floor where one of them smashed it with his boot. The red sand mixed with the rest on the ground. Eventually, it would be blown off into the water surrounding the platform they stood on. The faint scent of iron made her woozy.

She felt hands on her shoulders and someone took her arm to bear her wrist. Her body tensed as she wasn't sure what was happening. They were not dragging her away but holding her in place. Then she saw the scalding hot branding iron come towards her.

They were going to put it on the inside of her wrist. It would be hard to cover up in the summer. She had never asked where the mark went.

"Bear the mark of the betrayer, then leave. You are a Thornwell, no more," one of the council members said. The scalding searing pain on her flesh stole her breath and made her body jerk back, but the guards held her firmly in place.

She bit her lip to keep from screaming and forced herself to take deep breaths. She would bear this. She was going home.

Camille was free.

She walked out of the chamber and saw the silent guard standing there. He eyed her wrist for a moment then looked at her. "Your things are loaded into the car. I am to show you to it and see you off grounds."

She really didn't know what to say as so many emotions were hitting her.

"Yes sir,"

The silent guard smirked then started walking. She followed and when she reached the small sedan he handed her the keys. "See to it this gets returned to the company it was rented from. If you do not return it, they will seek retribution. I gave you your instructions. Do not pin this on me. Understood?" he explained in a very clear tone.

"Yes. I understand." She unlocked the door and opened it. This was it. She was really done with this place. Her eyes traveled to the academy, taking it in one last time. The rustic mansion style buildings her former coven owned.

"Good luck, Camille," the guard said.

The use of her name and not betrayer caught her by surprise. She looked at him, still unsure of what to say.

"I never learned your name," she said.

"Fletcher Devonshire." Then he turned and walked back towards the door. She never did ask him why he had changed his tune after their heated exchange. She figured she would never get the chance to know.

There were no more goodbyes, just her trying to ignore the pain on her wrist as she started the car and left. Her eyes welled up from the whirlwind of emotions within her but not once did she look back. Mt. Shasta was the only thing she wanted to see on the horizon.

That evening Willow and Evan had come over to Reyes's cabin again. They had arrived together and smiled at each other a lot, but when he had asked Evan about it, his friend just said they were talking. Reyes had been able to shift at will now but Willow informed him the full moon would always make him shift.

"How does it feel when you shift back now? I know the at will thing has been pretty recent."

"Not as bad. I'm likely going to take the day off after a full moon, though. I usually feel fine by the middle of the day, but I think the amount I eat is going to raise some eyebrows if I went into work. I'm eating basically from the time I wake up until I go to sleep."

"Well your secret is safe with me, wolf boy," Evan said.

Reyes laughed and glanced at the mountain. Sorrow cascaded over him.

Bring her back, damn it. The pleading in his mind never stopped. He looked at Willow. "How much longer do I have to wait?"

"I don't know."

"I want her back. I want her to see what I've done. I want her to know she doesn't have to worry about me."

"I know, Reyes. We want her back too. Have faith that she is doing everything she can."

"Five months isn't enough? After she was hauled away in a van." Reyes fought back his tears.

"Do you want to sit in the calming circle?" Willow suggested. "I have some of the oil in my bag."

Reyes sighed. "No. I will be alright. Sorry."

"It's alright. We can stay," Evan said, sitting forward in his seat.

"No. I'm going to try to relax. Thanks for coming over for dinner. I will see ya both tomorrow."

"She will come back to us. Don't give up on her," Willow told him. She gave him a brief hug then Evan pulled him into a tight bear hug.

"Stay strong, brother. Your witch will come back."

"Thanks."

After Reyes saw them out, he slumped on the couch and leaned his head back once again, looking up at the high peaked ceiling. Sitka nuzzled up against him and he put his arm around the bobcat, holding her close.

He couldn't fight the tears anymore.

"Camille. Please. Come back."

He set his beer down on the coffee table and wiped his eyes. Suddenly a sharp stinging sensation cramped his entire arm up, causing him to jolt.

"Fuck," he groaned and lifted his sleeve up, only to see the mark was gone. Not believing it, he ran into the bathroom and looked in the mirror.

The evocation was gone.

Chapter 42

Camille had parked her car a few shops down from her old bakery. The main street of Mt. Shasta was quiet and deserted. Much like it had been that night. She was tired and emotional, remembering the last time she stood here. It brought back so many more emotions she thought she had buried. It would be hard to see the sight of where her bakery once had been. Sure, the destruction she had last seen it in would be cleaned up, but it wouldn't say Bakewell's. It would be some other business.

There was a sign lit up above it but she hadn't gotten close enough to read it. The yellow loading curb had been freshly painted. Her eyes focused on the plants in the window of Willow's shop and she was relieved it was still there. Willow was still here. She hoped to see her tomorrow. The Apothecary looked much the same. A small, sad laugh slipped out of Camille upon seeing a candle called Sitka with a bobcat sketch in a crescent moon of flowers. Willow hadn't forgotten her and maybe that meant she had kept Sitka. There was still a chance she might be able to find her place here again.

This place she had felt the most at home. It still did. She smiled, recalling when she had first seen that mountain tonight, waiting for her on the horizon. Steady and steadfast as it always was. Now that she was here it was almost too much to think about what would happen when she saw Reyes again.

With a hard swallow, she walked a few more steps to the door that used to be hers then stopped dead in her tracks at what she saw.

A bakery was there.

The sign read 'Sitka's Bakery' with the same bobcat in the crescent moon sketch on the logo. The walls were accented with aged wood with dried floral arrangements in little jars hung and a large art piece of Mt. Shasta. It looked like a cozy haven inside. The cases were all brand new as were the counters. Everything had been renovated.

The sign on the door said 'coming soon' and tears welled up in her eyes. She knew in her very core that this was for her. Reyes hadn't forgotten about her.

A loud roaring engine came speeding down the road and a whimper of emotion spilled out of her upon hearing the tires screeching to a stop.

"Cami!" Reyes hesitated. Finally, she turned around and saw him. Sitka jumped out of the open window and ran up to her, ripping a sob from her as she knelt down to pull the bobcat close.

"Are you hurt? What did they do to you?" Reyes knelt down and pulled her into a warm embrace immediately. Sitka squeezed out from between them and nuzzled her.

She grabbed Reyes tightly, inhaling his scent and the sensation of his soft blue flannel on her fingertips. "Reyes," she whimpered, ignoring the pain on her wrist.

"Willow and I nursed Sitka back to health, and we told Evan what we are. I kept Sitka at my place. I begged that mountain every night to bring you back. I never gave up. Tell me you are home for good. Please tell me you didn't marry any assholes. Please." He pulled back and held her hands, looking for a ring but fixed on the fresh wound. She pulled it back, suddenly self-conscious of it. It looked horrible. "What is this? Tell me you are home, please?"

"It's the brand of the betrayer, every witch will know I rejected a legacy. They branded it today. It will never vanish. It's not an evocation, just a mark seared into my flesh."

"Let me tend to it. You didn't even wrap it?" he asked, pulling her to stand but being mindful of her wrist.

"I had to leave after they did it, I just wanted to be home, so I didn't stop. I only filled the tank up twice on the way home."

"You're free? Of obligation? The coven? Both covens? They will not come for you again?" he asked, tilting her chin up. She knew she looked exhausted and gaunt. Assuming she probably looked haggard, she looked away. "Camille. Please answer me. I cannot lose you again."

"I'm free. Nameless." She squeezed her eyes shut. "The bakery?"

"Willow and I cosigned on the business transfer. I fixed it up myself and hired contractors for what I couldn't do. I can't bake for shit but I wanted you to have something to return to. I took out a loan just to pay the rent on it until you returned." He cupped her jaw with both of his hands and brought her to look at him. "The bakery is yours. I have the keys back at the cabin."

She cried out. "I just—I lied to you and then you could have been hurt when they came for me. Then you did all this for me? And Sitka? Not knowing when or if I'd come back?"

"Come home, to the cabin with me. I have all of your stuff and your car. We started something and we were going to take it to the next level. I want to." He was nearly pleading.

"I love you. I was going to say it to you that night, I should have told you months before that night. I'm sorry," was all she could say before he kissed her deeply again.

He rested his forehead against hers. "I love you, Camille. I know you are free, and I want you to remain that way for the rest of your life, but if you don't want to remain nameless, Navarro is available. It may not be a prestigious legacy, but I promise you will be taken care of."

"Are you proposing to me?" she laughed.

"This isn't a proposal but if you say yes now, I will soon."

"Yes!" Camille proclaimed. "Yes, Reyes. I'd be honored."

Sitka swirled around their legs and purred.

"Let's go home then. Are you hungry? I have food at the house I am happy to make you."

"It's late. And you probably ate. I can forage," she said, feeling overwhelmed again. "And the car." She looked at the rental.

"It's in a spot. We will get it tomorrow." He took her hand and led her to the truck where he opened the door. She climbed in before Sitka jumped in and sat in her lap.

Before closing the door, Reyes leaned on the cab and waited for her eyes to meet his. "Let me take care of you before you dive back into that bakery. Please? Wife to be."

"Alright." She smiled widely. He leaned in and kissed her again before he closed her door and ran to the driver's side where he jumped in the seat. "What are we going to tell people? I have to cover this up. You have to cover it up."

"We'll figure it out. Right now I need you in our cabin and close," he said, giving her leg a squeeze. "I spent every night begging that mountain, those trees, and the stars to bring you back. I want to remain by your side, as long as I can, until my bones return to the earth and when they do, I hope it's beside yours when that time comes."

"I prayed every day that you would be alright, every full moon that you would be safe."

"I was. I will tell you about it over dinner."

When Camille got out of the truck, she looked at the cabin, the backdrop of the conifers, and the stars against the A-frame that made her feel so many emotions. Everything ranging from excitement, to hope, to curiosity about their future together.

Camille was home.

Her eyes welled up upon entering the cabin again. Reyes took her hand and guided her upstairs. She started breathing heavily, trying to fight the emotions as she saw the bedroom.

"Hey, take a deep breath. I'm not going to tell you not to cry, if you need to, but I'm here."

"I never stopped thinking about this place, about you."

Reyes led her into the bathroom and sat her on the counter. It was cleaner than she remembered. He pawed through a drawer and the cabinets then set to gently cleaning the burned mark.

Camille noticed he had a few salves and things from Willow's shop.

"Are those calming candles?"

"Yes. Willow insisted. We made a calming circle in the backyard, Evan helped. He's learning all of this too." He spoke of how the last few months went and how grueling they had been. How he connected to Evan first after eavesdropping on them; how he spoke to Sitka in some nonverbal he still can't exactly explain.

"You can change at will?" she asked, amazed. "You look like you bulked up a bit."

"Yes. I can show you tomorrow." He smiled. "I will wrap it after you shower, *if* you would like to shower, or I can do it now."

"I'm disgusting. I thought I had one more month to pay off my debt, but my brother granted me forgiveness from the council. He's in charge now. It's a long story."

"Relax. You're not disgusting, take your time. I will head up when I hear the water turn off," he said and kissed her again.

After washing the day and the last five months away as carefully as she could to not agitate her burn, she got dressed. A pair of sweats that now hung loose on her, a tank top, and one of his flannels.

Reyes walked up as she pulled the flannel on and he quickly adjusted the sleeve. "I missed seeing you in these." He kissed her head then he set to wrapping her wrist.

"Is this a shirt?"

"Yes, I bought a lot of them since I was ripping them to shreds. But I can change now and my clothes go with me. I don't want anything to get into the wound tonight but this is the best I have for now."

She nodded and followed him downstairs where a bowl of beef stew with a side of garlic bread was waiting for her.

"I made a batch over the weekend. I added a little of the calming enchantment Willow made me. Only two drops as instructed. I have some serums for Sitka which I keep in her supply cabinet."

Camille smiled and noticed the large water dispenser and stainless steel food bowl that had 'Sitka' engraved on the side. "She has a supply cabinet?"

"Yes. I usually toss her raw meat in the evenings, but there's some kibble in the cabinet along with a brush. I discovered that she likes to be brushed, and I installed a doggy door for her, so I don't have to leave a window open. I also am working on proper paperwork to legally "own" her so there are no issues. Seth is helping me with it. She hangs out at Willow's shop some days. Other days I leave her here."

Despite fighting her cries earlier, she felt tears prickle in her eyes. Only now, they were for a different reason she wanted to cry. She wiped them and started eating, noticing he had a bowl too.

"Has the shifter council contacted you?" she asked.

Reyes looked at her wide eyed. "No. Should they have?"

"I had my hearing two months ago, the California witch council was there." She then explained how the hearing went, what would be asked of her, and that the shifters were aware of him but deemed him not ready to be contacted.

"So you have to go alone? For how long?" he asked.

"I'm not sure. I'm not sure when they will begin to summon me. Or what will be asked of you. I might be able to go with you."

"We will figure it out. Together." He sighed and rubbed her back. "Those assholes. Willow wrote to them often and they said they were looking into it. They knew the whole time?"

"At least for a few months. Yes," Cami sighed and took another bite.

"They didn't hurt you, did they? Aside from that?"

She sighed and told him what the debt was and how her days were spent, how she probably wouldn't be able to hike very far. She spoke of the two guards, the visits from Leland, her brother, and the students. All of it. And by the time she was done, tears were running down her face. "I was never supposed to remain a Thornwell. Funny it took a Talbot to tell me to become the betrayer."

"That guard and Leland," Reyes muttered with disgust. "Bastards. Did you have the ring the entire time?"

"It was his ring I was supposed to enchant with my bond to him. He kept it on him. I pawned mine somewhere in Oregon before I moved here. He was supposed to enchant mine on the night of our vows. He approached my cell once a few days after I was thrown in there." Camille explained the exchange with Leland.

"You are a Navarro now. You are mine, not his. Not theirs," he said with reverence.

"Do your parents hate me? I am not sure I could ever go visit your sister. The thought of going back to Seattle is too much to think about right now."

"No. They don't hate you at all. They really like you, they were so sad you were gone. I didn't tell them what all happened exactly but it was so hard. I just would have gone silent, I gave so many people the silent treatment." He told her about how the police deemed him unstable and said he was going into shock. That he was fine with it since his fear would be being accused of having something to do with it. He was in therapy twice a month and he was usually really quiet but sometimes when he slipped and tried to speak, the memory lapses would happen.

"That sounds like so much more hassle. Like I downplayed how bad it really was, and they did that to you."

"It was hard, but honestly forgetting you felt like the biggest insult after what you have done for me, after what you have endured. You are home now and we get to live out the rest of our lives together."

Sitka brushed against her leg. "Thank you for taking care of her. It hurt me so badly to sever the bond."

"She wants to be your familiar again, she's worried you would have changed too much. She never left my side, even when I forgot her and chased her out of the house. She always came back." Reyes wiped his eyes. "I would just hug her and cry on her every night."

Camille smiled and felt overwhelmed by the many emotions within her, ranging from happiness to hurt that both he and Sitka had gone through so much. "She's bonded to you, too, you know. When they are cared for and tended to like this, they choose to open their connection to you. She was bonded to you the day we found her. It's probably why she always showed herself to you at the bakery. She knew you wouldn't really do anything."

Reyes laughed. "The day of the follow-up inspection, I begged that mountain that she wouldn't be in the bakery." He leaned down and scratched her head. "Sit in the circle tomorrow and let her be your familiar again. She missed you too."

They finished eating and she insisted on helping to clean up. He started to protest but soon gave up. Then he took her hand and led her upstairs to the loft where he pulled her into a deep kiss and his hands quickly found her waist.

"Reyes." She hugged him tightly. "I love you so much."

"I love you too. I imagine you are exhausted, but when you are ready, I really want to make up for lost time," he murmured.

Her hands pulled him closer. "I want you to claim me, Reyes. I want you all over me. Make me yours."

"Say no more. You were the only one I ever thought about."

She sighed and gripped him tighter.

He kissed her as her hands slid down to his rear. "You are all mine, lifemate."

"I love you, Reyes. Never doubt that."

Reyes began to undress her, and came down to his knees as he always did. Falling into that familiar rhythm again, like their first time, only there was no hesitation tonight. They were slower and more intentional until they finally drifted off into slumber, holding each other.

Epilogue

It had been a very happy reunion for the girls. Camille had surprised Willow in her shop before dropping the rental car off with Reyes. Evan, too, had stopped by when Reyes told him to take his break.

She was excited to see that Willow and Evan were spending more time together. Reyes had explained Evan's concerns and despite Camille being back, the divorce was not finalized so Evan still wasn't ready to rush into things. Reyes would slip occasionally and call it their courtship. The two witches told him it was common for shifters to use the more traditional terms for things.

A few weeks later, the four gathered at Willow's house.

"I gotta say, it's pretty wild knowing you're going to be a kept male now." Evan patted Reyes hard on the back, since he had properly proposed to Camille about a week ago.

"And I gotta say, I've never been happier," Reyes said, taking a sip of the beer in his hand. Camille smiled at the two.

Willow grabbed her notebook and opened a page then sat down. "I was looking up this enchantment and thought it might unlock the scents to be stronger. Have you tried it?"

As Camille looked over her friend's enchantments, worry cascaded over her face. "You have to be careful to get this one right. It is an unlocking spell, it can unlock some magical binds on people and things.

Even some evocations. I've never heard of it being used to unlock more potency of something, but I suppose it could work."

"Would it have worked on that memory thing I had on me?" Reyes asked.

Camille looked at him with a frown. "No. Not by Willow's enchantment. I don't know anyone who could undo an enchantment done by my parents. It would have to be another legacy coven leader."

"So it has to be an enchantment weaker than my abilities?" Willow asked.

"Yeah, that's usually how these things work."

"Then we should be fine, right? I'm not near as strong as you are."

"Did you put it in something already?" Camille asked.

"Just this candle but I haven't tested it. I wanted to get your opinion on it."

Camille vaguely noticed Evan finish his beverage and stand up, heading towards the sink.

"Does anyone need anything while I'm up?"

Reyes shook his head.

"Alright, go on and light it so I can see how it is. I want you to tell me what you get from it first though," Camille instructed.

With a nod, Willow grabbed the candle and the matches. The spark struck, igniting the match head with a flame. Camille noticed Reyes and Evan watching intently. Neither one had moved; they were so interested in this. Reyes had stopped fidgeting with his bottle cap and Evan remained standing by the sink with his beer bottle in hand.

Then Camille noticed Sitka too stood up from the ball she had been in on the couch and trotted cautiously over to them.

The strong scent of cedar and bergamot was certainly more potent than Willow had made in the past. It was almost overpowering. She had gotten something wrong. Her eyes widened and went to Reyes, hoping it wasn't going to trigger some feral impulse in his wolf.

"Wait!" Reyes exclaimed just before Evan cried out in pain, dropping the glass and causing it to shatter on the floor.

Camille's jaw dropped and Reyes leapt up, putting an arm in front of her. "Willow, get behind us," Reyes urged.

She looked as Evan doubled over and fell to his hands and knees, right into the glass. "Fuck!" he cried out again and held his bloody hand up. Then he appeared as if he were going to vomit and leapt up, hurling into the sink.

He braced himself on the edge, trembling as sweat broke out over his face and neck. Another retching caused him to strain and his hand smeared blood on the counter.

"Evan?" Reyes asked. "What do you feel? Something is different about you."

"It's magic. Witch magic," Camille stated, watching the red aura cascade around him. "Your magic was blocked? Why?"

"I'm not a witch though. I feel nauseous. My body feels weird. What happened? What did that candle do? The scent hit me and I felt a sharp stinging sensation on my leg, right on my knee. Then whatever this tingling sensation came over me made my stomach churn."

"A stinging sensation? That's what it felt like when the silencing evocation was put on me, it felt like that the night Camille returned too. It made me jump in the truck and drive to the bakery. I knew she had to be back. The evocation was removed when she came back, that was the deal. You had an evocation on you this whole time. Neither of you sensed it?" Reyes rasped, looking at Camille and Willow.

Sitka had at least relaxed.

"What was on your knee? I don't think I've ever seen you in anything but pants," Camille asked, stepping forward.

His hand was still bleeding and his back slid down against the cabinet to the floor.

"Evan!" Willow fretted and rushed to a drawer.

He heaved and knocked his head back against the cabinet. "I have a scar on my knee, I honestly don't even remember getting it. My dad said I fell and cut my knee on something in the backyard when I was little. A cactus? A rock? I don't remember. I was a pretty rowdy kid."

Reyes stepped forward and held his hand up above his heart. Willow set to picking out the glass. He winced in pain.

"Is the scar still there? Was it actually a scar?" Reyes asked, looking back at Camille.

"I don't know, I'm not exactly in a position to pull my pants down," Evan slurred out. "I still feel nauseous. There's a tingling sensation all over my body too. What's happening to me?" He looked at Camille, nearly begging for answers.

"That's your magic being released into your body, coursing through your veins. It's been suppressed for how long? When did you get the scar?"

"I don't remember. I'm not a witch." He panicked. Reyes braced his shoulder and arm with his knees.

"Calm down," Reyes said softly.

"Someone blocked his magic? And I just released it? This entire time, Evan was a witch, and Reyes was a wolf? I never sensed anything in them."

"You have gotten stronger," Camille said and stepped forward. "Evan, where were you born?" Cami asked, scanning his face.

"Phoenix. No wait. Tacoma. I grew up in Phoenix," he panted out, tapping his head against the cabinet again.

"At a hospital? Or at home?"

"What are you asking, Cami?" Reyes asked nervously.

"What is your last name?" she asked, ignoring Reyes's question.

"Myers! The most basic white dude name I could have, Evan Myers."

"Your father's family name, I take it? What was your mother's maiden name?"

"Smith. Again, as basic as can be."

"Did you know your mother?" She narrowed her eyes, taking in his features. The blue eyes and the sandy blond hair. *No. It can't be.*

"What kind of question is that? Yes, both of my parents raised me."

"Your biological mother?" Camille asked but she didn't sound convinced. She hadn't taken her eyes off him.

"Why are you asking?" Reyes repeated his question.

Camille now realized what she was doing. She was prying into family secrets that had been buried. She had done this to Reyes and it upset him immensely. The situation was completely different for Reyes than it was for Evan. No one had blocked Reyes from shifting. He just hadn't had exposure to enough magic before her. But Evan's mom had blocked his magic for fear of him being found. Willow had gotten strong enough to unlock it.

"I—I think your biological mother's name is Paige Talbot."

Acknowledgements

We have arrived at this section and I never feel as though I thank everyone even after doing three of these now but let's try.

Obviously I want to thank you, dearest readers. For giving this story a chance. I never saw myself writing paranormal romance and I still question if this even really fits in the genre or if it is in fact more of a romantasy. Regardless, thank you for reading this story of the bakery witch and the county health inspector set in the shadow of Mt. Shasta. I obviously wouldn't be able to do this without you.

Huge thanks to Siskiyou County, that land of enchanted waterfalls and Mt. Shasta. I was on my way to Crater Lake in 2023 shortly before Old Giants made it's debut and passed through the county. We stopped in Dunsmuir and made a quick trip to Hedge Creek Falls. It was packed but still magical. It wasn't until fall of 2024 did I ever venture back that way to fully explore all the other areas I mention in this book and later books. Now that county shares space in my heart alongside Humboldt.

Huge thanks to my editing team. Brittany, Kai, and Kristen for your dedication and patience dealing with my messes. You truly have helped me become a better writer.

The various discord groups I have found along the way, thanks for listening to me and liking all my pictures of beverages and hikes. Adalyn Grace's discord whom I have met some of the best bookish friends from. To Teagan and the rest of the creative place always in my heart

To Jill Tew, Lyssa Mia Smith, & Kika Hatzopoulou for your super fun street teams, thank you for making writer's channels and sharing your insight.

Alicia, Monica, Catari, Jenn, Hannia and Fira, thank you for being the bookish homies.

To the IG friends who have stumbled on this trail with me, Mina, Jenn, A.J. Sam, Morgan, Kaylee, Emmy, Rae, Rachel, Sim, Z, Stevie, Margot, Emily, Lorin, TR, KJ, Shiloh, Heather, and just so many more folks your support honestly means more than you can imagine.

To Shae, Emily, Arden, and everyone else at A Seat At The Table for your support and hosting writing groups and author events, thank you. Your support means so very much.

Jason, Alex, Rachel, Natasha, and everyone else from Writing Demystified and the FYDN crew thank you. This book truly would not exist without you. I wrote the bulk of it next to your stories.

The Panera crew: Ann, Pat, and Mel. Thank you for your support while tinkering with this.

Special thanks to Connie who I always think about while researching plants and trees and why they are the way they are. The camping trips to Wright's Beach and Burlington Campground will always remain with me.

I want to thank the talented artists who brought all my idiots to life. I have tagged them so many times on Instagram.

My coworkers who have kept my day job one of the best places I have worked at. (still the one agency I never mention but it's ok there isn't an office in Siskiyou anyways.) Yang, Gil, Linda, and Maire, thank you for countless coffee breaks, K-BBQ meetings, and the memes during those TEAMs meetings.

Of course thank you to my family for encouraging my love of travel and curiosity about this place I live. It's a big state and I am extremely lucky to have traversed a lot of it.

To my beta readers: Sam, Carly, Rachel and others who helped ask the hard hitting questions I never considered in this story. Yes, Sitka chose that life.

To Eden and DK for the hikes and craft days with Emily and Dee thank you for the snacks.

Of course the bestie, Danielle, who travels a lot of miles to wander off into the mountains and trees with me and then listen to me talk through all these plots I get stuck on. (The next two ES books especially.)

Of course to Rocky and Pixie, the animals that keep me company while I'm working. And my husband, Joe, who is always supportive and makes sure my tire pressure is good when I go on these solo trips. Who never hesitates to say we can order dinner when I'm deep in a manuscript or formatting to get these books out. Who found me a car better suited to get to the Black Butte trailhead. Love you.

Until we meet again in the shadow of the mountain.

Also by

<u>Short Stories</u>

Beacon

~

<u>Old Giants novellas</u>

Swift of Storm

<u>Old Giants</u>

Secrets of Old Giants

Unkindness of Old Giants

~

<u>Enchanted Senses</u>

An Inspection So Sweet

About The Author

Kelly Virens is a fantasy author with a love of all things trees, mountains, oceans, hiking, and storytelling. Born and raised in San Diego, California, with a two year teaching stint in Japan, she relocated to Northern California to find home in all the amazing areas nearby. When she is not writing, she is usually off hiking or exploring somewhere in the region where she finds inspiration. Following a hike, she always stops by a nearby bookstore and a coffee shop. Her imagination is usually dreaming and scheming new things to write, draw, or make. Follow along with her explorations on Instagram with her personal account @fireflirt and her bookstagram @KellyVirensBooks

Check out more Secrets of Old Giants & Enchanted Senses content below

linktr.ee/portfireflirt